S0-BOJ-737

The Last Girls

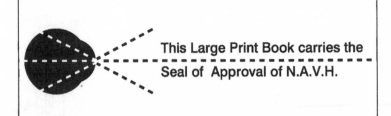

This Large Print Book carries the
Seal of Approval of N.A.V.H.

The Last Girls

Lee Smith

3 1489 00478 4276

Thorndike Press • Waterville, Maine

© 2002 by Lee Smith.

Lyrics from "Bad Moon Rising," by John Fogerty, courtesy of Fantasy, Inc. All rights reserved. Used by permission. Copyright © 1969 Jondora Music (BMI). Copyright renewed.

A portion of this novel was first published in a slightly different form in *Novello: Ten Years of Great American Writing*, edited by Amy Rogers, Robert Inman, and Frye Gaillard. Published by Novello Festival Press in 2000.

All rights reserved.

This is a work of fiction. While, as in all fiction, the literary perceptions and insights are based on experience, all names, characters, places, and incidents are either products of the author's imagination or are used fictitiously. No reference to any real person is intended or should be inferred.

Published in 2002 by arrangement with Algonquin Books of Chapel Hill, a division of Workman Publishing Co., Inc.

Thorndike Press Large Print Basic Series.

The tree indicium is a trademark of Thorndike Press.

The text of this Large Print edition is unabridged.
Other aspects of the book may vary from the original edition.

Set in 16 pt. Plantin by Minnie B. Raven.

Printed in the United States on permanent paper.

Library of Congress Cataloging-in-Publication Data

Smith, Lee, 1944–
    The last girls : a novel / Lee Smith.
      p. cm.
    ISBN 0-7862-4734-7 (lg. print : hc : alk. paper)
    1. Women college graduates — Fiction. 2. Mississippi River — Fiction. 3. Female friendship — Fiction. 4. Southern States — Fiction. 5. Class reunions — Fiction. 6. River boats — Fiction. 7. Large type books. I. Title.
PS3569.M5376 L38 2002b
  813'.54—dc21   2002028725

This book is for my beloved husband, Hal — pilot, shipmate, and running buddy on the continuing journey . . . and for Jane and Vereen Bell, who went down the river with us in the summer of 1999.

The Mississippi is well worth reading about. It is not a commonplace river, but on the contrary is in all ways remarkable. . . . It seems safe to say that it is also the crookedest river in the world, since in one part of its journey it uses up one thousand three hundred miles to cover the same ground that the crow would fly over in six hundred and seventy-five. . . .

It is a remarkable river in this: that instead of widening toward its mouth, it grows narrower; grows narrower and deeper. From the junction of the Ohio to a point half way down to the sea, the width averages a mile in high water: thence to the sea the width steadily diminishes, until, at the "Passes," above the mouth, it is but little over a half a mile. At the junction of the Ohio the Mississippi's depth is eighty-seven feet; the depth increases gradually, reaching one hundred and twenty-nine just above the mouth.

— Mark Twain
Life on the Mississippi

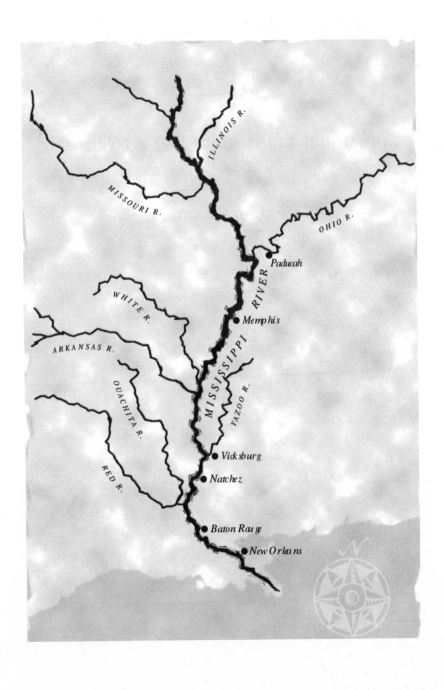

Sometimes life is more like a river than a book.

— Cort Conley

June 10, 1965

It's Girls A-Go-Go
Down the Mississippi

PADUCAH, Ky. (AP) — "We can't believe we're finally going to do it!" were the parting words of 12 excited Mary Scott College students about to begin their "Huck Finn" journey down the Mississippi River on a raft.

The adventuresome misses weighed anchor at 1:15 p.m. today, bound for New Orleans, 950 miles south. Their departure was delayed when one of the "crew" threw an anchor into the river with no rope attached, necessitating a bikini-clad recovery operation, to the crowd's delight. "Hey, New Orleans is thataway!" shouted local wags as the ramshackle craft finally left land, hours later than planned.

Their skipper, 74-year-old retired riverboat captain Gordon S. Cartwright, answered an ad that the girls had run in a riverboat magazine, writing them that he would pilot their raft down the river for nothing. He plans to make eight or nine miles an hour during daylight, tie up at night, and reach New Orleans in 10 or 12 days.

"I've carried more tonnage, but never a more valuable cargo," said the captain.

The girls include Ruth d'Agostino of New

York, N.Y.; Margaret Burns Ballou of Demopolis, Ala.; Lauren DuPree of Mobile, Ala.; Courtney Gray of Raleigh, N.C.; Jane Gillespie of Richmond, Va.; Susan Alexis Hill of Atlanta, Ga.; Harriet Holding of Staunton, Va.; Bowen Montague of Nashville, Tenn.; Suzanne St. John of New Orleans, La.; Anna Todd of Ivy, W. Va.; Catherine Wilson of Birmingham, Ala.; and Mimi West of Silver Spring, Md.

The raft, named the Daisy Pickett, was built by a Paducah construction company under Captain Cartwright's supervision. Resembling a floating porch, the Daisy Pickett is a 40-by-16-foot wooden platform with plyboard sides, built on 52 oil drums and powered by two 40-horsepower motors. It cost $1,800 to build. The raft has a superstructure of two-by-fours with a tarpaulin top that the "sailors" can pull up over it, mosquito netting that they can hang up, and a shower consisting of a bucket overhead with a long rope attached to it.

Living provisions are piled in corners of the raft, with army cots around the walls for sleeping. Some girls will have to sleep on the floor each night, or on land. A roughly lettered sign spelling "Galley" leads into a two-by-four-foot plywood enclosure with canned goods, hot dog buns, and other odds and ends of food supplies. The girls will take turns on "KP duty" and have a small wood-burning stove in one corner.

The Daisy Pickett left flying two flags, an American flag and a hand-painted flag sporting a huge yellow daisy.

Mile 736
Memphis, Tennessee
Friday 5/7/99
1645 hours

Harriet thinks it was William Faulkner who said that Mississippi begins in the lobby of the Peabody hotel. Waiting to check in at the ornate desk, she can well believe it. Vast and exotic as another country, the hushed lobby stretches away forever with its giant chandeliers, its marble floors, its palms, Oriental rugs and central fountain, its islands of big comfortable furniture where gorgeous blond heiresses lean forward toward each other telling secrets Harriet will never know and could not even imagine. Oh she has no business being here in Memphis at all, no business in this exclusive lobby, no business going on this trip down the river again with these women she doesn't even know any longer and has nothing in common with, nothing at all. As if she ever did. As if it were not all entirely a coincidence — proximity, timing, the luck of the draw, whatever. Harriet has read that they assign roommates now strictly by height, a system that works as well as any other. And in fact she and Baby were exactly the same height (five feet six inches) and exactly the same weight (125 pounds) — though Lord knows it was distributed differently — when they were paired as roommates at Mary Scott College in 1963. They could wear each other's clothes perfectly. Harriet remembers pulling on that little gray cashmere sweater set the minute Baby took it off, Baby coming in drunk from an afternoon date as Harriet rushed out for the evening; she remembers how warm and soft the cashmere felt slipping down over her breasts which no boy had ever seen. That was freshman year.

Oh this is all a dreadful mistake, Harriet realizes now as her heart starts to pound and she tries to breathe slowly and deeply in the freezing fragrant air of the Peabody hotel. She anchors herself by looking up the nearest column, so massive, so polished, really she is quite insignificant here beside it. Insignificant, all her unseemly heaving and gasping and emotional display. Harriet gazes up and up and up the slick veined column stretching out of sight into the dark Southern air of the mezzanine at the top of the marble staircase that

14

leads to all those rooms where even now, cotton deals and pork-belly futures are being determined and illicit lunchtime affairs are still in steamy progress. Oh, stop! What is *wrong* with her? Everything Harriet has worked so hard to get away from comes flooding back and she has to sit down on a pretty little bench upholstered in a flame stitch. She really can't breathe. She's still getting over her hysterectomy anyway. She gasps and looks around. The walls are deep rose, a color Harriet has always thought of as *Italian,* though she has never been to Italy. The lighting, too, is rosy and muted, as if to say, "Calm down, dear. *Hush.* Everything will be taken care of. Don't worry your pretty little head . . ."

A black waiter appears before her with a silver tray and a big grin (Doesn't he *know* how politically incorrect he is?) and asks if he can bring her anything and Harriet says, "Yes, please, some water," and then he says, "My pleasure," and disappears like magic to get it. The big corporation that runs this hotel now must have taught them all to say "My pleasure" like that, Harriet is sure of it. No normal black boy from Memphis would say "My pleasure" on his own.

But *was* it William Faulkner who said,

15

"Mississippi begins in the lobby of the Peabody hotel"? Or did somebody else say it? Or did she, Harriet Holding, just make that up? At fifty-three, Harriet can't remember anything, sometimes of course it's a blessing. But for instance she can't remember the names of her students five minutes after the term is over, and she can't remember the names of her colleagues at the community college if she runs into them someplace unexpected such as the Pizza Hut or Home Depot, as opposed to the faculty lounge or the library where she has seen them daily for thirty years.

Yet suddenly, as if it were only yesterday, Harriet can remember Baby Ballou's beautiful face when she married Charlie Mahan in the biggest wedding Harriet has ever seen, to this day, and they were all bridesmaids: Harriet and Anna and Courtney, suitemates forever, and now they're all gathering again. Oh, it's too much! Just because Harriet took care of Baby Ballou in college does not mean she has an obligation to do so for the rest of her life.

Harriet can't remember why she ever consented to do this anyway, why she ever called Charlie Mahan back when he left that message on her voice mail, considering it was probably all his fault anyway. Yet Charlie Mahan is still charming, clearly, that deep throaty drawl that always reminds Harriet of driving down a gravel road, the way she and Baby used to do when she went down to Alabama visiting. Joyriding, Baby called it. Harriet has never been joyriding since. Just driving aimlessly out into the country in Baby's convertible, down any road they felt like, past kudzu-covered barns and cotton fields and little kids who stood in the yard and silently watched them pass and would not wave. Just drinking beer and listening to Wilson Pickett on the radio while bugs died on the windshield and weeds reached in at them on either side, towering goldenrod and bee balm, joe-pye weed as tall as a man. Like everything else in the Deep South, those weeds were too big, too tangled, too jungly. They'd grow up all around you and strangle you in a heartbeat, Harriet felt. A Virginian, Harriet had always thought she was Southern herself until she went to Alabama with Baby Ballou. And now here she is again, poised on the lush dark verge of the Deep South one more time.

Harriet thinks of the present the bridesmaids gave Baby the night before her wedding, sort of a joke present but not really, not really a joke at all, as things have turned out: a fancy evening bag, apricot watered silk, it had belonged to somebody's grandmother. "Everything you need to live in the Delta," they had printed on the accompanying card. Inside the purse was a black silk slip and a half-pint of gin. Harriet could use a drink of gin herself just thinking about Baby's thin flushed face with those cheekbones like wings and her huge pale startled blue eyes and the long dark hair that fell into her face and how she kept pushing it back in the same obsessive way she bit her nails and smoked cigarettes and did everything else.

"Here you are, ma'am," the waiter says, coming back with a beaded crystal goblet of ice water, but when Harriet fishes in her purse for a tip, he waves his hand grandly and glides off singing out "My pleasure!" in a ringing gospel voice. Harriet fights back an urge to laugh because she knows that if she does, she will never, ever, stop.

A scholarship student all through school, Harriet often identified more with the blacks she worked alongside in the college dining room than with some of her classmates who had never worked one day in their privileged lives. A black person will tell you the truth. As opposed to rich white

Southerners who will tell you whatever they think you'd like to hear. They will tell themselves this, too, before they go ahead and do whatever it was that they wanted to do in the first place.

A beautiful coffee-colored nurse presided over the examination that decided Harriet's recent hysterectomy, shining a flashlight thing around inside Harriet while three white male doctors stood in a row and said "Hmmm" and "Humn" gravely and professionally. One of them, apparently her primary doctor, looked like he was twelve years old. The doctors were looking at her reproductive tract on a television screen set up right there in the examining room. Harriet, feet up in the stirrups and a sheet wrapped primly around the rest of herself, was watching this television, too. It was truly amazing to see her own uterus and ovaries and Fallopian tubes and everything thrown up on the screen like a map. It was a miracle of modern medicine and so, oddly enough, it was not personally embarrassing to Harriet at all. In fact, it was like she wasn't even there. The doctors discussed the mass on her ovaries, which they couldn't actually see, due to the fibroid tumors in her uterus. *"Hmmmmm,"* they opined significantly. Then the doctors withdrew, walking in a straight white line out the door to consult privately among themselves.

The nurse, who had said not a word during the entire examination, turned to Harriet. She cocked her head and raised one elegant eyebrow. "Listen here, honey," she announced, "in my line of work, I've seen about a million of these, and I want to tell you something. If I was you, I'd get the whole fucking thing took out."

Harriet did just that. She'd been bleeding too much for years anyway. (Somehow the phrase "bleeding heart liberal" comes into her mind.) But a person can get used to anything and so she had gotten used to it, used to feeling that tired and never having much energy and having those hot flashes at the most inopportune times.

"Didn't all these symptoms interfere with your sex life?" the young doctor had asked her at one point.

"I don't have a sex life," Harriet told him, realizing as she spoke that this was true. It has been true for years. The phrase "use it or lose it" comes into her mind.

Well, the truth is, she didn't *mind* losing it. In many ways, it has been a relief, though Harriet always thought she'd have children eventually. She always thought she'd marry. Harriet is still surprised, vaguely, that these things have not happened to her. It's just that she's been so busy taking care of everybody — first Jill, then Mama, then starting the COME-BACK! program at her school, sponsoring the newspaper and the yearbook; and, of course, her students have been her children in a way. She sees them now, sprinkled all across the Shenandoah Valley, everywhere she goes. "Hello, Miss Holding! Hello, Miss Holding!" their bright voices cry from their strangely old faces. She can't remember a one of them. Time has picked up somehow, roaring along like a furious current out of control . . .

If she hadn't had the hysterectomy, would she ever have agreed to Charlie Mahan's request, would she have gone along with this crazy scheme? Somehow she doesn't think so. But it's true that things started seriously slipping over a year ago, even before she consulted the gynecologist. She just didn't feel like herself. Her mind started wandering, for one thing. For instance, she might arrive in Charlottesville for a meeting without even the faintest memory of having driven all the way over there, what route she took, and so forth. She might walk from her living room into her kitchen and then just stand there, wondering what she'd come for, what she'd had in mind. Her friend Phyllis called it the Change. A big, bossy woman who teaches accounting at the college with Harriet, Phyllis has already gone through the Change all by herself, pooh-poohing doctors and eating huge handfuls of ginkgo baloba and ginseng from the health food store in Roanoke.

"You've got to go with the flow, change with the change," she advised Harriet. "Try some zinc."

"Or maybe a man," Harriet surprised herself by saying. The words flew right out of her mouth.

"Why, Harriet!" Phyllis was as surprised as she was. Phyllis herself doesn't want a man, she has announced, because if she got one now, she'd probably just end up taking care of him, and then he'd die on her. Men are like mayflies, Phyllis says.

But Harriet had found herself thinking about them anyway. Sometimes she woke up at night with her body on fire, thinking about them. She did not tell Phyllis about this. Harriet always *liked* men; she used to have dates with them, too, mostly decorous dates that stopped when they got too demanding. Or, to be accurate, that's when Harriet stopped seeing them. And they were nice men: the new minister at the First Methodist Church, a widower; the academic dean of her college, whose wife ran off with her yoga instructor; and, once, her own dentist, who asked her out for dinner while he was in the middle of performing a root canal on her upper left canine. Of course, she nodded yes, leaning way back in the chair like that. Why, he could have drilled right straight on up into her brain. Not that he would have, Henry Jessup — he turned out to be a very sweet man, actually — a dreamy, poetic sort of man, for a dentist, who had moved back here from Cleveland to take care of his aging parents. He really liked Harriet, too. For some reason he thought she was very funny; he really "got a kick out of her," or so he said. He took her on hikes, to picnics and outdoor bluegrass festivals. But anytime Henry Jessup tried to say anything serious, Harriet's mind flew right straight up in the air and perched in a tree like a bird. Finally he gave up. His parents died, and he returned to Cleveland.

But that was years and years back.

More recently, just three weeks ago, Harriet practically accosted a strange man on a Saturday morning at the farmers market in her own hometown. Well, that's an exaggeration. She didn't accost him. But she spoke to him first, which is not like her, to be sure. She still can't believe she did it. It was one of her first trips out of the house following her hysterectomy. He was a man she'd never seen before, a stocky, rumpled, pleasant-looking man about her own age with a bald head on top and one of those little gray ponytails Harriet has always liked. He was examining tomatoes.

"That's a German Johnson," she blurted out. "They're real good. You probably think it's not ripe, but it *is*, it's just pink instead of red. They're pink tomatoes, German Johnsons."

He turned around, smiling, to see who had so much to say about tomatoes. "Thanks," he said to Harriet. "I'll take two," he said to the tomato lady, old Mrs. Irons, still looking at Harriet. "Hey," he said, right out of the blue, "let's go get a cup of coffee, what do you say?" But he didn't give her time to say anything. "Just a minute, let me pay for these tomatoes, okay?"

While his back was turned, Harriet made her escape, ducking behind the quilt lady's booth, past the Girl Scout lemonade stand, around the corner and into her waiting car. Safe at last, Harriet burst into tears. She cried all the way home, and not only because her stitches hurt but out of some deep, sad longing she didn't know she felt. Now she's sorry, or almost sorry, that she ran away. She wonders who he was. And sometimes she finds herself — if she's stopped for a light downtown for instance — scanning the streets, looking for that blue denim shirt. Which is perfectly ridiculous. As is her continued crying, which continues to happen at the strangest times . . . this hysterectomy has given her too much time to think.

Harriet always thought she'd get her Ph.D. and publish papers in learned journals while writing brilliant novels on the side. Why, even Dr. Tompkins wrote "Brilliant" across the top of her term paper once — now whatever was it about? "The Concept of Courtly Love in . . ." *something*. So why *didn't* she ever get her Ph.D.? Why didn't she ever marry? Why didn't she have that cup of coffee? These things strike Harriet now as a simple failure of nerve. Of course, she's always been a bit shy, a bit passive, though certainly she's a *good* person, and loyal . . . oh dear! These things could be said of a dog. She's never been as focused as other people somehow. She's never had as much energy, and energy is fate, finally. Maybe she'll have more energy now, since she's had this hysterectomy. Maybe all that progestin was just confusing her, messing things up. Now she's on estrogen — "unopposed estrogen," her young doctor called it — writing out the prescription in his illegible script. "Go out and have some fun," he said.

Instead, Harriet is experiencing another failure of nerve here at the desk in the lobby of the Peabody hotel, the entrance to Mississippi. She writes her name on the line, she hands over her Visa card and her driver's license. She takes the massive gold room key which pleases her somehow; she's glad they haven't gone over to those little electric card things.

"Oh yes, a package arrived for you this morning, Federal Express," the frail clerk says in an apparent afterthought. He plucks the orange-and-purple cardboard box from the shelf of packages behind him and pushes it across the counter toward Harriet, who steps back from the desk involuntarily. She knows what it is. "El Destino, Sweet Springs, Mississippi," reads the return address. The clerk hesitates, watching her, watery-eyed. Has he been weeping? He slides the package a little farther across the counter.

"Shall I take that for you, ma'am?" the bellboy asks at her elbow with her luggage already on his cart. Dumbly Harriet nods. Then it's over and done, it's all decided, and it is with a certain sense of relief that she follows the back of his red-and-gold uniform through the lobby toward the elevator, past more ladies drinking in high fragile chairs at the mirrored mahogany bar. Baby should be here, too; she was raised to be a lady though she didn't give a damn about it. Sometimes Harriet actually hates Baby. To have everything given to you on a silver platter, then to just throw it all away. . . . If anything is immoral, Harriet believes, then that is immoral. *Waste.* Harriet follows the bellboy past the fountain where the famous ducks swim round and round.

Soon, she knows, the ducks will waddle out of the fountain and shake their feathers and walk in a line across the lobby and get into an elevator and ride upstairs to wherever they're kept. The ducks do this every day. What would happen, Harriet wonders, if somebody shooed them out the door and down the street and into the river? This is what's going to happen to Harriet.

For here is the great river itself, filling up the whole picture window of her eleventh-floor room. Unable to take her eyes off it, Harriet absentmindedly gives the bellboy a ten-dollar bill. (Oh well, that's too much but she's got a lot of luggage; she couldn't decide what to bring, so she just brought it all.) The bellboy puts the FedEx package down on the glass coffee table next to a potted plant and a local tourist magazine with Elvis on the cover. VISIT THE KING, the headline reads. Harriet moves over toward the window, staring at the river. She does not answer when the bellboy tells her to have a good day; she does not turn around when he leaves. Across the lower rooftops, past the Memphis Business Journal building and the Cotton Exchange and the big NBC building blocking her view to the right, across the street and the trolley tracks, there's Mud Island where the steamboats dock.

Improbable as something out of a dream, two of them sit placidly at anchor like dressed-up ladies in church, flags flying, smokestacks gleaming, decks lined with people tiny as ants. While Harriet watches, one of the paddle wheelers detaches itself from Mud Island and steams gaily out into the channel, heading upriver. The ants wave. The whistle toots and the calliope is playing, Harriet knows, though she can't really hear it, it's too far, and you can't open these hotel windows. But she imagines it is playing "Dixie." Now the steamboat looks like a floating wedding cake, its wake spread out in a glistening V behind it. Can this be the *Belle of Natchez* herself, the boat Harriet will board in the morning? Probably not. Probably this is just one of the day cruisers, maybe the sunset cruise or the evening dinner cruise already leaving. Harriet certainly doesn't have much time to get herself together before she is supposed to meet Courtney in the dining room. Now why did she ever say she'd do *that?* Married, organized, and rich, Courtney is everything Harriet is not. Each year she sends Harriet a Christmas card with a picture of herself and her family posed in front of an enormous stone house. Two sons, two daughters, a cheery husband in a red vest. Tall. All of them very tall.

The river is brown and glossy, shining in the sun like the brown glass of old bottles. Here at Memphis it is almost a mile wide; you can barely see across it. The Hernando de Soto bridge arches into Arkansas, into oblivion, carrying lines of brightly colored cars like so many little beetles. Light glints off them in thousands of tiny arrows. The sun hangs like a white-hot plate burning a hole in the sky all around, its sunbeams leaping back from the steamboat's brown wake and off the shiny motorboats flashing by. Harriet is getting dizzy. She's glad to be here, up so high in the Peabody hotel, behind this frosty glass. Across the river, along the low dreamy horizon, clouds stack themselves like pillows into the sky. A thunderstorm in the making? Too much is happening too fast. At her window, behind the glass, Harriet feels insignificant before this big river, this big sky. Surely it won't matter if she leaves now, quickly and inconspicuously, before Courtney finds out she's here. Oh she should lie down, she should hang up her dress, she should go back home.

The river . . . it all started with the river. How amazing that they ever did it, twelve girls, ever went down this river on that raft, how amazing that they ever thought of it in the first place.

Well, they were young. Young enough to think *why not* when Baby said it, and then to do it: just like that. Just like Huck Finn and Jim in *The Adventures of Huckleberry Finn* which they were reading in Mr. Gaines's Great Authors class at Mary Scott, sophomore year.

Tom Gaines was the closest thing to a hippie on the faculty at Mary Scott, the closest thing to a hippie that most of them had ever seen in 1965, since the sixties had not yet come to girls' schools in Virginia. So far, the sixties had only happened in *Time* magazine and on television. Life at the fairy-tale Blue Ridge campus was proceeding much as it had for decades past, with only an occasional emissary from the changing world beyond, such as somebody's longhaired folk-singing cousin from up north incongruously flailing his twelve-string guitar on the steps of the white-columned administration building. And Professor Tom Gaines, who wore jeans and work boots to class (along with the required tie and tweed sports jacket), bushy beard hiding half his face, curly reddish-brown hair falling down past his collar. Harriet was sure he'd been hired by mistake. But here he was anyway, big as life and right here on their own ancient campus among the pink brick buildings and giant oaks and long green lawns and little stone benches and urns. Girls stood in line to sign up for his classes. *He is so cute,* ran the consensus.

But it was more than that, Harriet realized later. Mr. Gaines was passionate. He wept in class, reading "The Dead" aloud. He clenched his fist in fury over *Invisible Man,* he practically acted out *Absalom, Absalom,* trying to make them understand it. Unfortunately for all the students, Mr. Gaines was already married to a dark, frizzy-haired Jewish beauty who wore long tie-dyed skirts and no bra. They carried their little hippie baby, Maeve, with them everywhere in something like a knapsack except when Harriet, widely known as the most responsible English major, came to baby-sit. Now people take babies everywhere, but nobody did it then. You were supposed to stay home with your baby, but Sheila Gaines did not. She had even been seen breast-feeding Maeve publicly in Dana Auditorium, watching her husband act in a Chekov drama. He played Uncle Vanya and wore a waistcoat. They powdered his hair and put him in little gold spectacles but nothing could obscure the fact that he was really young and actually gorgeous, a young hippie professor playing an old Russian man. Due to the extreme shortage of men at Mary Scott, Mr. Gaines was in all the plays. He was Hamlet and Stanley Kowalski. His wife breast-fed Maeve until she could talk, to everyone's revulsion.

But Mr. Gaines's dramatic streak was what made his classes so wonderful. For *Huck Finn*, he adopted a sort of Mark Twain persona as he read aloud from the book, striding around the old high-ceilinged room with his thumbs hooked under imaginary galluses. Even this jovial approach failed to charm Harriet, who had read the famous novel once before, in childhood, but now found it disturbing not only in the questions it raised about race but also in Huck's loneliness, which Harriet had overlooked the first time through, caught up as she was in the adventure. In Mr. Gaines's class, Harriet got goose-bumps all over when he read aloud:

Then I set down in a chair by the window and tried to think of something cheerful, but it warn't no use. I felt so lonesome I most wished I was dead. The stars were shining, and the leaves rustled in the woods ever so mournful; and I heard an owl, away off, who-whooing about somebody that was dead, and a whippoorwill and a dog crying about somebody that was going to die, and the wind was trying to whisper something to me, and I couldn't make out what it was and so it made the cold shivers run over me. Then away out in the woods I heard that kind of sound that a ghost makes . . .

This passage could have been describing Harriet; it could have been describing her life right then. Mr. Gaines was saying something about Huck's "estrangement" as "existential," as "presaging the modern novel," but Harriet felt it as personal, deep in her bones. She believed it was what country people meant when they said they felt somebody walking across their grave. For even in the midst of college, here at Mary Scott where she was happier than she would ever be again, Harriet Holding continued to have these moments she'd had ever since she could remember, as a girl and as a young woman, ever since she was a child. Suddenly a stillness would come over everything, a hush, then a dimming of the light, followed by a burst of radiance during which she could see everything truly, *ev-*

erything, each leaf on a tree in all its distinctness and brief beauty, each hair on the top of somebody's hand, each crumb on a tablecloth, each black and inevitable marching word on a page. During these moments Harriet was aware of herself and her beating heart and the perilous world with a kind of rapture that could not be borne, really, leaving her finally with a little headache right between the eyes and a craving for chocolate and a sense of relief. She was still prone to such intensity. There was no predicting it either. You couldn't tell when these times might occur or when they would go away. Her mother used to call it "getting all wrought up." "Harriet," she often said, "you're just getting all wrought up. Calm down, honey."

But Harriet couldn't help it.

Another day Mr. Gaines read from the section where Huck and Jim are living on the river:

Sometimes we'd have that whole river to ourselves for the longest time. Yonder was the banks and the islands, across the water, and maybe a spark — which was a candle in a cabin window . . . and maybe you could hear a fiddle or a song coming over from one of them crafts. It's lovely to live on a raft.

His words had rung out singly, like bells, in the old classroom. Harriet could hear each one in her head. It was a cold pale day in February. Out the window, bare trees stood blackly amid the gray tatters of snow.

Then Baby had said, "I'd love to do that. Go down the Mississippi River on a raft, I mean." It was a typical response from Baby, who personalized everything, who was famous for saying, "Well, *I'd* never do *that!*" at the end of *The Awakening* when Edna Pontellier walks into the ocean. Baby was not capable of abstract thought. She had too much imagination. Everything was real for her, close up and personal.

"We *could* do it, you know," Suzanne St. John spoke up. "My uncle owns a plantation right on the river, my mother was raised there. She'd know who to talk to. I'll bet we could do it if we wanted to." Next to Courtney, Suzanne St. John was the most organized girl in school, an angular forthright girl with a businesslike grown-up hairdo who ran a mail-order stationery business out of her dorm room.

"Girls, girls," Mr. Gaines had said disapprovingly. He wanted to get back to the book, he wanted to be the star. But the girls were all looking at each other. Baby's eyes were shining. "YES!" she wrote on a piece of paper, handing it to Harriet, who passed it along to Suzanne. *Yes.* This was Baby's response to everything.

Harriet shivers. She hangs up the new navy dress with the matching jacket she'll wear to dinner tonight. She orders all her clothes from catalogs; it confuses her too much to shop. She unpacks a jumble of cosmetics and medications (vitamins, cold cream, calcium, Advil, lipstick, the alarming estrogen) and tosses the old envelope of clippings onto the bed. She steps out of her sensible flats and takes off her denim jumper and white T-shirt (Lands' End) and hangs them up in the closet alongside the navy dress. All these clothes she might have owned in college, she realizes, confirming her suspicion that whatever you're like in your youth, you only get more so with age.

She remembers believing, as a girl, that wisdom would set in somehow, sometime, as a matter of course. Now she doubts it. There are no grown-ups — this is the big dirty secret that nobody ever tells you. No grown-ups at all, including herself. She cannot think of an exception — except, probably, Courtney, the suitemate she'll be having dinner with later tonight. The very thought of Courtney makes Harriet feel like her bra strap is showing or her period has started and she's got blood on the back of her skirt. But this is ridiculous! Harriet has had a complete hysterectomy and now she has to lie down. Her doctor has prescribed a daily rest for the first four months after surgery, and in fact, Harriet cannot imagine doing without it. She's so tired . . . They say that for every hour you're under anesthesia, a month of recuperation is required. Maybe that's an old wives' tale. One thing that's perfectly clear is that Harriet Holding will never be an old wife. It's too late now.

Though she doesn't really *look* old . . . Harriet slides off her slip to stand before the mirror in her white underwear. The only real difference is that her brown pageboy is cropped below her ears now instead of at her shoulders, the way she used to wear it. But her hair is not yet gray, only a softer, duller brown. Suddenly she remembers overhearing Baby on the phone once during freshman year, arranging blind dates for them all. "Harriet? I don't know exactly what you mean by 'good-looking,' but she's very attractive, and she's got the most interesting face . . ." It's just a bit asymmetrical, actually, with a wide forehead and big hazel eyes set slightly too far apart; a pretty, straight nose like her mother's; and a rueful, mobile mouth. The color comes and goes too easily in her face. Which has always embarrassed her. And she can't hide any of her feelings. Now flushed in the sunset's last glow which illumines the whole room, Harriet could almost be the girl who went down the Mississippi River on that raft so many years ago. She's still trim, her skin pale and softly freckled and luminous in this odd peachy light. Her stomach is flat, her breasts firm. Children have not worn her out.

But suddenly Harriet can't breathe. She leans forward clutching the dresser, staring into the mirror. The light flares up behind her somehow, throwing her face into darkness. Now she's a black cutout paper doll of a woman set against the glowing rectangle of sky, not a woman at all, nobody really, a dark silhouette. Tears sting her eyes; she gropes for the lamp switch and turns it on. The room comes back. Harriet throws herself down on the bed, heart beating through her body like her blood.

Here it comes again: she's all wrought up. Of course she can't rest. Finally she sits up, gets the envelope, and fishes out a faded newspaper entry from the Lexington, Kentucky, newspaper, dated June 10, 1965. OLD MAN RIVER, HERE WE COME! the headline says. Harriet scans the article, smiling. She has not looked through these clippings for years.

They'd named the raft for an early Mary Scott College alumna from Paducah whose sister, Lucille Pickett, had entertained them for tea in her gingerbread family home on the bluff several days before the launch. Harriet remembers that tea as if it were a scene in a play, the crowded musty parlor like a stage set, the old lady sitting up ramrod straight on one of those terrible tufted horsehair sofas, referring again and again to "Sis-tah Daisy," whose photographs lined the walls. A dark-haired beauty, Sis-tah Daisy had been a concert pianist, they were told. After her graduation from Mary Scott, she had performed in "all the grand capitals of Europe," settling at length in Paris where her brilliant career continued until a personal tragedy forced her to return to Paducah. Miss Pickett had said "personal tragedy" in such

40

a way that no one, not even Baby, dared to ask what it was.

"Here she gave private lessons at that very piano until her untimely death," Miss Pickett continued, pointing at the piano with her cane. (Catherine Wilson, on the piano bench, jumped up as if shot, then sat back down shamefaced.) "But I must say," Miss Pickett continued, "after her return from Europe, a certain luster was lost. A certain luster was most assuredly lost." She seemed lost in thought herself for a moment, then began banging her cane on the floor with such force that everyone was startled.

A tiny black maid who looked as old as Miss Pickett herself came scurrying out of the kitchen bearing a tarnished silver tray piled high with slices of fruitcake, of all things, and passed it around. Harriet ate hers dutifully, though she got the giggles when she happened to catch, out of the corner of her eye, Baby slipping her own slice of fruitcake into her purse. Of course it was left over from Christmas! Of course it was. Or maybe the Christmas before *that*.

Finally they escaped, running down the sidewalk toward the nondescript motel near the dock where they were staying, laughing all the way. Who could even imagine how *old* that woman was! And what about the *fruitcake?* By the time they reached the river, they'd named the raft: the *Daisy Pickett.* Harriet felt that they had cheapened the memory of the mysterious Daisy by doing so; she hoped that Miss Lucille would never know it, but of course this was impossible. They were celebrities in Paducah for the next four days as they bought provisions and made commercials to finance the trip. Everything they did was on the news.

Now she reads to the end of the article. "The girls wore white T-shirts with yellow daisies painted on them and sang, 'Goodbye, Paducah,' to the tune of 'Hello, Dolly' as the unusual craft departed." In fact, in Harriet's memory, they sang relentlessly, all the time, all the way down the Mississippi. They sang in spite of all their mishaps and travails: the tail of the hurricane that hit them before they even got to Cairo, a diet consisting mostly of tuna and doughnuts, mosquito bites beyond belief, and rainstorms that soaked everything they owned. If anything really bad happened to them, they knew they could call up somebody's parents collect, and the parents would come and fix things. They expected to be taken care of. Nobody had yet suggested to them that they might ever have to make a living or that somebody wouldn't marry them and look after them for the rest of their lives. They all smoked cigarettes. They were all cute. They headed down the river with absolute confidence that they would get where they were going.

How ignorant they were! But it was just as well, really, wasn't it? Because everything is going to happen to you sooner or later anyway, whether you know it or not. Maybe it's better not to know. Harriet flips through the rest of the soft yellowed clippings. Datelines read Helena, Arkansas; Caruthersville, Missouri; Vicksburg; Natchez; Baton Rouge . . . Here's a close-up of Baby and Harriet on the front page of the Memphis paper, bandannas tied around their heads, squinting into the sun, grinning raffish sailors' grins at the camera. Here's another one, a group shot of them all on the daisy-painted bow, waving and cheering except for Baby who stares moodily off to the side, Harriet notices now, across the wide water.

Harriet pauses at a photograph of activities on deck — Courtney and Suzanne are playing cards, several girls (is that Ruth under the brim of that Panama hat?) are reading, while Bowen does her nails and Baby sleeps. Smack in the middle of them all, clearly oblivious to the rest, Anna sits cross-legged, writing in a notebook. "If it looks confusing, you've got the right idea!" this article reads. "This literary crew contains several writers. At center, Anna Todd, junior English major from Ivy, West Virginia, is writing her first novel." Not even her first, Harriet thinks. And certainly not her last. Now she's written how many? Twenty or so? Thirty? All these romances, Harriet hasn't read them but she's sure they're terrible, simply because Anna is so famous, frequently mentioned in *People* magazine and even *Parade*. Oh dear. How will Harriet ever be able to ask Anna about her work? She should have *tried* to read them at least; her own mother had read romances all the time. Harriet's mother's bed was strewn with paperbacks, all those shiny lurid covers with the girls bursting out of their bodices and a castle in the background someplace. For this old newspaper photograph, Anna had taken an ostentatiously literary pose — pen raised, lips pursed, brow furrowed in concentration, red hair rippling all down her back.

But *she* had been writing, too, Harriet

44

remembers with a start. She was writing a novel. She'd begun it on the raft and then failed to complete it, of course, when everything happened. But yes — Harriet was writing a novel, in between stints as cook and navigator, in between hands of bridge. It was an initiation story. An eight-year-old girl trying to come to terms with the loss of her father, with her mother's promiscuity. Harriet had outlined it as precisely as she used to outline the pictures in her coloring books as a child, with thick dark exact lines, pressing down hard. Then all she'd had to do was color the insides. A snap. Harriet had written two or three pages of the novel every day on the raft. (Anna wrote a daily ten or twelve pages of *hers,* while Baby scribbled sometimes on little scraps of paper then jammed them down into the pockets of her cutoff jeans.)

They'd all been in visiting writer Lucian Delgado's creative writing class that spring, Lucian Delgado with his rumpled three-piece white suits and all the pain in the world behind his weary, hooded eyes. Terrible things had happened to him and were happening to him still. He conveyed this without words; they could just *tell.* Scandals, wrecks, arrests, divorces . . . "*Don't* write, my lovelies!" Lucian Delgado would tell them in class. "Stop if you possibly can!" Of course, this made them all work harder than ever. Once when Harriet went to his office for a conference, she found Lucian Delgado passed out cold across his desk, silk tie thrown on the floor, typewritten pages strewn everywhere. Harriet had picked them up and put them in a stack on a corner of the desk. She read one sentence, which said, "From his balcony, the pointed roofs of the city lay below him like a great sea, devoid of hope or even interest." Harriet tiptoed over and bent down to stare at him curiously, his mouth slack with a little drool in the corner, his cheek smashed down on an open copy of the *New York Review of Books*. A fly buzzed noisily at the window, striking the frosted pane again and again. Harriet had tiptoed out. Lucian Delgado gave everybody an A, then disappeared before the end of the term, never returning their final stories.

But on the raft, Harriet was writing a novel. It's all coming back to her now. She followed her outline resolutely. They had learned how plot works: beginning, middle, and end; conflict, complication, and resolution. It was as simple as that. Harriet was twenty years old. She knew all about plot. Her outline seems so silly to her now, ridiculous; such plots may have been suited only to boys' books anyway. Certainly these forms don't fit Harriet's life, or the lives of any women she knows, or the lives of any of the women she works with in the COMEBACK! program. In her Write for Your Life workshop, where Harriet tries to help her students tell their own life stories, she has learned that there are more ways to tell stories than she could ever have dreamed. And all the stories are different.

Mr. Gaines had explained that Huck — their inspiration — was an American Odysseus off on an archetypal journey, the oldest plot of all. According to the archetype, the traveler learns something about himself along the way. What did *we* learn? Harriet wonders now. Not much. Only that if you're cute and sing a lot of songs, people will come out whenever you dock and bring you pound cake and ham and beer and keys to the city, and when you get to New Orleans, you will be met by the band from Preservation Hall on a tugboat and showered by red roses dropped from a helicopter, paid for by somebody's daddy.

"A Raft of Girls," another caption reads, beneath a picture of them dancing on a dock someplace, Harriet believes it was Baton Rouge. Would she remember the trip at all if she didn't have the clippings? Certainly she wouldn't remember these details: Baby's bandanna and the captain's umbrella and all those tunafish sandwiches. They did an ad for some tuna company, wasn't that it? And an ad for some blue jeans company that photographed their butts from behind, leaning over the *Daisy Pickett*'s rail. If they made the same trip today, they would not be referred to as "girls" in any of these articles. They would be called "women." And they would never, ever, consent to that butt shot.

It's twilight when Harriet wakes, strangely and fully rested from her brief nap, yet flushed and disoriented. She springs up, her body tingling all over. She is drawn toward the window. A wide apricot swath of light lies now across the river, solemn and elegaic, fading even as Harriet watches. Buoys glow red and green. Lights twinkle across the bridge and move on the dark water. It's a "monstrous big river" out here, as Huck said. Harriet can feel it now, she can already feel its suck and pull and hear its whisper in her ear as she imagines herself floating farther and farther from shore, borne out into the current on a rising tide of unopposed estrogen.

Mile 736
Memphis, Tennessee
Friday 5/7/99
1900 hours

"I'll meet you at the entrance to Chez Philippe, it's right off the lobby," Courtney had said in her gentle North Carolina accent, and sure enough there she is now, waving. Harriet spots her the minute she alights from the elevator. Harriet waves back. Suddenly she's aware of her own bitten nails, no rings — as opposed to Courtney's hands which glitter with diamonds and taper to bright red oval nails. Magazine hands. In fact, Courtney herself could have stepped from the pages of *Vogue*, with her perfect black suit, her pearls, her elegant cap of smooth blond hair. Here beside her, Harriet feels like a caricature: the old maid in the deck of Old Maid cards they used to play with when she was a girl back home.

But Courtney is just as friendly as can be, kissing Harriet on the cheek, taking her by the elbow to steer her through the dining room to their table, keeping up a patter of small talk. She reminds Harriet of all the ladies who used to come to her mother's little sewing shop in Staunton, ladies who could easily make charming conversation all afternoon as they stood up straight and turned slowly around and around on the stool like music boxes while Harriet's mother sat cross-legged on the floor below, mouth full of straight pins, turning up their hems. They were not to look down, and didn't. Harriet's mother had held these ladies up to Harriet as a kind of model: this is how *she* should behave, this is how *she* should look, this is the life she should aspire to. Clearly, it's Courtney's life.

The waiter appears. They order, and then Courtney chooses a bottle of Chardonnay which goes straight to Harriet's head. She nods a lot as they eat and Courtney tells her all about her children and about her husband's success in business and about her own community work on behalf of the library and the church and rape crisis and Harriet forgets what else. "It sounds like you're so busy," she finally says. "I guess it was probably pretty hard for you to arrange to take a whole week away from home for this trip. Especially without Hawk, I mean."

"Oh no." Courtney signals the waiter, who takes their plates. "We often travel" — she hesitates — "separately. I'll be staying on in New Orleans for the weekend, in fact. Also, I wanted to see the plantations along the river, especially the gardens — I'm something of a photographer these days. But of course I wanted to see all of *you*, too, and in any case, it would have been almost impossible to turn down Charlie Mahan on the phone. It was not a request that one could refuse, was it?"

"No."

"I've found myself thinking a lot about Baby ever since I learned about her death anyway," Courtney goes on. "It was such a shock. Tragic, really."

"Yes." Harriet twists her napkin, suddenly fighting back tears.

"Did he say anything else to you about it?" Courtney leans forward. "How it happened or anything? Anything more than that brief report in the *Alumnae News*?"

"He said it was an accident," Harriet whispers. "An automobile accident just before Christmas. There'd been an ice storm the night before, so the roads were still slick. Apparently she drove off a bridge on

52

the way to Jackson to do some Christmas shopping."

"A *single* car accident?"

Harriet nods.

"Well, it makes you wonder, then, doesn't it? I mean, whether it was suicide or not. Remember how dramatic she always was? And how . . . troubled. Of course, he'd probably never say, if it was, because of the children and all. *I'd* never say, myself." Courtney takes a compact from her purse and looks in the mirror to reapply her red lipstick. "Well? What do *you* think, Harriet? You were her best friend."

Harriet opens her mouth, then closes it. No, I wasn't. Well, yes, I was. "I don't know if she killed herself or not," she tells Courtney now. "I'll admit, it came into my mind, too, but Charlie certainly didn't say anything that would indicate it. And remember how fast she always drove?"

"Well." Courtney clears her throat. "In any case, I presume you brought the ashes with you?"

"I just got them," Harriet says. "Charlie FedExed them here to the hotel. Or at least I'm assuming that's what's in the FedEx box. It's not very big. I mean, it's just *some* of her ashes anyway. But I haven't had the nerve to open the box yet."

"Just wait, then." Courtney pats her hand. "We'll all do it together, when we're coming into New Orleans, like Charlie requested. You shouldn't have to deal with it all by yourself."

Oh yes I should, Harriet's thinking as Courtney signs the check. "Wait," she says too late. "Let's go Dutch on this."

"Oh heavens no." Courtney waves to the waiter. "My treat."

In school, Harriet remembers, Courtney was poor, too, like she was. It's nice that she's apparently gotten rich now, she always wanted it. She was always so concerned about the "right" thing to wear or the "right" thing to do. Now she epitomizes the right thing. And yet she's still nice, too, she really is, just as nice as she was when she was a girl. Harriet remembers Courtney as wearing badges all the time which identified her as helpful in various ways: freshman orientation leader, student government representative, dorm counselor, Honor Court. She remembers Courtney staying up all night with Baby on a bad drunk, Courtney vacuuming their dormitory lounge. And Courtney's brown eyes still look out on the world with that same level gaze; her smile is just as frank

54

and open. Harriet fights back an impulse to throw herself into Courtney's capable manicured hands, to say, for instance, Okay now, Courtney, *what about me? Whatever happened to me?*

But Courtney is asking her something. "Weren't you from some place fairly close to school? Was it Lexington? Or Charlottesville?"

"Staunton," Harriet says.

"Oh yes, of course, I remember Staunton." Courtney is so polite that it's impossible to know whether this is true or not. "Staunton is a *charming* town. Historic, isn't it?"

"Yes," Harriet says. "Very. Yes, it is. Historic, I mean."

"And you went back there right after college?"

"Yes."

"And you never married, you smart girl?"

Harriet knows that Courtney is just saying it this way to be nice.

"No." Something more seems called for here, some further explanation, but Harriet can't think what it could possibly be. "I always thought I would," she says, "but then I didn't, somehow. You know."

Courtney nods, but of course she *doesn't*

know. "But really, Harriet, here you are, still looking exactly the same — it's eerie, honestly! How do you manage it? What's your secret? And you still live in the very town where you grew up . . . That's unusual, I think, at least by today's standards. So, whatever have you been doing all these years? Tell me about yourself."

Harriet drains her glass. "I don't have any secrets," she says apologetically, standing, a little wobbly. "There's really nothing to tell."

Nothing she *can* tell anyway. It all began in her mother's little sewing shop on Water Street in Staunton so many years ago, and in many ways, she's never really left. Oh, she has her own house now, of course, on Confederate Hill up near the hospital, she's been there for years and she loves it, really she does, with everything arranged just the way she likes. Flowered wallpaper in the dining room, stenciled borders in the hall (she did them herself), and the cutest little Chinese red library with a gas log fireplace, everyone comments on it. Her mother's old table Singer sewing machine sits in the library now, holding a lamp and a Boston fern.

But Harriet still gets the funniest feeling in her stomach every time she drives past the boarded-up sewing shop on Water Street. She would feel better if it were a yogurt shop or a travel agency or, well, *anything*. As it is now, Harriet has the awful sense that their life — her life — is still going on behind that blackened, dusty pane, those ramshackle boards, that nothing has ever changed.

The storefront room was narrow and high-ceilinged, like a shoe box; at the back, it opened into a smaller version of itself which was mostly used to store cloth and supplies. "Now don't you *even* look at my junk room!" her mother would laugh, guiding someone through. Someone . . . who? A man — it was always a man, and Mama was always laughing. A door at the back of the little room led into an alley, where the man had parked his sleek dark car, for reasons of discretion. A black iron stairway, oddly located in the middle of the second room, led up into their living quarters, which Mama called "the apartment." Actually it was a series of three rooms leading one into the other, right over top of the shop. The girls' room had twin beds and a three-sided bay window looking out on the street; then came the kitchen, tiny and jumbled yet strangely elegant with its round oak table and hanging Tiffany lamp;

then Mama's room with its own scent — cigarettes and talcum powder and musky perfume and something else, something mysterious. Mama's room was exotic and beautiful with its big brass bed and rose silk coverlet and piles of soft pillows and clothes strewn all around, its crackly piles of newspapers and magazines. How Harriet and Jill loved to snuggle in the bed with Mama, looking at fashion magazines!

"Now, what do you girls think of *that?*" Mama asked, pointing to a long dark cape worn by a skinny disgruntled-looking model.

"Yuck!" Jill giggled. "Ugly gull!"

In addition to her other problems, Jill had a slight speech impediment. She couldn't say her *R*'s. "Hawwiet," she called her sister, or just plain "Sissy." Mama and Harriet collapsed in giggles, paging through *Vogue*.

"You know Jill has very good taste," Mama often said. "I rely totally on her judgment." Mama was not entirely kidding.

In some undefinable way, Jill was the moral center, the heart of the little family. Her eyes were unnaturally large, unnaturally blue — "cornflower blue," Mama said. When she looked at you, it was like she could see deep, deep down into your very soul, and you could never tell her a lie. Jill called forth the best in everybody just by being there, and once she was gone, the best was gone, too, or so it seems to Harriet. Of course, she always knew that they wouldn't have Jill forever — Mama was clear on that from the beginning — from the "get-go," as she put it.

Mama also made it quite clear how she felt about it, too, nearly snapping off Mrs. Ellen Drake's head the day she ventured to remark, "Well, I must say, Alice, what with no husband and all, this poor crippled child certainly is a cross for you to bear, honey. A cross for you to bear!" Mrs. Ellen Drake always said everything twice.

"She is *not!*" Alice Holding snapped, scrambling up from the floor, hands on hips, blond curls quivering. "She is a blessing, Ellen Drake, do you hear me? She is the joy of my heart." Occasionally Harriet thought disloyally that *she'd* like to be the joy of her mother's heart, too, but mostly she was too busy being good, being helpful, to mind. Besides, it was impossible not to love Jill, as it was impossible not to love Mama.

Mama had the most remarkable sense of style, Harriet can't imagine where she got it: from the movies, perhaps, or out of magazines, or out of her own head, for she lived on images of glamour and elegance, though she rarely went out. Downstairs in the shop, which was really their living room, Mama's taste was reflected everywhere — in the curvy lavender love seat with the old mink coat thrown casually across it, like some exotic pet; in the low-hanging crystal chandelier which came, Mama liked to say grandly if somewhat inaccurately, from "Paris, France, Europe," neglecting to mention the rummage sale where she'd actually found it; in the soft old sofas spread with crazy quilts and velvet throws; in the round Moroccan leather coffee table covered with the most interesting things, eight little boxes that fit inside each other, a silver dagger, a filigree vase full of peacock feathers. And always, swirls of smoke — for many of the ladies who came here did not smoke in public, or even at home — and always, music from Mama's hi-fi. Though Alice Holding could glance at a dress and reproduce it exactly without a pattern, Harriet was sure that her ladies came to Mama as much for the atmosphere and the conversation as for her considerable dressmaking skills. Surely these ladies had needed a refuge, a little escape from the inexorable demands of their station.

Stories floated back and forth through the magic air of the sewing shop like the dissolving ribbons of smoke, weaving in and out of themselves, until it was almost impossible to distinguish one from another. *Oh, he did not! Oh, she did not! Well, what in the world did you do then, honey?* Harriet loved to fall asleep wrapped in the mink coat on the love seat with the soft murmur of stories in her ear. She loved to sit on the Oriental rug in the corner playing Old Maid with Jill or reading to her from the Nancy Drew books they both adored. Harriet loved Nancy's friends — boyish George Fayne, prissy Bess Marvin — and most of all Nancy herself, energetic and brash and smart, able to solve *any* mystery.

For they lived with mystery there in the sewing shop — didn't they have any grandparents, for instance? Children in books always had doting grandparents. *"Oh, please,"* Alice said when Harriet badgered her about it. And who was Harriet's father anyway? Alice was maddeningly mum on this subject, too, though she once said under duress that he was a Yankee sailor she'd met at Virginia Beach. And where was he now? "Gone with the wind," Alice said. "Ha!" Another time she called Harriet a "love child." Harriet liked this phrase as much as "joy of my heart" and said it over and over in her mind: love child love child love child. I am a love child. Though, judging by the mirror, it did not seem likely. Could a love child be so thin and pale and earnest? Rose Red, for instance, in the Snow White and Rose Red book, looked more like a love child than Snow White.

In contrast to Harriet, everybody knew who her sister Jill's father was, for he had actually married Alice. Hal Ramsey blew into the sewing shop like a big wind, stirring things up, turning their lives upside down. Harriet adored him. Hal Ramsey was a rangy man with a gap-toothed grin and an engaging way of cocking his head when he was talking to you, listening hard, as if what you had to say was terribly important. Harriet was five years old when he first showed up to service Alice's sewing machine. He knocked on the door in early September and didn't leave until right before Christmas. That Christmas, Alice cried and cried and didn't buy Harriet any presents, so some of her ladies pitched in and gave Harriet a drawing kit, a stationery set, some ugly new oxfords, and a beautiful Barbie bride doll.

They brought Alice some nerve pills.

Then in February, Hal Ramsey showed up in a brand-new red car, announcing to one and all that he'd come back to marry Mama. Two days later, it was done. Alice's ladies threw a big party for them at the country club. "Now," they said, "she'll settle down and that poor little girl will have a daddy."

This was the best part of Harriet's early childhood, when her mama and Hal were married and he was not on the road. His route covered sixteen counties, but when he was home, Alice cooked pot roasts and Hal Ramsey played his guitar in the kitchen and they drank something called Long Island iced tea and laughed a lot. When he was gone, Alice stood looking out the shop door and smoking a cigarette, tapping her foot. Hal Ramsey took Harriet fishing once at the beginning of trout season to a stream in the mountains outside town. "You got it! You got it!" he shouted, helping her reel in a big rainbow-colored fish that twisted in the sunlight, throwing diamond drops of water all over them both.

It seemed like no time at all had passed

before Alice was pregnant, then Jill was born, then Hal was gone like a shot.

"Son of a bitch!" Alice said, stomping around the shop in her pink peignoir, a gift from Hal, smoking cigarettes and telling everybody who came in how he had acted like everything was just fine right up until the minute he left, so she didn't suspect a thing. Not a thing! Nothing at all! Son of a bitch! Her ladies "oohed" and "ahhed" and "tsk-tsked," bringing casseroles.

"I'll tell you one thing," she said to Harriet. "If a man leaves his wife for you, then he'll sure enough leave *you* for another woman. You can mark it down."

Harriet registered this, though she knew even then that Mama's words would never apply to her, and she was nice to Mama's men friends who started coming by again after Hal Ramsey's departure. Harriet spent most of the time she was not in school taking care of Jill. Sometimes she thought about that fishing trip, though — the only one she's ever been on — and she remembered how the sun looked, coming up, and how the fish looked coming out of the water, and how it had turned from every color in the rainbow to dull, dull gray while she held it in her hands.

Years passed. A special lady came to the

apartment to teach Jill her lessons while Mama sewed. Harriet made straight A's in school where she did not distinguish herself in any other way; somehow, she felt, she *could not,* since Jill never would.

When Harriet was in seventh grade, Alice hit on the idea of teaching her how to dance, hoping that this would make Harriet more confident, at least, even if she'd never be popular. These lessons took place in the shop whenever Alice wasn't busy or when the door closed behind the last lady of the day. Mama would look up and grin at Jill and Harriet. "Party time?" she'd ask. "Sure, I guess," Harriet said as shyly as if her mama really were one of that mysterious race, *boys,* while Jill clapped wildly and bounced in her special chair. Jill's favorite record was "Hernando's Hideaway" which Harriet enjoyed, too, especially the part where she and Mama stomped one foot and threw up their hands on *"Olé!"* but her own favorite was the dramatic "Love Is a Many Splendored Thing."

Harriet and Mama were sweeping theatrically around the apartment to its exalted strains when Mr. Dabney Carr made his first appearance. The doorbell tinkled and in he popped like a man in a clock, dressed in the nicest dark suit, carrying a coat and

65

an umbrella. Harriet had forgotten that it was raining outside.

"Oh." Mama came to a quivering, embarrassed stop.

"But please continue," the man said, "I enjoy a waltz myself." Harriet found this hard to believe, as he was a man who looked like he was all business, a man who didn't enjoy anything.

Mama crinkled up her eyes at him. "Do you?" she said. "Well, then." She crossed the shop in her stocking feet and put the record on again. She wore her pink angora sweater and a long, full skirt.

The man put down his things and followed her. "May I?" he asked, and then off they went, round and round, Mama's skirt swishing out on the turns. Harriet sat on the arm of Jill's chair and watched them, understanding very well that something momentous had occurred. Though it was *not*, as one of Mama's ladies said pointedly to her afterward, anything that would ever do her any good in the long run. The ladies' general opinion seemed to be that Mama was "too sweet" and "incapable of looking out for herself." In this way, they were wrong. Mr. Carr would look out for Mama for the rest of his life, though he would never marry her, because his own wife was still very much alive in the famous old asylum on the hill. She had been there for two years when he ducked into the shop that day, on impulse, to get a button sewed onto his raincoat. Mama did that, too, biting off the thread with her full red bottom lip stuck out. When she was finished, Mr. Carr put on the raincoat, thanked her formally, and almost bowed as he pressed her hand. He also shook hands with Jill and Harriet. *Good-bye, good-bye.*

Mama stood in the middle of the floor hugging herself after he left. "Now girls," she said, turning to smile at them, "*that* was a gentleman!"

Mr. Carr lived in Richmond, Virginia; he visited them once a week. During his tenure, things got spruced up: a dishwasher appeared in the tiny kitchen, Jill was given a TV, and the whole upstairs got a fresh coat of paint.

One day about six months after Mr. Carr's first appearance, Mama pulled Harriet over and hugged her. "Mr. Carr will be bringing his son along with him tomorrow," she said. "They will be staying at the Willetts Hotel." Usually Mr. Carr stayed at the apartment. "He's about your age," Mama said. "So be nice."

Be *nice!* In her whole life, had Harriet

ever been anything other than nice? Was she even capable of being anything else? A *boy*. She felt sick. "What's his name?" she asked. "Jefferson Carr," Mama said, "but he goes by Jeff. He'll go to see his mother when they get here on Saturday, but then he will probably stay with us while Mr. Carr goes up there on Sunday afternoon. It'll be a long visit, as he has a hospital board meeting to attend, too. So I thought you and Jeff might go to the movies, or maybe you could go over to Gypsy Park."

"Mama, I . . ." Harriet said. She was twelve years old and very, very shy. She had just gotten so that she could shake hands with Mr. Carr without blushing.

Mama touched Harriet's lips lightly with one finger. "Thanks," she said.

It was even harder than Harriet thought it would be. Jeff Carr looked like Rock Hudson. And he was furious at his father for having a girlfriend, furious at being left with them for the afternoon, furious at his mother for being sick. He kicked rocks all the way to the park and didn't look at her. He wore a navy blue windbreaker with the collar turned up.

"Wanna smoke?" he asked when they got there. It was a cloudy, blowing spring day. He still didn't look at her.

68

"Sure," Harriet heard herself say.

Jeff Carr produced two cigarettes from someplace inside the windbreaker, put them both in his mouth at the same time to light them, then took a deep drag and handed one to Harriet. When she put the cigarette in her own mouth, the end of it was wet with Jeff Carr's spit. Suddenly he was grinning at her. "Take a drag," he said. "Quick. Or it'll go out."

"What?" Harriet felt like an ignoramus, one of Mama's favorite words.

"Like this." Jeff demonstrated for her. He sucked the smoke deep into his lungs and blew it out in a cloud where the March wind blew it away.

"Oh, sure." Harriet tried to sound blasé. She did it, then burst out coughing.

Jeff doubled over in laughter. "Oh, man," he said. "Oh, wow. Far out. You're really a big smoker, huh?"

"Well," Harriet said when she could speak. "Actually I've never smoked before."

"No shit," Jeff said.

"But I just *love* it!" Harriet added.

"*Sure.*" Like every boy his age, Jeff was a master of sarcasm.

"Can I have another one?" Harriet dropped her cigarette butt on the gravel walk and ground it out.

"Okay," Jeff said. This time, she put it between her own lips and he lit it for her, which went surprisingly well. "Where do you go to school?" he asked.

"Why, *here*," Harriet said. She didn't know there was any other choice, but Jeff said he was going to a boarding school in Massachusetts next year, that he was looking forward to it.

"You are?" Harriet could not imagine this. "Why?"

"Man, it's so depressing at home, you can't even imagine." He described their big old historic house full of antiques, with a pool in back. He said it felt even bigger these days with his two older sisters grown and gone and his mother in the loony bin. Once she'd tried to drown herself in the pool, he said, but had been rescued by the gardener. He wasn't even sure she really meant to do it, since she was in the shallow end. Hard to tell. Anyway, she was drunk and she'd swallowed a lot of water and the rescue guys came.

"That's *awful*," Harriet said sincerely. She was starting to feel light-headed from so much smoke. Jeff shrugged. The wind came up and they stood shivering in the bowl of Gypsy Park, surrounded by the wooded hill on one side and the highway fence on the other. Nobody else was there. Suddenly Jeff leaned forward and slapped her hard on the shoulder, then hopped backward. "Can't catch me!" he called and then he was zigzagging through the play equipment and Harriet was after him, right on his tail. Though she'd never tried out for any teams and was judged to be "not athletic," she could run like the wind. "Gotcha!" she cried finally, slapping him across the butt, and then she took off with him chasing her in and out of trees on the hill until he cornered her between a pine and the fence, and they dashed back and forth around the tree until she slipped in the pine needles and fell and then he threw himself down flat beside her. Harriet was laughing so hard she couldn't breathe, and so was Jeff. "Hey!" he said in a minute, sitting up. "Hey, guess what she said yesterday?"

"Who?" Harriet could not quit laughing.

"Mama," Jeff said.

"What?"

"When I went into the dayroom, she came over and grabbed me and took me up to everybody she knew and said, 'I don't think you've met my son, Dwight Eisenhower.'"

"No shit." It was the first time Harriet ever said that word.

"Yep," Jeff said. "I swear to God. She's in la-la land."

They walked down the hill and got on the kiddie play equipment for some reason. Harriet held on for dear life while Jeff pushed the little merry-go-round faster and faster and faster. Then they got on the swings and swung so high they went up even with the bars every time, up into the gray cloudy sky which was beginning to darken now. Every time she pumped, every time the swing rose forward on its perilous arc, Harriet's heart leapt into her throat and she thought, Now. Yes. Now, closing her eyes and leaning back and feeling her hair stream out behind her. She thought, Yes. I will die now, in a kind of rapture at the very top of the arc, but then she didn't, and finally when Jeff yelled, "I guess we'd better go," she stopped pumping and started dragging her feet every time she came down. It was a long dark walk home.

Just as they turned the doorknob, Mama threw open the door and cried, "Why, wherever have you been? I was so worried!"

"Just over at Gypsy Park, like you said." Harriet was indignant.

Mama leaned forward, peering at her. "Well, it must have been good for you," she said. "Look at those roses in your cheeks."

Harriet pulled back embarrassed.

"Come on," Mama said. "Aren't you cold? I've got some hot chocolate for you."

"Where's Dad?" Jeff asked.

"He'll be back in a little while," Mama said. "He just called. He's still at the hospital board meeting which has lasted longer than he thought." She ladled out two cups of hot chocolate from the little burner hot pot where she kept her ladies' coffee going all day long. "Here, honey," she said, handing one to Jeff. "I guess your daddy's pretty much of a bigwig, isn't he?"

"Bigwig," Harriet said.

"Bigwig," Jeff repeated. He started laughing.

"Bigwig!" Harriet was laughing so hard that she couldn't hold her cup. She had to put it down and collapse on the love seat.

"Bigwig, bigwig," they chanted, rolling around on the love seat. Jill started laughing, too, while Mama stood there in her silly frilly blouse and watched them with a puzzled hopeful look on her face that could break your heart if you thought about it. "Bigwig! Bigwig!" they screamed.

This is how Harriet met Jefferson Carr

who would fall hopelessly in love with Baby Ballou when she introduced them all those years later on the campus of Mary Scott College, an event that seems to Harriet in retrospect as inevitable as the passing of time itself, preordained from the very moment when Mr. Carr opened the door and came out of the rain and into the sewing shop.

Courtney has invited Harriet up to her room after dinner to look at her scrapbooks, the pride of her life, a work of art if she does say so herself. She has brought six of them, an overnight bag full of albums to show her friends on the *Belle of Natchez*. But wouldn't they all be amazed if they knew about the decision she faces as they steam down the river? Wouldn't they all be amazed if they knew that the most important person in her life is not even pictured in these albums? Her husband, Henry ("Hawk") Ralston, has often teased her by telling everybody that he hasn't even unpacked from a trip before she's already had the photos developed and put them into the current album, with appropriate captions. But Courtney doesn't care if he makes fun of her for being so organized. So what? *Somebody* has got to be organized. Courtney's not going to get down on herself about it.

As a matter of fact, the original raft trip — the only "wild" thing Courtney ever did in her life, until recently — never would have happened without her. She and Suzanne St. John organized it all — got the information, kept the books, got everything lined up. At Mary Scott, Courtney was on the Honor Court and yearbook staff. Now she is on the vestry of Saint Matthews Church right next door to Magnolia Court, Hawk's family home, circa 1840. "This home has *not* been restored," Hawk's mother told her severely when she turned the keys over to Courtney. "It has been *maintained.*" Courtney knew she could handle it. She is good at maintaining. She is president of the Dogwood Historic Preservation Society and Friends of the Library.

See, here she is standing in the historic cemetery at Saint Matthews, next to the Berry monument. Here she is convening the Friends of the Library, with her gavel. And here she is with Charles Frazier, the author of *Cold Mountain,* whose appearance constituted their most successful event yet, bringing in scads of money. Courtney still means to finish his book. It's just that it was taking *so long,* all that walking across the whole state of North Carolina, it was pretty slow. Also, recently and for very good reason, Courtney hasn't been able to concentrate. Whenever she tries to read, all she can think about is Gene Minor; all she can see is his silly face.

But here's the house, as photographed for *Southern Living*, 1984: *exterior*, looking up the long hill from Four Corners. It's a large stone manor house of a type uncommon in Raleigh, a house that would suit a moor except for those columns and the deep veranda which stretches across the front. This house is a testament to Hawk's Scots heritage, as he likes to say, and to his grandfather's monumental vanity. Eight huge old magnolias, four on either side of the long central driveway, have determined its name. The driveway runs all the way down the hill to Four Corners; here, the estate is shielded from the busy street by a high stone wall topped by wrought iron spikes. That wall means business. So does Hawk. And if you look closely at this photograph, you can see Hawk himself, in fact, standing by the massive front door, wearing slacks and a tie and a cardigan sweater, studiedly casual, sort of a corporate Mister Rogers. A handsome man, with that sharp nose and silver hair. A powerful man. A man to reckon with.

Interior. Hawk and Courtney stand in the library before the big stone hearth made by Moravian masons on their way west to build the Biltmore Mansion outside Asheville. You can tell that Hawk belongs in this house by the way he smiles so confidently into the camera, chin up, one arm outstretched on the mantel which holds an antique clock flanked by silver candlesticks and a militant army of family photographs going back a hundred years. This is Hawk's great-grandfather, Henry Giles Ralston, C.S.A.: this is Hawk's father in his naval uniform, World War II. The old sleigh bed in the master bedroom suite right upstairs is the bed where Hawk was born but scarcely ever sleeps in now. Courtney is used to it. She has been used to it for years, though at first her heart was broken again and again — right after the honeymoon, for instance, when he went to Charlotte on business and a girl's voice answered when she called the number he had left. Courtney had hung up without speaking. She cried all night long. The next day she'd attended her first Junior League meeting, at Buffy Sandover's house. In the afternoon, she took a tennis lesson. Two nights later, when he walked in the kitchen door, she turned from the sink and threw one of the new wineglasses at him. The wineglass hit the doorjamb just beside Hawk's head and shattered. He didn't even flinch. Just stood there looking at her, one dark eyebrow raised in a question.

"Who is she?" Courtney's voice was shaking.

"Where's Mama?" Hawk asked. "Where's Walter?"

"Your mother is out in her apartment. Why? Because you think I'm making a scene? Well, I *am* making a scene, by God. I don't care who hears me either. We just get back from Jamaica, and you're gone for two days. I asked you who she is!" Courtney threw another wineglass, not exactly at Hawk. It hit the edge of the sink, raining crystal down on the floor. Hawk shook his head, as if Courtney were an obstinate child. But at least he didn't lie.

"It doesn't matter," he said. "She doesn't matter. Let's get that straight right now, Courtney. You are my wife. This doesn't concern you at all."

"It *does* concern me!" Courtney was crying almost too hard to stop.

"No. You are mistaken," Hawk had said gently. He moved toward her across the kitchen floor, crunching glass. He caught her by the shoulders and spun her around.

"No —" Courtney twisted her head to the side. He took her chin in his hand and turned her face toward him and kissed her, slowly and gravely, for a long time. He was good at this. Then he took her out to dinner at the country club. By Christmas, she was pregnant.

She'd left him only once, when Scott was eighteen months old and Jeremy was a colicky newborn.

One April night, she'd been up with Jeremy for hours, her nerves on edge, when she heard a car coming slowly up the gravel driveway and looked out the window to note that its lights were off. It pulled right in front of the steps and stopped under the coach light. It was a red Cherokee which Courtney didn't recognize. Hawk got out, carrying his jacket over one shoulder and his bag in his other hand. He took a few steps toward the house and then turned and walked around the front of the car and leaned his head into the window on the driver's side for a long time, five or ten minutes, then turned and walked back around the car and stood to watch it pull away. He stood there until the car passed all the magnolias and reached the end of the driveway, red taillights winking away in the night. At the dark upstairs window, Courtney watched all this as if it were a movie. It was just starting to get light, pink sky above the horizon. Hawk reached out and broke a dogwood blossom off the tree by the steps and stood looking at it for a minute, then let it drop onto the grass. He turned and disappeared from view below and soon Courtney heard his step on the stairs, and then he opened the door.

He did not seem surprised to see her sitting by the window with Jeremy on a pillow in her lap. He walked over and kissed the top of her head. "I got a ride from the airport," he said. "I guess you've had a hard night." Hawk stripped and lay down on the bed and was instantly, soundly asleep. Courtney could always tell by his breathing. Finally she put Jeremy down and then she got in bed, too, pressing herself against Hawk's back. The bones of his legs were so long from knee to hip; he was a big man. She ran her fingers along his collarbone and his jaw and through the hair on his chest and then traced his nipples and his ribs one by one. Morning

came slowly in the window until everything soft and dark grew hard and visible.

As soon as Hawk went to the bank,
Courtney called and canceled a pediatri-
cian's appointment for Jeremy and a
"Mother's Morning Out" for Scotty, then
packed them up and drove over to her twin
sister's. She left a note for Hawk. It was
not a very good place to go, but she
couldn't think of another. Their mother
had died years before.

"I think you're crazy," Jean said when
she got home from work and heard the
whole story. "Maybe he *did* get a ride
home from the airport. How do you know
he wasn't telling the truth?" Jean was a
shorter, sturdier version of Courtney. Once
they'd been inseparable, Burton High
cheerleaders together. But then Jean had
enrolled at NC State and met Buzzy while
Courtney had gotten the scholarship to
Mary Scott. Their lives were different now.

"Oh, come on." Despite her lack of
sleep, Courtney felt more clearheaded than
she'd ever been before in her life. "No
plane comes in at four o'clock in the
morning. No friend gives you a ride at five.
Besides, he wouldn't have stuck his head in
the window like that, if it was a guy. You
don't do that with a guy."

"I guess you're right." Jean lit a cigarette and tapped it nervously on her ashtray. The ashtray said Kings Dominion. Under it were coupons Jean had clipped.

"I've had it," Courtney said. She sat on Jean's couch and looked out Jean's picture window at the neat yards and the neighbors' lookalike houses. Why couldn't she live in a nice little brick house like this one, like Jean and Buzzy, and get a job? Why hadn't she ever thought of *working* anyway? She'd had two years of college. But all she'd ever done was get married. A cement mixer rolled slowly down the street and it occurred to Courtney that her life had been like that, once she met Hawk it was just like that, a big machine set in motion and she was on it, by God, and it was going and going and there was no getting off. Courtney felt as brittle and clear as glass that day in her sister's living room, smoking her sister's Newports. They drank some wine and then took a walk in the arboretum, Jean pushing the stroller while Courtney carried Jeremy in a Snugli. Jean loved these kids — she and Buzzy were still trying, no luck so far. Courtney had always had all the luck.

When they got back to the house, Buzzy was sitting at the kitchen table drinking a beer.

"Courtney just came by for a little visit," Jean said.

"Yeah, well, that's good, because you might have forgot but tonight's my poker night, the guys are coming over, we gotta get ready, babe. You haven't been to the store yet?"

"I mean, Courtney needs a place to *stay* for a little while," Jean said.

Buzzy turned and looked at Courtney. His jaw dropped open. "Yeah?" he said. "You *sure*, little sister?"

Courtney nodded. Scotty was running a toy car along the kitchen table, then up and over Buzzy's hands. Buzzy picked him up and hugged him.

"Okey-doke," he said. "Why don't you take the kids upstairs and get them settled down? Just pull out that couch in the spare room, you know, my office, and make up a pallet for the kids on the floor. You want to go with me, Jean? We can pick up some pizza along with the beer. You know anybody that likes pizza?" he asked Scotty, who bobbed his head up and down so vigorously that everybody started laughing.

"Buy some milk, too," Courtney said.

But while they were gone, the doorbell rang, and when Courtney ran down the stairs to open it, she found Miss

Evangeline there on the stoop with her new gray Cadillac (big fins; it looked like a shark) waiting at the curb behind her. Walter was driving. He waved. Courtney waved back.

"Gramma, Gramma, Gramma," Scotty came bounding down the stairs.

"Oh my! Oh, my darling!" Miss Evangeline acted like they'd been missing for years, like they'd been kidnapped. She grabbed Scotty up though she was too frail for it, really, kissing his round little face again and again as he started playing with the pearls at her throat. Since Stephen had died in Vietnam, Hawk was her only child, these her only grandchildren.

Miss Evangeline didn't weigh ninety pounds dripping wet. Her yellow-gray hair was piled haphazardly up on her head; her filmy blue eyes had tears in them. "Come along now, dear," she said to Courtney. "Come along home." Then Miss Evangeline must have given some kind of signal to Walter because he got out of the car, tipped his hat to the curious neighbors who had gathered in their own yards to see what was going on, and came right into the house and went upstairs to get their things. Jeremy slept through it all.

Soon afterward, Courtney got a new car,

a Volvo station wagon, and Buzzy got the electric contract for Hawk's new downtown financial center. Little Evangeline was born, then Lydia. Without ever discussing it, Hawk and Courtney worked things out. Courtney ran the house and supervised the children, though Hawk was a good father, both strict and generous. He attended ball games, graduations, and recitals. He and Courtney chaired the Greater Raleigh United Way Campaign together. They were a team.

When Miss Evangeline finally died, they established a music scholarship in her honor at Meredith College, where she had gone to school. Hawk bought banks in South Carolina, banks in Tennessee. Following an antiques tour of England with several friends, Courtney renovated Magnolia Court. She became a famous hostess. Here in front of the hearth, she is poised, serene, beautiful. Those are the candlesticks she brought back from England, eighteenth-century coin silver. Courtney's hair is held back by a velvet band; she wears a close-fitting black velvet jacket and a floor-length red plaid skirt. Courtney and Hawk make a handsome couple as they stand before this glowing fire, which is not really a fire at all, though these new gas logs they make now are so realistic you just can't tell the difference. Courtney's bright red smile stretches all the way across her face. She holds a silver tray of hors d'oeuvres, one of her favorites — shrimp tarts, Miss Evangeline's recipe.

Oddly, the same hors d'oeuvres are visible on the table in *this* photograph, too, in the scrapbook devoted to Little Evangeline's wedding which Courtney held at home. Vangie wouldn't get married at Saint Matthews because she didn't believe in God, she said, and neither did Nate, her fiancé as Courtney kept referring to him, hopefully, as if this designation would somehow make him shape up and act like one — like a fiancé, like a husband, instead of like a bass guitar player, which he is.

In the photograph, Nate and Vangie are laughing hysterically and feeding each other bites of cake which is falling all over the seed pearl bodice of Vangie's wedding dress. It cost twenty-two hundred dollars. Vangie has taken out her nose ring for the occasion. The long lace sleeves nearly hide the vine tattoo on her upper arm, and of course nobody can see the butterfly on her thigh and who even knows what other tattoos or piercings she might have or where she might have them? Courtney shudders to think. Vangie has never told her mother much about her life, which is just as well. As with Hawk, she'd rather not know. The things Courtney *does* know about her daughter, the public things, are disturbing enough, such as the name of Vangie's band, the Friends of the Library. But at least Courtney has the satisfaction of knowing that *she* has done her duty, by all of them, her entire difficult family. This wedding alone took a full year of work.

She could never have done it without Gene Minor, that sweet thing. His presence is everywhere in this wedding album — everywhere and nowhere, for of course he is not pictured. His company, Florenza, handled everything. Gene Minor convinced her to be more, well, *theatrical* than she'd ever considered. "If it's not fun, don't do it" is Gene's motto, and since Vangie didn't care one way or the other — she was on a West Coast tour and hadn't wanted such a big wedding in the first place — Courtney did it all. She did everything Gene Minor suggested, and it was brilliant. People are still talking about it.

Gene was the one who held out for an evening wedding, the one who convinced her to go with the red roses for all the bouquets, Vangie's too, the one who ordered the tent and supervised its erection in the back garden and had it all rigged up with those thousands of tiny white twinkling lights and wound the tent poles round and round with garlands of baby's breath. Gene Minor personally created the spectacular soaring silver and red arrangements on each table ("Hey, baby, you gotta think vertical!"). He wove roses and silver sprays through the ivy of the old arched trellis where Vangie and Nate would say their vows, a project that could not be accomplished until the afternoon of the wedding itself. While Gene Minor was out in her backyard doing this, Courtney hovered between house and garden like a butterfly, too nervous to light down anyplace, though once she dared to tiptoe up behind him and actually touch his sweaty T-shirt. Gene Minor jumped as if shot, then toppled off his little ladder onto his back like a giant turtle, arms and legs waving helplessly in the summer air. "Why, Mrs. Ralston!" he exclaimed in that high squeaky voice. "Oh my, Mrs. Ralston, oh oh!" Courtney got so tickled she had to sit down right there on the grass, too, holding her sides in laughter. "Mom! What are you *doing?*" Vangie cried out the window. But Courtney couldn't quit laughing for the longest time — in all her life, nobody has ever made her laugh so hard as Gene Minor. He is such a *nut!*

He's the one who suggested the fireworks, too, which were fabulous, capping off the evening. Here's a photo of the grand finale when six or seven were fired off at once, exploding like an arrangement of celestial lilies in the sky over Magnolia Court. Looking up, the whole crowd went "ooh!" at once, three hundred faces bathed in the colored light. And who would ever guess that inside the potting shed which you can barely see in the bottom right-hand corner of this photograph, the mother of the bride and the florist were locked in a long, damp, passionate embrace?

Of course, Gene Minor is not pictured in photograph after photograph of the children — Gene Minor is just for *her,* just for Courtney. He has no business here among these boys in various groups and various uniforms, shining heads all in a row, smiling or squinting into the sun, holding different kinds of balls. There's Jeremy's little face, Scotty's big grin. Oh, if our children actually knew how much we love them, they'd never be able to hit any of these balls, they'd be simply immobilized by the force of it, by the awful force of our love. Probably in the long run it's best that our children are shielded from us, as they are, by schools and churches and teams, by teachers and friends and other people.

Then little girls in tutus, little girls on ponies; bigger girls in bodices, in dust caps, in plays; girls in bathing suits, with breasts. There's Lydia grown hugely tall and toothy, carrying her hockey stick, making a goal. There's Lydia hugging her teammates in an all-out way that makes Courtney vaguely uneasy. Lydia teaches now, history and hockey, at a prep school in Virginia. She runs marathons, and does not make hors d'oeuvres. Scotty is getting an M.B.A. at Duke. But Jeremy, well, something's wrong with Jeremy, though Hawk will not even admit it and no one seems to know what it is. "It's just a phase . . ." Courtney has been saying this for years.

But he was such a normal child. Look at him in these photographs, he looks just like every other boy on his Little League team, doesn't he? Like every other boy in his Rainbow Soccer league, like every other boy in his graduating class. But like Gene Minor, Jeremy is not really pictured here either. Courtney doesn't know where her sweet little Jeremy went or even when he disappeared. Why did his grades start going down, and why did he drop out of school freshman year at Williams College, despite his famous IQ? Courtney has no idea. Hawk is simply disgusted, calling Jeremy a "slacker." And now he's cut him off, which Jeremy seems not to mind or even notice. For several years now he's been in Boulder, Colorado, living in a rented room over the secondhand bookstore where he works. Courtney tells everyone who asks that Jeremy is "finding himself," though she doesn't really believe it and would be even more worried about him if she didn't have other, bigger fish to fry.

Speaking of fish, here's a picture to catch your eye: Hawk with that sailfish he caught off Cozumel two years ago on his annual trip with Scooter Bowles and Martin Hanes. Held upright by a block and tackle at the dock, this fish stands even taller than Hawk, who's grinning ear to ear behind his sunglasses, beneath his fishing cap. Barechested, barefooted, he's wearing those crazy, baggy old Hawaiian shorts he loves, looking just as much at home on this foreign dock as he does in a boardroom. A man accustomed to killing things — deer, birds, fish. Big fish. A man who can still stop a girl dead in her tracks just as he did — oh Lord, yes, didn't he? — so many years ago.

But Hawk's most recent fishing trip, earlier this summer, in May, is not pictured here.

Actually Courtney was in bed with Gene Minor when she found out about it. Wednesday afternoons are always theirs. Gene closes the flower shop and Courtney meets him at home — *his* house — with lunch, something delicious. It's fun to cook for Gene because he likes food so much. (Hawk, on the other hand, always carries a pocket counter for fat grams.) That particular afternoon (Was it only two months ago? God, it seems like years) Courtney had fixed lamb chops and new potatoes with mint from Gene's herb garden right outside his kitchen door. She'd left the door wide open, letting the spring sunlight and Gene's cats, Stan and John, into the dingy old fifties kitchen. She'd set two places at the red and gray plastic dinette table. She knew he'd bring her some flowers for lunch, which he did, five blue irises in a slim yellow vase.

"Beautiful," she said.

"You certainly are." Gene Minor kissed her, always an unsettling experience. Well, thrilling. Always a thrilling experience. Gene perused his pantry, chose a bottle of wine, and opened it with a grand flourish. "Ah!" he said, swirling the red Bordeaux around and around dangerously close to the lip of the wineglass, a parody of the connoisseur. He inhaled deeply. "An impertinent little red," he pronounced. "Good body, though. Nice ass." Courtney giggled. He winked broadly at her, behind his thick glasses. Gene Minor was legally blind, which might be the reason he thought she was beautiful. Or maybe he thought she was beautiful because he'd thought so in high school, and he was stuck fast in time. Whatever! Courtney didn't care. The fact was that when he took his glasses off to make love to her, his eyes were as round and blue and unfocused as baby-doll eyes, as plates. When he turned them toward her, she could see herself there as that hopeful girl, that cheerleader she used to be long before she grew up and got so old and so responsible.

Time stood still in Gene's house. Even the jeweled kittycat clock in his bedroom ticked along two hours and twenty minutes late, so that if you ever wanted to know what time it was, you had to add two hours and twenty minutes to whatever it said. The first time she came here, years ago, Courtney had been amazed by this system. She'd said, "Why in the world don't you get it fixed? Or just get a clock that tells time?"

But then she got to know him.

Gene is a big man, close to three hundred pounds. Courtney loves to lie in bed with her arms around him feeling that thick layer of fat. Gene Minor is like a seal, like a warm fur coat. He turns Courtney on and comforts her, both at the same time. Yet she's never able to fall asleep the way he can on those Wednesday afternoons after making love, instantly as a baby. In fact, Courtney never naps, she's always too keyed up. She's lucky to get four or five hours of sleep a night, often lying awake for hours as lists run through her mind.

Here, at Gene's house, she had finally learned to leave the dirty dishes on the table when they went to bed, but still she couldn't sleep. And today she was really on edge, she didn't even know why. Finally she had gotten up and put on one of

Gene's huge shirts and walked into the kitchen. It was an army-green work shirt she'd never seen before, with BOBBY stitched onto the pocket. Gene had probably bought it at the Twice As Nice store — he loved old clothes, costumes, and dressing up. To be as smart as he was, Gene was an almost childish man. Courtney smiled, remembering the time he had appeared for lunch in a pink silk kimono, to her horror. But it was hysterical, she had to admit. Stan and John were on the dinette table, gnawing at the lamb bones. They didn't even look up when she came in.

On impulse, Courtney had crossed the kitchen and called her home answering service. There was a message from Anne Weaver changing the date of the upcoming Friends of the Library meeting and a message from Ellen Henley, Hawk's secretary, saying that so-and-so was still waiting for him but would have to leave by noon, and then, that message from Hawk.

"Honey" — he hadn't called her honey for years — "where are you? I'm heading down to the coast to do a little fishing with the guys. Why don't you come on down, too, and pick up some barbecue on the way, will you? And some hushpuppies, you know, the works."

She knew. With Hawk, it had always been "the works." The barbecue place was right on the way down to their beach house at Emerald Isle. But Hawk hadn't said a word about any fishing trip, especially not in the middle of the week like this. And what about that message from Ellen Henley? Courtney had listened to the messages again, standing barefoot in the middle of Gene's kitchen floor while Stan rubbed against her legs and purred. Before Gene, she'd never known a man who liked cats. But there was something funny about Hawk's voice, there was something wrong. Courtney tiptoed in and retrieved her clothes from Gene's bathroom and dressed and left, as she often did, without waking him. On Wednesdays Gene liked to nap until about six o'clock and then stay up till all hours watching videos. He was a night owl and a movie nut.

Courtney pictured him as she drove to the coast. It usually calmed her down to think of Gene slumbering through the afternoon, her own sleeping giant, but today that didn't work and even the pokey little towns of eastern North Carolina, which she loved, failed to do the trick. It was a beautiful day, though. As she drove across the last big bridge over the sound, Courtney put her window down and drew in a deep breath of the familiar salt marsh smell. The wind felt good in her hair. She'd been finally cheerful by the time she turned into the concrete driveway of Miss Evangeline's old shingled beach house, an anomaly among the newer, smaller houses that surrounded it.

Courtney had pulled in next to Hawk's Land Rover and got out, wondering where the other cars were, the other guys. She climbed the outside staircase up to the deck carrying the box from Fat Daddy's, then went in the kitchen door and put it on the table next to Hawk's car keys and this morning's newspaper. The old house was completely quiet. Dust turned in the beams of sunlight slanting across the wide pine floors, covered with the myriad rag rugs that had been here ever since Hawk's parents were young and this house stood alone on its stretch of beach. Courtney hadn't been here since the past summer — funny, isn't it, how time gets away from you? The Copelands had come over for lunch, and she'd made that cold spinach soup; later, she walked up to the point by herself and saw a rainbow. It seems like yesterday. And only yesterday, too, since the kids were small and she brought them down here all the time. Right here on the kitchen wall are all the marks Hawk made with the ruler as they grew up. But where *is* he? Maybe they went off to fish in somebody else's car.

Courtney stepped out of her shoes and went out on the deck. Almost nobody was on the beach. The tide was out, tide pools glistening silver in the sun at different places, Courtney thought, from where they used to be. Nothing stays the same. She headed down the boardwalk which was partially covered with sand from the winter's storms, making a mental note to call Mr. Tabor, the caretaker.

But who was that on the last landing, just sitting there? Somehow, from the back, it hadn't looked like him. He turned as she approached, but did not wave or speak. He sat on the wooden bench, tackle box beside him, rod and reel propped against the rail. Cloud shadows raced across the beach behind him; a jogger passed and waved. He sat there. "Hawk!" she called. He looked at her for a second with absolutely no expression followed by a big surprised grin that lit up his whole face. "Courtney!" He had seemed delighted. "Hey, where's Baron? Didn't you bring Baron?" Their old chocolate lab, Hawk's pride and joy, Baron had been dead for fifteen years.

And now, in spite of all these tests they're doing on Hawk, Gene Minor has picked this *very week* to issue his ultimatum. It's all the fault of that life coach, he got her off the Internet, everything was going along perfectly well until she entered the picture. Courtney found the brochure two weeks ago, lying by the phone. "Rosalie Hungerheart," it read. "You can live your dreams! Like an Olympic coach, Rosalie guides her clients to the top levels of performance in their personal and professional lives. Discover what you want and *get it!* Life won't wait!" The back of the brochure had been torn off and sent in, Courtney presumed, to Rosalie Hungerheart, probably along with a check. Gene is so gullible.

But Courtney and Gene have a perfectly satisfactory relationship already. Courtney spends every Wednesday afternoon with Gene, plus the occasional overnight when Hawk is out of town or when she manufactures a shopping trip to Atlanta. Several times they've met at one of those cheap motels up in north Raleigh, though Gene finds this depressing. "I'm a big quality-of-life guy," he told her the first time, turning a terrible print of an Indian brave to the wall.

It was his idea to drive down I-95 to Pedro's South of the Border for an overnight. "It'll be a hoot," he promised. Courtney had seen those tacky Pedro's signs lining the highway for years, but of course she'd never thought of stopping. "This is a stolen weekend!" Gene had announced to the startled waiter, wearing that silk kimono. He cast a little flurry of dollar bills at him before slamming the door in his face, bearing the tray of margaritas and enchiladas over to the giant bed where Courtney waited, naked, in hysterics. Before Gene she hadn't laughed, really laughed, in years.

The best thing about Pedro's was that they did not have to hide out. Courtney was absolutely sure that she would never, ever, meet anybody she knew there. Not in the giant gift shop where Gene bought her a ring that said BABE in fake pink diamonds, not by the gaudy tiled pool, not in the dark Sombrero Lounge where she let him run his hand all the way up her leg under the table. It was so dark in there, nobody could see a thing. They've never gone back. It was just too far, too risky. But

Courtney has often thought about it. That overnight at Pedro's existed outside of time and space, like their whole relationship, which is why it's so perfect. Courtney can't believe Gene Minor wants to wreck it now. It has been just perfect since the very beginning. *Look.*

"My goodness!" Harriet Holding says politely when Courtney pulls out the aqua blue vinyl scrapbook with MY PROM on the cover in gold script — Gene found it in a thrift shop someplace. Suddenly Courtney can't wait to open it, to see him again, her darling, her love. She can't wait until the end of this trip when he is going to meet her in New Orleans for a stolen weekend at the Royal Orleans Hotel. "Don't you *dare* bring that kimono!" she has already told him. But secretly, she hopes he will.

Harriet Holding would not look so sleepy and bored if she knew the truth about these pictures. She'd be astonished. Courtney is astonished, too. She still considers herself the last person in the world who'd ever have an affair, the very last. She'd never have done it at all if it had been anybody real, anybody that people knew.

This is how we met, she does not say,

opening the scrapbook. Gene Minor materialized in her life under the most improbable circumstances, really, circumstances as improbable as he was. It was eight years ago. Courtney was forty-four, over the hill by anybody's standards. And a little blue, to tell the truth. It was the first year that the kids were all gone, or mostly gone — they'd never live here again anyway, not in the way they had, though she'd keep their rooms just the same, of course, monuments to their happy childhoods. Courtney had always assumed she'd feel relieved at this point, free to devote herself to her various causes, to travel with her women friends — to paint, perhaps. Though she'd never had time, she'd always wanted to paint, and she certainly had a flair for color and design. Perhaps she'd go over and take some courses at NC State. What was it everybody said? You'll have more time for yourself.

Courtney had been wandering the house that day ("That fateful morning!" as Gene would deem it later) thinking about it. Her house, huge and silent, was in perfect order. It was Lucille's day off, and Hawk had gone to Switzerland on bank business, or so he said. Courtney picked up the card that had been on her kitchen table for a week now, an invitation to her high school reunion. Jean, in charge of the food apparently, had left two messages begging them to go, not understanding that it was the kind of thing she'd never even mention to Hawk. But Hawk was gone.

"ENCHANTMENT UNDER THE OCEAN"
Class of 1963 Reunion and Prom Night
Had a terrible time at the first one?
Well, you've got another chance!
Dress to impress.
Volunteers needed to decorate.
Call 939-0335.

Well, Courtney had certainly had a bad time with, who was it? Pee Wee Raines, Lord only knows whatever happened to *him*. Now, she didn't have anything else to do. Of course, she could go shopping, but she didn't really need anything. Or she could go over to the club and slip into the Round Robin tennis group. Or she could go to Dina's for a manicure. Or she could just lie down here on this nice thick Oriental rug and scream her head off.

The reedy voice which answered her call sounded oddly familiar. "Hey now," it said.

Courtney reconsidered. Then she said,

"Hello, this is Courtney Ralston, and I'm calling about the reunion, I know I'm a little late, but —"

"This is Courtney? Courtney Gray? Oh my God, be still my heart! Courtney Gray, as I live and breathe! I can't believe it!" He sprang into her mind as fully as if he'd never left it for all those years — Gene Minor, that geeky boy. He used to make her laugh so hard in study hall that they'd both have to go to detention. He used to do those harelip readings from the English anthology: "Thith ith the forest primeval . . ."

So that afternoon Courtney found herself driving over to Robertson Elementary, a little abandoned schoolhouse which was "being transformed absolutely as we speak," according to Gene Minor on the phone. Inside, it was a time warp — the entrance hall with its institutional-green paint, its brown woodwork with coat hooks at intervals, its antique drinking fountain that Courtney would love to have out by her pool, actually. In the auditorium, several women were nailing fishnets full of blue balloons to the ceiling. One bald guy who looked vaguely familiar sat on a folding chair blowing up the balloons, while another man, on a ladder, installed a hanging mirror globe. Up on stage, a big man with long gray hair was making gold coins spill artfully out of a pirate chest onto a pink-sand beach. He wore a voluminous white shirt, thick glasses, and sweated profusely. "Right here," he was saying to two boys who struggled out on the stage carrying what appeared to be a real palm tree in an enormous pot.

"Why, Courtney! Hello!" Several women rushed over to greet her, including her old cheerleading buddy, Stephanie Speer, who had gained about fifty pounds. Courtney felt better immediately. And Beverly Midgett had let her hair go completely white, Courtney couldn't imagine why. But she was really, really glad she'd come. And when Carla Potts, whom she'd never even particularly liked, came up to her, too, she found herself blinking back tears. Honestly, it was so stupid! But clearly there had been life before Hawk; these people obviously recognized her, so obviously she had existed then, too.

"Listen, where's Gene Minor?" she asked Stephanie. "I thought he'd be here. He's the one who got me into this."

Stephanie pointed to the stage. "Right there."

"*That's* Gene Minor? That guy? But he

used to be so skinny." Courtney couldn't believe it.

"Well, he's not skinny now," Stephanie said. "But then I'm not one to talk, am I? Anyway, he's a real character, just wait. I think he got some kind of an arts degree, I'm not sure, but then his father died and he started helping his mother run the flower shop and he's been there ever since. He's never married, obviously."

"Obviously," Courtney said. But even then, staring up at Gene Minor on the stage wearing his cowboy boots and those thick glasses, she'd thought he was cute. In a weird way. But definitely cute. Though he was clearly crazy — after the palms had been installed to his satisfaction, he began dancing around the stage singing "All night, all day, Marianne, down by the seashore siftin' sand," fingering an imaginary instrument.

"Air ukelele," he announced, looking out at his impromptu audience for the first time. "Courtney!" He jumped right off the stage. "I'm so glad you made it!" He towered over her, crushing her hand.

"Yes, well, I am, too." Oddly, she meant it. Then she looked down at his hand.

"Oh, those aren't real," he said with his high-pitched giggle. "I'm just getting used to them for tonight." He wore three huge rings on one hand, four on the other, all of them gaudy.

"Why?"

"The *Elvis act*, silly," Gene Minor said. "I do it at every reunion, it's a tradition. But I guess you haven't been to any of our reunions before, have you?"

"No, this is the first one, but I'm certainly looking forward to it." Courtney's practiced social voice rang false even to herself. "My husband is out of town" — she didn't know why she said that — "so I'll be coming with Jean and Buzzy."

"Hey, I've got a better idea. Why don't you pick me up, and Elvis can be your date? I might need a little help with my costume, wig adjustment, whatever. My house is right on your way."

"How do you know that?"

"Easy. We've delivered to you a lot. Miss Evangeline used to order all her flowers from my mother — Miss Evangeline, what an old horror *she* was!"

"Okay," Courtney heard herself saying. "I'll pick you up. What time?" The address turned out to be surprisingly near Magnolia Court, though it was a street Courtney had never heard of, and she had a sudden sense of worlds within worlds, another Raleigh, a secret Raleigh down inside the one she knew. Or maybe she was inside *that* one. It made her nervous to think this stuff. Still holding the phone, Courtney phoned Jean to say she was coming to the prom after all. Jean screamed when she heard who she was coming with. "But I guess he's harmless," she said at the end of their conversation.

"Hello," Courtney called three hours later, pausing at Gene's gate which was partially open anyway. She couldn't even see his house, hidden deep in the trees.

"Hey now. You look beautiful." There was Gene Minor himself, wandering around his wild overgrown garden with a watering can, not even dressed. Except for those ridiculous white satin bell-bottoms and that big flashy belt. His breasts were as large as Courtney's. "This is for you." He picked up a white box from an old glass-topped table.

"A wrist corsage?" Courtney hadn't seen one for years. It was a pink orchid.

"Yeah. But wait a minute, I need to get you to help me do something before I finish getting dressed, if you don't mind."

Curiously, she didn't.

"It's my chest hair."

"What?"

"Well, there's some things you just can't do for yourself, you know what I'm saying, and one of them is dye your own chest hair. You think you could . . . ?"

"Sure."

"Well, then, walk this way." He did a funny Harpo Marx duck walk into the house with Courtney following. They mixed up the dye at the kitchen sink and Courtney began applying it gingerly with the corner of a tea towel. "You don't have to do it all," he said. "Just put some right up here, where it'll show." She dabbed it on. Elvis's jeweled V-neck shirt hung over the kitchen door. His black wig lay on the kitchen table.

"You know one thing I'll never forget about you," Gene Minor said, almost whispering. "It was junior year, on the trip to Spring Lake, and you had that green two-piece bathing suit, and you kept diving off the float in the middle of the lake. You were doing swan dives, back flips, everything. You dived all morning. You were amazing."

Courtney nodded. She used to be very athletic as a girl, before she realized that boys didn't like this.

"You were *great*," Gene Minor said sincerely. "I was out on the float the whole time, watching you. I'd reach over and pull you back up." He hesitated. "I remember one time, I was pulling you up when your strap slipped off your shoulder and your top fell down and I saw your breast, just for a minute. Then you flipped your strap back up and grinned at me. It was just a second. You knew I saw it, and you didn't even care. You were so cool. That was the coolest thing, the sweetest moment." He paused while Courtney, hardly breathing, dabbed the dye into the pulsing hollow in the middle of his collarbones. "And you don't even remember it."

"I —"

Gene Minor put his finger to her lips. "It's okay. I know you don't. You wouldn't. I wasn't the kind of boy that a girl like you would even notice."

"I do remember you, though —"

"Sshhh." Gene Minor continued to run his finger around her lips, almost absent-mindedly. "We're old. It's okay." He stood very close to her, then closer, pushing her against the sink. She leaned back as he pressed his hips against hers, staring into her eyes.

"Gene!"

"Surprise!" He grinned.

"But I thought you were gay."

"Everybody does, darling," he said. "You can't imagine what an advantage it is for me."

"Now listen here, you quit that." But she was laughing just as hard as she ever did in study hall. "If you get dye on this dress, I'll kill you. Besides, we're going to be late."

"Just one little kiss," he said. "Just one. Doesn't count. Won't hurt a bit, I promise. Anyway, Elvis can be as late as he wants. The show won't start without him."

Now Courtney shows Harriet the eight-by-ten picture of herself and Elvis at the prom, posing in a giant seashell. Elvis points at the camera, displaying his rings, while Courtney stands radiant in her tacky pink dress with those funny dark stains on the front of it, wearing her wrist corsage. The last photograph shows Elvis closing his act with "Heartbreak Hotel." His wig looks awful, but by then Courtney had understood that it was supposed to. This act was not so much Elvis as Gene Minor *doing* Elvis. Gene's whole life is like this, in a way. An elaborate put-on, a lot of fun. Oh, why does he have to change, especially *now?* Why does he have to get so demanding? Courtney knows it's all because of that life coach, what's her name? Rosalie. This is all Rosalie's fault. In the

112

photograph, Elvis's glasses have clouded up. His blue eyes swim in mist. His belly hangs over his belt. His dark chest hair glistens with sweat in the jeweled V of his stand-up collar. Courtney smiles, remembering. Then she almost cries remembering how he had turned and looked straight at her right at the end of this song, at the end of his act, on "I'm so lonely, baby, I'm just so lonely I could die." Because it was *her*, not him, that those words referred to, Courtney Gray Ralston, who had everything she ever wanted, who was just so lonely she could die.

Anna pulls the brim of her trademark black hat down over her trademark auburn curls, right down to the rims of her enormous black sunglasses, and sweeps grandly up the *Belle of Natchez* gangplank on Saturday afternoon. *Ta-da!* She has always imagined herself boarding a steamboat and now, just like everything else she has always imagined, it is happening. Dare to dream! This is her main message to the world. Dreams really do come true; you just have to be careful what you dream. Anna inclines her head graciously to the various uniformed staff who assist her onto the Cabin Deck, taking her arm, her bag. Too bad Robert couldn't make this trip with her, he'd just love all these cute smiling boys in uniform. The Forward Cabin Lounge is decorated like a whorehouse with its flowered carpet and all these tasseled Victorian lamps and curvaceous brocade love seats and marble-topped coffee tables. It is just *divine*.

Hand to her breast, Anna stops to catch her breath and appreciate it all. When she finally finishes this damn Confederacy series, she'll have to get back in shape. A personal trainer, that's it. And she can buy some of those shiny little workout outfits you see on the Home Shopping Channel late at night when you can't sleep. "How much farther?" she calls to the slim-hipped steward, but now he's too far ahead to hear her, dodging blithely through all the luggage placed outside the stateroom doors, bouncing up the magnificent Grand Staircase with its brass rails and the hand-painted trompe l'oeil ceiling replete with cherubs and doves. Tiepolo, for heaven's sake! Or Michelangelo! It doesn't matter, she's going to *die*. These steps will be the death of her. Thank God — finally the steward is waiting for her now on the landing of the Promenade Deck, grinning like Huck Finn himself, towheaded and cute, a college student no doubt.

Now *there's* an idea: towheaded young man — let's call him Huckleberry — older woman, one week in paradise, drifting down a river of love, outside of time and place, she's got so much to teach him, he's got so much to learn . . . Too racy for a category romance — maybe a Silhouette Special Edition or Gothic Contemporary. Isn't that what they call this style of architecture anyway? Steamboat Gothic.

"Here you are, ma'am. The Verandah Suite." Huckleberry opens the door with a flourish. He heaves her three enormous suitcases inside, placing two on the luggage racks and one — for lack of anyplace else — on the velvet daybed.

"I just love the way you say 'ma'am,'" she says to make him blush, which he does, charmingly, obligingly, waving away the twenty-dollar bill she thrusts at him from her cleavage.

"Oh no, ma'am, no tipping until the end of the trip."

He's too adorable! Anna waggles her fingers at him as he closes the door. Well! It's certainly snug in here; if *this* is the most luxurious suite they offer, then she can't even imagine the rest of them. Little boxes. Anna begins to unpack as best she can; she misses Robert, who always insists on doing this for her, wherever they travel. He has a real nesting instinct.

Anna pulls a golden cord to open her thick lace curtains; the window gives out upon her own private balcony and the busy

Mud Island dock, with Memphis in the background. She sees a woman who might be Courtney Gray heading down the hill in a smart white suit. She looks terrific, damn it. Ah well. There'll be plenty of time to renew her acquaintances, not that these women have ever showed the slightest interest in doing so. But Anna herself has never even attended a reunion — they always seem to fall in the middle of a book tour. And perhaps it's true that the more successful you are, the more people are afraid to approach you. God knows, she's been successful — why right now she's at the top of the heap with a new book just out (at number seven on the best-seller list) and another in the pipeline.

Anna pours herself a tulip glassful of cognac from the cut-glass decanter on the candle-stand table. There! She tosses the hat and the Italian scarf on the bed, kicks off her black patent leather sandals, hangs up her white silk blouse and black jacket. She'll have to call for more hangers. She loves the way her full breasts spill over her bustier, never mind her somewhat pleated cleavage. *Too much* is always preferable to *not enough*. Damn all this sunlight anyway. What is it Robert always says? "Hell is direct lighting." She removes her black slacks and folds them just so over the back of a chair, then finds her billowing purple caftan in the suitcase and slips it on. There now. Three hours to write before they even leave the dock — good. She can knock out the first chapter of the new book, perhaps, or do a little brainstorming for the next one. Those women will just have to wait to see her, no matter how curious they are.

She closes the curtains; Memphis disappears. She dims the chandelier. She opens her folding file, puts her notes and special fountain pens out on the spindly desk, then the custom-made notebook with its famous pink unlined paper that she always uses for her first drafts. Interviewers are so surprised to learn that she doesn't even own a computer. "Romance is physical," she has explained again and again. "I don't want anything mechanical to come between my body and the page. This way, my emotions simply flow from my body through my fingertips, straight onto the paper." The interviewers always nod, enraptured. Now Anna lights a scented candle — ah! that's better. She thrusts the fountain pen between her breasts, for luck. Touch, she thinks. See, smell, hear, taste. *Feel.* It is her mantra. *Feel.* And out of the blue, out of the creative empyrean, a title

118

comes to her. *The Louisiana Purchase*, she writes at the top of the pink page in her flowing, flamboyant hand. Perfect! — or *parfait!* — as it *all* begins to come to her in a rush, the hot lush Louisiana swamp teeming with gators and gars and snakes, cypress trees rising like wraiths from an earlier, more primitive time . . .

Morning. Morning on the bayou. Morning on Frenchman's Bayou, the hot pink dawn fading ever so slightly now as Vanessa . . . no, Jewel . . . no, *Jade* turns the rusty key in the ancient lock of her grandmother's dilapidated mansion set on its own tilted hummock in the spreading steaming (teeming? No, just used it) alluvial world of the swamp. Strange birds cry out in warning as they swoop low over the black water. A lizard races up a weathered porch column like a bright green streak. Behind her, the putt-putt-putt of enterprising developer Jean St. Pierre's motorboat grows fainter and fainter, then disappears. Oh, she should not have angered him! She should not have been so haughty. She should have accepted his offer of aid, should have allowed him to accompany her into the deserted house despite all those warning signs (the lingering touch, the eager moist gaze) that told her his interest was more than entrepreneurial. Jade stomps a delicate foot in frustration which only mounts as her shoe goes right through the rotten boards and disappears forever into the secretive black water. She leans down awkwardly to free her delicate foot from its painful vise.

"Bonjour, mademoiselle!"

Jade almost jumps right out of her creamy skin! Who can it be, out here in this godforsaken swamp in the middle of nowhere? Jade twists around to see, hot breath catching in her throat at the first glimpse of Adrian Batiste. It is as if he is a part of the swamp itself, a force of nature, a natural man. He sits low and easy in the water in his sleek pirogue. His chiseled face is dark and commanding; his eyes flash silver. A man as wild as his surroundings despite his loose open shirt and that ridiculous rakish hat — honestly, a pimp's hat! — which he sweeps off now, inclining his head in the mockery of a bow. His shoulder-length black hair gleams in the rising sun. *"Dis-moi qui tu es, mignonne. Dis-moi ton nom."* His voice is husky.

Jade pulls herself up to her full five feet four inches with as much dignity as she can muster, aware that the tight skirt of her Chanel suit is riding up her thighs and that her stockings are in shreds.

"I do not believe I have granted you the right to address me with the familiar pronoun," she spits at him.

His lazy grin is scornful. *"Pardon,"* he says, still with the French accent. And then, in heavily accented English, "My name is Adrian Batiste." He pronounces it Ah-dree-ahn. "My family has lived here in Frenchman's Bayou for seven generations. And you must be —"

"Jade Cameron," she says.

"Ah! I knew your *grand-mère,* a lady without peer."

"Indeed. Well, she has left me her house, in fact she has left me this entire island, and I've come to decide what to do with it."

"Then I am zee man for you." In one fluid catlike motion our hero has tied up the pirogue and sprung onto the porch. He kneels to retrieve her foot from its splintery trap, his touch like fire on her instep. "I will tell you what to do with zis property, *mam'selle — rien!* It is to say — nothing! Theese property belong to the birds and the feeshes and the other wild things of the earth, eet must remain as eet is, a sanctuary . . ."

With all the strength she can muster,

121

Jade kicks free of his hard, capable hand and stomps her little foot indignantly. In the back of her mind, she replays Pierre's suggestion for Creole Corner, the planned, gated community that could make her a very wealthy woman. "I will be the one who decides what to do with my own property! Now, get off my grandmother's porch!"

But the audacious Cajun is in no hurry, lounging insolently against the rail. "Ah, *ma petite,* well do I remember all the eve-e-nings I spend here avec your *grand-mère.* How she loved music, old Marie! I come to fiddle jus' for her, '*Jole Blon.*' How she loved to dance . . . She was-a something, your *grand-mère.* You resemble her, I tink." Without warning, he reaches out to stroke Jade's cheek with a caressing finger.

"Ooh! That does it! Get out of here!" With both hands, Jade pushes at his well-muscled overwhelmingly masculine chest — the old rail breaks — and now he is splashing in the black water. Furiously he retrieves his hat, claps it down over his dark, streaming locks, hoists himself into the pirogue and glides out into the bayou, silver eyes shooting sparks like bullets back at Jade.

"*Au revoir!*" His voice is harsh, yet warm.

"I will see you again, *mam'selle*." It is a threat as much as a promise.

The calliope cuts into Anna's creative frenzy; the deck shudders beneath her feet. As always, time has gotten away from her. That fugitive thief, he has stolen most of her life. But she doesn't begrudge him a minute of this afternoon, for *The Louisiana Purchase* promises to be every bit as successful as the rest of the Confederacy series: *Tupelo Honey, Rainy Night in Georgia, Angel from Montgomery, Carolina on My Mind, Stars Fell in Alabama, The Tennessee Stud, The Missouri Compromise* . . .

Anna puts down her pen, pours more cognac into the tulip glass, and goes to stand on her private deck. Sure enough, high-rise Memphis is receding from her eyes, turning into a toy town, though commercial enterprises still line the shore. The whistle blows twice. The engine throbs. The *Belle of Natchez* moves out onto the water like a dream.

Without warning, Anna's mind slips back to that other, earlier embarkation on the *Daisy Pickett*. She stood at the rail then, too, gripping it so tightly that her fingers hurt, laughing like crazy as Baby kept banging the champagne bottle against the corner of the raft, and it just wouldn't break . . . but no. Anna pulls that particular curtain closed in her mind. She has trained herself not to revisit certain times in her life, for obvious reasons. Pain serves no function at all — as opposed to, say, *romance*. And Anna wasn't even herself then, not yet, she was just some earlier trial version of Anna, a dreadfully mousy little hillbilly from West Virginia, now deceased. Anna can scarcely remember that girl, and considers it just as well. She hopes the others on this trip won't insist on resurrecting her.

Forget the past, let the dead be dead, and live each day as it comes. This is Anna's message, saying her mantra on the deck: feeling the breeze in her face as the *Belle* picks up speed, watching Tennessee slip farther and farther away, smelling that old river smell which still threatens to send her right back — *damn it* — to Paducah, while the manic calliope shrills in her ears and the cognac burns down her throat . . . feeling, *feeling* this moment for all she's worth. This is Anna's message: *be here now.* And that Huckleberry boy is really not such a bad idea for a hero, not at all, though most heroes are brooding and dark, of course, and a freckled towhead would certainly be a departure . . .

Harriet and Courtney sit at a round table on the upper level of the Paddlewheel Lounge, sipping giant steamboat stompers — billed as the Drink of the Day — which have turned out to be sweet, icy, and bright orange, appropriately enough, as the sun sinks lower and lower over Arkansas. From here they have a fine view down into the bandstand area and out back past the great red paddle wheel as it turns up the muddy wake.

"Heavens!" Courtney fishes around in her stomper, removing all manner of fruit and other tropical debris. "This drink is enormous."

"That's okay," Harriet says, sucking it down through the straw. "I need it. I'm terrified."

"Oh, come on." Courtney smiles warmly; she's decided that she really likes Harriet, such a character.

"This music is so loud," Harriet says as the albino Little Bobby Blue launches into a tinny version of "Frankie & Johnny" on his honky-tonk piano. Then she leans forward. "Is *that* Anna, do you think?" She indicates an elegant woman coming up the curved staircase, but no, the woman turns back to laugh with the man behind her. Anna will be alone. The bar is filling up, good thing they grabbed this table.

"I have never seen so many fat people in one place." Courtney surveys the crowd. "And they're so tacky." She would think that the price of this trip would make for a certain, er, level of traveler, but this is clearly not the case. There's a tattooed, potbellied man at the bar in a red tank top, for instance, chasing his beer with little shot glasses of something vile, laughing too loudly — certainly not the type one would expect to find on a cruise that cost nearly three thousand dollars. Surely he'll change for dinner . . .

"Well, it's the *river*, I think," Harriet says. "There's such a romance to it, the idea of going down it, I mean. Why, back in Staunton, when word got out about this trip, people I scarcely knew started coming up to me at the bank or the drugstore or just anywhere, all kinds of people, dying to talk about it. A lot of people have always wanted to do it, I think. It's sort of a universal fantasy."

"I suppose so." This music *is* loud; these people *are* fat. Courtney is not sure she'll be able to bear it for a whole week. Though on the other hand, she can't wait to tell Gene about it. It's really his kind of thing.

"Harriet?" But this large woman with the actressy voice bears absolutely no relation to the schoolgirl Anna with her little nasal squeak.

"Anna?" Harriet leaps up to hug her. To their own surprise, both women start squealing in exactly the same way they did after every break and every vacation at Mary Scott when they were girls. Courtney can't help herself either. She stands up and squeals, too.

"My God, I just can't believe it!" Catherine Wilson has let her long hair go gray; it curls around her broad, tan, smiling face. She approaches them with a big bearded man in tow, and then they all have to squeal some more. The bartender sends over five big orange stompers on the house.

"Those look lethal," says Russell Hurt, Catherine's husband. This is not the husband they were expecting.

"They're pretty good, though. I think they have ice cream in them." Harriet is really getting into hers now.

"*Jesus.*" Russell heads for the bar.

"He just wants a martini." Catherine leans forward to grasp Anna's plump, jeweled hand. "My God, Anna. It's been so long, hasn't it? And you're so famous now. What does it feel like?" Catherine was always direct.

Anna purses her plummy lips. Her big glasses have shaded lenses, even indoors; you can't really see her eyes. "Well, it's a burden, of course, yet it's quite gratifying all the same. But it has been a *lot of work,* believe me!" Her lip starts to quiver.

Catherine squeezes her hand some more. Russell comes back to stand behind his wife's chair and raise his martini. "To you!" he addresses them all. "To the girls of the *Daisy Pickett!*"

"The last girls," Harriet adds oddly, involuntarily, causing everyone to glance at her as they drink. "I mean, they'd call us *women* in the newspaper if it happened now."

"To the last girls, then," Russell Hurt repeats, chuckling. "That's good."

"Could you take our picture?" Courtney

asks him. "Before you sit back down, I mean."

"Sure." Russell puts his drink down on the table, taking Courtney's expensive camera from her. He backs up a pace or two while the women bunch together.

"It's all automatic. Just push that little green thing," Courtney says.

Russell focuses. "Got it! Okay, girls, say 'Fortune 500' . . ." The flash goes off.

They will be red-eyed and happy in this photograph, with Courtney poised and expectant on the left; Catherine on the right, head thrown back and laughing, down to earth and natural as ever; Anna in the middle, sitting among her jewelry and scarves and fringes like a foreign idol, smiling mysteriously; then Harriet, whose wide-eyed grinning face pops up behind the others like a hand puppet, like a joke. Later Harriet will look again and again at this picture, just as she looked hard at Anna that afternoon, searching for any trace of the sweet serious friend of her youth. Maybe if Anna just weren't wearing so much makeup or so many clothes . . .

"Thanks." Courtney takes the camera back from Russell, already envisioning this photograph in her *Belle of Natchez* album. She'll call it, "First Day Out for the Last

Girls." Courtney scoots her chair back to make room for Russell next to his wife, whom he clearly adores, touching her hand constantly, unnecessarily. Hawk never did this, not even when they were young. "So tell us," Courtney asks them brightly, "how did you all meet?"

"Well . . ." Russell hesitates. Catherine nods at him. "Okay. I was deputized by the other guys in my law firm in Birmingham to buy some kind of sculpture for the courtyard in our new office building. We wanted something local — we like to support local artists. I'd been struck by this huge concrete figure I'd seen over at the public gardens; it was sort of a woman, reclining, and sort of a planter. You know, ferns. They had several of them, actually. One was placed half in and half out of a stream. It made a little waterfall. I think that one was some kind of mythological animal or something, wasn't it, honey?"

"No," she says. "I just made it up."

"You're a sculptor now?" Courtney asks. They all look at Catherine, who looks down at her bare sandaled feet.

"Hell yes, she's a sculptor." Russell seems surprised that they don't know this. "Shit, her work is everywhere, you've probably seen it, you just didn't know it. She's a very well known artist."

"Oh, Russell, come on. It's just stuff for the garden. Yard art," she tells them. "I really got into it after Steve died."

"*Steve?*" Courtney and Harriet look at each other.

"Oh, well, of course I was married to Howie first —"

"For a little while," Russell winks at them.

"I see we've got some catching up to do," Courtney leans back in her chair.

"Steve was my second husband, a physician, who died. It was a . . . an accident." Catherine swallows hard. "It was some years later that I met Russell. He came by the house, as he said. I've always worked out of my house. Of course I *liked* him, I liked him right away, but I never thought I'd marry him or anything like that. I wasn't looking for a husband. I'd had husbands. I thought he was just — I don't know — an interim man."

"That's a great title." Anna scribbles it down in a little notebook which she produces from somewhere within her person. "Can I have it?"

"Be my guest, I'll never use it. It's funny, how much I used to love to write in college. I mean, I know I wasn't ever particularly good at it" — Catherine waves her hand to override them — "no, I really wasn't. But I loved it. Or maybe I just loved going to that class and hanging out with y'all. I can still remember the way I always felt when we used to climb up that hill to Miss Auerbach's house on faculty row, or to Lucian Delgado's. That feeling like, well, like anything could happen. It was so exciting."

"Oh, I felt that way, too," Harriet says. *The crackle of leaves beneath your loafers in the fall, the crunch of hard frost under your boots in the wintertime, your bare feet sinking into the cool wet grass of spring.*

Bells ring all over the steamboat. They file into the huge dining room, which takes up at least half of the Observation Deck. Red lips gleaming, a pretty girl in a hoop skirt directs them to their table.

"Hi, I'm Maurice, I'll be your server." A black boy pulls out their chairs; he looks like a running back.

"Well, Maurice, you've got your job cut out for you on this trip," Russell says. "Think you can help me take care of all these women?"

"No problem!" Maurice flashes a world-class grin, handing the menus around.

"My God, no wonder these people are

all so fat!" Courtney takes in the five-course menu selections.

"But they were *already* fat," Harriet points out. "Maybe they just picked this cruise because they know they'll get enough food." Then she blushes, looking down — she forgot, momentarily, that Anna is clearly a very big woman underneath all that stuff.

"I'll bet everybody orders every course," Courtney says. "To get their money's worth. That's what my father used to make us all do whenever we went on a trip and the food was included. We all had to be in the clean plate club."

Prix fixe. Anna knows this term now, but suddenly she remembers all too well a time when she *did* not, when she knew nothing and said everything wrong because there were so many words she had only read, never heard pronounced, such as the time in American Lit when she said that Hester Prynne was not immoral, but rather had been simply misled, pronouncing the word to rhyme with "chiseled." Everybody had sat in silence until they got it and then started laughing, one by one. Anna herself never found this incident amusing. The point was that she'd *read* all those words, but had never said them aloud before she went to college.

"I'm with your dad," Russell is saying to his wife. "I still like to get my money's worth." He orders artichoke bottoms with crabmeat, rack of lamb, and Black Forest cake. "Go, girl! This is the clean plate club," he tells Catherine, who orders next. They seem like the perfect couple, which doesn't surprise her old friends. She's easy to get along with. She and Howie seemed like the perfect couple, too, which they were until she left him. And now, secretly, Catherine sometimes feels like leaving Russell who is driving her crazy with this midlife crisis of his which has been going on forever, it seems to her. "Just hush," she wants to say. "Quit whining. Act like a man." She knows she ought to be glad that Russell is so sensitive and verbal, but she's not. She's tired of it. She wishes he'd just shut up. Now, now. Be nice, Catherine cautions herself. She read someplace that the three rules for a successful marriage are: *Be nice. Be nice. Be nice.* This ought to be simple, but every year it gets harder and harder to do. Catherine is older now. She gets tired, too. And this is her only life.

Courtney orders the consommé and two salads. There's scarcely a thing on the menu that she can eat if she expects to remain a size six by the time she gets to New Orleans.

"Look over there," Harriet says suddenly. "It's Mark Twain."

"Actually it looks more like Mr. Gaines, remember him? Whatever happened to him, anyway?" Catherine asks.

"No, that's the Riverlorian," Courtney has been studying the daily *Steamboatin' News*. "He's the guy who lectures about the river. I think his lectures start tomorrow morning."

"Mr. Gaines went to some college in Florida, I believe, when he didn't get tenure at Mary Scott, the year after we all left. And his marriage broke up after that," Anna offers, and they suddenly remember that Anna had an academic husband herself, what was his name, that skinny pale guy . . . Kenneth. That's it. He was getting his doctorate at UNC. Whatever happened to Kenneth? "I believe Mr. Gaines was taking advantage of his students," Anna adds primly. "Of Baby, for instance." She hadn't meant to say it. She doesn't say, *of me.*

"Now Anna, I'll bet you don't know that for sure." Harriet looks like she might cry. She always loved Mr. Gaines. In fact, it's hard for Harriet to imagine that Mr.

135

Gaines is not right there still, at Mary Scott, just as it's hard for her to imagine that all these other girls have run through whole marriages, whole lives.

The first course arrives in a flurry of little dishes deftly served by Maurice. Russell orders champagne. Courtney and Catherine compare pictures of their families. Between them, Catherine and Russell have six children, seven grandchildren. How can this be? Harriet wonders. The champagne arrives. Russell approves the bottle, looking over the rim of his reading glasses. Out on the parquet dance floor, couples are moving with intricate steps and turns. Arthur Murray, Harriet thinks darkly. They've all been to Arthur Murray.

Courtney clears her throat. "I'd like to propose a toast," she announces. "To Baby."

"To Baby."

"To Baby."

"To Baby."

They lift their glasses.

"She must have been a helluva girl." Russell is the only one who didn't know her.

"Oh Lord! You can't even imagine!" Catherine says. "There was nobody like her. Thank you," she says as Maurice arrives with her salmon.

"Nobody," Harriet whispers, twisting her napkin.

"Well, no wonder," Courtney says. "Don't you remember her *family?* I think Baby did pretty well, considering."

"What was her family like?" Russell is the perfect straight man.

"They were just so rich," Courtney says. "They'd been rich for generations. You should have seen her parents' house in Alabama — antebellum, of course. Ten columns across the front."

"Twelve," Harriet murmurs. "Miles and miles of land . . ."

Catherine puts down her fork and leans forward. "Okay. Here's the perfect anecdote, the anecdote that captures it all. You probably remember this, too — you were there." She nods toward Harriet, who looks doubtful. "Anyway, I was in your room — we were working the Ouija board, you and me, Harriet."

"Oh!" Harriet had forgotten all about the Ouija board.

"And the phone rang, and Baby picked it up. 'What?' she said real loud, and then, 'Well, are you okay?' and then, 'I'm just so glad you're okay.' Then there came this long silence during which she was listening, and twisting her hair around her finger the way she did" — they all nod — "and then she said, 'Well, all I can say, Troy, is that if *I* were *you,* I'd go right out and get him another one just like it before he gets back from his trip.' "

"Oh my God," Harriet says. "I do remember that."

"What was it about?" Russell asks. "Another what?"

"Another station wagon," Catherine says. "See, she had these wild twin brothers, Troy and —"

"Boy," Harriet says.

"Troy and Boy," Catherine goes on. "Troy being named for her father, Troy Beauchamp Ballou, though I can't actually remember Boy's real name right now, but it was a long string of family names, very impressive. Anyway, they were about sixteen, I'd say, maybe seventeen, and they got drunk and went driving around the golf course in the middle of the night, of all things, and somehow they had managed to drive their father's station wagon straight into one of the water hazards, actually I think it was a lake, where it was completely submerged."

"Good God," Russell says.

"Did they manage to buy him a new one

before he got home?" Courtney asks.

"I doubt it." Catherine smiles. "But the very idea of suggesting it, the possibility that anybody could even think of doing such a thing, was just staggering to me at the time."

"I guess so." Russell stands, holding out a hand to Catherine. "Honey?"

"You'll be the youngest on the floor, in this crowd," Harriet calls after them as they make their way through the tables toward the tiny dance floor. The band is named the Steamboat Syncopators. "I really didn't understand there'd be so many old people on this trip, did you?" She turns to the others.

"No," Anna says, and Courtney shakes her head. "No."

"But we're old, too." Harriet goes on as though she doesn't quite believe it herself. "How old do you think *that* woman is, for instance?" She indicates a white-haired couple dressed almost alike in madras plaid. "I'll bet she's not a day older than we are."

Anna squirms uncomfortably. "Please," she says, refusing to place herself for even a minute among these aging hoi polloi — not a bad title, either: *Among the Hoi Polloi,* a class that Anna has risen above, she hopes, forever. "I never have old people in my books. Never. We'll all get there sooner or later anyway. There's no sense rubbing our noses in it."

"I disagree," Harriet surprises herself by saying stubbornly, waving away Maurice who keeps trying to refill her coffee cup. "I teach these community workshops at my school, in the COMEBACK! program?" Her voice rises at the end of each sentence when she gets flustered. "It's mostly women? And they write their own life stories?"

For the first time, Anna removes the big glasses, to stare at Harriet. "Whatever for?" she asks. "Who would want to read about people like *that?*" Anna has dark violet smudges, like bruises, beneath her eyes.

Harriet swallows. "Well, Anna, nobody's going to read them, really," she explains. "Except me, of course. The idea is that it's good for them to think about their lives and write down anything at all, it's a way of gaining understanding — and maybe, I hope, control. It's empowering."

"Shit," Anna says.

Courtney jumps.

"What?" Harriet has to lean forward to hear, as a little ripple of applause runs through the dining room. Catherine and

Russell sit back down at the table.

"It is *not* good for them!" Anna snaps.

"Well, I've been working with these women for years, and I disagree." Harriet won't let it go. "I mean, these may not be stories in the way *you* think of a story, I realize, with a strong plot and all, of course. These stories are more like the one Catherine told about Baby's brothers and the station wagon, an anecdote, maybe, that captures a whole life, or just a few sentences about something they feel strongly about."

"A story *must* have a plot," Anna announces in the tone of a decree.

"But sometimes it just doesn't," Harriet says.

"That's ridiculous!" Anna stands up, swishing her layers, adjusting herself. "You are quite wrong. I'm in this business, remember. You're not. I ought to know."

"How about a stroll around the Observation Deck?" Russell comes back to address them all, with Catherine at his side.

"But isn't there something going on right now in the Grand Saloon? Just a minute, I'll see —" Courtney consults her *Steamboatin' News* schedule.

"No doubt. There's *always* something going on in the Grand Saloon." Harriet, relieved by the change of subject, watches the Riverlorian out of the corner of her eye as he works the crowd, moving from table to table. Surely Anna can't be right about Mr. Gaines.

"Tonight's show is called 'Showboat Jubilee,'" Courtney reads aloud.

"I think we'll have to skip that one," Russell says.

"I believe I will turn in now, actually," Anna announces somewhat grandly, rising. "I was up before five in order to get to the airport — it has been a very long day." But then she smiles at them all, not her professional book-tour smile but a real smile, flooded with that Paducah feeling she seems unable to control today. These women were the only friends of her life, actually. She's worked so hard ever since, she's never had time to make any more. Oh Lord! This trip might be too much for Anna after all. She told herself it'd be useful, allowing her to do some research for the Louisiana book, but now she wonders if this is even true. She researched all the other states in the encyclopedia. Anna grasps the edge of the table to support herself. Why did she come? And damn Robert. Why didn't he come? Now she can't even remember. It is an effort for

Anna to assume her regal bearing. "Good night, all. Don't look for me until after-noon."

"Anna —" Harriet says, but just then the Riverlorian approaches their table.

"Good evening, ladies," he says with a stiff little bow. "I'm Pete Jones, your Riverlorian. Just wanted to welcome you folks aboard the *Belle of Natchez*."

"Why, thank you!" Courtney's all smiles.

Close up, the Riverlorian doesn't really look much like Mark Twain, except for the moustaches and the suit. He doesn't look like Mr. Gaines either. Actually he looks more like Kenny Rogers, only heavier, but he's wearing those horn-rimmed glasses that Kenny Rogers would never wear. He turns to Harriet. "How about a dance?" he asks right out of the blue.

"Oh, I —"

"She'd love it!" Courtney pokes her in the side.

"No, I — actually I have to catch up with my friends right now. Thanks a lot anyway," Harriet throws back over her shoulder as she races out of the dining room.

"Ma'am?" The Riverlorian turns and bows to Courtney.

"But isn't it time for the 'Showboat Jubilee'?" If it's printed on the schedule, Courtney is bound to do it.

"Right you are." The Riverlorian consults his very official-looking watch. "I ought to head that way myself," offering Courtney his immaculate white sleeve. They move toward the Grand Saloon.

"Anna? Anna?" Harriet perceives Anna's wake, a kind of shimmering in the air, and follows it through the crowd and up to the front of the boat where she finds Anna leaning against the rail smoking a thin, nasty, black cigar.

"My little indulgence." Anna waves the red end of the cigar. "Sorry."

"No, *I'm* sorry," Harriet says sincerely. "I'm sorry I was so strident back there at the dinner table when we were talking about stories, I mean. I wanted to tell you that. Please don't pay any attention to me. I should never drink. I don't know how to act in public anyway. I think I have some kind of social Tourette's syndrome."

"Don't be silly." But Anna permits herself a smile.

Hair blowing, they look out at the river ahead which drops away to darkness before them now on either side. Occasionally a beam of light from the pilot house above them sweeps across the black water. "I

144

can't believe we did it, can you?" Harriet says softly. "This river is just huge. It's really dangerous. Somehow it didn't look so big from the raft. I guess you can't tell how big things are when you're right in the middle of them anyway."

"Thank God!" in that throaty voice. "It's just as well. If we could ever really see what we're doing, then we'd never do any of it, I imagine."

Harriet takes heart. There's something of Anna here after all, she's sure of it, as they stand in the windy dark.

Courtney just can't believe it. She's scarcely awake on the very first day of the trip when there's a knock on her cabin door, a short businesslike knock, and then, as she sits up in bed clutching the covers to her chest, the note slides under her door. Gene! It's a message from Gene already. Courtney jumps up to grab it, then has to find her reading glasses before she can read it. Nobody can receive telephone calls on this boat, which is a big nuisance, though they can phone out with some difficulty, using something called WATERCOM.

"Call home immediately," the note says. "Mary Bell." Damn. She might have known. Of course it would be from Mary Bell, Hawk's first cousin who has volunteered to stay at Magnolia Court in Courtney's absence. "For as long as I'm needed," as Mary Bell put it modestly, eyes cast down, when she arrived.

"What does *that* mean, until I'm dead?" Hawk had demanded. The three of them laughed uneasily. It was a joke but not quite a joke, not really a joke at all, as Mary Bell is famous in the family for showing up unannounced in times of crisis to help out.

An unmarried woman of indeterminate age, Mary Bell is very good at helping out. With her gray hair pulled back into a plain, tidy bun, her sensible lace-up brogans and her print button-up dresses (Where did she even *find* dresses like that anymore?) Mary Bell assessed the situation with her pale, pale unblinking eyes, and did whatever needed to be done. Quietly. Just like that. She had come to them once before. Upon finding Miss Evangeline in a state of extreme agitation, Mary Bell had sent the home health nurse away, lowered the shade, washed Miss Evangeline's face, attended to her nails and makeup, then disappeared for an instant only to reappear with a mint julep in a silver cup on a little silver tray. Courtney couldn't remember ever seeing that tray before. It was uncanny. Miss Evangeline had calmed right down.

"Tell me, Bell," she'd said, "do you remember those brothers from Ahoskie who came visiting us that time? And one of them played the banjo?"

"Mack Durand," Mary Bell said without missing a beat. "He was mad about you. Don't you remember? Why, Uncle Ned had to threaten to run him off with a shotgun, the way he mooned around town after you and Henry were engaged. It was embarrassing to all concerned."

"Why, I believe he took a room in town —" Miss Evangeline had said dreamily.

"Over the stable," Mary Bell finished her sentence, then stroked her cheek, and finally Miss Evangeline slept.

Three weeks later she was dead.

And now, Mary Bell has reappeared.

Courtney tries to throw off her forebodings as she dials. Mary Bell will be up, of course, and fully dressed. She seems to scarcely sleep, or scarcely eat, living on trouble.

"Ralston residence." Mary Bell sounds like some kind of servant.

"Hi, this is Courtney. How is he? How are you? What's happening?"

"Oh, we're doing just fine here, dear." Mary Bell's voice is icy sweet. "You go right ahead and enjoy your trip. Everything here is just fine. Don't you worry about a thing." Her voice is too cheerful.

"Can I talk to Hawk? Where's Hawk?"

"Oh, he's at the gym, I believe. He was already gone when I got up."

He might be at the gym or he might not be, Courtney thinks. He might not have come home at all last night. But in any case, it sounds like he must be feeling better. "That's good, I guess," she says. "What's the message?"

"Call Ellen Henley at home." Mary Bell is obviously reading off something. She repeats the number three times, as if Courtney is retarded. But of course she is just trying to be helpful.

"All right," Courtney says. "I'll call her right now." Ellen Henley is such a workaholic, she's sure to be up, too, even at this ungodly hour.

"And I presume it is all right with you if I put up some fig preserves," Mary Bell says. "You've got all these figs out in the side yard going to waste before my eyes, I just can't stand it."

Oh God. Courtney forgot all about the damn figs. After thanking Mary Bell profusely, she hangs up and glances out the window at the Arkansas shore sliding past. Courtney shakes her head to clear it, then dials. She waits a long time for the

WATERCOM operator to come on the line.

Ellen Henley is all business, as usual. "I wanted to talk to you before you got away," she says pointedly. "I left several messages . . ."

Oh God, Courtney remembers. Of course you did. The truth is, she wanted to go on this trip so badly that she forgot them. Just forgot them — how unlike her. "Yes," she says, sitting on the edge of her bunk. "What did you want to talk about?"

"It's Mr. Ralston." Suddenly the supercool, supereffective Ellen Henley is blubbering. "Something awful is happening," she says. "I didn't want anybody to know. I thought he might get better. Maybe that was wrong, but —"

"Slow down," Courtney says. "It's okay. I'm sure you've done the right thing, Ellen. You always do. Now tell me what you're talking about."

"Well, it started awhile back. Six months ago, maybe. Maybe it was even a *year* ago, I'm not sure."

"*What?*" Courtney asks. "What started?"

"Mr. Ralston," Ellen begins. "Mr. Ralston, he" — she pauses to collect herself. "Oh, he just started forgetting things. Little things, insignificant things, like where are the paper clips when he knows perfectly well where they are. I've kept his paper clips in that very same little red lacquer box on his desk for *eight years*. One day he forgot Charlie Poole's phone number, and another day it was the number of the club. That's when I really started to notice it. But I just thought, oh well, Mr. Ralston is starting to slip, we all slip a little bit as we get older, it's nothing to worry about, and so I —"

"Covered for him," Courtney says. "Of course you did." For the first time in years, she wishes she had a cigarette.

"But it wasn't ever anything *big*, mind you, just little things, and it didn't really matter. So much of what we do is just routine anyway. Mr. Ralston is very good at delegating responsibility, and at this level, there's not really so much we have to do, not in this office, I mean . . ."

So he's been a figurehead for years, Courtney realizes. Somehow it doesn't surprise her. Going out to lunch or off to golf while smart, efficient Ellen Henley ran the show, taking on more and more . . .

"Then it got worse," Ellen continues. "There was one week back in June when he actually missed several appointments, even missed a closing on that property in

Rocky Mount. Oh, he got on the phone every day and checked in with all our key people, and returned his calls just as he always had, so I thought things were going along as usual and I was amazed when they called from Rocky Mount to ask where he was, just *amazed*. But then the next day it was the same story, he never showed up for a very important meeting at the bank, and he didn't even call. Didn't call them, didn't call me, either . . ."

Courtney has never heard normally quiet Ellen Henley run on so. Was that the week of Hawk's fishing trip? "Where was he?" she asks.

"Well, that's just it. I don't know. I still don't know. And you know what? I'm not sure he does either. He got the funniest look on his face when I asked him. I can't even describe it to you."

"What about recently?" Courtney asks. "This week, for instance? Right now?"

"Oh, he acts as if everything is fine, normal, business as usual. He went to the Century Club luncheon on Monday. You know he goes every year. He seemed real chipper when he came back, too, telling jokes and whatnot, really he seemed just fine. And he looked so nice too, he was wearing that yellow tie with the little blue diamond pattern on it." She pauses. "*Well.* But since he's been out of the office so much, I went through those two boxes on his desk, you know the ones I mean, of course I'd never dream of going through his personal desk drawers, Mrs. Ralston, but I must say I'm finding a *lot* to straighten out here. Why, there are several letters I typed weeks ago that he's forgotten to send out at all. I never thought to check on them, and here they are! So I FedExed them out yesterday afternoon. But I don't want you to worry about this, Mrs. Ralston, because I can handle everything, I really can. Business will go on as usual, I promise you. But when Mr. Ralston mentioned that he'd be out having some tests today and tomorrow, and gave me the doctor's number, and I looked him up and saw that he is one of the head neurologists at Duke, well, I put two and two together and decided to call you. I hope you don't mind. I just felt I *should* tell you these things, so you can tell the doctor. I didn't really feel that I could call him myself. I knew it wasn't my place, but I've been so concerned, you see I just didn't want to believe —"

"*Ellen,*" Courtney says. "Ellen. I think you should call the doctor. You do it, not me. It's very difficult to make a call out from this boat. Please. Just call him up and tell him exactly what you've told me. He needs to know these things. I certainly didn't realize there was any problem at the office, so this is very helpful. You're doing the right thing."

Ellen draws a deep breath. She chokes off a sob. "Then I'll do it," she says. "I *will*. Only you must promise me, Mrs. Ralston, that you will never, *ever*, tell Mr. Ralston that I spoke to you about this or that I called the doctor. And the doctor mustn't ever tell him either." Her anxiety trembles across the wires.

"Of course not," Courtney says in her brightest, firmest voice.

"I would rather die than embarrass Mr. Ralston" is the last thing Ellen says before they exchange good-byes.

Courtney lies back on her bed and stares up at the ceiling. Now she can hear footsteps on the deck above her, voices in the corridor outside her door. Ellen loves him. This is perfectly clear. Poor, plain little Ellen Henley, thin blond Ellen Henley who has worked for Hawk for years, ever since she was a country girl fresh out of secretarial school. Doesn't she have a husband, or didn't she have a husband once? Suddenly Courtney remembers a fat young man in a red plaid jacket, drinking too much at the company Christmas party. Then he was gone. He has been gone for several years. Yellow tie, indeed! But so many, many women have loved Hawk; Courtney wonders if Ellen knows this. Certainly he has never fucked her; Hawk's taste runs to big brunettes, and he'd never be that stupid anyway. Courtney can just hear him — "It's easy to find girls, but it's damn hard to find a good secretary." She can picture how he'd wink when he said this to one of the guys. Maybe Ellen covers for Hawk about women, too. Courtney can imagine what Ellen tells herself to justify it: "Everybody knows a man like Mr. Ralston has greater needs" or "His wife is frigid."

But she's *not*, damn it! She's *not*. Though the sad truth is that she has never loved Hawk in the way a woman should love a man, a way she didn't even know existed until she met Gene Minor again after so many wasted years. And now she's headed to New Orleans for a stolen weekend with him, a weekend she deserves, damn it, because she has *put in her time*. She's furious with Hawk for getting sick right now; it's like he's done this on purpose to thwart her. But that's not true, or fair. *None* of this is fair, Courtney thinks, remembering back suddenly to her days on the Honor Court at Mary Scott, meting out justice every Wednesday night. She was so proud of her impartiality, her fairness. She had actually believed then that justice existed and that she was dispensing it.

"Courtney?" It's Harriet's voice, and Harriet's light tap outside her door. Courtney freezes, but in a minute she can tell that Harriet has moved on. Poor Harriet. And poor Courtney who came so close to being just like her, to never knowing real love either. The steam whistle sounds for breakfast as sun streams in the little window and Courtney runs her hands over her own body, her breasts, her flat stomach, her thighs, down between her legs the way Gene does. *Will.* The way Gene will touch her only five days from now.

Mile 664
Prairie Point Towhead
Sunday 5/9/99
0800 hours

The Riverlorian Chat turns out to be so popular that Harriet puts her notebook down on a chair in the Grand Saloon, to save herself a seat while she goes to the breakfast buffet.

"Hey, wait up!" Catherine tosses her sweater across the chair next to Harriet's, and hurries to catch her. "Good morning," she says. "How'd you sleep?"

"Like the proverbial rock." Harriet joins the buffet line, takes a plate. "I thought maybe the engine sound would bother me, but it didn't at all. In fact I sort of liked it. Like white noise. What about you?"

"I had a little trouble at first. Or maybe that was just because Russell snores. He's always asleep before his head even hits the pillow. But once I got to sleep, I was fine."

"Where's Russell now?"

"Oh, he's walking his laps around the deck. He's already got it figured out, exactly how many laps it takes for three miles. At home he does three miles every day. He'd die if he missed his exercise. He's obsessed with it." Catherine laughs. "Men!" She puts two sausage biscuits on her plate. "Is that all you're having?" indicating Harriet's bagel.

"Why, yes, I —"

"Do you remember my mother? Mary Bernice?" Catherine spoons scrambled eggs onto her plate.

Harriet nods. Who could ever forget Mary Bernice? Or that grand Tudor house up on top of Shades Mountain in Birmingham, where she presided?

"Well, one time I took her out to a deli for breakfast and ordered bagels for both of us. Mary Bernice took one bite of her bagel, then put it down and said, 'Catherine, my dear, anybody who thinks *this* is *good* has clearly never tasted a biscuit!' " Catherine leads the way back to their chairs. Mile after mile of densely wooded shoreline slides past the boat; here the trees grow right down to the water's muddy edge. Periodically, Russell rushes past outside the windows, wearing a headband and old gray gym shorts and a Doc Watson T-shirt and sweating profusely. He flashes them a peace sign as he goes.

"Gosh, he's got good legs, hasn't he?" Harriet didn't mean to say this.

Catherine turns to look at her husband's retreating form. "Well, yes, he does," she answers, as if noticing them for the first time, which can't be true, as Russell's legs really are exceptional.

The crowd settles down as Pete Jones enters, looking very nautical this morning in a long-billed navy cap and navy shorts with high white socks and clunky black lace-up shoes. The shoes are all wrong. It's entirely possible that he was a nerd in youth, Harriet realizes, before becoming a Riverlorian.

"Okay, folks," he says into the hand mike. "On behalf of Captain John Dulaney and the entire crew of the *Belle of Natchez*, I want to welcome you on board. We're going to relax you, we're going to entertain you, we're going to take you back and slow you down. Currently we are traveling south down what is called 'the Big River,' which extends from Cairo to the Gulf of Mexico. For those of you who like to keep up with such things, the length of the lower Mississippi — the Big River — is exactly 953.8 miles. We're making about ten miles per hour right now.

"You'll be seeing a lot of shipping as we

go down the river — this is America's biggest highway, after all. It's not uncommon — as I'm sure you've already noticed — to see a tow pushing three barges of fifteen tons each. That makes a floating island, folks, 195 feet long. That one there, for instance" — with a jerk of his head, he indicates the river side of the *Belle* — "that one's carrying coal for power plants, and just think what it would be like without it. Why, on Monday nights, we'd have to sit around watching football in the dark!" Everybody laughs except for Harriet, who doesn't get the reference. The Riverlorian continues, "Later in the summer, you'll see the Midwest's grain harvest heading down the river. The barges also carry sand, gravel, salt, and chemicals, especially below Baton Rouge. And incidentally, folks, you won't be seeing any freighters until we get to Baton Rouge. They can only come upriver as far as the upper Baton Rouge bridge, because they require a deep draft of 45 feet. People say that Huey Long built that bridge low on purpose, so Louisiana could keep all the freighter trade."

"What's this bridge we're coming up to right now?" an old man's voice rasps from the back of the Grand Saloon.

"That's Tunica," the Riverlorian answers. "And if you folks will keep an eye out toward starboard — that's *right,* for you landlubbers — you'll see all the gambling casinos in a minute."

The Grand Saloon erupts in exclamation: "Oh, look! Oh, I read about this! Aren't we going to stop?"

"Don't worry, folks, there'll be a casino every place we dock, all the way down the river. Just hang on to those quarters, you'll have plenty of chances to use them," says the Riverlorian.

The casinos are ornate, fanciful, and improbable, like photographs Harriet has seen of Las Vegas, like illustrations from a fairy-tale book. Silken banners fly from the pink towers of one castle; another features turrets and a moat. And that one's Moorish, with onion domes.

"Oh, look, there's a hotel, too, right here — or is it part of the casino?" Catherine points. "Twenty-five dollars a night! That can't be right."

"Yep, that's it, miss." A heavyset old man in a Budweiser shorts set leans forward to tell her. "See, what they figure is, they make it all back at the casino. Oh, they've got it down to a science, they have."

"Why, that's horrible," Harriet says.

"Honey, that ain't nothing." Now the man's wife leans forward, her breath hot in Harriet's ear. "Listen here, my sister lives down in Natchez, where we'll be day after tomorrow, and her own next-door neighbor got so hooked on gambling, she left her two perfectly darling children and a marriage of ten years for it. She won't come home, they say she's stripping to get more money. Her husband is a state trooper, so he can't stay home with the kids, so everybody in the neighborhood has pitched in to help with the babysitting. It's just pitiful."

But the Riverlorian has already gone on to the Battle of Vicksburg, in which a total of nineteen thousand men were killed, wounded, or missing. When the siege ended on July 4, 1863, putting the river into Union hands all the way down, President Lincoln said, "The Father of Waters again goes unvexed to the sea." You can tell the Riverlorian likes this phrase, the way he rolls it off his tongue with a flourish. Harriet writes all these facts down in her notebook. She's horrified when Catherine takes some cross-stitching out of her bag and starts to whip her needle briskly in and out of the tiny squares. Russell charges past again, waving. Catherine's mouth moves as she counts stitches: "One, two, three." Everyone else is getting restless, too, they get up for more coffee, look out the windows, rustle around in their chairs. Undaunted, the Riverlorian keeps right on, discussing the history of the river and the Louisiana Purchase. How would a person become a Riverlorian anyway? You wouldn't just decide as a boy, *What I really want to be is a Riverlorian,* surely . . .

"The two most momentous events that ever happened on the river happened in the same year, 1811. One was the great earthquake, folks, centered at New Madrid, the most powerful earthquake that ever took place in North America." Sometimes the Riverlorian sounds like a preacher, Harriet thinks. "The river ran backwards for three days, folks" — can this be true? — "leaving a vast sunken lake in western Tennessee, Reelfoot Lake, and changing the course of the river forever. Now this was happening just at the very same time the first steamboat, the *New Orleans,* constructed by Robert Fulton at a cost of thirty thousand dollars and owned by Nicholas and Lydia Roosevelt, sailed down the Mississippi River for the first time, with its owners on board. And Lydia Roosevelt, that brave young woman, was *pregnant!* Well, here they came, folks, headed downriver on their historic voyage just days after the earthquake. All along the river, everybody ran down to the bank to cheer and gape. They had never seen anything like it in all their lives. And the Indians? Well, the Indians thought it was a sign from their gods. They *blamed* the steamboat for the earthquake. They got so scared, they fell down in fits all along the river. And when the steamboat *New Orleans* reached the city of New Orleans in late January, Mississippi steamboating was born."

The Riverlorian consults his watch. "That's all, folks, have a lovely day, and don't forget it's a special Mother's Day supper tonight, so if you've got a mother, why, think about her! Write her a letter! If your mother is here with you, give her a kiss for me. Or, better yet, bring her up here, and I'll do the job myself! And if you *are* a mother, do something nice for yourself. How many mothers have we got here in our group today?" Almost all the women's hands go up. "Well, then, ladies, Happy Mother's Day! from all of us to all of you."

Harriet puts her plate on the stack as they leave the Grand Saloon. She looks back over her shoulder to see the Riverlorian kissing three old women, one of them in a wheelchair. "What about *your* mother?" she asks Catherine. "Mary Bernice. Is she still alive?"

"No, she died last year," Catherine says, "at ninety. Oh, she was something, she was amazing, right up until the end. She wore high heels every day of her life. After she broke her hip, I took her shopping because the doctor insisted that she had to buy some of what he called "sensible shoes," and come to find out, she couldn't even wear them. She had worn high heels for so long that her ankle was permanently fixed at that angle, the high heel angle. Even her bedroom shoes had heels."

"I remember her out gardening in a linen dress and spectator heels." In her mind's eye, Harriet sees Mary Bernice poised against bougainvillea.

"She called it gardening, but it was really more like directing the help. I remember I got so tickled one time when I came home from school and found her stretched out on a sofa, all dressed up, with a wet cloth across her forehead. 'Why, Mama, what's the matter?' I asked. I thought she'd had a heatstroke. 'Oh, Catherine,' she said, 'I'm just so exhausted. I've had three men in the yard all day long.' " Catherine smiles wryly. "I just drove her crazy, when I started building things and working outside myself. I was a big embarrassment to her. She never had a clue about what I was up to. I stopped expecting her to after a while."

They pause on the shady side of the deck to look out at the river. You can barely see across it here; you can barely tell the water from the sky, with only the faint shimmering horizon line floating between the two.

"But what about you, Harriet?" Catherine asks suddenly. "Your mother was a widow, wasn't she? Wasn't your father already dead when we were at Mary Scott?"

Harriet looks out at the dreamy, slow-flowing water.

"Not exactly," she says.

Harriet's mother, Alice, had harbored a guilty wish that her lover's wife, Mrs. Dabney Carr, would "just up and die" in the hospital on the hill. And since she immediately spoke whatever came into her mind, she'd said so, many times. Then, "Why, Alice, I'm ashamed of you!" she'd chide herself immediately, leaping up in

166

mock horror, her pretty face suffused with a deep, becoming blush. "You bad thing!" she'd cry, slapping her own face. This performance never failed to delight Mr. Carr, whose delight in Alice knew no bounds anyway. He grabbed her hands and gave her a kiss on each flaming cheek to calm her down. "It's not that I wish her ill," Alice sighed dramatically, "it's just that I want you all to myself, all the time." And then how he had beamed: that plain, stoic, no-nonsense businessman Dabney Carr. He never flinched as he drove his wife's family's cigarette business farther and farther into the black, amassing a legendary fortune; yet he was putty in the tiny, delicate hands of Alice Holding.

Harriet had thought of Mr. Carr as very old in those days, yet he was not really old at all, merely formal, in the mold of a Virginia gentleman of an earlier age. Once, near Christmastime, he gave Harriet a candied orange slice; her pleasure had so impressed him that he never appeared thereafter without a candied orange slice wrapped in wax paper in his pocket just for her, Lord knows where he got them all. Finally Harriet got sick of candied orange slices though she was too polite to say so, and he was too polite to stop bringing them. To Jill he brought those paper-weights with snow in them, one for each holiday and one for each business trip he made, until her collection took up the entire windowsill in the front room of their apartment, overflowing into a special bookcase with glass shelves which he brought for her, too. Jill loved to pull her chair right up to her bookcase and lift the paperweights one by one, turning them upside down, until the whole shelf was snowing.

Mr. Carr was generous and kind and not really old at all, so when the intercom crackled in the middle of Harriet's French class that January of her junior year in high school, followed by the nasal voice of the assistant principal summoning Harriet Holding to the office, please, and Mrs. LeRoux came over to her desk and whispered that she might as well take all her books and her coat "as it's likely to be bad news, dear," Harriet thought first, hopefully, of Mrs. Carr, then mentally slapped her own face.

Alice was waiting in the office, a sure indication that something terrible was wrong, as she never came to school for *anything*. Her hair was wild. She was wrapped in a stained trenchcoat Harriet had never seen before; she couldn't imagine where it had come from. Alice thrust her car keys at Harriet, who had just gotten her learner's permit the week before. "You drive," she said, "and step on it." Then she started crying.

They did not go home.

Instead they drove the snowy road straight to Richmond, where Dabney Carr lay hooked up to tubes and monitors in a private hospital in the Fan District. Swept along by Alice's firm grip on her elbow, Harriet did not even get a good look at the distraught family and friends gathered in the waiting room, nor at the nurses in their official station, though they leapt up as Harriet and Alice raced by. "Just a minute there!" one of them called. But Harriet and Alice did not pause before pushing through the large steel double doors marked INTENSIVE CARE, NO ADMITTANCE and then into Room 2 where he lay perfectly flat on a high white bed under a bright white light. Blips and lines flashed across the screen. Little pale oxygen tubes ran out of his nostrils. A bag of fluid hung at the side of the bed, its tubes looping down, then taped to his arm. Another tube was taped into his other arm. His eyes were closed, his cheeks sunken in a way that Harriet had never seen. She realized that they must have taken his dentures out, though she hadn't actually known that Mr. Carr had dentures, and she didn't know how she knew this. But Mr. Carr's mouth was wide open in the most undignified way; his breath rattled in and out of his chest. Harriet knew instantly that he was dying.

"Oh, honey," Alice said almost to herself, letting go of Harriet's arm finally to cross to the bed and kiss his parchment cheek. His eyelids fluttered, he made a sound. "I'm here, baby," Alice said. "I'm here now." She kissed him again and sank down in the chair by the bed with her arm thrown across his neck, her curly hair covering half his face. The door flew open. Alarms went off. Two nurses and a doctor entered, followed by a thin woman in an emerald green wool pantsuit who pointed at Alice and said, "Don't you think you can come in here like this, you whore! We know who you are." The bigger nurse took the woman's arm, as if to restrain her. The doctor came forward and tapped Alice on the shoulder. "Ma'am?" he said politely. "Ma'am?" until she raised her streaming face.

But Mr. Carr opened his deepset dark

eyes. He struggled to sit up though the other nurse tried to hold him down. "Please, sir!" she said. Mr. Carr's breath came and went in awful gasps. "Let — her — stay," he said. Then his head rolled back on the pillow. His chest seemed to collapse. The moving blips on the screen changed, and the doctor pushed Alice aside as he leaned forward to listen to Mr. Carr's chest.

The woman in the green pantsuit threw up her hands. "All right! I give up!" she shrieked. "I just give up!" She pushed past Harriet as though she were invisible, leaving the room.

The nurse smiled at Harriet. "You okay?" she asked, and Harriet nodded, her lips dry.

"Suction!" The doctor snapped his fingers.

"You need to go now," the nurse told Harriet.

"Mama, I'll be right outside in case you want me," Harriet said clearly over the hubbub even though Alice did not appear to hear her.

"You sweet thing," Alice said into Mr. Carr's ear.

Though Harriet had dreaded going into the waiting room, she had to; it was the only place to sit, and she couldn't desert her mother. But luckily she was still invisible, in the way her mother had always been invisible until that very day. All afternoon Harriet sat in the corner of the waiting room drinking Tabs and doing her homework — thank God she'd brought her books along — also *Tess of the d'Urbervilles*, which she was reading for AP English. She did her algebra, then her French (the pluperfect), then read the assigned chapter on Andrew Jackson in the American history book and answered all the stupid questions at the end.

Weeping and talking and smoking cigarettes, the family came and went. "It's hopeless," the thin woman in the pantsuit hissed at them all. In her mind, Harriet had nicknamed her the Ice Princess, but in reality, she turned out to be Mr. Carr's oldest daughter, Marianne; the other daughter was thin, too, but nicer, crying silently into a wad of Kleenex and tapping her slender foot. Her worried young husband sat beside her, stroking her hair. Cousins and servants came and went. Jefferson Carr did not come, as he was far away, at the boarding school up north. A plump young Episcopal minister who looked like something out of *The Canter-*

bury Tales appeared with his tight collar, his bulging cheeks. They admitted him immediately; he came out shaking his head. Harriet ate a bag of Fritos and read *Tess*. Several nice men in suits showed up. They spoke reassuringly to the family, nodded to Harriet as if they knew her, then arranged themselves in chairs by the bay window, which gave out onto a wintry little park.

A black woman named Viola appeared with a big silver tray of fried chicken, deviled eggs, and roast beef sandwiches. Until then, Harriet had not realized she was starving. She ate and ate. "This is the best chicken I've ever had," she said, taking another drumstick. Viola beamed, squeezing Harriet's hand. Jeff loved her, Harriet remembered. He was always talking about Viola.

A general flurry ensued as the outer door opened again and a heavyset woman came in pushing a wheelchair and calling out, "Here she is!" It was Mrs. Herring, Mr. Carr's secretary. Harriet recognized the deep Southern drawl she'd heard so often on the phone. And the woman in the wheelchair must be Mrs. Carr, who didn't look crazy at all, only frail and sick. Someone had given her a hairdo that very instant, it looked like, spraying her thin blond hair into a transparent halo around her head through which the scary outline of her skull was visible. Her bright red lipstick made a garish gash across her face. "Mama!" her daughters cried. Cousins crowded around. The men in the suits stood up at their chairs.

"Oh, Viola," Mrs. Carr said, ignoring them all, "there's a bat in the Florida room, you'll have to get it out immediately, I won't go back in there until you do."

"Yasm," Viola said.

"How many times do I have to tell you to close that flue? *Always close the flue,*" Mrs. Carr went on. But she seemed to have thought of something else by then, mumbling, looking down to pick at the sleeve of her gray wool suit.

"Doesn't she look pretty?" Mrs. Herring said to them all.

"Doesn't she know about Daddy?" the younger sister asked.

"Well, I've *told* her," Mrs. Herring said. A little silence fell. Violet arc lights came on among the dark branches of the trees outside the window. Mrs. Carr picked at her sleeve. "Mary Tate, Mary Tate," Mrs. Herring said. "Look here, Mary Tate, your whole family is here, isn't that nice?"

Mrs. Carr held her head up then and

looked around, balancing her luminous hairdo carefully. "Well, they're all going to hell!" she snapped.

But Mrs. Herring was wheeling the chair forward. "I suppose this is as good a time as any for her to pay her last respects to Mr. Carr," she said to the assembled crowd, clearly relishing her role.

"Dabney is going to hell, too," Mrs. Carr announced cheerfully over her shoulder. "Dabney will burn, burn, burn."

"Code blue, Room 2, code blue, Room 2," the intercom crackled.

"Oh!" the younger sister began to wail.

"My God, it is too late." Mrs. Herring pressed her hand to her heart.

Viola grabbed the wheelchair. "Less us just go on home now, Miss Mary Tate," she said. "You come along with Viola. I bet you haven't had no decent supper yet neither."

"They don't know how to cook a thing up on that hill," Mrs. Carr said. "They make a pancake as hard as a rock."

Everybody in the waiting room was crying now. Harriet put all her books in her book bag, then stood up and put on her coat. One of the men in suits came over and thrust something into her coat pocket just as the steel doors opened; later, she'd see it was a hundred-dollar bill. "Mama!" Harriet rushed forward to her but the other two men were already there somehow, escorting Alice out, dragging her really, Mama's blond curls wild and her cheeks fiery red like the circles of rouge on a kewpie doll. She sobbed uncontrollably. A magic path opened before Mama and the men, like the Red Sea, Harriet thought, grabbing two more pieces of chicken and some sandwiches from Viola's abandoned tray and stuffing them into her bookbag as she followed.

They did not go back to Richmond for the funeral.

Courtney pauses at the door before heading out onto the deck where they're all to meet before the Captain's Champagne Reception. The warm breeze stirs her hair and she can feel it curling, well, *frizzing* around her face, it's something about the humidity out here on the water. Thank God for curling irons — Courtney uses the large two-inch diameter kind, which actually straightens her hair out. Suddenly she remembers the day Gene burned his hand on it; she'd plugged it in in his bathroom while she showered.

"Oh my God!" he screeched. "What is this instrument of torture? My darling? Is this yours? What ghastly thing are you planning to do with it? Should I flee while there's still time?"

Courtney stepped out of the shower to grab Gene's hand and run cold water over it at the sink. "I'm so sorry," she said.

177

"Here, this'll help."

"Butter," Gene said. "What about butter? That's what my beloved sainted mother always used to put on a burn, bless her heart."

Courtney laughed. "Oh, nobody believes in that anymore," she told him. "That's old hat. It's all cold now — cold water, ice."

Gene slipped his free hand around her wet waist. "Very impressive. How do you know all that?"

"Easy," Courtney told him. "I'm a mom."

"*Such* a mom," Gene said into the wet hair at the back of her neck.

"Gene —" One of the unwritten rules for their Wednesdays together was that they never mention her kids.

"Listen" — he had both arms around her now, while the water ran on in the sink — "I think you're a great mom. I really do. I wish you were my mom."

Courtney had to laugh. "Oh, stop it," she said.

"But then I couldn't do this, could I?" Gene had asked. "Or this —" Courtney stands dead still on the deck as the memory of what Gene Minor did next sweeps over her like the hot breezy Arkansas air. She was watching him in the mirror the whole time. Later Gene refused to let her use her diabolical curling iron, so her hair sprang up in loopy curls all over her head while they sat out in his garden for it to dry. (She had smoothed them out, of course, the minute she got back home, not that Hawk would have even noticed, but still . . .) "I am enchanted!" Gene had announced, standing behind her, running his fingers through the curls, holding her head like a ball in both big hands. "You little pre-Raphaelite mom, you!" He massaged her head, the most wonderful sensation. Nobody had ever done that to her before. Courtney leaned back in the old Adirondack chair. "Did I mention that I'm a licensed phrenologist?" Gene asked.

"Why, no," she said dreamily.

"An oversight, then. But let me just tell you, you have some very promising bumps on this head, Mrs. Ralston, bumps that augur extremely well for your future happiness. This one right here, for instance" (he rubbed it) "would be your lump of Venus. I find it to be extremely well situated and highly developed —"

But now Anna and Harriet are waving to her, all dressed up for the reception. They must wonder why she's standing here like an idiot staring into the sun when the truth is, she just has to talk to him right now, no matter what.

"I have to make a call." She waves back to them. "I almost forgot. I'll be back in a little while. I'll be back for dinner if not before."

They nod and smile, uncomprehending. Courtney waves again, then dashes back to her stateroom where she unlocks the door and dials. She has to look up the number of the flower shop in her little leather book.

"Gene?" she asks.

"Baby?"

"It's me," she says. Then she can't talk anymore.

"Hey, baby, hang on, I'm just going back here for a little privacy, these dizzy broads I've got in here, they're hanging on every word." Courtney can hear the high-pitched voices of Miss Violet Perdue and Eugenia Reap; in spite of herself, she smiles. "I'm almost there, just a minute now." Suddenly his voice is clearer, closer.

"Exactly where are you?" she asks.

Gene chuckles. "In the cooler. Along with three thousand dollars worth of roses, lilies, and baby's breath, all white. We're doing the Pennypacker girl's wedding and reception. Her daddy's name is Worth

Pennypacker. It really is. Ain't that a trip? *So Dickens.* Okay, baby, what's on your mind? Aside from the fact that you miss me horribly and life isn't worth living without me and you realize this completely now."

"Oh God," Courtney says. "It's true."

"And you're going to tell old what's-his-name to kiss your ass the minute you set foot on dry land again —"

"Gene, be serious."

"I am serious, baby. I am serious as a heart attack, as my beloved sainted mother used to say."

"Gene, you know I can't do that. We've already had this conversation."

"But *why* can't you do it, babycakes, light of my life, joy of my heart, my sweet babushka, my popsie, my little cabbage rose?"

"Gene! Gene, stop it, listen —"

Gene breathes heavily into the phone. "I am listening," he says.

"I just talked to Ellen Henley today — that's Hawk's secretary — and I'm afraid this is all a lot more serious than I thought, more than just a ministroke, I mean, or some kind of temporary thing. Ellen Henley claims that this memory problem has been going on for months, and she's been covering it up. Oh, Gene, I'm afraid there's something terrible the matter with him. I'm afraid he's really sick."

"So? Look, the guy has been unfaithful to you for years, Courtney. He's embarrassed you, he's treated you like shit. I'm sorry he's sick, but that doesn't change anything. He's done what he's done, and you know it. You've got to stand up for yourself no matter what, whether he's sick or not."

This conversation is not going the way Courtney hoped. "Look, Gene, I just called because I was thinking about you. I didn't mean for us to get into all this stuff again. We already talked about it, and I explained to you that you're just not being reasonable. You know I want to be with you more than anything in the world, darling. But this is my duty."

"What if I told you that you have a duty to yourself, Courtney? A duty to be honest, for a change? What if I told you that you have a duty to me?" Gene doesn't sound like himself at all.

"Gene, that's ridiculous. I certainly can't leave Hawk right now."

"When, then? When can you do it?"

"Well, later. I'm not sure, exactly. Whenever Hawk gets through this medical crisis, whatever it is."

"Courtney, that could be years. Or never."

"Oh, I don't think so, I'm sure it's really nothing to worry about. We ought to know something by next week, I feel sure of it. Then we can talk about this other." The tone she knows Vangie hates has come into her voice; Courtney hears it herself, but there's nothing she can do about it now. This is the way she is. It's even what Gene loves about her, he's said so, many times: the polished preppy exterior, the predictable behavior hiding the woman within — like a bag lady in a porn flick, he says, who looks just awful until she starts taking off her clothes. Gene Minor is the only one who knows she exists.

"*This other?* That's how you think about us, about you and me? This other? Other than what? Your real life, I suppose."

Exactly, she does not say, thinking of her photograph albums, all those pictures where Gene is *not*. It kills her to think this. But no decent person could leave somebody who's sick, for heaven's sake! "Darling, you know that's not what I mean. You know how much I love you. But it will take me a little time, that's all, to work things out."

"How much time? Until Hawk gets well?

Because he may never get well. What if it's Alzheimer's? People live with Alzheimer's for years and years. So how much time are we talking here? How about until all the children get married?"

Courtney nods and starts to agree but clearly he's not serious, he's going on and on, it's like a long bad joke.

"Or how about this? How about until all the children *die?* Of course by then we might be dead, too, but what the hell, at least we wouldn't have upset anybody, would we?"

"Gene, what has gotten into you?" But suddenly Courtney knows. "It's that woman, isn't it? That woman with the stupid name, what is it? . . . Rosalie Hungerheart. You called her, didn't you?"

"Well, I can't talk to *you,*" Gene says. "You're off on some goddamn boat."

"I knew it!" Suddenly everything falls into place. This is not Gene at all, not the real Gene, her Gene, her Wednesday lover, her secret prince. "I can't believe you would be so susceptible to that pop psychology."

"It's not pop psychology."

"No? Well, what is it, then?"

"It's common sense," Gene says. "It's talking turkey."

Courtney just cannot believe this.

"Look" — he goes on in the most reasonable voice imaginable, it's driving her wild — "look, it's very simple. There's a clear choice here. You can choose love, which is life, or you can choose not love, which is not life, which is death, which is the way you've been living for years and years. Look, Courtney, most people don't even get the choice. They lead lives of quiet desperation, as the fellow said."

"Oh, Gene, quit being so dramatic."

"Sometimes I'm dramatic," he allows. "But this is real. I want my life, Courtney. I want you."

"But —"

"No buts. Either you want me or you don't."

"But Gene, you have to understand how hard this is for me. I've never done a thing I wanted to in my whole life, except for being with you. I've done as I was told and then as I thought I should."

"I know that, honey. It breaks my heart. You've been breaking my heart for years."

"Then why can't we just go on like we have been until things calm down? Why not? Why can't we just have this weekend together in New Orleans? I know it's that woman. I know she's put you up to this."

"She did not put me up to anything, Courtney. She just helped me to see the issues more clearly, that's all. I needed some help. You do, too."

"You know her name isn't really Hungerheart." Courtney can't help saying this. "Nobody's name is Hungerheart."

"This is me, baby," Gene says. "Just me. Just forget Miss Hungerheart. And I'm telling you that I don't want to go on like we've been going on for years now. I'm old, you're old, and I'm just not willing to do it anymore. So I'm offering you a choice, that's all. I'll meet you in New Orleans on Saturday the way we've planned, and we'll have a great weekend, and then we'll go back to Raleigh and you can tell Hawk that you're leaving, and he can mobilize Mary Bell and Ellen Henley and Lucille and all his girlfriends and his vast millions to take care of him. You know they'll do it. They'll all snap to. They won't even miss you. Besides, you'll be replaced by next year with a newer, younger, blonder Mrs. Hawk."

Courtney is terrified that this is true. "But I can't do it right now," she whispers. This is true, too.

"Okey-dokey, then. That's it. Then I can't make it down for the weekend either — you'll just have to shop instead of having breakfast in bed with me. You'd probably rather shop anyway."

"Gene —" Dammit, now she's crying. But then something snaps inside causing her to sit up straight on the bed, fists digging furiously into her eyes. *How dare he?* This — this — *florist!* She hasn't been Mrs. Henry Ralston IV all these years for nothing. "I can't believe you actually have the nerve to put me on the spot like this. I do not have to suffer this kind of abuse," Courtney says, "and I refuse to be coerced. Do you hear me, Gene? I simply refuse."

"Whoa. You sound like a rich lady I used to know," Gene says.

"Well, I'm certainly not going to respond to this — this — ultimatum."

"Okay." Suddenly Gene sounds tired. "That's it, then. Call me sometime, after you get back. I'd like to keep in touch anyway."

He *can't* be serious. "Gene —"

"Look, baby, I'm freezing my ass off in here. It's damned appropriate though, if you think about it."

"What do you mean?" she can't help asking.

"Oh, none of this 'gather ye rosebuds while ye may' shit, not for Mrs. Ralston. Freezing our rosebuds on the stem, that's more like it. Nip them in the bud while there's still time or else, God forbid, they might actually *bloom,* and we can't have that, can we, Mrs. Ralston? Can we now? No late flowering for Mrs. Ralston. No Indian summer, no second spring. In fact, Mrs. Ralston prefers silk flower arrangements in general, so much more practical, so much easier, so much less mess —"

Courtney takes a deep breath. "Gene," she says decisively in the voice that has run a hundred committees. "I'm not even going to listen to any further nonsense. I'll see you at the Royal Orleans on Saturday. I'll be waiting in bed, with a little surprise for you," she adds on the spur of the moment, without a clue as to what the surprise might be, but surely she'll find something, maybe a bottle of very good champagne or some little something from one of the antique shops along Chartres Street. Or a hat from that wonderful hat shop, maybe a Panama.

"I don't think you heard me," he says. "It's my way or the highway, take it or leave it, angel buns." He sounds like her old sweet Gene but he's not, something is really different now.

"Gene, you know you don't mean that! *I* know you don't mean it!" Courtney affects a laugh. "I'm sorry I bothered you at work, I know you're just tired, I can tell you're not really yourself. I'll call you tomorrow night, darling. I love you and I can't wait to see you this weekend. Bye-bye!" she places the receiver down firmly on the phone before he has a chance to say another silly word. He'll come to his senses, she's sure of it. But she'd better hurry, now she has to redo all her makeup from scratch, thanks to Gene for making her cry like that. Honestly! Who does he think he is?

Harriet feels like "country cousin come to town," as Alice used to say, entering the Grand Saloon in Anna and Courtney's wake for the Captain's Champagne Reception. Courtney's long black sheath is slit up the side. Anna wears a flowing cape and those enormous dark glasses that cover half her face. Heads turn as she makes her way grandly through the crowd. "Who *is* she?" Someone puts a hand on Harriet's arm. Harriet shakes her head, smiles, pulls away. This trip isn't exactly what she expected, with all these silly events happening every few minutes. But then the first trip wasn't what they'd expected either. Too many mosquitoes, too much rain, too much hard work, too many people both on the raft and on shore to have it be anything like a real Mark Twain experience. But it *was* an experience, all the same. Harriet remembers Mr. Gaines

saying, "There are only two plots in literature. The first one is, somebody takes a trip;
and the second one is, a stranger comes to
town." He was right, Harriet realizes now,
holding on to the back of Courtney's dress.
Everything she can think of fits into one of
those categories. *The Odyssey*; *Absalom, Absalom* . . . "Where's the captain?" she asks.

"Oh my God." Courtney stops so
abruptly that Harriet runs into her. "I
guess that's him in that sort of wishing well
thing." Flashbulbs are popping somewhere
ahead of them.

"It's an *arbor*," Anna turns back to say
sternly. "But what a gorgeous man! What a
hunk!"

"Straight out of central casting." Harriet
grabs a flute of champagne from a waiter
gliding past with a giant silver tray.

"Oh, look, everybody's having their picture made with him," Courtney says.
"Let's do it, too. Here, get in line."

"Wouldn't all this be awkward if the captain was really ugly? Say he had a harelip
—," Harriet wonders.

"Don't be ridiculous," Anna says. "The
captain couldn't possibly be ugly."

"But how do you know? I mean, is that
one of the criteria?"

"Of course it is! He's got to look like

this. Anybody can run a boat, and besides —" But Anna's words are lost in a ground-swell, a surge that carries them forward right up to the area around the arbor, roped off with a silken cord. "Names, please?" asks an efficient girl with a clip-board, who looks familiar, too . . . Oh yes, it's the girl who runs the gift shop, the Steamboutique, Harriet realizes. Now she's the photographer's assistant, and the photographer is one of the Steamboat Syn-copators, Harriet can't remember his name. Or maybe he just looks like one of the Steamboat Syncopators, they all have these little beards . . . Harriet puts her empty flute down on a white-draped serving table and grabs another one. Courtney's pulling her sleeve, spelling out their names for the picture girl. "Come on," she says.

Harriet will treasure this picture in which they all look so happy, Anna smiling enigmatically on one side of the glamorous captain; Courtney on the other, with a bright, startled expression; Harriet sort of squinched in between, up against the cap-tain's prickly shoulder with the braided gold epaulets and all the medals. Close up, the captain's curly hair glistens with oil. His eyes are large, dark, and liquid in the manner of Omar Sharif. He smells of breath mints and something else so male that Harriet nearly swoons. *What is she doing here?* The captain says something and presses their hands. Then before they know it, they've been whisked off the stage, out of the little arbor or the wishing well or whatever the hell it is. More champagne arrives. The band whips up their tinkly background jazz and the drummer goes into a prolonged drumroll.

The captain steps forward and raises both arms. "Welcome to my world," he sings in a big hearty baritone.

"Oh my God!" Anna exclaims.

"I guess you actually have to audition to be the captain," Harriet whispers.

"*Hush.* I can't hear." Anna is rapt.

Harriet has the sudden awful premonition that Anna is going to climb back up in the arbor to join him and that then they will belt out a duet. Harriet has always hated musicals, the way people dance with lampposts and burst into song whenever they feel like it; it's just so embarrassing. The captain switches into "Shrimpboats Are a-Comin'." Flashbulbs pop everywhere. He ends with "Ol' Man River."

"I could just *eat him up,*" Anna whispers.

The captain stretches his arms wide and

holds the last note forever. The crowd goes crazy. It's over. Courtney leads Harriet and Anna out to three rocking chairs on the deck facing the open river where an endless barge slips past, followed by another. Even though they're on the shady side of the *Belle*, it's hot out here. It would be very hot without this breeze.

Anna lights one of her nasty little cigars and turns to the others. "Well, that was quite an experience," she says. "I wonder where Catherine and Russell are. It's a shame they missed that performance."

"I think it's just as well," Harriet says. "Russell is so ironic, I'll bet he just hates things like that."

"In that case, we probably ought to sign them up for the Renewal of Wedding Vows Ceremony." Anna smiles behind her glasses.

"Oh, *let's!*" Harriet says.

"I'll do it tomorrow," Courtney makes a note. "Of course they'll never actually go through with it —"

"No, but think how embarrassed Russell will be when the list comes out in the *Steamboatin' News*." Anna taps ashes over the railing. They rock while the boat steams around an island with a sandy beach. "So," Anna says into the silence.

"Baby's husband called us all, I take it? I'm still wondering how he got my number."

"Charlie Mahan." Harriet nods. "I have no idea. He's a very wealthy man. I guess he has the means to get whatever information he wants."

"But didn't he call any of the others on the raft? Suzanne or Jane or Bowen, for instance?"

"No, I don't think so. Just us suitemates — and then, of course, Catherine was her roommate senior year. I don't think Baby kept up with anybody, really — I mean, we always exchanged letters at Christmas, but that's about all. I haven't seen her for years. Catherine says she hasn't either. I know she never went to any of our reunions." *Like me,* Harriet doesn't say, for she has had no excuses — no husband, no kids, no reason not to go. And she lives so nearby.

Anna snorts. "Nor have I, obviously."

"Oh, you should both come, they're fun!" Courtney has been to all of them, even though she didn't graduate. "We should *all* go next time."

"Probably not." Anna smiles, but you can't see her eyes.

"I believe I've been scared to come."

Harriet suddenly leans forward into the hot breeze. "I've been . . . oh, so *busy*, I guess, for so long, and then I guess I just didn't want . . . well, I didn't want to have to stop and really think about anything, you know? Or remember anything . . ." She pauses, rocking. They both turn to look at her, Anna exhaling slowly. "I think a reunion would be like — well, like *this* trip, in a way. Like the *Belle of Natchez*. It's all fake, isn't it?"

Harriet has a vision of herself the way she must have looked on the first day of college, sitting primly upright on the wide immaculate front seat of Miss Padgett Parsons's big Oldsmobile as it crept through the old brick gates of Mary Scott College while Miss Parsons, who had sponsored Harriet for the alumnae scholarship, talked a mile a minute about her own college experiences, about the Classics Club, the Honor Club, and Freya, the secret organization with the secret handshake, blah, blah, blah. Miss Padgett Parsons's hair was lavender. She had been Harriet's Latin teacher as well as sponsor of *Inklings*, the high school literary magazine Harriet had edited. In high school, Harriet had loved Miss Parsons. But that day, everything

Miss Parsons did got on Harriet's nerves — the way she pursed her lips, unconsciously, like an old cow chewing its cud, the way she smoothed her blouse over her ample bosom for no reason at all.

"There's the chapel," Miss Parsons was saying as they inched their way along in the stream of traffic. "And there's the Little Theater, I do hope you will try some acting courses while you're here, dear, I believe it would bring you out some." Harriet nods; she would rather die. All her life, people have been trying to *bring her out.* "Now that's the post office," Miss Parsons went on, "and that lovely octagonal building is the dining hall, isn't it pretty? We had to dress for dinner in my day, with gloves."

The campus really *was* beautiful, but Harriet already had it memorized from the map in the orientation guidebook because she was so afraid she'd get lost and be late for classes. Traffic was stopped dead as cars pulled in and out of the dorm lots, unloading, while returning girls ran toward each other for big hugs, all of them screaming, screaming. Harriet was perfectly sure that nobody would ever be that glad to see *her.* Nobody would ever scream.

Her last vision of the sewing shop rose

up in her mind's eye as still and quiet and perfectly framed as an old daguerreotype: Mama and Jill standing in the open door as she and Miss Parsons drove away. Their arms were entwined about each other's waists, their faces white and sweet. They blinked in the sun as if they had ventured forth into a bright new world not wholly their own. Their little hands fluttered like moths as they waved good-bye. Harriet fought back tears. There was certainly nothing insubstantial about any of these screaming, hugging girls at Mary Scott, dauntingly healthy with their shiny hair and muscular legs and summer tans. Finally, after being stuck for twenty-five minutes in the campus traffic, Miss Parsons was able to park behind Old South, Harriet's assigned dormitory. Harriet's hands were shaking as she pulled her largest suitcase from the trunk. Her luggage was as nice as anybody's, paid for by Mr. Carr, taking care of them in death as well as life. Followed by Miss Parsons, who insisted on struggling along with both the smaller bags ("for balance," she maintained), Harriet started up the little hill on the brick walkway.

But the lattice gate at the top was blocked by a boy and a girl who were kissing passionately. He had pushed her back against the wooden arch, among the blooming roses; she had one knee raised, showing a lot of leg as her wrinkled skirt rode up her lanky thigh. Her feet were bare and dirty; her toes curled up as he kissed her. The boy wore a white shirt. You couldn't see his face, though, nor tell his dark hair apart from hers, which cascaded all down her back. They did not stop kissing as she and Miss Parsons approached. Harriet set down her heavy suitcase. The boy was putting his hands all over the girl's back.

"A-hem!" Miss Parsons said loudly. The kissing intensified.

Harriet picked up her bag and walked around the arch, that's all you had to do, really.

"The proper authorities will hear about this, you can mark my word," Miss Parsons said as she marched past. The girl giggled. Miss Parsons had said "mark my word" all the time in class; Harriet was sick of it. She was sick of Miss Parsons, sick of Mama and Jill, sick of herself, and in fact she wished she could die right here on the spot, instead of checking into her dormitory, which is what she had to do next.

"Let me tell you," Miss Parsons said,

charging up to the desk like an old nightmare, "one of your students is making the most disgusting spectacle of herself not twenty yards from this building." After that, Harriet was so embarrassed that her mind left her body and went way up to the stained glass skylight at the top of the curving *Gone with the Wind* staircase. From this distance Harriet could just barely hear the dorm mother as she welcomed her to Old South, and she could just barely see Miss Parsons as she smoothed her blouse again and again and pursed her lips and finally charged away to disappear, Harriet hoped, forever.

"You lucky girl!" Mrs. Malcolm, the nice, plump dorm mother, handed her a key. "Everybody always wants to be in the Tower Suite."

"How did I get in, then?" Harriet asked. "Being a freshman."

"Luck of the draw, that's all. This year, it's a freshman suite." Mrs. Malcolm patted Harriet on the shoulder, immediately acting more maternal than Alice ever had. "Go on up, dear. Your suitemates have already arrived. There's an orientation meeting at four-thirty, then dinner at six. See you later." Sweetness oozed from Mrs. Malcolm's every pore.

The minute Harriet started up the stairway, the girl named Courtney came rushing down to help. She was as blond, crisp, and efficient as a girl in a commercial. In ten minutes' time, she had introduced herself, stowed all Harriet's bags in her room, and found out absolutely everything there was to know about her, which was clearly not much. Harriet sat down on her single bed, exhausted. Courtney stood poised on the balls of her feet, arms akimbo, smiling her wide red smile, still radiating energy. Not a shadow crossed her pretty face, nor hid in her big brown eyes. "I'm going out to see where my friends' rooms are, there's a bunch of us up here from North Carolina. My roommate, Anna, went over to the bookstore or something, but she ought to be back pretty soon, so you look out for her, okay? She's got red hair. A *lot* of red hair."

Harriet nodded dumbly, not sure what "look out for her" meant.

"Tell Anna I said let's all sit together at dinner, okay? And I'll see y'all at the orientation meeting." Courtney checked her watch, then bounced off down the stairs. Harriet started putting underwear in a dresser drawer, stepping over and around piles of clothes, record albums, Mardi

Gras masks, shoes and books. Margaret Burns Ballou, whoever she was, had come in here like a hurricane and left the same way. At least the books were reassuring. Harriet hadn't thought to bring any books from home except her new dictionary, a graduation gift from Miss Parsons. Margaret Burns Ballou had about ten times as much stuff as Harriet, who was through unpacking in a depressingly short time. She went over to the window and stood looking out at the duck pond with its rose garden over to the side, its weeping willows, its stone benches and that naked statue of somebody mythological, turning into a tree.

"It looks just like a fairy tale, doesn't it?" the voice could have come from inside her own mind. "I'm Anna."

Harriet turned to see the girl standing right behind her. "I'm Harriet Holding. From Staunton, just up Route 81. Where are you from?"

The girl bit her lip, hesitating. "Where would you reckon?" Anna asked.

Harriet considered the question. With her milky white skin and the cloud of frizzy red hair, Anna did not look like any of the Mary Scott girls Harriet had seen so far. Her luminous gray eyes were set far apart beneath the high white forehead, the pale arched brows. She was oddly dressed in a long full skirt and a white peasant blouse.

"Europe?" Harriet was sort of kidding and sort of not kidding.

"Nope. It's *West Virginia*," Anna said in a mock whisper, "but don't you tell a soul. I'm hoping to get beyond it." Then she giggled, as somewhere a bell began to ring. "Oh no, I guess we've got to go to that meeting now. You know what? Right now I wish I'd gone to the Cornerstone Baptist College in Wartsburg, West Virginia. I really do. I'm just scared to death."

For the first time that afternoon, Harriet felt herself beginning to relax. "Me too," she said. "Me too."

"Well, where in the world *could* she be?" Anna asked the others, gathered in Harriet's room. It was a good question. Since freshmen were not allowed to have cars, the choices were limited. But Margaret Ballou had failed to appear at both the orientation meeting and dinner. "Clearly she's here somewhere, or at least she's been here . . ." They all looked over at Margaret's chaotic side of the room. Though it was past nine o'clock already, it was just getting dark outside. Fireflies rose from the garden below.

Courtney leaned forward and snapped on a desk light. "We have no choice. Something must have happened to her. We'll have to notify Mrs. Malcolm right now."

"Hey, don't do *that*." The same girl Harriet had seen earlier, the girl who had been in the trellised arch kissing the boy, came stumbling in through the doorway, grinning from ear to ear. Her tangled black hair fell into her eyes and down her back, curling around her thin shoulders, her yellow linen skirt as wrinkled as a skirt can be. A little line of dried blood ran down her face from a cut high on one cheekbone: The roses, Harriet knew immediately. That's from a thorn in the roses. She watched as the girl floated across the room to drop on the end of her bed and curl up like a cat. Without even thinking about what she was doing, Harriet got up and went over and closed the door and locked it behind her.

"Thanks, honey." The girl had smiled at them all then, each in turn, that slow but reckless toothy grin that no one could ever resist. They smiled back — first Harriet, then Anna, then Courtney, too, though tightly, gritting her teeth. The girl dumped the contents of her purse on the bed, then rummaged through the pile, coming up with two Nestlé Crunch bars which she proceeded to unwrap and divide into their tiny little squares with surprising precision. She put them all on a Beatles album cover, then held it out like a tray.

"Dinner?" she asked. She had a low, raspy voice almost like a boy.

"We've had dinner," Courtney said.

"Dessert, then?" the girl asked. "I recommend the dessert."

"Sure," Anna and Harriet said together, then looked at each other and laughed. The single lamp held them all in the soft yellow pool of its light. The warm chocolate melting on Harriet's tongue was delicious. She took another piece, then another, then watched as the girl licked her fingers thoroughly, like a cat, looking at them one by one.

"Hey, y'all," she said. "Thanks. I'm Baby Ballou."

So the pattern was set. From the very beginning, Baby had never gone by the rules, seeming almost to assume that they were meant for other people, and Harriet had always covered for her. Harriet hadn't minded either. In a funny way, she loved it. She had always been so dependable, so drab, so good, so boring; her vicarious new life had the double advantage of being exciting, yet not dangerous. Often, it was almost glamorous — the gold dust on the butterfly's wings touched Harriet as well. For Baby's life was full of drama and intrigue. Only two weeks after school started, a disheveled boy in a black raincoat strode back and forth in the dewy grass outside Old South at 3 a.m. yelling, "God damn it, Ballou! I know you're up there!" until every light in the dorm came on and all the windows were full of tousled heads. He bellowed until Baby ran lightly down the stairs wearing only the Harley-Davidson T-shirt she slept in; she hadn't come back until the next day around noon. At dinnertime she joined the others in that lovely octagonal dining room where she ate three helpings of meatloaf and two helpings of scalloped potatoes, then pushed back her plate and lit a cigarette and smiled at them. "Don't even ask," she said.

At that moment Baby seemed entirely exotic to Harriet, another order of being. And yet they had a lot in common, too. Surprisingly, it turned out that all four suitemates had signed up for the yearlong Introduction to Creative Writing course.

The first semester, Introduction to Poetry, was taught by Mr. Holland, a poet himself, a brilliant, slight, ashen-faced young man with a recent Ph.D. from Iowa. He was widely assumed to be homosexual.

For their first assignment, Mr. Holland had them read several chapters in Joseph Campbell's *The Hero with a Thousand Faces*, then invent a constellation, then write a poem in the form of a myth explaining it.

"Cool," Baby sang out in class.

"Does it have to rhyme?" Courtney raised her hand to ask.

Mr. Holland's pale eyelashes fluttered contemptuously. "Of course not," he said.

Baby had already told them all that she didn't even want to come to college, this or any college — all she'd ever wanted to do was write, she said, but she'd made a deal with her daddy, and anyway a person has to be someplace, and Alabama will drive you fucking nuts. Harriet had never heard a girl use this word before; a thrill shot through her every time Baby said it.

Anna had announced her own intentions of becoming a writer, too. "Listen, I grew up in a holler surrounded by mountains you wouldn't believe, it was like I lived in a trap. If I hadn't been able to read, I would have died. I'm not kidding. I would have been a twelve-year-old suicide. Books were the only thing that got me out of there. And I'll tell you, I'm *not* going back!"

"I don't know if I can do this or not," Courtney told Harriet as they sat around, procrastinating, the night before the first poems were due. "I just thought it would be a little fun thing to take, you know, an easy A. Now I'm getting real nervous about it. What about you? Do you really want to be a writer, too, like Baby and Anna?"

"Yes," Harriet surprised herself by saying; suddenly it was true.

But Courtney seemed perfectly poised in class, where it turned out that each student had to read her poem aloud to the others, then receive their comments. Harriet would not have signed up for the course if she had realized that this would happen. Even worse, Mr. Holland had placed all their desks in a circle so everybody could see everybody else all the time.

Anna's hand shot up immediately when he asked for volunteers. She cleared her throat and in her twangy plaintive voice proceeded to read one of the darkest poems Harriet had ever heard, about an unhappy young wife in the mountains who took a lover from over the ridge; when her jealous husband found them in bed together, "under his mama's quilt," he killed them both, then cut off her hands and "made banjo frets of her little finger bones." He was never caught or punished for this crime. Instead, he became a legendary musician who "sang the dark heart of the world." This poem's title was "Little Finger Bones," which was also the name of the constellation, and in a certain way, Harriet decided later, it set a standard for the class. Anna looked up and stared at them all when she had finished reading it, her hair a crazy red halo around her old-fashioned face. *She* could have been the mountain girl herself, the murdered wife. No one spoke. Even Mr. Holland seemed taken aback.

"Well, ah, Miss Todd," he said finally, "I admire the way you have taken the traditional material of the mountain ballad and adapted it into this atonal free verse, a comment perhaps on the darkness underlying our stereotypical image of folk culture."

"Thank you," Anna said simply.

Harriet didn't have a clue what they were talking about. Her own poem, finally written in desperation at the last minute, seemed ridiculous to her now, nothing more than a little ditty inspired by a stuffed animal she'd brought from home, a big cat-shaped pillow Alice had made for her years before. She'd made up a little story about the cat, but it was trivial by comparison with everybody else's, obviously.

Courtney read next, however, a singsong poem which made Harriet feel a little better because even she could tell it was sappy, all about an old maid in a small town whose only sweetheart was killed in a wreck on the way to pick her up for a dance. She wore a heart-shaped corsage he'd sent her until it turned to brittle stems, then dust, "as do we all." Upon her death, the corsage took its heart-shaped place "above," which rhymed with "love."

"It is very hard to write about certain loaded themes, such as, ah, romance and death, without falling into, ah, trite language," Mr. Holland opined judiciously, swaying back and forth on his feet with his eyes closed. You could knock him over with a feather, Harriet thought.

"Is that *bad?*" Courtney wrinkled up her pretty face at him.

"Ah, *no,* of course not, but what we want to do whenever we can is to understate, especially in cases of extreme emotion, ah . . . any other comments here?"

Suzanne St. John raised her hand. "They don't make heart-shaped corsages in New Orleans," she said, and everybody laughed. But Suzanne was serious. Then she read her own poem which got by without much comment, followed by Lauren Dupree and Catherine Wilson. Harriet was fascinated by Catherine Wilson, who never seemed to care what she looked like or what she said, or what anybody else thought about it, either. Usually she wore jeans — nobody else wore jeans then — and a T-shirt, streaked with paint. She was invariably late to creative writing, coming straight from the theater. "Sorry," she'd say sweetly in her scatterbrained way, sliding into a seat at the back of the room. But it was clear that she wasn't really sorry at all. Catherine moved through the world with no pretense and a practical ease that Harriet found enviable. Her poem was about a dog whose master died in the Civil War yet he was still searching for him, eternally, all across the sky. This poem was named "Prince," for the dog. It almost made Harriet cry. During the readings, Baby alternately scowled out the window, fiddling with her pen, or sketched everybody in the class with amazing accuracy. Harriet had had no idea that Baby had any artistic talent at all. It didn't seem fair. But Harriet was growing hopeful. The allotted hour and a half was almost up.

"Margaret?" Mr. Holland asked.

Baby shuffled the papers on her desk, then read her poem straight through in a husky monotone without once looking up. The poem was all about abortions, which somehow turned into "starbabies of the night sky, waving their shiny hands."

"Well, I think that's just *gross*," Suzanne said into the silence that followed.

Baby said something under her breath, looking down at her desk.

"That is a wonderful poem," Anna announced precisely, definitively.

"So it's *good* to be gross?" Courtney was distressed. "I thought poems were supposed to be pretty."

"Those are greeting cards," Baby said.

Mr. Holland seemed on the verge of wafting clean away. "Ah, no," he said. "That is to say . . . but a poem need not be pretty. Ah, no. Pretty will not be our aim here."

This was news to Harriet, whose time had nevertheless come. Mr. Holland opened his whitish eyes and aimed them in her direction. "Miss, ah, Holding," he said.

Harriet took a deep breath which lasted two-thirds of the way through her poem, then gasped again, finishing at breakneck speed.

"Could you read that again, Miss Holding? Somewhat more slowly, please?" Mr. Holland requested of the ceiling, leaning back, rocking.

"I don't think so," Harriet whispered.

"Hell, *I'll* read it then." Baby got up and grabbed it, smoothing the wrinkled paper out on her desk. "Supercat," she announced. This time it sounded much better, even to Harriet.

"Thank you, Miss Ballou," said Mr. Holland. "Now girls, what do you make of this?"

"Obviously Supercat is a God figure," said Alexis Hill, who would make Phi Beta Kappa in their junior year.

What? Harriet would have spoken if she could.

But Mr. Holland nodded, eyes closed. "Ah, yes. Yes. Or some sort of celestial superego, perhaps related to the parent, watching over the speaker in absentia."

"Listen," Harriet finally said. "This poem is actually about a stuffed animal. A *pillow*."

"Hush, Harriet," Baby said.

"That's right," Mr. Holland agreed. "The fact is that it doesn't really matter what your intentions were in writing this poem, Miss Holding. Now the poem exists as an entity in the world quite apart from you, as it must, subject to our interpretation. You, the writer, cannot dictate that interpretation to us. You cannot protect this poem. In fact, Miss Holding, you have no further control over this poem at all."

That's ridiculous, Harriet did not say, but then thank heavens the bell rang anyway and they all scattered into the September sun and big old trees of actual afternoon in the real world, what a relief.

From the minute she started living with Baby Ballou, Harriet's whole life had become more intense, more interesting and colorful, than it had ever been. Sometimes it was *too* intense and colorful, and confusing — like being caught inside a kaleidoscope. Just when Harriet thought she knew what was going on, everything would get scrambled into a completely different configuration.

One bright September afternoon when Baby was in biology lab, Harriet got up from typing a humanities paper to answer a hesitant knock at the door. There stood a pale, plump young woman with large nostrils and kind of a pig face, squinting as if she might be nearsighted. Harriet knew she didn't go to Mary Scott College and also that there was something wrong with her.

"Hey. Is —" The girl peered past Harriet into the room.

"Baby's in lab right now," Harriet said, "but she ought to be back in about fifteen minutes. Why don't you come on in and wait for her? You can sit right over there, that's her desk."

The girl plodded through the piles of Baby's junk on the floor to sit at the desk where she did nothing, absolutely nothing. She did not read or look at anything on the desk. Instead she sat hunched over staring vacantly at the wall, breathing through her mouth.

Harriet cleared her throat. "Are you from Alabama, too?" She was trying to put the girl at her ease. "Are you a friend of Baby's from home?"

"Well, I knew her in the hospital," the girl said, and that was all she said. It was the longest fifteen minutes in the world before Baby came back and Harriet could escape to the snack bar.

"Who *was* that?" she couldn't wait to ask Baby later, but Baby just shook her head, eyes hidden behind the screen of her long dark hair. "Nobody," she'd said. Her checkbook lay open on her desk and for a minute Harriet got the wild idea that Baby might have written the girl a check — impossible to tell, of course, since Baby never filled in her check stubs or kept her bank balance. Apparently she didn't have to: her account seemed to be replenished miraculously, like a magic well. The girl did not return.

And then there was the matter of the blouses. Baby had started out with a lot of blouses. But as the first weeks wore on, the pile of dirty blouses on the floor grew, while more and more empty hangers gathered in Baby's closet. Twice she went shopping at the Little Shoppe across the street, coming back with still more blouses in their cellophane wrappings.

Finally Harriet couldn't stand it. "What are you *doing?*" she asked. "Lord knows, you don't need any more blouses. Why don't you just wash the ones you've got?" And get them off our floor, she did not say.

Baby turned to look at her. "You want me to make up something or tell you the truth?"

"Tell me the truth," said Harriet.

"I don't know how." Baby grinned. "I know that's pathetic, but I don't."

"Well," Harriet said, "I'm just the girl to teach you. Come on."

Harriet marched Baby down three flights of stairs to the bowels of Old South, where she professed amazement at the gleaming white rows of washers and dryers, the soap dispensers, all the choices for hot and cold and load size.

"This is just too hard!" Baby had wailed.

"No, it's not," Harriet said. "It's really not. I've been doing the laundry at my house since I was about seven. If I could do it when I was seven, you can do it now."

"You're kidding!"

"No, I'm not. I figured, since Mama made all my clothes, the least I could do was wash them."

Baby turned from the open washer to stare at her. "Wait a minute. Your *mother* made your clothes?"

Harriet laughed. "Everything. All of them. She still does. She made this dress I've got on, for instance. That's what she does for a living, Baby. She's done it all her life."

"She *made* that dress? I thought that dress was a Villager."

217

"That's the idea. We rode over in the car as soon as I knew I was coming here, me and Mama and Jill, so we could see what everybody was wearing. So I would have the right clothes." Harriet was starting to get nervous, the way Baby was staring at her. Baby had an unnerving way of paying very close attention, total attention, to what you were saying. "What does your mama do anyway?" Harriet asked. "Doesn't she sew, even a little bit? I thought all mothers had to sew, I thought it was the law."

Baby started stuffing all her clothes haphazardly into the washer. "My mother is dead," she said without turning around.

Then who keeps writing you all those little monogrammed notes and signing them "Mom"? And asking for you on the phone in that amazing drawl, with all of Alabama in her voice? But Harriet already understood that part of being Baby's friend was to bite your lip, bide your time. And sure enough, on Parents' Weekend in November, here came Baby's parents all the way from Alabama in a long yellow Cadillac: her stepmother as round and blond and luscious as a peach, wearing tons of makeup and diamonds, her father as huge and handsome as a movie star. "Oh God, aren't they *awful?*" Baby asked sincerely, watching them get out of the big car in back of the dorm. "Daddy is going to find a way to put how much money he's got into every conversation, just wait. And she's got a brain the size of a pea. Thank God, at least they didn't bring the twins." Baby had two fifteen-year-old brothers who were "holy terrors," she said. But Harriet thought Baby's parents were great, bending over backward to be nice to Harriet and Anna and Courtney and their parents, too, taking everybody out to a private club called the Shenandoah which they had apparently joined just so they'd have a place to entertain Baby's friends while she went to Virginia for college.

Harriet rode back from dinner at the Shenandoah Club in Alice's new green station wagon, paid for by Mr. Carr's will. Alice wrinkled up her nose and put a light hand on Harriet's arm just before she let her out of the car at Old South. "I want to ask you something," she said. "Your roommate . . . Baby . . . is she *okay?*"

"Well, sure." Harriet was taken aback. "I mean why are you asking me this?"

"I don't know," Alice said. "Something . . ."

"They're just *nice*, Mama," Harriet said

irritably. "They're very, very nice and very, very rich, that's all." But Harriet knew what Alice meant, though it wasn't until later that she'd learn what made Baby's parents so solicitous.

It was January. Harriet had been to Winter Frolics at the KA house at Washington and Lee with Thomas Lee, a prelaw student from Tennessee. Back home, he apparently rode horses and hunted a lot; after law school, he'd go into practice with his father. His whole life was mapped out; all he had to do was live it. Harriet had met him through Baby, of course, or some friend of Baby's at the KA house. Somehow Baby had arrived in Virginia already knowing about half of all the boys in the neighboring men's colleges, so she was always fixing the rest of them up. Harriet had gone from having no social life at all in high school to having more social life than she could handle. Her grades dropped from A's to B's, though her scholarship depended on them. Yet Harriet loved going out, she loved seeing herself as a social butterfly. She loved calling home and telling her mother where she'd been, and Alice loved hearing it — she always wanted every detail.

Harriet couldn't figure out what Thomas Lee saw in her; she suspected he liked her just because she was Baby Ballou's roommate. Nevertheless, after the party when he drove her back to the chaperone's house where Mary Scott girls were supposed to stay, Thomas Lee fell heavily across her in the front seat, trying for her breasts, which were luckily unattainable since both their coats and the gearshift were in the way.

"Thomas, I have to go in," Harriet said, struggling under his weight. He did not respond, breathing heavily, one hand finally inside her coat, then down her skirt, inside her panty hose. Next time she would wear a panty girdle. Even though she didn't really need one, it was a lot safer.

"Come on, baby," Thomas said into her hair. He pulled her panty hose down until they were like fetters around her knees. His fingers hurt inside her. His thing was out, and hard. Immediately Harriet's mind went up above the two of them, up above Thomas Lee's little red MGB convertible which he was so proud of, up above the crowd on the chaperone's lighted porch where lingering kisses went on and on. Harriet's head hurt, pushed against the door. But somehow, with a sudden burst of strength, she was able to reach back and open the latch, catapulting both herself and Thomas Lee out onto the icy bank, where he let out a yelp of pain. "Bitch," he said. "You goddamn bitch." Harriet didn't care, trying to pull her panty hose up far enough so she could walk. In the light from the porch, Thomas Lee's breath came out in little white puffs like cartoon conversation. Finally Harriet stumbled up the stone steps and into the house, leaving Thomas Lee there by the side of the road leaning over the top of his little car. He stood like that for a long time after the other boys had left, stood there until Harriet started to get really worried about him, but then finally he got back into his car and drove off into the night.

Forehead pressed against the cold glass of the dormer window, Harriet watched his red taillights wink out of sight. She knew he wouldn't pick her up tomorrow morning for the Bloody Mary party at the KA house, she knew he'd never call her again. She had broken one of the cardinal rules in the elaborate game of dating at Mary Scott; she had not been charming, she'd embarrassed him. Therefore she would be penalized. She didn't care; she could work on her Milton paper in the morning; in fact, she'd rather do that anyway. By then

Harriet was starting to worry there was something a little bit wrong with her, as far as dating was concerned. She hadn't understood that the whole object of college was to graduate with an engagement ring as well as a diploma, though everybody else seemed to understand this very well — everybody except Baby, who didn't give a damn, and was already becoming famous for it. At Mary Scott, girls either fell into the Whore or the Saint category, at least until they became engaged. Then, and only then, was it okay to Do It. In fact it was required, Harriet believed. But if you made a miscalculation and lost your Most Precious Possession somehow along the way, or bet on the Wrong Boy, you lost everything. In spite of this — in spite of the seriousness of what you had to lose — the boys tried valiantly to make you lose it, getting you drunk, sweet-talking you, telling you lies ("My mama just died" or "My sister's got this incurable disease, we just found out"). Harriet understood that the boys were not *bad*, to do this. They were just boys. This was their role. The girl's role was even harder. Girls were supposed to get turned on, be sexy, yet not quite *do it*, ever, without that ring. Simply by ignoring it, Baby had escaped the whole system of dating at Mary Scott. But for Harriet, it was all exhausting, and she was glad to be out of it for that Sunday morning at least, glad to stay in bed and read Milton. She could not help remarking that the devil was much more interesting than God, just as Baby was much more interesting than, say, Courtney.

Ironically, Harriet had to ride back to Mary Scott with a girl who had gotten engaged that very weekend, a senior with the unlikely name of Muffy Tortuga. Muffy almost drove off the mountain road three times, admiring her own ring. She went on and on about the merits of her fiancé, a Deke. Harriet's whole face ached from smiling by the time Muffy finally dropped her off at Old South.

They were gathered in the lounge waiting for her: Courtney, Baby, and Anna. Courtney turned off the Carole King album, and they all stood up when she came in. "For God's sake," Harriet said from the doorway. Something seemed to be draining out of her head and down into her stomach, leaving her light-headed and nauseated and very, very tired. "What is it?"

Baby came over and wrapped around Harriet like a vine. Anna stroked her hair.

"Jill died last night," Courtney said. "Actually it was early this morning, around four o'clock."

"But she . . ." Harriet started. "Mama didn't . . ."

"It was a surprise," Courtney said. "Your mama said Jill's heart just gave out. She said you'd known it could happen, all along. A failure of heart, she called it."

"I'll have to . . ."

Anna had kept on stroking her hair. "Some doctor friend of your mom's is going to pick you up first thing tomorrow morning," she said, "and then we'll all come for the funeral, which will be on Tuesday."

Later Harriet could scarcely remember the funeral at all. It was very small and very sad, held in the Methodist church because one of Alice's most loyal clients was Marge Hammond, the minister's glamorous wife, for whom Alice had slipcovered all that ugly old furniture in the parsonage when the Hammonds first came to town. So Jill had a proper Methodist funeral even though as far back as Harriet could remember, neither Jill nor she nor even Alice had ever been to that church, or to any church, not even once in all their lives. Harriet had lost her gloves, so her hands were still cold long after the burial in the Methodist church-yard, still cold that night back in her room at Mary Scott when she finally got to bed after what had seemed the longest day of her life. Still she could not sleep. She lay in bed jerking at each sound — each high-pitched laugh, each slamming door, each car horn, each tower chime — until nearly midnight when the dorm finally quieted down. Everybody had been so nice. Notes, cards, and four bunches of flowers had awaited her return. Several times, as she lay sleepless in bed, steps had approached their room and then retreated once they saw the index card she had taped to the door: SLEEPING. Finally (it must have been well after one) Baby came back. "Harriet?" she said into the darkness. Lord knows how she got into the locked dorm.

"I'm here," Harriet said.

"Oh God, thank God," Baby said. She stripped down to her T-shirt and panties and got in bed with Harriet, hugging her from behind, covering up Harriet's cold hands with her own, twitchy and nail-bitten as always. Baby's hair spread out over Harriet's shoulders smelling like smoke, like bourbon, totally familiar some-how, and totally comforting. They breathed in and out as one. "Listen," Baby said. "I had a brother once."

"You've got two brothers now," Harriet said.

"No, no, that's not what I mean. Those are Daddy and Elise's twins. I mean I had a real brother. He died when I was ten."

"Baby! You never told me that! How old was he?"

"Thirteen," Baby said. "His name was Richard. Richard Ross Ballou."

"That's a nice name," Harriet said.

"He hanged himself," Baby said. "Or maybe not. Maybe he fell out of a tree. He was fooling around with a rope in the woods, we had this fort."

"Oh, how awful. How awful, awful," Harriet whispered.

"Depends."

"Depends on what? What do you mean? Of course it was awful."

"Listen, I know more than you do. I was there, remember. But now sometimes I think, oh well, at least he didn't have to live to see all this shit."

"What shit?"

"Nothing. Never mind. It's just that I'm sorry, okay? I am just so fucking sorry, honey, that's all." Baby spoke into Harriet's hair, each word a warm breath on her neck.

"How come you never told me about your brother before?" Harriet asked.

"I never tell anybody," Baby said. "It's okay. It's all in the past. I just wanted you to know, that's all. So, look, are you still pissed at your mom?"

"No." Harriet was so tired now that she couldn't remember why she had gotten so upset in the first place. Why shouldn't Alice have a new "friend," this little Dr. Piccolo, with his shiny bald head and his stupid Mensa watch chain? Mr. Carr was gone. Jill was gone. Harriet's whole life was gone, gone in an instant, as if it had never existed. And only Harriet seemed doomed to remember and remember and remember, to remember everything. After a while Baby's arm relaxed its grip on Harriet's waist and her breathing slowed down. The tower clock chimed three. Harriet kept staring at the soft, glowing rectangle of the window, where the light from the lamppost by the duck pond caught the blowing flakes of snow which seemed not to fall so much as to whirl around and around, dancing, like the snowflakes in Jill's paperweight collection from Mr. Carr.

"After you, ladies" — Russell Hurt ushers his women into the Night Owls Club in the Paddlewheel Lounge. They're lucky — they get the last available table before the show starts. Little Bobby Blue is already seated at the piano playing bebop. Russell orders grasshoppers all around.

"I *never* drink after dinner," Anna remarks, sipping hers, "though for the life of me, I can't remember why not." She joins the laughter; she's loosening up. Tonight she wears all black, her flaming hair pinned up with rhinestone combs. But after all, it's the captain's special dinner, and what a fine-looking man *he* has turned out to be! Anna imagines a lonely young woman, recently widowed in a tragic freak accident, locked up in her cabin sobbing for two days on a cruise down the Mississippi with her dotty aunt Dot. Reluctantly,

229

this young widow dries her tears, puts on her dowdy pathetic best, and attends the Captain's Champagne Reception. He's a dark swarthy passionate Mediterranean type of the sort she has always hated. He steps forward and opens his brawny commanding arms. His medals gleam on his chest. "Welcome to my world . . ." he sings in a deep baritone packed with testosterone. He is magnificent. The crowd presses forward. But suddenly, he glances *her* way. Their eyes lock. An electric current shoots between them. (Little does he know that the tragic young widow has just inherited this whole steamship company . . .)

"Well, I suppose they're basically all right, but I still don't see why they had to put them at our table." Courtney's referring to the couple who were seated with them at dinner earlier. "What are their names again?"

"Leonard and Bridget," Russell says. "Oh, they're okay. In fact, Bridget's pretty much of a fox." He winks at Catherine.

"How old do you think she is?" Harriet asks.

"Oh, I don't know. Thirty-five, maybe? She's a lot younger than he is, that's for sure."

"Russell, you don't know anything. She's at least forty-five. I mean, she's forty if she's a day. She's had a lot of work done — can't you tell? She's a trophy wife," Catherine says.

"And what are you — an atrophy wife?" Russell shoots back as a singer billed as Diamond Lil comes to the piano and launches into a sultry version of "Smoke Gets in Your Eyes."

"On the other hand, *she's* not very foxy, is she?" Harriet means Diamond Lil. "Don't you think she looks like a big hefty milkmaid in that get-up?" Diamond Lil wears a low-cut peasant blouse and a full red skirt. Her breasts swell as she leans forward.

"Milkmaids have their charms," Russell says. "I wouldn't mind meeting her two friends either."

"Russell!" Catherine slaps his hand.

Diamond Lil sings "Summertime" and "Crazy." She really does have a very good voice in addition to those impressive breasts. Harriet wonders what *her* story is, why she's here on this boat singing with the albino Little Bobby Blue instead of in some famous nightclub in New York or New Orleans. Something must have happened to her, Harriet thinks. Something happens to everybody.

Diamond Lil sings "The Sounds of Silence," one of Russell's favorites, he remembers when it was a hit back in the sixties, sung by, who was it? Simon and Garfunkel. It was on the juke box in the basement of the Beta house, Russell remembers punching A5 again and again, sinking back into that old leather couch while it played. There was something about it, it was so plaintive. "Hello darkness, my old friend." The strangest feeling used to come over Russell then, it was indescribable, really, and yet here it is again, years later. Many years later.

"Really, I have to go to bed," Anna is saying. "I can't believe I've stayed up this late."

"We'll see you tomorrow," says Courtney. "Are you going on the battlefield tour? Or just into Vicksburg?"

"Neither, I'm afraid." Anna adjusts her layers. "I'm here to work, you know."

No, Harriet does not say. No, don't you remember? Doesn't anybody remember anything but me? We're all here for Baby . . . For some reason Harriet remembers the way Baby used to sit on her bed with her legs flat out to the sides. She was double-jointed . . .

"Harriet, Harriet, listen, you've got to hear this!" Courtney is laughing, Anna is laughing, Russell is laughing, Catherine is poking her in the side. Up front at the piano, Diamond Lil has changed the words of "Can I Have This Dance for the Rest of My Life?" She's singing, "Will I wear Depends for the rest of my life?"

"I'm not so sure this is funny," Russell says.

"Look, look." Courtney is hysterical. "They don't even get it." And in truth they don't seem to, most of the older people in the bar nodding to the music with the same vague smiles they've worn all night. Two couples are waltzing. Diamond Lil finishes up with a flourish. "That's it! Good night, ladies and gentlemen!" Harriet stands up with the others, and Diamond Lil sings them all out the door with "Goodnight Irene."

"Good night! Good night!" Russell and Catherine echo, slipping off. "See you in the morning." Courtney disappears, but Anna pauses at the rail, even though she seemed to be in such a hurry to get to bed, so Harriet lingers, too. The air out here is thick and steamy.

"I was just thinking," she says, "some of those old couples in there must have been

233

married for more than fifty years. Why, even Courtney and Hawk have probably been married for thirty-five years. I just can't even imagine it."

"You could imagine it," Anna says, "if you'd ever run into the right man."

"Did you ever do that, Anna? Run into the right man, I mean?" Darkness gives Harriet the courage to ask.

"Eventually," Anna tells her, lighting up a cigar.

"But it wasn't that graduate student," Harriet prompts, as a horn from another boat sounds across the dark water.

"Kenneth Trethaway?" Anna gives her snorting laugh. "No. Hardly."

"We never really knew him, did we?" Harriet's trying to remember.

"You never really knew me either," Anna says.

Even her closest friends in college — these suitemates — didn't know her real name, Annie Stokes. Nor did they know that the plain woman who showed up sometimes at Mary Scott for Parents' Day was not actually her mother.

Ernest Stokes, Anna's father, was a free-lance evangelist who'd moved from church to church all over West Virginia, hauling his family along. By the time she was thirteen, Anna had been to seven different schools, though she did not always go to school, as her mother was sickly, and often Anna had had to stay at home to take care of the little boys. This she'd never minded, for they were adorable, blond angels all three — David, Mark, and John — each a year apart. They had nearly killed her mother. Helen Stokes was frail anyway, a beautiful girl with red-gold hair that fell to her waist who liked to sit by the kitchen door in the sunshine smoking a cigarette and listening to the radio which had to be turned off when Daddy came home, unless it was gospel, which Daddy approved of. Daddy did not approve of much. Anna was not allowed to dance, to take gym classes, or to try out for cheerleader at school. She could not wear jeans or sleeveless blouses or drink Coca-Colas either. But she had loved her daddy, who was handsome and sweet, tossing the little boys up in the air whenever he came back from a revival, ruffling her hair. He had a beautiful speaking voice, deep and resonant, like God. Anna could see why her mother had taken up with him when she was just a girl, not much older than Anna. He had come through her town and saved her, then baptized her in the river, then married her. Then they had been fruitful and multiplied. But Anna's mother started coughing blood. She went away to a hospital the year Anna was thirteen, and then Anna was in charge of everything, though people from the church were real nice, bringing food and hand-me-downs. When Mama came home, she was very thin, with red cheeks. She got Anna to put the radio on the table beside her bed so she could hear Randy's Record Shop out of Gallatin, Tennessee. She loved Patsy Cline. At first all Mama would eat was cream of mushroom soup, but then she wouldn't eat anything.

The day she died, the boys were playing ball up the road and Anna's daddy was preaching a funeral someplace else. Anna was folding the wash. Her mama had been asleep but all of a sudden she woke up strangling. "Oh my God!" she said, looking at Anna. Then she fell back against her pillow, then she died. Her fingers had curled up like ferns. Spit came out of her open mouth and ran down her neck into her nightgown.

The day after the funeral, Daddy yelled bloody murder and broke up the kitchen furniture with the ax while Anna sat huddled in bed with the little boys, hugging them.

Three weeks after that, Daddy married Mrs. Loretta Goudge, a widow in their church, twelve years older than he was. Everybody except Anna thought this was fine. "A man has to have help taking care of younguns," they said, nodding. "A preacher has to have him a wife."

But though Mrs. Goudge was nice enough, Anna shriveled in her presence. At school, her grades went down. Her teacher sent her over to see Miss Todd, the old missionary health nurse. "Don't tell your daddy," the teacher said. Miss Todd was not from around there. "Child, child," Miss Todd said, stroking Anna's hair.

When her daddy and Mrs. Goudge left town for a new church in Ohio, taking the boys, Anna had stayed on with Miss Todd to finish high school. Miss Todd had a leather-bound set of the classics in her living room; Anna went right through them. Under Miss Todd's tutelage, she learned Latin and table manners and geography and memorized a poem a week which she recited to Miss Todd every Sunday morning before church, Miss Todd's church, which was Presbyterian and not emotional. Anna declaimed from the stair landing to Miss Todd who sat below, sipping her tea:

Breathes there the man with soul so dead,
Who never to himself hath said,
"This is my own, my native land"?

Miss Todd liked to tie back Anna's hair with a black velvet ribbon and kiss her on the mouth, but that was all; and even later, in Anna's mind, it was more than a fair exchange.

Anna did not see her father and the boys again, as they moved next to Indiana. At school she took a role in the class play and won a poetry contest. She got a job at the local dimestore where she worked after school and on Saturdays. In her senior year she was valedictorian and had her pick of college scholarships. She chose Mary Scott on a whim because she liked the way the white chapel steeple cut into the blue sky on the day of her visit and the surrounding mountains made her feel comfortable and the girls were nice. Boys would have been too much to deal with right then, though she had managed to kiss one several times at the church camp where she was a counselor during the summer before college began.

At orientation, she enrolled as Anna Todd, and kept the name even though Miss Todd was absorbed with another underprivileged girl, Anna's successor, by Christmastime. Anna didn't mind. In fact she felt curiously relieved, free to form her own friendships with other girls for the first time. She loved her suitemates.

She loved her classes. At Mary Scott it was possible to admit her secret wish to *be a writer,* to actually say it out loud, which she had never done. Nobody laughed at her for it. Her teachers were encouraging. Though she intended to write nice poetic stories that would demonstrate her large vocabulary, the stories came out different from that, surprising her. Yet nobody flinched when she read them aloud in the workshop, those first short gritty stories set in West Virginia, all of them about people she had known or heard about. She wrote one story about two abandoned, starving children who set their house on fire to summon help and another about a church organist who was so fat she didn't know she was pregnant until the labor pains began during Wednesday night prayer meeting while she was playing "Amazing Grace." She wrote a story about a girl who killed her young husband by accident with a tractor, then left her children with her mother and disappeared. These stories were seriously discussed in the workshop and then published in the college literary magazine. It was easy. Anna was amazed. Everybody thought she was tough, like her stories, but she wasn't. She didn't understand where these stories were coming from but they poured out of her onto the page like milk from a pitcher. They scared her.

On the strength of the first four chapters of the novel she was writing for her senior thesis, Anna was awarded a national Helen Levitas Creative Writing Fellowship which would pay her first year's tuition in graduate school at Columbia University, where she had already been accepted. She opened the official letter in the old post office at Mary Scott early one Saturday morning in February and stared at the black typed letters on the page until they all slid together into words and the news sank in. Then she turned on her heel and ran across the front quad to Mr. Gaines's office. It was a wet, foggy morning. Nobody was up yet. Mr. Gaines had been Anna's lover for the past two years. Of course she had had boyfriends, too, starting with all the dates Baby had fixed them up with that first year, but in most cases Anna felt much older than the boys from the neighboring schools. She liked to tease them, though; sometimes she could wrap them around her little finger. In general Anna found that most boys could take her or leave her, but the ones that liked her, liked her a lot. Graduate students had proved more interesting, but were usually too poor to take you anyplace nice for dinner. By senior year, Anna had broken two hearts that she knew of, in spite of her longstanding relationship with Mr. Gaines.

This relationship was a *relief,* in a way. It kept her from having to be in love. Mr. Gaines was a good husband, a good teacher, and a wonderful father to Maeve. Anna knew he would never leave Sheila. She didn't want him to. Oddly, the knowledge that their affair had no future enabled Anna to enjoy it all the more. Until that Saturday morning in February, the day she received the letter announcing her fellowship.

The English department was located in Bartlett Hall, one of the oldest buildings on campus, and the door was always open. Anna ought to know — she'd spent enough time there during the past four years. Of course, Mr. Gaines wouldn't be in his office now, he'd be at home where he belonged, with his family. Probably he was still fast asleep. But Anna could leave him a note. She couldn't wait until Monday to let him know the good news. Monday was a whole weekend away! Anna pushed the door open and entered the wide, shadowy hall which was as familiar to her now as her own room. Here was Miss Auerbach's office with Virginia Woolf's picture on the door; Mr. Duff's office with its incomprehensible quotation from Joyce; the crayon grave rubbing of William Faulkner's tombstone hanging on Mr. Goldman's door; Lucian Delgado's office which he was so rarely in; and Mr. Gaines's office with yellow light spilling out from under the door and falling from the transom in a golden rectangle on the heart pine floor.

Anna stopped dead. The fine hair rose on her arms. She heard Baby's unmistakable giggle. And then Mr. Gaines's low voice saying something she couldn't quite hear and then Baby giggling again. But Baby was engaged to Charlie Mahan; the wedding was set for June 10. Anna would be a bridesmaid. Surely Mr. Gaines was just helping Baby with a paper. Anna crept closer. She knelt and pressed herself against the door. She stayed there for almost an hour, unable to leave even when she knew she should, unable to leave until the big front door swung open and old Mr. Hash came in and turned on the hanging overhead lights and threw that brown grainy stuff on the wooden floor and started sweeping it up. Anna stood up then. She had no wish to see Baby. " 'Lo, Mr. Hash," Anna said to him, leaving.

So she went ahead and fell in love with Kenneth Trethaway, a graduate student from the University of North Carolina who had been pursuing her in a hopeless, reckless, relentless way for some time, and married him in the summer after Baby's wedding, when she realized she was pregnant. Normally morose, Kenneth had exhibited more delight than Anna had thought possible when she told him the news. His parents, too, both postal workers in Raleigh, seemed pleased and bought the newlyweds an enormous Naugahyde couch for the little house across from the police station in Chapel Hill where they would live for the next four years while Kenneth finished his Ph.D. Kenneth's parents were simple people, astonished by their moody, brilliant son. They hoped the marriage would settle him down.

Anna and Kenneth made fun of the

couch, wondering aloud how many naugas had died to produce it. Anna even did a pencil drawing of the nauga, a strange little mythological creature which looked to be half bird and half armadillo. They made love on the couch, on the floor, on a mattress they pulled out into their tiny backyard to look at a meteor shower which was gorgeous in spite of the sirens wailing from the police station. Kenneth and his friends smoked dope all the time, but Anna did not after she got pregnant. Kenneth and his friends called her "the Madonna." Kenneth adored her then. He wept wildly when she lost the baby at five months, having already used her Helen Levitas fellowship to buy a washer and dryer and pay off Kenneth's car loan.

She didn't need to go to graduate school anyway in order to finish her novel. Kenneth was the scholar, not she. She could keep her job and write on the side. She could write in the early morning and at night and on holidays. Actually, she ended up writing at work sometimes, too, behind the shelves in the big hospital basement where she filed patients' charts all day long; and because of this, she did not get angry when she'd come home on the bus well after five o'clock — sometimes it was actually *dark,* in the wintertime — to find Kenneth and his friends still smoking dope and listening to jazz and talking about literature in a frenzy (as if anybody cared) with no thought of supper. *She'd* have to go out and get supper, if they were to have any, sometimes just hamburgers from McDonald's, or macaroni and cheese out of a box from the 7-Eleven. Sometimes she'd get high, too, and then fuck him when his friends finally left.

Anna and Kenneth were thin, poor, and generally *wrecked* in those years. But she loved this heightened life unaccountably, as she loved Kenneth. What *was* it about him? For starters, he was a genius — everybody said so. Anna didn't even understand his field of study; "deconstruction," it was called. He was the hot new thing. Anna couldn't read a word he wrote.

At six feet six inches, with poor eyesight, Kenneth was so tall he was always tripping and stumbling over things or bumping into other things with his head. He had bleeding scabs. He was the most physically awkward man Anna had ever known, except in bed, where he was wonderful. He had pale gray eyes like Anna herself, but so huge and defenseless behind his thick glasses that to look into them made her weak with love. He called her "Anna," with a broad *A*. He read Proust aloud to her every night they weren't stoned.

At the university, he won a teaching award, then a graduate fellowship, then published a paper on postcolonialism. He presented it at the MLA in San Francisco. At the hospital, Anna received a promotion, with supervisory duties and more money, only it didn't seem like much of a promotion since it was so demanding that she couldn't write on the job anymore.

"Take it — it'll only be until graduation," Kenneth promised.

But after receiving the Ph.D. with highest honors, Kenneth was kept on by the department for another year, and then another. When Anna finally finished her novel, she didn't know what to do with it, so she wrote to Mr. Gaines asking for advice, but she never heard back from him. Miss Auerbach recommended an agent who took the book. The agent called Anna at the hospital to say that she loved it, that it was "fabulous." Anna wondered if the agent had read the same book she had written which was, she knew, depressing, like a lot of her stories rolled into one. Or like a landslide, like the slag heap which slid down the mountain and covered nine houses in the mining town in the book.

She bought champagne on the way home.

"Great." Kenneth, usually so intense, exhibited a notable lack of fervor. "To you." He raised his glass.

"What's the matter?"

"Nothing's the matter. What do you mean? Down the hatch!" Kenneth had never said "down the hatch" before.

Anna eyed him suspiciously. "Honey . . ." she said.

"It's okay," he said. "Congratulations. Only . . ."

"Only what?"

"What name are you going to publish under?"

"Well, I hadn't thought . . . Anna Trethaway, I guess. I mean, that's my name."

"I should think you'd want to keep your own name."

"Anna Todd? What's wrong with Anna Trethaway? Are you *ashamed* of this book or something? You haven't even read the last chapter or that revised middle section."

"No, it's just . . . I just . . . well, surely you understand, Anna, it's a little embarrassing for you to publish a book before I do. Why don't you use your own name?"

"But people would know anyway. I mean, our friends would know . . ."

"Not necessarily," Kenneth said.

"*Of course* they would! There'd be reviews, and interviews . . . and we'd tell them, too, wouldn't we? *Kenneth* —"

"Fuck it. Of course. Just fuck it. I'm sorry." Kenneth put his glass down on the telephone table so hard that it tipped over, spilling several phonebooks and the Rolodex address file onto the floor. And then he was gone, leaving the door wide open. Wintry wind rushed all around Anna as she tried to gather up the cards from the Rolodex. Sirens wailed from the police station. Finally Anna stood up and slammed the door. Then she sat down on the couch — that same tacky couch Kenneth's parents had given them years before — and took a drink of champagne straight from the bottle. She thought she ought to call somebody with her good news. She looked through the cards in her hands, almost all of them Kenneth's friends. She should call up Baby, everybody had thought Baby was so goddamn talented. And she ought to call up Harriet and Courtney, too.

But she won't. She'll finish this champagne and then she'll drink some vodka from the freezer where Kenneth puts it now to keep it cold for the martinis which he has taken to drinking lately, ever since he got his Ph.D., and then she'll drink some more vodka, and then she'll throw up and be sound asleep when Kenneth gets home.

The next day she will throw up again, and the following day. But even when she is sure she is pregnant, even after trying to get pregnant again for so long, she won't tell Kenneth. Nor will she show him the letters from the publishers, which say "too raw" and "not commercial" and even "Since Miss Todd is undeniably talented, perhaps she should consider writing about a better class of people." Anna will work on at her hospital job, typing theses and dissertations at night for extra money. Kenneth has to have a new suit and a root canal. She's waiting for him to apologize, which he never does. Instead, he buys the suit and flies all over the country, interviewing for jobs. He does not take her with him. He does not fuck her when he comes home; he says he is too depressed. The whole process of applying for jobs is so demeaning.

The night he came back from Chicago, she was sitting in the dark in their tiny living room, watching for him out the window.

"Hi," she said when he opened the door. She had on his soft old wine-colored flannel shirt which smelled like him, kind of peppery somehow.

"Anna! I thought you'd be asleep." He looked flustered, exhausted, wearing the new suit and a bottle-green trench coat she'd never seen before. The streetlight came in the window on his anguished face.

"Nice coat," she said.

"Thanks."

"So, did you get the job?"

"I don't know yet. You know that. I told you how it works."

"Kenneth, I'm not going, am I? You're going, but I'm not."

He sank to the floor by her feet, face in her lap, sobbing. "I'm sorry," he said over and over again. "I'm just so sorry."

Anna twisted her fingers in his wiry dark hair and looked out the window where sure enough, another siren went off before long and a cop car shot away from the curb, tires squealing. Danger was everywhere. But the thing was, she really loved him. It was like her love was something independent of herself that had taken on a life of its own and grown larger and larger with time, like the baby which she was carrying. It didn't matter if Kenneth was worthy of this love, nor if he loved her. Her love was beyond all that. For Anna knew, even in that moment, that she was privileged to be such a lover, that she was stronger and greater than he.

Kenneth knew it, too. He packed his clothes the next day and moved in with the other girl. After a week or so, Anna realized that all those friends in the Rolodex really *were* Kenneth's. She had been too busy putting him through school to make any, except for the girls in her filing unit at the hospital, of course, who were gratifyingly furious, hatching wild revenge plots.

"I know where we can get some *E. coli,*" little Barbara volunteered. "I'm not kidding, either. All you have to do is put it in his yogurt."

But Kaye held out for arson, which would kill *her,* too.

Anna had to laugh, shaking her head. She wasn't even attractive. Anna had already driven over there and parked in front of the apartment. *She* was tall and thin and black-haired, like Olive Oyl, and looked even more depressed than Kenneth. Her field was eighteenth century.

Somehow it seemed inevitable to Anna

when the agent wrote saying that much to her regret, she was unable to place this novel which was finally, she felt, "too disturbing," but she would be willing to see any future efforts from Miss Todd.

"Kiss my ass," little Barbara said.

"But you know," Cindy spoke up timidly, "maybe you ought to listen to her, Anna, and try something different, something romantic, something people really want to read, especially since you're going to have to support yourself entirely for a while" — and she didn't even know about the baby — "unless you want to work here for the rest of your life."

All the girls groaned.

"Like what?" Anna felt wild and strong, open to anything. She knew she would have a girl.

"Like *this*." Cindy handed her a paperback named *Mortal Passions*, featuring a bosomy girl on the cover, running through a graveyard with a castle in the background. "No, it's *good*," Cindy insisted over the general laughter. "I'm not kidding, just read it, you'll see, it'll make you feel *so much better* . . ."

These words echoed in Anna's head all the way to South Carolina where she planned to live on one of the barrier islands while she waited to have her baby. She'd chosen this location on a whim, having read about the area in a travel article. She read *Mortal Passions* in a motel room in Cheraw, South Carolina. She was not worried about being followed; she knew that Kenneth would feel too guilty to see her again. She had enough money for a while. She'd cashed in their joint bank account and taken their car and one small print she'd always liked, of the Blue Ridge Mountains around Linville Gorge where they'd camped on their honeymoon. On her next honeymoon, Anna vowed, there would be no camping.

Mile 437.2
Vicksburg, Mississippi
Monday 5/10/99
0500 hours

Harriet sits out on the little balcony in her nightgown watching the river stream past, dark at first, then that pale ghostly luminescence as dawn comes near, so you can just barely tell the water from the tree line from the sky. She's all wrought up. She feels like she never even slept, though that can't be right, can it? A person *has* to sleep. She has read that a lot of times you're actually asleep, lightly, even when you think you're not. She hopes that's true. She remembers how Baby used to stay up for days on end sometimes. Harriet's dreams — or memories or thoughts or whatever they were, depending on whether she was actually asleep or not — were full of Baby, and now she should be exhausted, but she's not. She feels more alive than she has felt for years, a terrifying, exalted feeling. Her nerves are like wires in the wind. She leans forward to look at the river.

Mist — or fog, which is it? — floats in patches on the surface. Birds swoop low then rise on flapping wings. The sky is pearl. The water lightens. Now Harriet can pick out buildings and docks along the shore. She hears men's voices. Peering down over the railing, she sees them all out on the deck below, waiting with giant coils of rope. The engine grinds into a lower register. The boat slows down. *Vicksburg.*

Suddenly aware of her nightdress, Harriet goes back inside and lies down on her bed in the dark, air-conditioned stateroom. It's actually chilly in here, completely different from the rich, sultry, river-smelling Mississippi air outside. Harriet pulls her covers up to her chin. If she could just sleep. If she could just relax and enjoy this trip as the others seem perfectly capable of doing in spite of the circumstances . . . But it's amazing, really, how little they seem to remember or care about why they're here. Why just yesterday, on the way to the captain's reception, Anna turned to her and said, "Now Harriet, wasn't Baby in love with some boy before she married this man who called us all up? I seem to recall something like that. Who was that boy anyway?"

"It was Jefferson Carr." After so long a time, it gave Harriet a shock to say his name.

"And didn't he go to some odd school? How did she meet him anyway?"

"Oh, Anna, don't you remember? She met him at that literary festival when Jim Francisco made the pass at you, sophomore year. And I introduced them."

The literary magazine, *Redbud*, had come out in late fall with five of Baby's poems and two of Anna's stories, one of them named "Ring around the Moon," in which a boy and a girl are taking a bath together in a motel after having sex. During the workshop discussion, Suzanne St. John had been much more upset by the sleaziness of the motel than by the story's graphic nature. "I just can't believe a nice girl would go to a place like that," she squealed. The story had created a little furor on campus, and all the copies of the literary magazine were snapped up immediately, a first. Harriet had had a poem in that issue, too, but nobody mentioned it. Probably it wouldn't have been published, she thought later, if she hadn't been a junior member of the *Redbud* staff. Or perhaps that was too harsh.

It was in her official capacity that Harriet had been presiding over the registration table for the college's annual Fall Literary Festival that year. Draped with a white sheet, the table sat under one of the oldest oaks on front quad. Its bright leaves fell all around, spangling Harriet's snowy table and the lush green grass. Harriet was there to give out programs, answer any questions, and make sure everybody had a name tag. She had worn a name tag herself. Anna had been sitting with her for a while but had disappeared to wash her hair in preparation for picking up Big Jim Francisco, the visiting poet, at the airport. Jim Francisco had a terrible reputation, but it was felt that Anna, with her coalfield smarts, could "handle him." Baby had a date that weekend with Kevin Cahill, a picturesque graduate student from UVA, a poet with long, curly reddish hair and nearly translucent skin and green freckles. ("They are *not green!*" Baby cried, giggling, but Harriet maintained that they were.) In any case, he adored Baby. He always dressed in army coveralls with poetry books and wine bottles sticking out of various pockets, and he kept his dog, John Donne, a black lab with a red bandanna around his neck, with him at all times.

Baby was cutting chemistry lab that afternoon to go hiking up Morrow Mountain with Kevin Cahill and John Donne.

Harriet sighed, sitting at her table among the falling leaves. Why hadn't *she* been asked to pick up the visiting writer? Why wasn't *she* on top of a mountain with a poet? Already she was beginning to suspect that she might be better suited for editing, or teaching, than writing. She had picked education as her minor, just in case. But she smiled politely as she checked off names and gave out name tags and directions to the visitors who did not even notice her, no more than if she'd been Marion Faw, the thousand-year-old English department secretary who had psoriasis all the time. In another forty years she might *be* Marion Faw, think of that.

Hunky Mr. Gaines wandered by, an arm around his beautiful wife. "Hi, Harriet!" little Maeve cried, riding her Big Wheel along behind them. A bunch of bearded, booted graduate students from UNC registered, having driven up from Chapel Hill. Some nuns arrived from St. Mary's, attracted by the reputation of C. E. Reed, whose small body of work was visionary even though he turned out not to be. A morose, egglike little man, he had disappeared into the campus guest house upon his arrival early this morning and had not yet emerged. His student hostess, Lauren Dupree, hovered in the garden, waiting to escort him to the upcoming events. A whole poetry group from the nearby community college signed in, along with their two teachers who did not look like writers at all, thought Harriet. They looked like ministers' wives, with their shirtwaist dresses and perfectly even bangs and sensible shoes. Now their own Marilyn Auerbach — who *looked* like a poet, at least, with that cape (though it was too hot for the cape) — came roaring across the grass with her usual giant, furious strides, smoking her Luckys. Marilyn Auerbach never walked on the sidewalks.

Harriet sighed, fiddling with her pencil. She knew she did not look like a poet.

"Harriet?" he said.

She looked up. The clear air went iridescent. *"Jeff?"*

"Harriet Holding," he said. "I can't believe it."

Later she would not be able to figure out how he had walked across that big expanse of leaf-studded grass toward her, as he must have done, without her seeing him. How he had simply *appeared*. Yet it seemed inevitable, as if something missing had suddenly slipped into place. She stood up behind her table. Jefferson Carr smiled the same big open smile he had had as a boy. He walked around the table and hugged her, picking her right up off the ground. He spun her around and around until the blue sky and yellow leaves and old pink brick buildings began to blur and she felt like a girl in a kaleidoscope. She was dizzy when he set her down.

"I guess we've got some catching up to do," he said. His brown hair was cut in some kind of a buzz cut; she had an immediate urge to touch it.

"Just a minute." Harriet grabbed a legal pad from the registration table and wrote, SIGN YOURSELF IN AND GET A NAME TAG in a shaky hand. Then she simply walked off with Jefferson Carr, leaving her sign propped up against a filing box on the table. She knew this was irresponsible, yet she felt proud of herself for doing it. "Let's go down to the snack bar and get a Coke," she said. Jefferson Carr had grown tall and broad-shouldered. He didn't look anything like his father. His mother was dead now, too, he told her: suddenly, a virus, last winter. Just about when Jill died, as it turned out. "I'm sorry," they both said at the same time, and then laughed. They kicked through the thick leaves side by side.

"How is your mother?" he asked. "I always loved your mother."

"Just the same," Harriet said. "Well, maybe more so."

"A couple of times I started to drive down there and see you all. Once I even made it all the way to Staunton, but I couldn't get out of the car somehow. I just drove around. I saw the shop, and some women going in and out, and so I thought, 'Fine, they're fine,' and then I drove back to Richmond. I should have come in," he said.

"No," Harriet said. "Maybe it's better not to. Not to go back, I mean. I don't know." I don't know because I really never left, she did not say. In any case, it would not have been good, she felt, for Jefferson Carr to run into Dr. Piccolo who was still in residence these days, Dr. Piccolo who cut his pointed beard with the kitchen shears and left the coarse black bristles in the sink, a practice which Harriet hated so much that she and Baby had made up a name for her reaction: *cillaphobia,* fear of hair.

Jeff was at Shenandoah Military Institute

in Lexington, it turned out, surprisingly. After years up north, he'd been ready to come back to Virginia for college. But he loved military school, he'd gotten good at it after all those years. In fact, he was the head prefect of his class right now, at SMI. Then Harriet understood why his khaki pants were so neatly creased, his loafers shined to a high gloss, his blue oxford cloth shirt so perfectly ironed. The Washington and Lee boys were sloppier and took pride in it, their rumpled shirts straight out of the dryer, their shoes held together with electrical tape. If sports jackets hadn't been required, they'd never have worn them; as it was, they wore the oldest, tattiest jackets they could find. Jeff Carr's blue blazer was immaculate.

"Your father would be so proud of you," Harriet said suddenly, without knowing she was going to say it. She knew it was true. Dabney Carr had been such a decent and honorable man.

"I hope so." Jeff cleared his throat. "You know, you probably spent more time with him than I did." His dark eyes filled up with tears. "Sorry," he said.

"Don't be sorry. *I'm* sorry." Harriet covered his hands on the table with hers and held them. Jeff's hands were square,

262

strong, and totally functional. He caught the waitress's eye and ordered two more Cokes.

"I didn't know you could, you know, get away like this from SMI," Harriet said.

"Oh, sure. In fact, I actually rent an apartment in Lexington with some other guys. We get to use it a fair amount of time for R&R. After all, SMI is not a prison." Jeff flashed her another big white smile. He was drop-dead handsome in spite of that military haircut, anybody would have to say so. Several girls Harriet knew had come into the snack bar and were staring at her and Jeff. They think it's a date, she realized, and then she thought, Well, why not? She straightened her shoulders. This would look *very much,* no, *exactly* like a date, to anybody who walked into this snack bar right now.

But actually Jeff was majoring in English at SMI, he was telling her, he figured it would be his last chance to spend any time on something like that. He'd go into the military right after graduation, of course, and then he'd probably go into the family business with his brother-in-law. There were no sonnets in his future. He had come down today on a whim, with a couple of buddies, but the buddies could take care of themselves. "*Now*. What about you?" he asked.

Harriet took a deep breath and it all came tumbling out pell-mell, as if she'd upended her pocketbook: all about school, her suitemates, her job on the *Redbud*, the writing class she was taking then with Marilyn Auerbach, the one she would take with the famous Lucian Delgado in the spring. "But I'm not really very good," she said.

Jeff started laughing. "You haven't changed a bit," he said. "Little Miss Nobody, remember that book Jill had? I used to read it out loud to her and then we'd kid you about it."

"Little Miss Nobody lived up the stair —" Harriet chanted.

"And when she went out, she went nowhere," Jeff said. His square hands had square nails and little tufts of dark hair on the knuckles. Jill's skin was so white, Harriet had sometimes thought she could see through it to Jill's small blue veins, her delicate, pulsing heart.

"Well, looky here. Party time." Baby and Kevin Cahill stood in the doorway, blocking the slanting sun. Somehow it had turned into late afternoon. Baby wore a boy's white shirt and blue jeans with beggar's-lice all over the legs; her hair hung down in her face. Kevin stood behind her with his arm around her waist.

"Oh, Baby!" Harriet half stood, thinking how wonderful it was for the people she loved the most in the world to know each other. "I want you to meet my old friend Jefferson Carr."

Baby sat down. Kevin Cahill turned a chair around backward and sat down, too, straddling it. Baby ran her hands through her hair. She pushed it back. She shook her head in that way she had, like a dog coming up out of the water, settling her hair around her shoulders. She smiled at Jeff. "So, are you from Staunton?" she asked.

"Richmond," he said. "But I haven't really lived there for years. I went away to school. So I probably won't know anybody if you're going to ask me." He smiled at her.

Baby was looking at him. "How did you meet Harriet, then?" she asked. "To hear her tell it, you'd think she grew up under a rock."

Jeff leaned forward into the same serious, straight-ahead way of talking he had had as a child. "Haven't you met Harriet's mother yet?" he asked. "Alice is great. Our parents were friends, so we used to play together when we were kids."

With a single sentence, he had normalized Harriet's whole weird childhood. "Excuse me," she said, or thought she had said, but maybe she didn't because by then Kevin was asking Jeff where he went to school, and nobody seemed to notice when she slipped off to the bathroom to cry, hard, for about ten minutes. When she came back, Kevin was saying, "You're kidding, you mean you're going into the army *voluntarily?*" in a loud voice, and Jeff was smiling back at him, frank and confident.

"Sure," Jeff said. "It's not for two more years, remember. A lot can happen over there in two years. Anyway, I want to."

"Man, I can't believe this shit," Kevin said.

Baby looked back and forth between them, her eyes that intense light blue. She was no longer smiling.

Jeff checked his watch. It was a serious watch with lots of extra dials on it. "Well, since I drove all the way over here to go to this thing," he said, "let's do it." He stood up. "Harriet?" he said. He held out his arm like an old-fashioned boy in a play.

"Oh, fuck," Kevin said. He put a cigarette in his mouth and offered one to Baby.

Ignoring him, she stood up and came around the table. "Take me, too," she said.

"Gladly." Jeff held out his other arm to Baby, who threw back her hair and took it, and like that he walked them both out into the brilliant blue afternoon and all the way across campus through the skittering leaves to Kenan Hall, all of them talking and talking, though Harriet could never remember, later, anything they said. They got the last seats in the house, with Harriet in the middle. Jim Francisco was everything the *Redbud* committee had expected, big and haggard, wearing a black cowboy hat which was even more than they had hoped for. He read about deserts and dogs and bleached white bones and once he stopped in the middle of a poem to look up from the page straight out at the audience and say, "Damn! Ain't that good?" He was greeted by thunderous applause. He was full of shit but there was something more than that, something huge and real which didn't have any place here on this tidy campus among these students and academics who could only study him, Harriet realized. They could never *be* him.

"He's an asshole," Anna glided up afterward to whisper, as they stood caught in the crowd leaving the auditorium. "He's already trying to get me to spend the night with him, can you believe it?"

"Oh no," Harriet whispered back. But she could believe it.

"He's staying at the Hitching Post Motel, which is funny anyway, considering he's from Montana, but he keeps calling it the Whipping Post. He keeps saying stuff like, 'Hey, baby, I've got something big to show you later at the Whipping Post.'"

"Maybe he's kidding. What did you tell him?"

"Well, nothing. I mean, not yet. I don't want to piss him off before Miss Auerbach's party. I'll think of something," Anna said. "There's plenty of time."

"Anna, I want you to meet my friend Jefferson Carr," Harriet said over a sudden crush of people. "Jeff, this is one of my other suitemates, Anna." Her heart felt like it would burst as Anna and Jeff shook hands.

"Wow, where'd you find *him?*" Anna whispered before she disappeared into the throng.

Harriet felt the steady pressure of Jeff's hand on the small of her back as they finally began to move slowly onto the portico.

Baby arched her back, stretching. She

leaned back against one of the massive columns. "I need a drink," she said.

"There's your boyfriend." Jeff pointed down the hill at one of the big oaks where Kevin lay in the grass, reading ostentatiously, John Donne sleeping by his side. Kevin did not look up from his book as they all came out.

"He's not my boyfriend," Baby said.

"No?" Jeff asked.

Baby shook her head vehemently. "God no," she said. "Listen, I'll see you all at the party later, okay?" She walked down the steps and across the grass to Kevin. They stood on the steps and watched her go. Harriet had forgotten she was barefoot. Baby leaned down and spoke to Kevin, or maybe she kissed him; her hair fell across his face.

Jeff cleared his throat. "I need to find the guys I came with," he said, "and then we'll buy you some dinner."

"It comes with the price of your registration." Immediately Harriet could have killed herself, missing the chance to go to a restaurant with a bunch of guys. "It's kind of a box supper, out by the duck pond."

"Sounds good." Military school had turned Jeff into the kind of boy who said "sounds good" and "roger" a lot. It developed that the other cadets, Tom and Price, had struck up an acquaintance with two seniors, serious longhaired girls Harriet liked but didn't really know, so the six of them sat together on the bank of the duck pond and ate their boxed suppers from the dining room, fried chicken and potato salad and brownies, while the night fell fast around them and a chill came over the water. It was, after all, October. Price, the big cadet with the black-rimmed glasses, was very funny talking about how weird it was to try to edit a literary magazine at a military school. "All the poems have perfect cadence," he said. "Everything rhymes. But the magazine gets very few submissions."

"Why not?" asked Harriet.

"Oh, we're too busy polishing our boots all the time." Jeff winked to show her that he wasn't entirely serious. "We have to march a lot. Not much time for poetry. Hey, you going to eat that?" He indicated the chicken breast which Harriet had scarcely nibbled, and when she shook her head, he said, "You mind?" and she shook her head again and he picked it up and ate the rest of it.

It was almost dark, almost time for C. E. Reed's reading when Harriet flew up and up to hover above the duck pond. This is me, she thought. This is me having a picnic with Jefferson Carr, looking down at the scattered groups around the shore, the water rippling in the chill breeze, the sudden flurry of blowing leaves, the lights coming on like magic among the trees along the path and all across the campus. This is me, she thought before she took Jeff's outstretched hand and was pulled to her feet and set back down in the world, cheeks wet with tears she hoped nobody could see in the dusk.

"Harriet? Ready?"

"I just need to run up to the dorm for a sweater," she said, because it was suddenly too much, she felt *too much,* she couldn't stand it anymore. "I'll meet you at the reading, okay? It's in the same place, just save me a seat." The pounding of her feet filled her whole body as she ran up the hill to Old South. Their room looked like a hurricane had hit it: light on, door wide open. Baby was not there. Harriet grabbed a sweater and raked a comb through her hair.

"Harriet, honey, what's wrong?" Courtney stood poised in the doorway, waiting for Hawk, her new boyfriend, to pick her up.

Instead of answering, Harriet hugged her, fast and hard, and ran out the door. Wasn't this how she was *supposed* to feel, finally? A girl with a boy she liked, waiting for her? She ran down all three flights of stairs and made it over to the auditorium just as C. E. Reed began to read from his famous book in a deep lugubrious voice. "He sounds like that guy, you know, on *The Munsters,*" she whispered to Jeff, slipping into the seat he had saved for her.

"Herman," Jeff said. "You're right. He does." Jeff started laughing and then Harriet was laughing too, uncontrollably, even though she knew she couldn't make a sound. Every time they looked at each other for the next ten or fifteen minutes, they started up again.

Finally the essay came to its depressing end (man falling forward into the snow, crows reeling overhead) and Harriet led them all over to the party at Miss Auerbach's house up on faculty row.

"Why . . . Harriet!" Miss Auerbach seemed very surprised to see her show up with so many boys. "Er . . . come in!" It was funny to see the big cadets push through Miss Auerbach's bead curtain into the world of art. Miss Auerbach ran her house as a sort of literary salon which she presided over unguently, pendulous breasts and lots of beads swinging with her purple caftan. English majors were everywhere: on the Turkish rugs, on the batik cushions, on the floor around Big Jim Francisco who was playing his guitar in a corner. "As long as we keep him playing the guitar, he keeps his hands to himself," Anna told them, coming up with two beers.

Now Anna was wearing a long crinkly yellow dress, with her frizzy red hair pulled straight back in a way that gave her a slightly surprised expression. "You all go on in the kitchen and get a drink," she said, heading back to the corner. Harriet introduced Jeff to Mr. Gaines, who embarrassed her by launching into a testimonial about what a good baby-sitter she was, as if he were giving her some kind of recommendation for marriage. Harriet's face grew warm at the very idea, while Mr. Gaines went on and on.

Finally, she was able to pull Jeff into the crowded kitchen where he fell deep into conversation with Mr. Duff, the old Yeats scholar with the goofy smile and the wild white hair. Everybody adored him, the way he leaned toward you cupping his ear with his hand and seemed to really care what you said in class, no matter how dumb it was. Mr. Arlington, the new drama professor, dressed all in black, glowered against the green refrigerator. His wife had left him, rumor had it, a week after they moved to Mary Scott. He gestured wildly with his hands, talking to Catherine Wilson. So much intensity would have terrified Harriet, but Catherine didn't seem to mind, nodding and sipping her beer, smoking a cigarette, throwing her head back to laugh. A skinny, agitated young man Harriet had never seen before stood in front of the stove, talking to Kevin and some of the other guys from UVA. "So I write this novel about this alienated guy in Memphis who can't deal with real life, so he goes to the movies all the time, right? It take me three years, right?" They nod solemnly, nursing their beers. "Then what happens? Walker Percy publishes *The Moviegoer* and it gets all this attention. So what happens to me? I had this publisher who was really interested and now he says, 'Sorry, man.' I mean you really can't blame him, it's pretty similar, I admit it. But then my *agent* surprises me by saying, 'Sorry, man,' too. So here I am, kicked out in the cold on my ass. Now, what are the odds on *that?*" Kevin shook his head. Harriet managed to slip past them to the sink which was filled with ice and beer. She grabbed two and handed one to Jeff who took it and pressed her arm in thanks without ever looking away from Mr. Duff. But he held on to her arm, so Harriet stayed by his side.

"Hey, try some of this." Suddenly Baby was there, too, pouring straight bourbon into a lot of little paper cups she'd lined up on the kitchen counter. She smiled at Jeff. "Haven't I seen you someplace before, soldier boy?" Jeff smiled back. He picked up his paper cup and tossed it down in one gulp, so Harriet did the same.

"We didn't go to the reading," Baby said. "How was it?"

"You didn't miss anything," Jeff said.

"That's right," Harriet said, but nobody heard her because somebody put on an album just then, the Beatles singing "Can't Buy Me Love." Jim Francisco must have finally gotten tired of playing his guitar, Harriet thought.

Baby started moving in time to the beat. She loved to dance. "We had a fight," she said over the music.

"I'm sorry," Harriet said.

"Don't bother." Baby closed her eyes, dancing, still barefoot. Soon she was joined by Catherine Wilson and Bowen Montague who had all done a Supremes act to "My Girl" for Spring Follies last year. They'd called themselves the Virginia Wolves. Harriet and Jeff and the guys from UVA moved back to make room. Harriet filled up all the paper cups again. "What the hell, fiction is dead anyway," Kevin told the guy who wrote the novel about the moviegoer. The music switched to James Brown's *Live at the Apollo* album: "Please please please please." Some of the guys from UVA and the biggest cadet, Price, joined the girls in the middle of the floor. People jammed the doorway, trying to see. Harriet's back was pushed against the counter. Baby danced with her eyes closed, a streak of dirt down the back of her shirt. Catherine Wilson did the pony while everyone cheered. The bourbon was good, Harriet found, fiery but sort of calming, too, you could feel it go all the way down. The girls were dancing doubletime.

And then, though Jeff kept his hand on her arm and Harriet was still pressed right up against him, so close she could feel his hip joint, his actual *bones,* she knew he had left her. He was there, but somehow he wasn't. She realized that she was rubbing an inch of his oxford cloth shirt back and forth between her fingers and that she had been doing this for quite some time, the way her mother used to finger clothes surreptitiously in a store, say, a dress she was planning to copy, or the way Jill played with the satin edge of that baby blanket she dragged everyplace for years and years. The oxford cloth felt strong and grainy, a little bit damp with his sweat. Harriet rubbed it back and forth between her fingers and her thumb. She did this until the music stopped and Jeff Carr gently loosened her hand and gave it sort of a pat. "Hey, it's been *great* to catch up with you, Harriet," he said into her ear, over the noise of everybody suddenly talking. "We'll see each other again soon, okay? Real soon." And then he was gone, out the kitchen door, with Baby. They left the door wide open when they went.

Kevin's face was suddenly inches away from Harriet's. "Well, fuck it," he said. "Let's get drunk." He waved a wine bottle at her.

Harriet smiled, or tried to smile. "Okay," she said, and they did, but it wasn't much good really and then Miss Auerbach was kicking everybody out. Harriet left Kevin passed out in a hammock on Miss Auerbach's porch and walked back across the campus by herself, breathing the crisp air. There was smoke in it from some place far away. She fell across her bed fully dressed and did not even awaken for the famous scene which took place a little later, when Anna, trying to escape from Jim Francisco, told him that she'd go to the Whipping Post with him if he'd just let her run back to the dorm first to pick up her nightie and her diaphragm. But she never reappeared, leaving him stranded in her car in the Old South parking lot. Soon Big Jim was in a rage, bellowing "Anna! Anna!" exactly like Stanley Kowalski in *A Streetcar Named Desire*, as several people pointed out later. Security finally came to haul him away. Big Jim did not show up for the coffee and Danish good-bye party the next morning, nor did Anna, nor did Harriet who was hung over all day long and even into Monday, when her first class was Irish Literature with Mr. Duff, whose wild white hair looked even wilder than usual, electrified, a dandelion going to seed. They had been assigned a group of poems by William Butler Yeats; Harriet had read "The Song of Wandering Aengus" over and over.

"You know, Harriet," Mr. Duff stopped her in his formal way as she went back to find a seat in his classroom, "it was nice to see you at the reading this weekend, and I so much enjoyed meeting your friend the cadet — Jeff, isn't it? — at the gathering on Saturday night. He is a lovely young man."

She turned to look at him, at his blotchy skin, his pale blue vulnerable eyes. "Yes," she said simply. "He is a lovely man."

Baby was campused for a week, turned in by Louise Burr, that fat bitch, who would clearly never have a date in her whole life and hated everybody who did. At first Baby was furious, claiming this was ridiculous, that she would *die* if she couldn't see Jeff Carr for a whole week, but she calmed down after talking to him for an hour on the phone Monday night. "I can't ever see him during the week anyway," she told Harriet, in a surprisingly cheerful mood. "You wouldn't believe what all they make them do over there, it's just amazing. So I might as well write my goddamn Shakespeare paper and get it over with." Baby gathered up her books and headed for the library, a first. "Oh, Harriet" — she paused on the stairs, looking back at Harriet framed in the doorway — "let's drive up there next weekend for the Grand Parade, okay? I can't wait to see him do his thing, you know. He invited us to come."

"I thought you were going down to Duke."

Baby made a face. "Oh hell no," she said, as if it were the farthest thing from her mind. "Will you come with me? *Road trip.*" She grinned.

"Sure," Harriet said.

From the very beginning, Harriet was part of it — it was like being in love herself, but not as scary. Jeff and Baby suddenly became the most beautiful couple on campus, the most visible. Everybody noticed them — you had to notice them whenever they walked into a room. It was like they had a light around them. You couldn't quit watching them. They insisted on taking Harriet everywhere: to the campus movies, to the snack bar, over to Lexington for parties, fixing her up with Jeff's friends, none of whom ever fell in love with her, though it didn't seem to matter — *they* loved her, Baby and Jeff, and it was enough. Somehow Harriet was necessary. She completed them. And everybody said it was the most beautiful autumn in many years, day after day of clear blue weather with Morrow Mountain a blaze of color in the distance. Harriet felt it was happening just for them.

"Doesn't it seem like the stars are *bigger* than they used to be?" Baby asked one night when the three of them were lying on a quilt beside the duck pond looking up.

"You're right. At least they're brighter than they used to be," Jeff said.

In a way, this seemed true of everything.

As days turned into weeks and then a month, then two, it became clear that Baby was undergoing a transformation. She stopped biting her bottom lip and drawing in her breath with that little gasp when she talked to you. She quit chewing her hair and her nails. She started turning in her assignments when they were due, or mostly, since the time she could spend with Jeff was so limited that she actually started studying. She quit drinking so much. She gained some weight. "I never thought I'd even *like* anybody who was a good influence on me!" she told Harriet, giggling. Every night she slept in his SMI T-shirt with his name stamped across the back. She spent hours writing to him, even though they talked on the phone every day. She did not return calls from other boys, and after a while, they quit calling. Baby's parents flew in for a day on their way home from a trip to New York, "to meet Margaret's little soldier boy," as her glitzy stepmother Elise put it, but even their approval didn't seem to bother Baby. The only people who didn't like Jeff were those few, such as Miss Auerbach, who didn't take to his politics. ("Hey, I don't *have* any politics," Jeff said. "Miss Auerbach is the one with the politics.")

Though Harriet considered herself "not political" either, it was undeniably stirring to see the cadets come marching across the field in their weekly Grand Parade, eight hundred strong, all those white hats and white shoes and belts, the flags flying, the band playing John Philip Sousa, the sun glinting off the guns, the inexorable drumbeat underneath it all. Harriet cried every time they played the national anthem and raised the flag, she couldn't help it. It was thrilling. The whole thing was thrilling.

Only one warning bell ever rang, in February after Harriet and Jeff had visited Baby in Alabama over Christmas vacation for her first cousin's much-heralded debut. This cousin, Nina Wade Ballou, was two years younger than Baby, who had already made her own debut, apparently, though she had never once mentioned it. Sometimes Harriet felt that there were two

Babys — one, the moody wild girl who stalked around Mary Scott; and two, the other girl Harriet saw fully for the first time on this trip, the lady-in-waiting who was also a lot like all the double-name cousins she introduced Harriet to: Nina Wade, Martha Fletcher, Emma Dell — it was impossible to keep them straight. They looked alike, too, all blonds.

Harriet had been really nervous about the whole thing, but her green satin dress, made by Alice, was perfect. Both Elise and Baby's aunt Honey exclaimed over it when Harriet emerged like Cinderella for the ball. Then Aunt Honey pinned her hair up, while Elise clipped some dangly diamond earrings to her ears.

"Are those real? What if I lose them?" Harriet couldn't quit looking at herself in the pier glass mirror in the downstairs hall — maybe it was the curve of the mirror, or the smoky old glass, but she really did look, well, *beautiful*.

"Oh Lord, I can't remember if they're real or not," Elise was laughing. "But if they are, I'm sure Troy has got them insured. Anyway," she went on, "you *won't* lose them. My, aren't you just a picture? Isn't she a picture, Honey?"

And Honey, a fat replica of Elise, sitting

squarely in the middle of a pink love seat with her legs stuck straight out in front of her like sausages, said, "Yes indeed, yes indeed," sipping her sherry judiciously.

"But look here!" cried Elise, and all three of them turned to the winding staircase to watch Jeff come slowly down with Baby on his arm, one step at a time, her red beaded skirt trailing out behind her. Jeff wore his gray dress uniform, its brass buttons shining. "Oh my! Oh my!" Aunt Honey dug her fists into her eyes as if she might cry and then she *did* cry, loud boo-hoos that Baby and Elise ignored.

"What is the matter with your aunt?" Harriet couldn't wait to ask as soon as they got into Elise's little sports car, Baby driving.

"Well, she's crazy, of course!" Baby said. "They're all nuts, I'm telling you. I mean, she had this fiancé or something, I forget. Who knows? She just cries at the drop of a hat." Baby was struggling with her big skirt. *"Shit!"* She finally pulled it up to her waist and slung it back over the seat, pumping the accelerator. You could see her panties. "Sorry," she said to Jeff beside her and Harriet in the tiny seat behind, both half covered in the glittery drift of satin.

"Hey, I don't mind," Jeff said, squeezing

her bare knobby knee. This was the Baby that Harriet knew, the one who went bare-legged no matter what.

"Light me a cigarette, will you? If you think you can do it without burning us all up," she flung back to Harriet, who did, immediately woozy on that first great rush of nicotine.

It seemed to Harriet that Baby drove for miles out into the vast empty countryside. Alabama was enormous anyway. Even Baby's father's farm was enormous, its stubbly fields rolling out forever to those sketchy feathery bare trees on the far horizon. You couldn't even see to the end of his land. Baby went through a crossroads and over a black river and headed down a long lane lined with flaming torches for the last half mile. Massive and white-columned, the house rose up from the dusk like a vision before them, its upper gallery festooned with green magnolia branches. Harriet decided not to tell anybody that she'd never been to a debutante ball before. Uniformed boys were waiting to take the car. Heading up the great steps, clinging to Jeff's arm with Baby on his other side, Harriet felt as if she were about to burst out of her skin. This is me, she thought. I will never be so beautiful again.

Nodding, smiling, drinking the fizzy champagne, Harriet tried her best to notice the red poinsettias, the pearl and stephanotis arrangements, the chandeliers and candelabras and mirrors everywhere, tried to remember all these details to tell Alice, but then the music started and a boy came up and she was swept away, around and around the hall trying to keep up with him. Out of the corner of her eye, she could see Baby dancing with Jeff and then she couldn't see them anymore and then when she saw Baby again, she was dancing with her father whose thick, handsome face was full of pain and pride at the same time. ("Oh, sure, he loves me," Baby had assured Harriet not long before. "He loves me too much. This is why he can't stand to have me around.")

Baby and her father were the best-looking couple on the floor.

The next day the girls slept until afternoon, getting up just in time to greet Baby's family which was arriving from everywhere, dozens of them, to congratulate Nina Wade and meet Margaret's soldier boy and eat the little fish deep-fried in a big drum of hot oil and a whole pig cooked on a huge iron spit over an open fire. Black men did all the cooking, out in the yard.

You ate the whole fish, bones and all. You crunched them between your teeth.

Baby's brothers loved Jeff, following him everywhere. They all shot mistletoe out in the woods and then rode motorcycles down to the river, full speed ahead across the frosty fields, Baby hanging on behind Jeff. Harriet sat on the front porch and watched the three motorcycles disappear into the big red sky of sunset while she answered Baby's relatives' questions as best she could. Now, where was *she* from? And where was that boy from? And who were his people? And what did they do? These old women were much too curious, Harriet thought. In fact, it wore her out, how much everybody in Alabama liked to talk. They went on and on about nothing, really, but nobody — *nobody!* — ever said one word about Baby's mother, who was not pictured among all the portraits lining the long gallery, most of them old, serious, stern-faced Ballous, but some of them more recent: teenaged Baby on Satan, her much-mourned horse, winning a ribbon, winning a trophy; Mr. Ballou and Elise someplace tropical, pictured in evening dress; the twin boys, little, playing in the sand on a wide, sunny beach — and that must be Baby's other brother, that tall dark thin boy standing with her in front of a church. They look just alike. Maybe it's Easter. Baby, about eight, wears a striped dress with a wide white collar and a straw hat with cherries on it. The boy wears a light-colored suit that has gotten too short for him — suddenly, Harriet imagines — maybe he's in a growing spurt. Though other people are also in the picture behind them, walking up the steps into the church, Baby and her brother stand stock still facing forward, hands barely touching, staring into the camera. Baby smiles happily. But it's as if her brother can see into the future somehow; his hollow boy's face looks haunted and sad.

"There you are! Want to play bridge?" It was Aunt Honey, huffing and puffing, hand to her heart.

Harriet turned away from the wall of photographs with a shiver, glad to join Aunt Honey and some of the two-name cousins, glad that Alice had taught her how to play bridge.

Harriet was amazed by the extent of Elise's Christmas decorations. "Oh, she does it for *months!*" Baby said scornfully, but yet, Harriet thought, the house *was* beautiful, a work of art, each mantel draped in greenery, each door with its wreath, each tabletop with its bit of holly. Harriet's favorite was the wooden manger with all the little wooden animals and people and angels on the table in the hall. It had been carved, Harriet was told, by a black man who worked for Baby's daddy. Harriet could never pass it without picking up the little Jesus and marveling at him, carved from a walnut, big as a fingernail.

Especially Harriet was amazed by Elise's Christmas china, a full set for sixteen, each piece with a seasonal picture in the middle surrounded by a border of evergreen.

"Isn't this *tacky?*" Baby whispered, drying a platter with a Santa on it. It was the cook's night off, and Harriet had volunteered them for the dishes.

"Well, actually, no, I think it's kind of cute. I like it." Harriet was glad she'd said this because Elise swooped into the kitchen suddenly, enveloping them in the heady cloud of her perfume.

"You'll have one, too," Elise said. "Everybody does."

"Have one what?" Harriet asked.

Baby kept drying pans. She was mad because her father had taken Jeff off with him to Rotary.

"Christmas china, of course. Everybody needs three sets — your good china, your

everyday china, and your holiday china."
Elise ticked them off on her perfectly manicured hands. "You'll have yours before
you know it, girls."

"I will *never, ever,* have any Christmas
china." Baby gritted her teeth.

"Oh, Baby, you do say the silliest things!
Of course you will, if you want any!" Elise
left the kitchen in a trail of laughter. "You
girls are just angels," she called back. "I
don't know what we'll do without you,
Harriet, I swear I don't. You be sure and
come back as quick as you can."

"No hanky-panky!" Baby had told Jeff,
wagging her finger, showing him to his
room on the day they got there. "And Harriet stays with me." Yet whenever Harriet
awoke, Baby was never beside her in the
heavy canopied bed, and on the last night,
she stayed awake until early gray light
came in the window through the wavy old
glass and Baby came to sleep beside her
like a child. Harriet lay propped up on one
elbow watching Baby's shallow breath slip
in and out, in and out, until the alarm finally went off and it was time to get up
and pack and leave.

Back at school, winter dragged on forever, gray and messy. Harriet was doing re-

search for a play about Mary Shelley which she planned to write as her big project in Mr. Arlington's modern drama seminar. She had a secret crush on Mr. Arlington, but she'd die if anybody, even Baby, found this out. It was a pretty safe crush, actually, since the only student Mr. Arlington really seemed to like was Catherine, who had a steady boyfriend at W&L. It was close to curfew one Sunday night when Harriet came back from the library and entered their dark room to the ringing of the telephone. She threw down her book bag and picked up the receiver. "Hello?"

"Is she there?"

"What?"

"Baby. Is she there?"

"Well — I — don't know. I just came in, actually."

"Okay. I'll wait. Look around." Brusque, nearly rude, Jeff didn't sound like himself.

"Listen, I — what's the matter?"

"I just need to know if she's there."

"I thought she was with you. In Lexington."

"Harriet. *Please.*"

"Okay. Hang on." Harriet put the receiver down and switched on the lights. Baby might not be here right now, but clearly she had come back from Lexington.

There was her black dress, thrown across her unmade bed, there was her overnight case on the floor. The bathroom door was closed.

"Baby," Harriet said outside it. "Baby, are you in there?"

It was not a sound, but almost a sound.

Something made Harriet pause, then turn on her heel and go back to the telephone before she opened the door. "Jeff, she's here someplace, but I don't know where, exactly. I mean, her bag is here. Maybe she went down to the snack bar."

"Well, tell her to call me whenever you see her." Jeff sounded relieved. "And Harriet . . ."

"Yes?"

"Thank you." He hung up.

Harriet went back to the bathroom door. "Baby," she said loudly and — she hoped — calmly, "I'm coming in there. I'm going to open this door."

But it wasn't locked. Baby was sitting in the tub with her legs drawn up, arms crossed on her knees, face down on her arms. She didn't look up when Harriet opened the door.

"Baby!" Harriet drew her breath in sharply. The water in the tub was red. Baby's dark hair hung down into it. Finally she looked up, her face dead white in the stark fluorescent light. She had black shadows like smudges under her eyes and no expression, none whatsoever, in them.

"Let me see your arms," Harriet said.

Baby stared at her.

"Arms. Hold out your arms!"

Still staring at her, Baby held out her arms one at a time. Harriet had never noticed how thin they were, actually the word was *scrawny*. A short diagonal red slash crossed Baby's left forearm, halfway between elbow and wrist. It was still bleeding.

"Is that the only one?"

Baby nodded.

"You didn't really mean it then, right? Or you would have gone for the vein." Harriet swung from fear to fury in an instant, shocking herself. What was the matter with her? "I just can't believe you would do this to us."

Baby sank back against the tub, knees drawn up again, watching her. "Don't be mad," she said like a little girl.

"Don't be mad!" Harriet repeated. "Mad! Are you crazy? Come on. Get out of there, right now."

"No." Baby shook her head so hard that a long wet strand of her hair stuck against her cheek.

"Yes," Harriet said firmly. "We're going to the infirmary."

"No." Baby struggled to sit up, looking a little bit more like herself. "No, please, it's not even deep, you can see for yourself. I didn't really mean it. Haven't we got some Band-Aids someplace? I feel a whole lot better now." She stood up, holding on to the edge of the tub. Her hipbones stuck out, you could see her ribs. Her breasts looked like something stuck onto her skinny chest, their nipples all shriveled up. Harriet held out her hand for balance as Baby stepped out of the tub. The minute Baby touched her, Harriet's anger disappeared, leaving a profound anxiety in its place.

"Are you sure we shouldn't go to the infirmary? Maybe they could give you a pill, like a tranquilizer or something." In the back of her mind, Harriet thought that it might actually be breaking the rules not to take Baby to the infirmary. She put a big towel around Baby's shoulders as she stepped from the tub.

"No, I'm fine now, really I am." Baby managed a fake smile, pressing a wad of toilet paper against the cut. "See? It's quit anyway." She moved the paper and together they watched the drops of blood come up like little red beads on a string.

"Well, *almost* quit," she said.

"I think you need stitches."

"No, please, Harriet, then I'll just get in a lot of trouble like before, please don't, please don't make me go, and please don't tell. Just get a Band-Aid, I know we've got some around here someplace."

Harriet knew where they were. "If you promise," she said, "really promise, that you will never, ever, do anything like this again. I *mean* it, Baby."

"Cross my heart," Baby said solemnly.

"Okay then." Harriet rummaged in her desk drawer and found the Band-Aids and put two across the cut. "There now," she said. "Get dressed. Here, put this shirt on. But call Jeff before you go to bed."

"Okay." Baby pulled the SMI T-shirt over her head. "But you have to promise me that you won't tell on me, okay, Harriet? You won't tell Jeff or anybody."

"Why should I promise that?" Harriet was exhausted, and disgusted with her.

"Because I'll never do it again, Scouts honor."

"You weren't a scout."

"Neither were you. Listen" — Baby looked at her — "it's just something that I used to do, okay? I really wasn't trying to kill myself."

"Well, then, what the hell *were* you trying to do?"

"Feel better," Baby said.

"Wait a minute. It makes you feel *better* to cut yourself?"

Baby nodded. "It . . . it . . . takes the pressure off, some way."

"What pressure?" Harriet didn't get it.

"The . . . I don't know how to tell you," Baby said. "It's just, I just can't stand it sometimes, that's all." She was shaking inside the big shirt.

"Can't stand *what?*"

"Oh, Harriet, I'm so bad for Jeff, can't you see that? I'm so bad for him, I should just leave him alone, but I can't, you know. I just can't, I never could. But I'll ruin him, I know I will, I'm just so bad."

"You are *not bad,*" Harriet said. "But what happened? Something must have happened."

"Oh, well, we — first I got caught up in his room when it wasn't visitors' hours, and then also he was late for drill, whatever that is, and then his grades are dropping, too, and then I guess the final straw was, he let me hold his gun."

"His gun?" Harriet repeated stupidly.

"Well, I wanted to see it, I really did, you know I grew up knowing how to shoot, so

296

he took it along when we went up to Goshen yesterday, no, *today* I guess, this morning, it seems like so long ago. And he was showing me how to shoot it out in the woods up there. Nobody at all was around. It *kicked*" — a little light came into her eye — "and it was really, really fun. But then we got caught."

"Who caught you, way up there?"

"Oh, some dumb guy from SMI. Some stupid little history professor up there on a picnic with his stupid little wife and his stupid little kids."

"So what happened?"

"Oh, I don't know, they're going to hold an inquiry, it's something like a court martial only not such a big deal. But anyway, Jeff got stripped of his title or his rank or whatever it is. He's not the prefect anymore."

"What does *he* say about that? Jeff, I mean?"

Baby managed a little smile. "He said he doesn't want to be the prefect anyway. He said he doesn't care. He doesn't care about anything but me. That's what he said. And now he'll have more time to spend with me. But I'll ruin him, Harriet, you know I will. He shouldn't be having anything to do with a girl like me."

"That is ridiculous," Harriet said firmly

just as the phone began to ring. "He called a minute ago, and that's probably him calling back."

Baby squeezed Harriet's upper arm so hard it hurt. "You didn't promise yet. Promise you won't tell Jeff."

Harriet hugged her. "Scouts honor," she said. Baby smiled. Baby's shoulder bones felt like little bony wings beneath Jeff's T-shirt.

"Okay." Baby picked up the phone. "Hello," she said, and then she listened for a minute, and then she started crying. "You know I love you," she said.

Harriet went into the bathroom to clean the tub, shutting the door behind her.

All during second semester the romance continued, intense as ever, but the best part had passed. Baby flirted with other guys and made him jealous. She didn't mean to, she said. She couldn't help it. She said she had never loved anybody like this before. She loved him so much she was scaring herself to death, she said. "Then why don't you just leave him alone?" asked Harriet, who didn't understand any of it. Harriet loved Baby but felt sorriest for Jeff, who had lost about ten pounds through pure suffering.

"I can't," Baby had said simply. "Oh, honey, I will never, ever, do that." They'd fight, make up, fight again, make up again. The struggle seemed huge and almost mythic to Harriet, like the stories of the gods and goddesses in Greek mythology. Often, Harriet was the one who made it work. She took and delivered the messages, sometimes rephrasing things. After all this time, she felt she knew what Jeff Carr really intended to say and what he didn't. Baby was harder to interpret, even more prone to say things she didn't mean. Harriet had to edit her carefully. It was a hard job. Harriet felt exhausted and exalted all at once.

Sometimes she couldn't decide what *she* wanted either. Clearly, Jeff would be better off without Baby. He could get back on the straight-ahead career path he'd been following before he met her. But Baby would probably die without him. And if they broke up, would Harriet ever see Jefferson Carr again? She couldn't stand that; she'd die, too. Now, Harriet got to talk to him constantly and see him every few days. Since he was no longer a class prefect, he drove over to Mary Scott even more often.

Spring came in too fast, too hot; summer

rushed straight at them, gathering speed. Baby was flunking math and chemistry, but the poems kept pouring out. It was like automatic writing, like taking dictation, Harriet often thought, watching Baby jot them down as she stared into space, listening. What did she hear? Not the poem, she'd told Harriet once, but the *voice* of the poem. This didn't make any sense to Harriet. And it wasn't fair either, she thought, struggling with her own stories. Visiting writer Lucian Delgado was lukewarm to these stories in workshop, but Harriet loved his class anyway, held on Wednesday nights at the Abbot Guest House where they'd put him, up on faculty row. Lucian Delgado gave them beer and wine and let them smoke. He smoked a pipe himself, wearing a deep-blue velvet jacket and bedroom shoes, his hooded eyes surprisingly intent while they read their work aloud.

Just before exams started, Harriet and Baby cut their Tuesday afternoon classes and went swimming with Jeff in the quarry halfway up Morrow Mountain behind the college, officially off limits to Mary Scott students. They had to pull apart the strands of barbwire fence and hold them up carefully in order to duck inside. The lake was like a bowl of black water surrounded by rocks, then tangled green woods with kudzu-covered trees, then high blue sky arching above it all. They were the only people there. Dozing on her stomach in the sun, Harriet lifted her head just in time to see Baby stand up on the big rock by the deepest part, shuck off her red bathing suit in one swift movement and take a running dive into the dark water over Jeff's loud "No!" He waded furiously into the lake, hands on hips, waiting for her to surface, then grabbed her as she swam in, pulling her up, shaking her shoulders until her head snapped back and she struggled in earnest to free herself. He slapped her once, across the face; she cried out; and then he was kissing her.

Heart thudding, hot all over, Harriet put her face back down on the towel. They were crazy. She could not stand to see this, yet she could not stand *not* to see it either. She hated them both. She hated herself. When she looked up again, they were gone. They had disappeared into the woods. Harriet lay flat on her stomach in the sun and felt her blood running through every vein in her body; she could feel her whole body pulsing in the heat. She touched herself until she was gasping in delight or dismay, she couldn't even tell which. Harriet was glad when the raft trip came up in Mr. Gaines's class, to distract them all a little bit, to siphon off some of that awful energy that kept Baby up until all hours even when she wasn't out with Jeff, kept her shooting off poems like firecrackers. Harriet was even glad when Jeff had to leave in mid-May for summer "maneuvers," a word Baby always said with a sneer, as if it had quotation marks around it.

"We'll kill each other before we're done," Baby had said once, but Harriet thought they'd kill *her* first. They kept her all wrought up. What had seemed so much like love now seemed almost like hatred sometimes, at least to Harriet, who hated being with them as much as she loved it, as much as she loved them. But the sweet part was already gone.

The fog has finally lifted; sun sparkles on the water. Harriet hears people in the corridor outside her door. She gets up. On the dock, men are unloading boxes off trucks and onto the *Belle*. Passengers are walking across the gangplank. There's Russell already doing his leg stretches against a concrete post. Vicksburg rises steeply behind the dock. All Harriet can remember about it from the raft trip is a lot of statues, Confederate cavalry, somewhere up there on the hill. It was late, dark. They'd been drinking, walking down a street full of statues shining white in the light of the moon. "But what about the *citizens?* Where are the citizens?" Baby kept asking, which cracked them all up. They seemed to have the whole town to themselves.

Now Harriet is ready to look at the poems again. She unzips the pocket of her big suitcase and removes the battered folder, then spreads them all out on the bed as best she can, though some are so crumpled that this is impossible. Baby wrote most of them in pencil on pages torn out of the little spiral notebook she kept in the back pocket of her cutoff jeans. She left them all in the drawer of her bedside table in the room she shared with Harriet at the Royal Sonesta Hotel when they reached New Orleans, along with some loose change (Baby never kept change), an empty pack of Winston cigarettes, a man's comb, two strings of Mardi Gras beads, and the address of a boy in Indianola, Mississippi. Harriet found them there after she'd left.

OLD LIARS ON THE AIR

The crackly burst
of men's voices
on the shortwave radio:

Where they at?
You seen em yet?

Yeah, I seen em
Back around Friars Point
They're all riding topless
It's a sight for sore eyes
I'm telling you.

MAMA I

Mama wore red short shorts
and high-heeled sandals
       she was too much
       for this town

PLEA

When Jeff first put me up here
I liked it
Oh I liked it a lot
On a clear day

I could see forever
in the words of the song
Sweet breezes
blew sun on my face
Nothing I had to do
Except my nails
So I got a great tan
Watched TV
Read novels
Ate petits fours
pepperoni pizza
anything I wanted
Drank champagne
But, though idyllic,
this surface is very hard
And the ladder has proved
Retractable
So if you could possibly
Assist me off this pedestal please
It's hurting my ass

MAMA II

drank gin like water
all day long
in the pink glass goblet
with the twisted stem
Daddy bought her in Venice
on their honeymoon

BIG BROTHER

either out
or in his room,
door closed
wouldn't talk to anybody
he called Elise *that whore*
drinking hard liquor
at eleven or twelve
with the boys in Dinkins Bottom
I said, Dinkins Bottom! Isnt that funny?
Isnt that funny, Ricky?
I lived to make him laugh
I lived for a word, a glance
from that face the most like mine
in all the world

DAY ROOM

They all think
They're Jesus
Why?
Maybe the first Jesus
Wasn't Jesus either
Maybe he was only
        Schizophrenic

BRONCHITIS

Cool pressed sheets
curtains drawn
Shutters down
Spirit lamp hissing
in the corner
Mama's special medicine
on my nightstand
Jack Daniels, sugar, and lemon juice
mixed in a china cup
with a silver spoon
Take as much as you want
you know what you need
Mama said

COMING OUT

Baby Ballou
how do you do
at your debut

Ricky Ballou
how do you do
pushing up pansies
two by two

VANITY

Mama's dressing table
with the rose silk skirt
held her sterling silver
comb and brush,
a million bottles, tubes, and vials,
little balls of cotton in a Chinese jar.
Cigarettes spill from the crumpled pack.
Ashes on the carpet,
ashes on the gold-and-velvet chair.
One high-heeled satin mule —
a pool of pink chiffon.
The oval mirror framed by lights
            is glamorous
            or clinical
depending upon her mood.
(but always theatrical)
Larger than life as they say

I stood at her elbow
as she made up her face
I mean *made it up*
created it from scratch
and claw and slash and burn.
She covered it over
smoothed it out
rouged those cheekbones
painted on the pouting lips,
the arched surprise of brow.

Cobalt liner. Cat's eyes
were all the rage then.
Sweet, sweet powder
from a feather puff

Perfume: *Je Reviens*
again and again.
Standing, smoothing, she
stoops to kiss my cheeks
before she leaves.
The air quivers,
charged with her beauty.

Now in the mirror
I, too, have cheekbones
          To die for.

Mile 437.2
Vicksburg, Mississippi
Monday 5/10/99
0900 hours

Courtney has decided that it'll be okay for
her to go ahead and smoke on this trip —
after all, she's under such pressure, and she
can quit the minute they steam into New
Orleans. Or sooner — she'll quit the night
before, so Gene won't even be able to smell
it in her hair. She often has a cigarette or two
when Hawk is out of town anyway — just a
little boost, a little present, something for
Courtney. So she might as well go ahead and
buy herself a whole pack while they're
docked here in Vicksburg. Wearing her
walking shoes and her dark glasses, she
heads up the long hill. This is a real workout.
But what a seedy, wretched town Vicksburg
is, in spite of all its history; don't they have
any civic pride here at all?

Weeds grow up through cracks in the
sidewalk. Many houses and businesses are
advertised for sale; two very old brick

buildings on her right are being demolished. Others stand vacant, their gaping windows like blind eyes gazing down the hill, brooding over the muddy river. A little wind has come up, blowing dust and bits of paper trash all along Grove Street, swirling them around Courtney's ankles. At the top of the hill sits a Shell station with a big sign on it that says smoke shop. Courtney buys a carton of Ultralights since they don't really count anyway, you hardly get any tobacco. Then she goes outside to the phone booth. The phone at Magnolia Court rings four times before she hears the click that means voice mail is picking up. But then a girl's high breathless voice says hello.

"Vangie?"

"Mama?"

It *is* Vangie, with a funny little note in her voice. Now Courtney remembers. Vangie's band was at the Cat's Cradle in Chapel Hill last night. How could she have forgotten? She even wrote it on the calendar in the kitchen at home, where Vangie is right now. Maybe Courtney is the one with Alzheimer's, not Hawk, only of course it's not Alzheimer's, he's too young.

"Mama? Hello, Mama, is that you?"

"Oh yes, hi honey. How are you? And

311

Nate? How was the show?" Thank God Courtney wasn't at home in Raleigh, she'd have had to go over to Chapel Hill for it.

"Oh, it was okay," Vangie says. "You know." Vangie says "you know" and "like" all the time, it drives her mother wild. "Mama, when are you going to come home?"

"Monday," Courtney says. "My schedule is right there, taped on the refrigerator. It tells you exactly where we are all the time. See it?" Courtney hears herself going on brightly about the *Belle of Natchez*, the food, the weather —

"Mama." Vangie interrupts. "Can't you come home sooner?"

"No, I can't," Courtney says. "I absolutely cannot. You can't get off a cruise once you're on it," which is not true at all, especially not this cruise, since it stops at so many towns. "Why?" she finally asks.

"Why didn't anybody tell me Daddy was sick?" Suddenly Vangie sounds very young and very angry, like she used to as a teenager.

"Well, honey, he's *not* sick, he's just having some tests this week, that's all, it's no big deal. We didn't see any reason to bother you while you are on tour. It's just an evaluation, basically."

"But Daddy *is* sick," Vangie says slowly. Each word sinks like a stone into Courtney's consciousness. She thinks of those boys she saw on the bank earlier this morning, throwing rocks into the river; each stone made a widening circle on the water. Courtney leans against the warm metal side of the phone booth. "It's all these lists," Vangie says.

"Oh, you know your father, he's always made lots of little lists." Courtney's voice sounds hollow to her own ears. "He's a very organized man."

"But he's *not*," Vangie wails. "He's making too many lists. It's like, his bedside table is covered with lists, I saw them when I went in there to get some aspirin. There's something the matter with him, Mama. And we've got to leave for Philadelphia."

"Now?"

"Yeah, we'll drive all day. Or, like, Van will drive. We'll be asleep, you know. In the back. Then wow, presto, we're there."

Presto, indeed, Courtney thinks. Kids are supposed to grow up and leave and go everywhere and do everything. But *we're* supposed to stay home, frozen in time exactly the way we were, and they don't like it if we leave. Or if we change. Not one bit. It's getting so hot in this phone booth.

Right in front of her, a fat man drives a long blue Buick up to the curb and gets out, mopping his face with the biggest handkerchief Courtney has ever seen. He's waiting. He wants to use the phone.

"I wish you'd come home," Vangie says. "Just fly home from the next city, what is it?"

"Natchez."

"Fly home from Natchez, then." Vangie is the voice of responsibility, certainly a bizarre turnaround considering all those nights when nobody even knew where she was. Why, one summer she was gone for three weeks, Courtney was just beside herself with anxiety, but did Vangie care? Heavens, no. Finally she called from Austin asking for money, which Courtney wired to her. Then she came waltzing back home with buzz-cut hair, dyed maroon. Friends of the Library, indeed! But Courtney was so glad to see her that she bought her a new electric guitar and never told Hawk.

"Dad looks different, too," Vangie says unexpectedly.

"What do you mean, different?"

"It's like, he's like, looking out of his face. It's hard to describe. It's not all the time, either. Like right now, this morning, he's just fine. He's being the nicest he's ever been to Nate, for instance. Nate never even really spent any time with Dad before, he's always been sort of like, well, scared of him. You know. But it was yesterday I'm talking about, when we came in and there he was, just sitting at the kitchen table reading the paper only he wasn't really reading it, you know, he was just like sitting there looking out of his face and when I said 'Hi, Dad, surprise!' he came back."

"Came back?"

"Uh-huh."

"Look, Vangie, what's your dad doing right now?" Courtney asks. "I'd like to talk to him, too."

"He and Nate went out to pick up some doughnuts. Mary Bell was determined to make a big deal and set the table and cook up this huge breakfast, but we don't have time. So right now Mary Bell is upstairs lying down or pouting or something, God knows, she's so weird, Nate can't even believe how Gothic this whole thing is, but anyway, Daddy got, like, all excited about this new Krispy Kreme place over on Glenwood, so that's where they went. I guess Dad seems like he's pretty happy to see us. He put the top down on his car."

"See? Everything's going to be just fine."

Vangie sounds tired. "Mama, you have spent your whole life saying that. But this time, I'm telling you, it won't work."

Courtney feels the sides of the phone booth closing in, a vise around her heart. The fat man is walking up and down on the sidewalk; he catches her eye and points to his watch. "Listen, honey, I've got to go. It's so hot in this phone booth, I feel like I'm going to faint. You have a great show, and give Nate and your daddy big hugs from me. I'll be back on Monday night."

"Whatever," Vangie says. The line goes dead.

The fat man heads for the phone booth as Courtney comes out. Sidling much too close to her, he catches her eye and winks, licking his bottom lip. His sweat smells like beer. Courtney turns on her heel and runs, all the way down Grove Street onto the dock and back to the boat.

Mile 437.2
Vicksburg, Mississippi
Monday 5/10/99
1015 hours

Catherine has been married for as long as she can remember, stretching out luxuriously in the big bed in their stateroom, this bed that goes on forever, it seems to her now. She can't remember a time when she wasn't married, or at least when she wasn't with a man. But to be honest, she's never thought much about it one way or the other. Men have simply occurred, like images, the way they'll come to her at the most surprising times and places in the midst of life, when she's doing something else completely, such as unloading the washing machine, and suddenly she'll see a shape in her mind's eye, a triangle, for instance, then a chair made out of triangles, and she'll just have to leave the wash or whatever she's doing, and go out to the shop and start making that chair. All her life, Catherine has been easily overtaken: by her husbands, by her children, by her images

317

and ideas, by life itself.

On the original raft trip, for instance, she was overtaken by her engagement, or by the *idea* of her engagement, to be exact. She was much more interested in her romance with Howie than she was in the river, or the trip itself. She didn't give a damn about Mark Twain, who reminded her of her uncle Walt anyway, a filibustering Alabama legislator she despised. She was working on her tan, with her upcoming engagement party at the Club, given by Howie's parents, in mind. To this end, Catherine basted herself each day on the raft with her own special mixture of iodine and baby oil, roasting first on one side, then the other. She timed the whole process, keeping her eyes closed with damp cotton balls on them so she wouldn't get those squinty little wrinkles in the corners, opening them only to check the time or to look at her brand-new square-cut diamond engagement ring as it winked in the sun all the way down the river.

She was a kind of a creation of herself. Her mother — the great belle, Mary Bernice — had instilled in Catherine and her younger sisters the idea that the whole point of college was to marry ASAP, and it was a vast relief to everybody that

Catherine had already gotten this taken care of. In fact, that phrase "as soon as possible" seems to capture Catherine's entire life. Everything has happened lickety-split with never a pause until now — menopause, actually, how ironic.

Catherine props herself up on one elbow to glance out the window which gives out on the long brown sweep of the river, then the faint line of green trees, then the blue sky. Three lines: brown, green, blue, going on and on forever out of the frame.

The horizon reminds her of those summers she used to spend down on the farm at China Hill with Wesley when they were kids, visiting Gran-Gran and Pops. Dorothy and Frances never went. They were too little. But Catherine loved it. Things were different there. Slower, as if you were living in an earlier time. Gran-Gran never dressed until noon, for instance, and it took Pops ten minutes to light his pipe, and Sunshine cooked dinner all day long in the big old kitchen with its heartpine floor. Dinner was at three o'clock. Then you had to lie down in front of a fan, in summer, or on a pallet before the hearth in the wintertime.

Catherine sees her China Hill self as a little girl in an old sepia-tinted photograph in somebody's album in the bottom of somebody's chifforobe in the attic of an old, old house. In this photograph she and Wesley are pictured from behind, holding hands, walking into the woods, like children in a fairy-tale book. They are very small and the trees are huge, arching over them. They wear identical overalls and straw hats and carry trot lines all rigged up by Pops, though you can't see the trot lines in the photograph nor can you see the Coosa River beyond the trees. They have been told to "go outside" which is what they are told every morning, with no suggestion as to what they should do there, unlike Birmingham where there are piano lessons and math tutoring and social dancing and homework. Down at the farm, they can do whatever they want as long as they come back when Sunshine rings the bell. Sometimes they ride the mules. Sometimes they walk all the way out to Dodson's Crossroads for a Nehi orange drink and free penny candy from Sis Puckett, who chews tobacco like a man and don't take no shit, she says, from nobody. Sometimes they walk the other way, down the river on the Dark Path to the railroad trestle bridge and climb up the steep bank into its web of steel arching over the river where they hang on for dear life, teeth chattering, while the Dixie Special roars overhead.

They've built a house on a little point of land by the river, too, out of tar paper and plywood and for the roof an old piece of aluminum siding they found on the road and dragged down there. The drumming rain on the roof sounds wonderful and this is Catherine's favorite memory of her childhood, sitting on the old car seat in the river house with Wesley watching the rain come across the river in spatters and swirls on the water and gusts in the willows along the bank. Wesley's face was little and smart and pointed like a fox. They were sixteen months apart, "Irish twins" said Mary Bernice. Catherine was bigger, though Wesley was older. There was a wooden chest in the corner of the river house where they kept Wesley's art supplies and their treasures gleaned from the river itself: a lady's necklace, silver filigree entwined with weeds; a tin cup and two tin plates; a leather box with the initials E.E.M. embossed on the top; old coins; a white china figurine of a Japanese lady; and best of all, a wooden foot that Catherine liked to pick up and turn over and over in her hands. They smoked Sunshine's cigarettes in the river house, and drank crème de menthe filched from the sideboard. Catherine knew she would never love anybody else as much as she did Wesley, ever.

They went to the river house on every visit to China Hill, from the time they built it when Catherine was eight until the year she was twelve, the year everything changed. It had been raining all that June and the river was up so high it covered the cypress knobs and the big round rock and the bottom of the willows, so high it lapped at the river house itself with a white frothy licking wave like hot chocolate with marshmallow topping.

"Don't you think we ought to move everything out?" Catherine shouted to Wesley over the sound of the rain on the roof. She was already hoisting the treasure box, but he shook his head, no.

"If it goes, it goes," he said flatly, staring out at the water. Huge limbs and logs floated past. Earlier they had seen a doghouse go down, spinning like a top. Then Wesley shaded his eyes and moved forward. In a flash he was out in the rain, hanging on to a willow, leaning over to scoop something up from the frothy tide.

"What is it?" Catherine yelled out into the rain, but he ducked back into the house with the dripping box clutched to his chest.

"What is it?" she asked again.

"A hatbox, stupid." Lately there had come this distance between them that was breaking her heart.

"What's in it?"

"How do I know?"

Wesley put it down on the floor and got out his new buck knife and started cutting the twine which securely bound it.

"Look at all those knots," Catherine said admiringly, over the drumming rain.

Wesley cut the last piece of twine and pried up the top and closed it immediately, with a look on his face that Catherine had never seen there before.

"What is it?" She came forward.

Wesley shook his head.

"I want to see." She touched the box.

"Listen, Catherine, you *can't* see. Go on back to the house, okay? I'll be there in a minute."

"Come on, Wesley." She grabbed the box and pulled.

"Damn it, Catherine, *quit*. Go on. Get out of here, okay?"

"No." She struggled with Wesley until the box slipped from his hands and fell to the plywood floor where the top popped off and a baby rolled out in a gush of bloody water.

"Oh my God." A feeling like a slow electric shock came over Catherine in a wave. She sat down on the floor and leaned over to peer at it. "It's a girl," she said.

"Shit," Wesley said.

"We have to tell somebody." Catherine was getting up now. The roar of the rain on the roof was driving her crazy, she had to yell to be heard.

"No," Wesley yelled back, and before she knew it, he had scooped up the tiny baby and thrown it back out into the rushing river, followed by the box. "Let's go," he said, stepping out into the rain. He didn't come back, and after a while she followed.

They never told.

Pops had a stroke at breakfast on Easter Sunday the following spring while he and Gran-Gran were visiting them in Birmingham. By coincidence, Catherine's period started that morning, too, only in the general rush of the emergency there was nobody to show her where to stick in the Tampax. Finally she figured it out by herself but when she came out of the bathroom, Mama had already gone to the hospital in the ambulance with Pops, siren wailing, and Gran-Gran was crying on the horsehair sofa in the wide front hall filled with neighbors. In Catherine's mind, life has not slowed down since. When Pops died later that spring, they sold the farm so that Gran-Gran could come live with them in Birmingham, a big mistake since all she did was sit by the window and weep. She never dressed.

As a teenager, Catherine was the apple of her daddy's eye and the bane of her mother's existence, messy and dawdling and daydreaming and talking on the telephone and taking up with all the wrong boys. She made A's in art and C's and D's in everything else, defying her mother in numerous flagrant and sneaky ways until finally, in exasperation, Mary Bernice sent her off to St. Anne's, in Virginia, in the wake of Wesley who earlier had been sent to Harmon Military Academy which was supposed to "make a man of him," which didn't work. At least Daddy eventually agreed to pay for Wesley to attend art school in Boston, when it became clear that he would never be a Phi Delt at the University in Tuscaloosa, like Daddy, or get his law degree.

Catherine knew this was one reason Daddy had liked Howie so much, because he was a Phi Delt at W&L, because they could do the secret handshake. Russell thought this was hysterical when she told him about it. He laughed so hard she wished she hadn't told; she'd always thought it was sort of sweet. Actually, Howie was sort of sweet, and actually, she'd sort of loved him.

Catherine stretches again, and again. It's nice to lie in this big bed alone. It's already ten-thirty. Russell dressed and went without making a sound. Well, he is considerate, damn it, it's a shame he's driving her crazy. Anyway, it's great that he's gotten so interested in the Civil War, especially since it's not even *his* war, being a Yankee and all, as she pointed out to him yesterday.

"What do you mean, it's not my war?" he demanded.

"Well, you know . . ." Catherine's voice trailed off in the way it does when she can't find the words she means.

"No, I don't know. What the hell *do* you mean? Shelby Foote said that any understanding of the United States as a nation must be based — 'and I mean *really* based,' he said — 'on an understanding of the Civil War.'" Russell has been reading Shelby Foote's whole narrative history of the Civil War, big old book after big old book, to get ready for this trip.

"I mean just what I said, it's not your war. It wasn't ever your war. You're a Yankee. It's the *South's* war."

Russell walked off chuckling and shaking his head, to get her a mint julep. He thinks he's a lot smarter than she is. Her other husbands thought this, too. Catherine has always believed it is to her advantage for them to think so.

At least Russell agreed to go on the Vicksburg battlefield and headquarters tour today without her. Usually he makes her take every tour, every side trip, with him because he's so afraid he'll have a heart attack when he's alone. But luckily he found out from the roster that there are forty-four doctors on board the *Belle of Natchez* this trip out — an entire group of doctors from Indianapolis. Unfortunately they are ENT doctors, not cardiologists. Russell loves cardiologists. But Catherine has reminded him that *all* doctors have done a rotation in cardiology, no matter what their specialty is.

She knows this because of her second husband, Steve Rosenthal, a physician who was in the first year of his residency when she took her son William to the emergency room after he fell off the porch and cut his forehead. It was bleeding like crazy, and Catherine was a wreck, too.

Dr. Rosenthal was tall and skinny, with a long, serious face and little round granny glasses which she had never seen before on a man. He wiped off William's forehead and held a piece of antiseptic-soaked gauze on the cut, pressing him tight to his chest where Will miraculously quit screaming. Suddenly Catherine could not remember any time when Howie had ever held William or done anything else but walk out of the room when he cried. Dr. Rosenthal smiled his grave smile at her. "He'll be fine," he said. "It's very vascular tissue, the head. He'll need a few stitches, however, so I'm going to call in Dr. Erskine, who's a plastic surgeon, to do it. You might have to wait a little while, but it'll be worth it. No sense in him having a scar."

"All right," Catherine said. She would have said all right to anything. When he handed Will back to her, Dr. Rosenthal's nice white coat was all bloody.

"Oh," she said involuntarily. "I'm so sorry." She reached out and touched his bloody collar. He looked down at her in a way no one else had looked at her before, a hungry, intent way. He was skinny as a pole. "Don't you want to call anyone?" he asked.

"No." She was amazed that this was true. The thought of Howie crossed her mind, wearing a seersucker suit, and disappeared. It wasn't working out anyway. He had liked the slapdash girl she was at Mary Scott, but somehow she had not shaped up into the wife he had apparently expected. Ever since she'd had Will, in particular, she couldn't seem to keep anything straight or get anything done — except play with Will, of course. Will was the best thing that had ever happened to Catherine so far. Now he sucked on her finger while she started crying again for no reason at all.

Dr. Rosenthal cleared his throat and said, "I want to see you."

"All right," Catherine said.

Suddenly he leaned down and put his mouth against the top of her head, into her hair. "Shit, I must be crazy," he said. Dr. Rosenthal turned on his heel and left with his giant ungainly strides, like some huge strange bird. Hours later, after Dr. Erskine finally came and sewed William up, and after Catherine had put him to bed and gone to bed herself beside Howie (who had been frantic, who was actually very nice, there was nothing really *wrong* with Howie at all), Catherine felt that she had simply made Dr. Rosenthal up, like a character in creative writing class.

But then he appeared on her doorstep the next Wednesday morning in the middle of a spring rainstorm, dark hair plastered to his forehead, glasses streaming, carrying a dandelion. He held it out to her. "Surprise," he said. First he looked stricken. Then he grinned at her.

Catherine had been nursing Will. She leaned out the door and looked both ways, up and down Country Club Lane. Then she grabbed Dr. Rosenthal's wet jacket collar and pulled him inside through the hall and into the kitchen where they both started laughing and couldn't stop.

Of course, when it all came out eventually, Mary Bernice was furious, summoning Catherine over for the official interrogation. Steven Samuel Rosenthal had come to medical school at the University of Alabama on a full scholarship, Catherine told her mother. His father was a butcher in Buffalo; his mother taught piano.

"A butcher!" Mary Bernice spilled her whole cup of coffee onto her dining room table. "Oh dear. Fronsie," she called, and Fronsie came to wipe it up.

"You won't have that," Mary Bernice said to Catherine. "You won't have any help at all. You'll have a hard, hard time, because I personally will never give you a nickel. Not a red cent. Do you understand that, Catherine?"

"Yes, ma'am." Catherine held William on her lap. Sunlight came through the open window in her mother's house. It felt good on her head, like somebody's hand.

"You'll have to give up the Junior League," Mary Bernice said.

"I never joined." Catherine had already moved out of the house on Country Club Circle and into married student housing with Steve, though they couldn't get married, of course, until she was divorced. Catherine bounced William on her knee. "This is the way the lady rides," she sang.

"Whatever will people think?" Mary Bernice said, almost to herself. The doorbell rang in the hall and Fronsie answered it and there were voices, then the closing door. Everything was hushed in this house, and cushioned, and comfortable. Silver candlesticks gleamed on the dining room table. Catherine and Steve would never have any silver, since she'd left everything — the china, too — for Howie.

"I always knew you'd be the death of me." Mary Bernice sounded almost gratified.

Thank goodness the little sisters married well and did not cause scandals, and so eventually Mary Bernice was mollified, if never entirely reconciled, to Catherine's choice. She even seemed to enjoy visiting the grandchildren who arrived punctually every two years, dark curly-headed babies who looked nothing like their mother. "Steve's little jewbabies," Catherine called them, nursing Amanda, changing Page's diaper, while blond William solemnly rode his red bicycle through the sprinkler. Mary Bernice kept her eyes carefully averted from the nursing; why *wouldn't* Catherine use bottles? Even black people used bottles these days. "Mama, could you hold Amanda just for a minute while I get another pin?" Catherine asked, and Mary Bernice did, but then she stood abruptly when Amanda spit up on her shoulder. She thrust the baby back at Catherine. "This is just too confusing," she announced. "I'm going home," and stalked off in a wide detour around the sprinkler which made a rainbow over the back yard. But Mary Bernice always paid for the diaper service, and eventually she came to rely upon her serious son-in-law who would listen to her so intently when nobody else would. She declared he was "smart," referring to him as "our psychiatric."

"Catherine doesn't even bother to keep house," Mary Bernice confided in her friends, "and our psychiatric doesn't even care." In fact, Steve loved to see Catherine out in the yard, surrounded by children — her own, the neighbors' — and plants. She built trellises and fences. She poured a concrete walkway. Steve encouraged her when she made the first heart-shaped steppingstones, then the suns and moons and cat-shaped steppingstones that would become her trademark. By then they had four children. They bought a big old house on the outskirts of town. Here Catherine made a fountain out of tractor seats, a porch rail out of antique bed frames, tables from old wooden doors with wrought-iron legs and inset tiles. She bought a welding torch and a kiln. Steve was gone a lot. He had chosen the state mental hospital over more lucrative private practices. He liked the big stuff, he said. He specialized in schizophrenia. In fact he was very excited about the clinical trials he was running for the new drug clozapine, when he was shot and killed in a robbery at the 7-Eleven where he always stopped for coffee on his way home. Five hundred people, all kinds of people, showed up at his memorial service. Catherine didn't even know many of them. When it was over, she thought she would die, too. But she didn't. She had to take care of her children, and she did, in the haphazard way she did everything. They fixed their own breakfasts, filled out their own permission forms. They went to school. They grew up. Catherine was working. Men occurred, then disappeared. She was working. Eventually she started making those big concrete women with mosaic tile dresses and hats. People bought them for crazy prices. One day a lawyer named Russell Hurt came by to discuss a commission, three of her concrete women for the courtyard in his new building. Three weeks later, he moved in.

But Catherine's whole life, even her life with Russell, seems distant to her right now, not nearly as real as the days when she used to wander the woods and fields with Wesley when they were kids. It's all because of the river. If Catherine closes her eyes, she's there yet and it's morning, early morning, her sneakers are wet with dew. She smells the honeysuckle so strong as she climbs up the stile; she hears the pot-rack, pot-rack sound of the guineas back there in the foggy woods.

Catherine props herself up on one elbow

against the pillows and looks in the mirror which Russell took off the wall last night and set up on the chair at the end of the bed so they could watch themselves making love, which turns them both on. "I wish I had a movie of this." How many times has Russell said this? How many times have they done it, over the past twelve years? Catherine can't even imagine. And wouldn't the children be shocked, really shocked, to know they still do it? Wouldn't it "gross them out," as "the girls" themselves used to say? It would gross out Johnny, the youngest, for sure. But, maybe not Amanda, who is more sophisticated, having worked in France for a year before entering graduate school in comparative literature, whatever that is, and who would have ever dreamed it? But certainly Page, now with her own twins and a busy lawyer husband to take care of, and certainly Will, in real estate with his father. Like Howie, Will works all the time. Howie will never retire, he's a millionaire many times over by now.

Watching herself in the mirror, Catherine lifts one heavy breast to her mouth and licks the nipple, sucks it just for a minute to get that little twang — like a single note plucked on a banjo — between her legs. She never was as intellectual as Anna and Harriet, was she? Or as focused and organized as Courtney. Actually, she was more like Baby though she didn't know it at Mary Scott, she thought Baby was so wild then, never dreaming how wild she could be herself. She's a middle-aged wild woman now. Oh, Catherine *does* like being married to Russell who is still likely to put down his newspaper any morning and stare at her until she quits tidying up the kitchen and comes to him, or to just cancel his tennis game in the afternoon if he gets in the mood and Catherine is available. He will even cancel *doubles*. Catherine likes that. As she has liked having all the children, their many comings and goings and friends and dogs and muddy shoes and sweatshirts flung down in the hall, the phone always ringing, the TV on, the school lunch menu taped to the refrigerator, brownies to bake for the bake sale. Catherine loves her children, she loves her grandchildren, she still loves to paper a bathroom herself or move the furniture around, to cook from scratch. Catherine loved those lists that she made out every day when the kids were all at home, so many many things to do, she loved to write things down on those lists and cross them off knowing that there were always more, more things on the list for any given day than she or anybody else could ever possibly do. She did not mind. She just did what she could every day and then drank a gin and tonic and fed the kids and sat down to help them with their homework while Steve worked late. Catherine was prodigal with her energy, generous with her days. There were plenty of days. Years flew by. The harder she worked, the happier she was. Messy, spontaneous and exuberant, Catherine was as unlike the cool and glamorous Mary Bernice or even Steve's mother, prissy little Claudia Rosenthal, as night from day.

In fact, Claudia could scarcely stand to visit, once flying into a little fit after Thanksgiving dinner upon observing, from her perch on the living room sofa, that the dining room tablecloth was uneven. "Do you think you could fix it, dear?" she'd asked Catherine, who was busy putting rain boots on the children. "Don't you think you could just pull it down there on the left, dear?" with a high shrill note of hysteria creeping into her voice until finally Catherine went over and gave it a yank, who cared?

But Claudia's most telling moment came

when she insisted on coming to "help" when Johnny, the last child, was born. Catherine woke in the night to nurse the baby, trying to figure out why she heard water running in the bathroom at that hour. Finally when she'd fed the baby and burped him and put him back down, she made her way into the bathroom blinking against the light to find Claudia in her threadbare white gown scrubbing the tiles with a toothbrush. "Hi," she said sweetly, looking up. "You need to buy some Tilex."

"Oh Lord!" Catherine had stumbled back to bed. Better a belle than a cleaning lady, she thought later, comparing her mother to Steve's, though there were times when she had felt differently.

Something about herself in the mirror reminds Catherine of Mary Bernice and she leans forward, breasts swinging, to peer at herself more closely. It is her mother's face this morning for sure, like that time years ago when she was so mad at Will and she heard her mother's voice coming out of her own mouth saying those words she and Wesley hated most when they were kids: "You *know* you don't think that!" Wesley used to run around in little circles, he'd get so mad at Mama. Catherine smiles, remembering. It's a shame that Johnny never even met Wes, that her other kids scarcely remember him. She wonders if she's the only person in the world who remembers his birthday: November 1. Scorpio. But she *does* look more like her mother than she used to, especially around the eyes. Catherine is determined never to drift off into euphemism the way Mary Bernice did at the end, denying everything, remembering nothing, refusing even to meet Wesley's lover who came all the way from San Francisco after his death. Wearing all her makeup and that ratty yellow silk dressing gown, Mary Bernice looked ridiculous, like a character actress in a movie, at the end. At least Daddy had had the good sense to keel over dead on the golf course.

Catherine read someplace that you never love your parents as much as you love your children, which is true. But isn't it strange how you can carry on arguments with them for years and years after their death? And you can *never* win.

Catherine steps into the tiny bathroom and turns on the shower which is nice and hot and has plenty of force, thank God. She shampoos her hair and then closes her eyes and leans back to let the water run all over her, down over her breasts and between her legs. She soaps herself good, pausing suddenly on her left breast — *what is that?* What the hell is that? She takes a deep breath and arches her back and lifts her breast so she can feel underneath it and all along her left side near the armpit. It's perfectly obvious. She can't believe she has never felt it before. It's because of Russell, she thinks, the constant presence of Russell, he's so loud, he's so distracting. But she can't believe that Russell hasn't felt it himself, and oh God, what if she has to have a mastectomy? Breasts are really important to Russell. What if she dies? Two of her friends have died from breast cancer already. The question is not *why me?* she realizes suddenly. The question is *why not me?* Well, shit. Shit, shit, shit. Catherine puts creme rinse on her hair anyway, you might as well look good even if you're dying. Might as well put on body lotion, too, life goes on even if you're dying. And even after you're dead. Oh, *stop it.* Maybe she's more like Mama than she thought. Histrionic. But this lump is *really big,* actually, almost as big as a golf ball. Anybody with smaller breasts would have noticed it ages ago. And Russell will be gone all day long on that stupid tour.

Catherine dresses as fast as she can, avoiding the mirror. It's time to meet Harriet anyway, they're supposed to walk into town together. Maybe she'll tell Harriet. Catherine walks quickly through the hall on the flowered carpet past all these pictures of people who are dead, dead dead.

"I remember Vicksburg as being bigger than this, don't you?" Harriet stops to catch her breath and look back down the long hill toward the river where the *Belle of Natchez* is docked right next to Harrah's Casino, a juxtaposition that must mean something, though she can't think what.

"Yes. No. I mean, I really can't remember Vicksburg very well at all." Catherine stops too, crossing her arms so that she can touch her breast.

"Ruth blew the bugle when we docked," Harriet says.

"Oh yes. That damn bugle!" Catherine kneads her breast. Now the lump feels huge, held up by her bra.

"And the mayor came, don't you remember, and gave us those little charms and Civil War minié balls, I've still got mine at home. Then they took us out to a restaurant and fed us hushpuppies and fried catfish which I remember especially well because we didn't have to cook that night. And Ruth had never eaten catfish," Harriet adds. "Then those people from the Mississippi River Commission took us to see that big model of the river the next day, before we left, and gave us sandwiches. We didn't have to fix lunch that day either."

"The reason you can remember so well is because you've never had children. I've blown out whole lobes of my brain," Catherine says. Her breast feels separate from her already. She has a sudden image of it rolling down the hill and then it's as if she's losing her whole body bit by bit, as if pieces are falling off and tumbling down the bluff to disappear into the river forever, and she can't stop them.

"Oh, but you have such a nice family," Harriet says. "I'm envious."

"Don't be. There are times when I wish I had no one at all."

Harriet stops and turns, shading her eyes, to stare curiously at Catherine. "You mean that, don't you?"

Catherine nods, still clutching her breast as they continue up the hill toward the austere old courthouse, now a museum, which sits on the highest point of the bluff, its columned porticos facing in every direction. Despite its grandeur, the court-house is as seedy as the rest of Vicksburg. Run down. Grass straggles up between the marble slabs of the portico floor; the columns are streaked with dirt. But it's really quite a view from here, like a lookout. No wonder Vicksburg was considered so strategic in the war. "The Wa-wa," Catherine's Gran-Gran used to say. Pops called it the "Silver War." Catherine and Harriet gaze out at the whole town running away down the bluff to the river before them. A wind comes up. Clouds skid across the patchy blue sky. Being up here is like being in the sky itself. Catherine feels nervous, exposed. "We'd better go in before it rains," she says.

The inside of the courthouse is as stern as the exterior, damp and dim, with cast-iron stairs leading up to the courtroom on the second floor. Harriet and Catherine climb them and move forward to join a little group gathered around an ornate iron dais where the judge must have presided. "This siege was the story of moving forward inch by inch," an ancient lady in a hoop skirt is saying in a whispery, cultured voice. They strain forward to hear her. "At the start, they were five football fields apart. By the end, they were so close they could speak to each other. The siege lasted forty-seven terrible days." Her small voice shakes.

"Oh, honestly!" one of the younger women from the *Belle of Natchez* says to her friend. This woman wears shorts with a matching sequined T-shirt and visor and that kind of fashionable mushroom haircut which looks just awful. "I swear, I don't see why they all go on and on and on about the damn Civil War so much. I mean, I'm from the South myself — Knox-ville's the South, isn't it? — but nobody in *my* family ever carried on about it like this. I just don't get it." Her nasal voice holds all of east Tennessee in it: hard times. And a recent, lucky marriage.

"Listen!" Suddenly the little old guide lady is on her like an insect. "My father ate *rats* at the siege of Vicksburg! Rats!" Her filmy eyes and yellow teeth are right in the younger woman's face.

"Damn, lady!" The girl breaks free, straightens her visor, and runs from the room with her friend following right be-hind her. They clatter down the iron stair-case.

"Rosalie, come along now." Another old lady in costume leads her away. "Rats!" Rosalie spits back at them out of her puckered, furious face. *"Rats!"*

"Let's get out of here." Catherine pulls Harriet down the stairs and out into the windy, changeable day. This courthouse gives her the creeps anyway, sitting up here on its hill in some kind of judgment, looking out — for what? You can't see the worst things come. Catherine carries her breast down the hill like a chalice, and though they eat a fine lunch together, fried oyster po'boys and potato salad and wine at a little restaurant called the Biscuit, and though they talk about all kinds of things, she does not tell Harriet about the lump in her breast. She can't tell Russell yet either. For it seems to Catherine, after her second glass of wine, that she has given her body nearly away already, to her children and her husbands, and now she wants to hold on to what she can.

Mile 437.2
Vicksburg, Mississippi
Monday 5/10/99
1600 hours

For the longest time Harriet has been debating whether to attend the afternoon Riverlorian Chat or not. On the one hand, she wants to take the opportunity to learn everything she can about the river; on the other hand, it's a good chance for a nap, since she hasn't been sleeping — but then, she can always sleep when she's dead, and the Riverlorian really is such an attractive man, she might as well admit it to herself, and his lecture starts in five minutes . . . Almost before she knows it, Harriet has taken a seat near the back in the Grand Saloon. She's the only one of their party in attendance. There are plenty of empty chairs, she sees. Many of the passengers are still out sightseeing, while a surprising number of others are going back and forth onto the casino boat. Harriet can see them out the windows. She thinks she might try a little gambling herself, maybe in Natchez. Finally Pete Jones comes in wearing clean creased khaki shorts with a lot of pockets in them and a white shirt with still more pockets (a man like that shouldn't have to do his own ironing). He looks like he's on safari. His knees are square and cute.

Harriet takes notes as he tells them about the Natchez Trace which she has never thought of before as actually having anything to do with Natchez, oddly enough. But the Natchez Trace turns out to have been the land route north through the wilderness taken by flatboatmen after trading their cargo in Natchez, or even down in New Orleans. They sold their boats for lumber and walked home. And since they were known to be carrying cash, land piracy was a big problem. Harriet wonders why Pete says "land piracy" instead of "robbery." Suddenly she glances up to find him staring straight at her as he talks. The rest of her notes are a mess, but she troops out dutifully with the group as they follow him up to the Observation Deck for a tour of the Pilot House. Pete introduces them to the pilot at the wheel, Rupert Middleton, who looks like a professor. Then Pete begins to speak. The boards on the big red paddle wheel are called bucket boards, Harriet learns.

"We use pine boards because if we hit anything, the boards will break and absorb the shock. This is a whole lot easier than replacing the Pittman bearing," Pete says. All the old men on the Pilot House tour nod sagely, as if they know what a Pittman bearing is! Honestly!

"All boats show up on the radar, which sees for a mile and a half, allowing us to continue in rain, fog, or at night. The radar also picks up buoys. Then we can hit the buoy with our six-million-candlepower spotlight, which picks up the buoy's fluorescent tape. One time we saw two white-tailed deer, swimming across right here." Pete smiles directly at Harriet. Next he explains the sonar or depth finder. "We're sitting nine feet down right now, with four feet of water under that." This doesn't sound like *much*, to Harriet. In fact, it doesn't even sound safe. Pete explains how they used to have a system on the river involving puffs of steam and whistles to signal to oncoming ships which way they'd pass them; one whistle or puff of steam meant port to port, two meant starboard to starboard. Now they do it all with radio. "Any questions?" he asks. To her own horror, Harriet finds herself raising her hand. "But how do they decide?" she asks. "Who has right of way?"

"The boat coming downriver, of course." He grins at her, showing the square yellow teeth under his snowy moustache. "It can't stop."

"Oh, of course." Harriet's response is lost in the general laughter.

Pete explains that the phrase "get the lead out" meant to drop the lead overboard on its hemp line to measure the depth. The line had one-and-one-half-foot marks on it. Twelve feet, or two fathoms, was safe water. "Mark Twain," the boy would cry, meaning okay. Captain John Dulaney of the *Belle of Natchez* started out on the river twenty years ago, literally "learning the ropes" (*Oh!* thinks Harriet), eventually working his way up from pilot to master's license, and now he's a captain. He's a good example, Pete says: "If you work hard and study and leave the girlie books at home, you can make something of yourself." Then Pete actually winks at her! "Captain Dulaney has been on the river for thirty years, since he was seventeen years old. By the way, to get your first-class captain's license, you have to be able to draw the river from memory, all of it, every bend and town and island. You have to know it like the back of your hand." He doesn't say, You also have to be picturesque and able to carry a tune. Harriet remembers old Captain Cartwright sitting at the wheel in his rocking chair under the red umbrella, pointing out the sights along the way.

Pete says, "That's about it, folks. Go ahead, take your time, look around at everything, Rupert here will enjoy the company. But don't touch these instruments." His lecture done, Pete crosses the Pilot House, heading straight for (oh no) Harriet. "I didn't mean to single you out or make fun of you," he says to her. He's really a very nice man.

"Oh, I didn't think so, not for a minute. I just blush so easily, I'm afraid. It doesn't mean a thing, though."

"Hey, I like a woman who can still blush," Pete says. "Hey!" — again, startling her — "How would you like to eat lunch with me tomorrow in Natchez? There's a pretty good restaurant right by the dock named the Magnolia Grille."

"Oh no, I couldn't do that," Harriet says immediately. Her eyes come up to the V in his open shirt. His chest hair is white, too.

"Well, another time then," Pete says easily, turning away to leave, then stopping to listen to a question from the dapper elderly man with the dog-headed cane.

"Are you sure you saw those deer swimming across this river, young man? I would tend to doubt that."

"Well, sir, all I can say is, they did it, and I saw it with my own eyes. Of course you know that every hair on a deer is hollow, so that might account for it. And now, if you will excuse me —" Pete's gone. He must be making that up, Harriet has never heard of such a thing. Isn't it irresponsible for a Riverlorian to make things up?

Harriet is perspiring so; she reaches in her purse and gets out a Kleenex, then shreds it to bits. She pushes her way past a little clot of ladies flirting with Rupert. They all wear those flowered short sets. "Pete!" she calls into the wind on the deck. "Pete!" But he's gone. Harriet runs into the passageway, then starts down the metal stairs. She rushes out onto the Observation Deck, where several people are playing shuffleboard and others are sunning themselves on deck chairs or observing the shore through binoculars. Some instinct tells her to head down the forward stairs. She's just in time to see one foot — his foot, in the black shoe — disappear. "Pete!" she races down the stair steps.

"Harriet?" Suddenly he pokes his head back around the divider, scaring her to death.

"Yes," she says breathlessly. "I mean yes."

He just keeps grinning at her in the most uncomprehending way.

"*Lunch,*" she has to say. "Yes I will have lunch with you tomorrow."

"Twelve o'clock then," he says. "Meet you at the landing." He doesn't seem to be a bit surprised that she followed him. And then he's gone again.

During dinner the *Belle* moves out of the Yazoo cut and back into the Mississippi, steaming down the setting sun's red path in the river. It's turned into a clear, beautiful evening with a nice breeze — a little cooler than it was. A momentary hush has fallen over the table, each face enlivened, for a minute, by the dying sun. Then while Maurice pours coffee all around, old Leonard and his pretty wife, Bridget, describe the casino boat where they have apparently spent the better part of the day. Bridget hit the jackpot on the Wheel of Fortune quarter slot machine. "So then I moved over to the next one, I think it was Wild Cherry, but nothing happened. I just lost quarter after quarter, while the guy who had taken over my machine won again. I never should have left, I knew it. Don't quit when you're ahead, there's a lot of truth in that.

But then *he* wouldn't leave, so I couldn't get it back. I tried Elvis, and Jeopardy, but I never got another run like that one." Leonard whispers in her ear. "Oh yes," she says, "I won seventy-two dollars, in case you're curious."

"That's a lot of quarters." Catherine smiles at her. Actually, Bridget reminds Catherine of her daughter Page, it's the same haircut, the same bright willing expression on her face.

"I learned about something today I'd never heard of before." Russell stirs cream into his coffee. "All of our associations with Vicksburg have to do with the siege, right? But come to find out, one of the biggest naval disasters in the entire history of the United States has an association with Vicksburg, too. Right after the end of the war, the steamboat *Sultana* put in at Vicksburg to get its boiler patched because they were having trouble with it, and no wonder. The *Sultana* was carrying 2,400 men on a boat designed to carry about 450. It was taking Union soldiers home from Andersonville. The captain got paid by the head — that's why there were so many on board. But his greed killed him. The patched boiler blew up north of here, killing 1,900 men — why, that's more than the 1,600 killed on the *Titanic*. Amazing."

"That *is* amazing. If I ever knew about it, I don't remember it either." Anna slides her chair back from the table.

Courtney stands up. "I'll see all of you later," she says pointedly, "at the dance." She's talked them into going, though Catherine is still trying to get out of it for some reason, and Harriet seems panicked at the idea of dancing.

But Bridget clears her throat. "Ahem," she says in the stagiest way. "Leonard wants me to tell you something." She leans forward. Leonard nods vigorously, with his sly grin. Courtney struggles to hide her annoyance. Who *are* these people? Harriet sits back down.

"Well" — Bridget surveys her audience — "Leonard likes to share our story with others; he feels it is his duty to spread the word. He and I were married in Hawaii nine years ago and only four months after the wedding, he developed prostate cancer." Perky as can be, Bridget acts like she's conducting a board meeting.

"Oh my God!" Russell can't help it.

"Wait." Bridget holds up her hand like a traffic cop. "Of course it was a terrible tragedy all around, since he had to have the entire prostate taken out immediately. I just couldn't imagine doing without him — I mean, we were virtually *newlyweds* after all, so luckily we ran into a surgeon who suggested a penis pump, and Leonard decided to go for it." Leonard smiles his lizardy smile at them all. "It was quite expensive, but let me tell you, it was worth every penny, every hour of surgery."

"You mean the thing works?"

"Russell, don't *yelp*," Catherine says sharply.

"It works great," Bridget assures them, "but it takes a while. The first step is that when you go home to recuperate, you have to leave it pumped up for the first three weeks so that it will heal in such a way you can get an erection later. So you do have to maintain an erection for the first three weeks."

"Jesus," whispers Maurice, who has joined the rapt circle.

Leonard says something in Bridget's ear.

"Oh yes!" She nods brightly. "The biggest problem we had during the entire time was when Leonard got this terrible abscessed tooth and had to go to the dentist for a root canal. Well, we didn't know what to do, because of course he'd just been staying at home ever since he got out of the hospital. But he was in awful pain."

Leonard puts his hand up to his face and grimaces, to demonstrate. "Well, I thought to myself, now how can we do this? Without attracting undue attention or even getting arrested, I mean. I knew we had to walk across a huge parking lot and into an office building and then of course we might have to wait in the dentist's office . . . Finally I got creative and made him this little harness contraption out of an old Kotex belt and one of those orange juice concentrate cans with the ends cut off."

Leonard whispers again.

"A *large* orange juice concentrate can," Bridget adds. "He wore some of his baggiest old sweatpants and then I had a real inspiration; I tied his matching sweatshirt around his waist and let the ends just droop down, you know, like this, to cover his erection, sort of casual California style, and off we went. Nobody even noticed. And at the end of those three weeks, we tried it out, and it worked like a charm." Bridget is radiant. Leonard nods slowly and constantly, eyes nearly closed, like a gator on a log. "Leonard thinks we should tell as many people as we can, so they won't give up hope if this happens to them." Bridget beams at Russell, who squirms in his seat. She reaches for Leonard's spotty old hand and squeezes it. "Now I call him Ready Freddy," she announces.

"My goodness!" Courtney jumps up from the table. "That certainly was interesting. And now, if you'll excuse me —" She's gone, Anna following, but Harriet, secretly hysterical, can't even get up from her seat, oh, she's going to wet her pants, she's going to *die*, but of course she can't laugh out loud. Catherine looks amused, too, biting her full bottom lip as if she can't trust herself to speak. Leonard whispers again to Bridget; finally they stand up.

"See you at the dance," Bridget says. "We're going to have a little rest first." She winks broadly. Leonard grins like a jack-o-lantern. Holding hands, they leave the dining room.

"Have you ever? I can't believe it." Catherine is wiping her eyes. "I mean, I know it's not funny, it's very serious, but —"

"It's — the — orange juice can!" Harriet finally manages to say.

"Oh man," Maurice cracks up, clearing their table.

"So how about it?" Russell says to Catherine, his lovely Catherine, putting his arm around her. "How about a little roll in the hay, hey hey?"

"See you later." Harriet is out of there.

"Baby?" Russell pulls her close against him and squeezes her, touching her breast. He nuzzles her hair.

"Way to go," says Maurice.

"Russell, stop it. What do you think you're doing, right out in public like this? You're disgusting." Catherine breaks away from him and leaves the dining room, fast. She does not look back.

By morning, 250 five-by-seven-inch color photographs of the dance will have been posted on the wall to the left of the dining room doors. They include:

No. 111. A group shot of Russell Hurt with his arms spread wide to embrace all his "girls": Catherine, serious and striking, at his side, with her long gray hair falling dramatically to her tan shoulders; Anna, enigmatic beneath a dressy pair of jewelled, smoked cat's-eye glasses, on his other side; Courtney next, caught in an unfortunate expression, mouth open, lip curled, as if she's about to tell somebody off; and then Harriet next to Catherine, standing straight and still with her lips pursed and her feet together just so, as if she were a girl from the previous century who had somehow strayed into this photograph.

No. 112. Another group shot of the now-disheveled "girls" who appear to be doing something like the can-can, all turned to the side with their arms around each others' waists, kicking their left legs up in the air. *"Can* we do it? No, we *can't!"* Courtney was chanting. Their eyes are red and their teeth look shiny white in the flashbulb's cruel glare. Their red mouths are open wide, very wide, laughing. (Courtney will humorously entitle this one "Can-Can Girls from Hell" later, when she puts it in her *Belle of Natchez* scrapbook.)

No. 128. Russell and Catherine Hurt, posed in the flower-twined wishing well, embracing for the camera. Bending down to kiss her, Russell wears a white dinner jacket, Teva sandals with no socks, and a Hawaiian shirt with bright green parrots on it, neck open. His right arm encircles her; his hand on her waist looks startlingly big. Catherine's white lace dress is not really vintage, just old — actually, it belonged to Mary Bernice. Normally she never dresses up, and Russell can't get over how good she looks. Her left arm rests gracefully, if somewhat ornamentally, on his shoulder. Catherine's head is back, her face tilted up, though we can't see it; we can't see Russell's face either. You can't even tell who they are. They could be anybody, anybody in love.

Mile 364.2
Natchez, Mississippi
Tuesday 5/11/99
0600 hours

Harriet wakes up suddenly, too early again. She's startled to see that they have already docked, with the landing right there and the ramp already down. The muddy river beats against the rocks. She remembers those rocks. And the narrow road winds up the steep bluff just as she remembers it, too. A fine gray rain falls on everything, turning it all pastel. Water color, impressionist. Two men carry a heavy box up the ramp to a waiting van that moves off slowly into the mist, lights blinking. Other men go into a lighted café across the way promising BEST COFFEE IN TOWN in pink neon, haloed by the mist. And there's the Magnolia Grille, right on the water, still shuttered and closed. It is — let's see — six hours until her lunch date with Pete. Harriet shivers again. It's silly to keep it so cold on this boat when it's so hot outside. It's unnatural. Her eyes rise to the top of the bluff where, she knows, stand the great houses Natchez is famous for — Longwood, Rosalie, Stanton Hall, Melrose. She's read about them in the guidebook. If she ever saw them the first time, on the raft, she certainly can't remember it.

Her memory of Natchez is altogether different.

It had been raining then, too, all afternoon as they ran downriver toward Natchez, a warm hard rain that sometimes seemed almost horizontal, driving under the tarp they'd lashed to the two-by-fours which made a frame on top of the raft. The rain soaked everything, going straight into your eyes. You had to keep your sunglasses on in order to see at all, but even so it was hard looking through water. It was already getting dark. Everybody was starving; they hadn't eaten since breakfast. There hadn't been any point in trying to make sandwiches in all that rain. Catherine had passed around apples and little packs of peanuts which worked just fine if you ate them fast enough. They all strained to see the Devil's Punchbowl, a huge depression in the bluff that the captain was determined to point out to them despite the rain. "Some say Sir Henry Morgan hid his treasure there, and there's folks looking for it yet, to this day." Finally they rounded the bend and there was Natchez, the steep bluff, the ragged little settlement along the water. "There used to be four streets running along there," the captain said. "Now there's not but one."

"What happened?" somebody asked.

"River took 'em." The captain removed his glasses and wiped them with his wet bandanna. "All right now girls," he called. "Prepare to land. You're going to have to go in the water on this one."

"I'll go," Jane said.

"Let's go with her." Baby grabbed Harriet's hand.

Then Harriet was in the water with a rope, sunk up to her ankles in mud, straining against the steady hard pull of the current.

"That's it, girlies! Keep a-coming, keep a-coming!" the men called from the bank. Harriet and Baby and Jane staggered up and handed their ropes over to the waiting men, then collapsed in a heap on a big revetment stone. Its rough surface was still warm, in spite of the rain. The captain gave orders and the others snapped to. The raft rocked at its moorings while they secured it. Finally the captain was satisfied and the rest of them clambered onto the revetment, lugging bundles of clothes and sleeping bags, calling out to the group of locals who were rapidly gathering to welcome them. Just then the rain stopped. Everybody cheered.

Baby touched Harriet's hand. *"Look,"* she said, pointing across the river. In the sky above Vidalia the clouds suddenly turned pink and parted like a curtain, revealing a window of blue. "Hey, everybody," Harriet called to the others, but there was too much noise at the dock, and no one saw it but them.

The captain sent everybody scurrying for driftwood, and soon a big fire was roaring between two revetment stones. Jane and Lauren had just started unwrapping the food when two beautifully dressed women appeared like apparitions, each of them carrying a covered tray. They were followed by two boys lugging a giant cooler between them. After so long on the river, Harriet thought the women looked bizarre in their linen summer dresses and white heels, their sleek blond hairdos.

"Hey! I'm Mary Lane Biggs and this is Sissy Watkins," the blond announced. "Mary Scott Class of '51. We've been watching you all on the news every night and I said to Sissy, I said, 'Sissy, I'll bet they'll be hungry when they get here, don't you reckon . . .' " She prattled on while the girls fell on the food like jackals. Fried chicken, tuna salad sandwiches, little pecan pies, and the best deviled eggs Harriet had ever eaten. "Did you make them?" she asked Mrs. Biggs.

"Oh Lord no, honey!" Mary Lane Biggs laughed and laughed at the very idea.

Harriet can still close her eyes and remember that meal exactly: the girls' sunburned faces in the firelight, how tired the captain looked, those beautiful women who vanished as quickly as they had come, like good fairies, when all the food was gone. Then Bowen went back to the raft for her guitar and somebody started passing a bottle of bourbon around. They were singing "The Lion Sleeps Tonight" when the sheriff appeared, looming up suddenly in the firelight, a fat red-faced man with flapping jaws. His gut hung over his belt and his gun hung at his hip. "Girls!" he shouted above the singing. "May I have your attention, please?" The singing stopped abruptly. The bottle disappeared.

The sheriff introduced himself as Bull Tate. "Now we're mighty glad y'all have chose to visit us here in Natchez," he announced, "and I want to make sure your visit is a safe one. You girls may not be aware that there is some undesirable elements in this part of the world right now, and it's a bad area you're parked in. So I've brought you some protection. Rusty! Ralph!" he barked, and a little bowlegged guy with a weaselly face came forward, followed by a blank-faced giant of a man. "These here are my trusties, and I'm leaving them with you for the night," Sheriff Tate said. "You have any trouble, they'll take care of it, ain't that right boys?"

"Yessir," the trusties said.

"Oh no," Baby whispered. "You mean they're going to stay here all night long?"

All the girls were scared of them. Eventually the captain convinced the trusties to stay back from the revetment near a big sycamore tree where they soon fell asleep, but Suzanne organized a watch anyway. "Why, we could be raped, or — or — anything could happen!" she said. "Those men are criminals."

"I wonder what the sheriff meant, 'undesirable elements'?" Ruth asked. "Don't you think he probably meant black people?"

"I think he meant civil rights workers," Lauren said softly. "You know they're all over the place this summer, registering voters and such as that."

"Of course he does," Harriet said.

"Well, I'm going up that hill to find some cigarettes," Baby announced.

"You can't go by yourself," Courtney said immediately.

"Then come with me."

"Oh, Baby, it's too far. Why don't you just go to sleep? Or bum one from somebody."

"I'm jonesing," Baby said, "but I want my own pack. Bye. I'll hitch a ride or something." Sure enough a car stopped for her almost immediately, its red taillights blinking in the night. Courtney shook her head. Bowen strummed her guitar and started singing "Four Strong Winds."

"Harriet! Harriet!" Harriet hadn't even realized she'd fallen asleep when Baby was back, shaking her shoulder. "Ssh! Come on, wake up. Come with us."

Harriet sat up and looked around the smoldering campfire at the sleeping girls, the captain lying spread-eagled on his air mattress snoring like a chainsaw with his glasses still on. The trusties were snoring, too, under the sycamore tree. Nobody was keeping watch. "Baby! What are you doing? Where have you been?" she asked.

Baby grabbed her notebook and some other things out of her pack. "Hush," she said. "Come on, let's go. I met the neatest guys."

"Guys! What do you mean?" But because she always did everything Baby suggested, Harriet put on her shoes. She stood up.

"Sssh." Baby pulled her out of the circle of firelight and into the dark.

"Who *are* these guys? Don't you want to get some sleep?"

"Look, we can sleep when we're old. We can sleep when we're dead. These guys are Bull Tate's worst nightmare."

"What do you mean?" Harriet breathed in the steamy air. She looked back at the cozy circle in the firelight. But now the moon had come out, big and low. It made a shiny path across the river to the landing where the raft lay at anchor and the old car stood idling, lights off.

"This is Jesse and this is Noah," Baby said, opening the car door. "Okay, y'all. This is Harriet."

"Cool," said Noah, sticking out his hand.

"Pleased to meet you," said Jesse, driving.

Both boys had long dark curly hair.

Noah's was pulled back into a ponytail. Baby jumped into the front seat. When Harriet got in back, Noah handed her a paper cup that held a liquid that burned the whole way down her throat. "Lord! What is this?" she asked.

"Local product." Noah smiled at her. "I'm developing a real taste for it." When the old car reached the top of the bluff, Jesse turned on the lights. "We can't really take you girls out anyplace," he said. "We're not welcome in the white bars, even if they were still open, and it might not be a good idea to take you into a juke joint this late at night, either. So if it's okay with you, we'll just go back to our place."

Baby said, "Sure, that's fine," before Harriet could open her mouth. *What are you doing?* she wanted to shriek. But as they drove through the dark town with its boarded-up stores and its Confederate statues in the center of the intersections, she began to relax. These guys went to Antioch, which she had at least heard of. Noah was from New Hampshire and Jesse was from Boston. They were only here for the summer. They had taken a politics course from a radical professor who had convinced them to come down here with him this summer to register voters. The girls would meet him, too, later when they got to the house. Now they were driving along with flat open fields on either side, broken by the dark lines of trees.

"This summer is a turning point in my life," Noah said earnestly. "I don't think I can ever go back to the way I was."

"What do you mean, 'the way you were'?" Harriet edged across the torn seat to hear his answer.

"Privileged," Noah said. "You know, a car at sixteen, daddy's a doctor, the whole bit. I just didn't know *shit*," he said, shaking his head, passing her the paper cup again. "I couldn't have even imagined how people live." For some reason he reminded her of Jeff, even though of course they were very different, but yet there was something . . .

"Let's turn off the lights." Suddenly Baby lunged across the front seat.

"Hey, whoa, what the hell are you doing?" Jesse asked as the dashboard went dark.

"Now, see? We didn't even need them. Isn't it beautiful?" Baby said softly.

It was. The road stretched out like a silver ribbon ahead of them, while the fields lay vast and soft on either side; they seemed to go on forever, gently rolling to the horizon. The moon was so bright that the telephone poles cast long shadows behind themselves. The old car glided down the highway like a ghost car, like a dream.

"Oh wow." Noah pulled Harriet over to him and kissed her as if it were the most natural thing in the whole world, which at the moment it seemed to be, even to Harriet. Jesse turned the lights back on when he pulled off the road into a long rutted driveway that ended abruptly in the overgrown front yard of an old farmhouse. In the headlights, the farmhouse looked like it was in such bad shape that nobody could possibly even consider living there, but Jesse put on the brakes and turned off the key. "Home sweet home," he said. Two other cars were already parked in the overgrown yard.

"I don't know . . ." Harriet began.

"Hush. Come on," said Baby.

Noah in the moonlight turned out to be taller than Harriet had expected. He wore an old blue work shirt, cutoff jeans, and work boots. He took her elbow to guide her up the rickety steps onto the porch. Wind chimes tinkled somewhere. "You live here?" Harriet asked.

"We've got it for the summer rent-free," he said. "Only problem is, it doesn't have water, so we have to carry it up from the well." He gestured vaguely with one hand. "Oh yeah, the toilet's over there, if you need to go. It's the old-fashioned kind. An outhouse, I mean." He switched on a bare hanging lightbulb in the front room which had a large table in the middle of it covered with leaflets and papers. A side door opened.

"Boys?" the most beautiful girl Harriet had ever seen stepped out blinking into the light. Her hair was like a black cloud down to her waist; she wore a man's wrinkled white shirt. Her legs were dark and strong. "Oh, hello," she said to them easily. "I'm LaGrande." LaGrande was no older than they were. A man with a red beard materialized behind her, squinting so that you knew he needed his glasses.

"I'm Art Frazier," he said. "It's not much, but you're welcome." Everybody laughed. "Make yourselves at home." Art Frazier and LaGrande went back inside their room. Then Harriet had realized that they were actually going to spend the night there, she and Baby, at that farmhouse out in the middle of nowhere, and that nobody even knew where they were; but in that instant she had also realized that she wanted to, that she wanted to be here more than anything. Noah's hand felt like fire on the small of her back as he guided her up the stairs. "This is my room," Noah said, lighting a candle. The room had no furniture at all except one caneback chair and some kind of wooden trunk stacked high with books and papers. Most of Noah's stuff was piled in a corner, the rest of it strewn across the room. A bare mattress had been pushed right up to the floor-to-ceiling window, its shutter propped open by a pole. It had no screen.

"Come here," Noah said.

As if she were sleepwalking, Harriet let him lead her over to the mattress.

"Look." The dark woods stretched away down a slope at the back of the house to a little farm pond which shone like a lady's oval hand mirror in the moonlight. Harriet sank down on the mattress just as a strange sound, almost like a woman's cry, came from the dark trees. "My God! What's that?"

"Just an owl," Noah said softly. "We have a lot of owls out here. They're hunting now. There's a lot of squealing and thrashing around when they get something." He put his arm around her, under the T-shirt, and pulled her close. He told her that he was a humanities major, that his mother was a law professor, that they were Quakers, that he had gone to the George School, that he had two little sisters named Daisy and Rose. He cupped her breast in his hand. She could feel his erection. He told her that he had an old yellow lab he adored named Gatsby, that he was reading *The Magic Mountain*. He unzipped her jeans and she started to cry.

Noah sat up on his elbow. "What's the matter?" he asked.

"I can't." She was sobbing into the pillow, she felt so dumb. "Actually I haven't ever . . . this is not . . ."

"It's okay." Noah stroked her hair. "It's okay, don't worry about it, it's no big deal. Just forget it." He lay back down and settled his arm around her waist again. "Listen to the owls. Go to sleep."

When Harriet woke up, it was early morning and all the birds were singing and it was already hot. A thick blanket of yellow sunshine lay across Noah, curled on his side on the old stained mattress. He looked very young, slack-jawed in sleep. She nestled up to his back. She could smell him. She could smell herself. Chickens scratched in the yard outside and a cock was crowing someplace. This is my own life, Harriet said to herself. This is the real thing. Noah had two mosquito bites on one shoulder. She could count his ribs. "Hey." She poked him gently. "Noah. Wake up. We've got to go. We've got to get back to the raft."

Noah turned over to her, smiling. "Aw," he said.

When they came downstairs, Art Frazier said "Good morning" and LaGrande gave them thick mugs of steaming coffee. "This is New Orleans coffee," she said. "It has chicory in it." Her plaited hair was wound up on top of her head. They drank the coffee sweet and black. It was wonderful coffee.

"You'd better go up and wake Jesse," Art Frazier said. Noah took the stairs two at a time while LaGrande went out back to search for eggs. Harriet stood on the front porch looking off into the tangled woods while Noah pounded on a door upstairs. She heard Baby's voice, then their clatter on the stairs. "Harriet?" Noah came out on the porch and stood close behind her with his arms around her waist. LaGrande came back around the side of the house with five fresh eggs cradled in the tail of her shirt. "Look, it's an omelet," she said. "You'd better stay for breakfast," and she flashed her pearly grin. To Harriet she seemed the epitome of elegance and freedom.

"I wish I could," Harriet said sincerely. The last thing she saw as they drove off was Art Frazier and LaGrande standing in the knee-high grass in front of the sagging porch with their arms wound tightly around each other's waists, smiling straight into the sun as they waved good-bye. The trip back to the dock seemed short in the steamy morning. Jesse drove as close to the camp as he could, stopping at the edge of the revetment to let them out.

What the hell —" The biggest trusty suddenly appeared beside the car on the driver's side.

"Go. Go!" Baby cried, hitting the top of the car, which took off in reverse, spewing gravel.

"Son of a bitch," the trusty said.

"Good morning." Baby gave him her biggest smile.

He dropped his head and backed up, mumbling something they couldn't hear. The old captain grinned at them, shaking his head, as they picked their way over the rocks toward the camp. Most of the girls were still asleep. Baby mixed up some instant oatmeal with hot water from the kettle on the fire but Harriet couldn't eat a thing because the most awful thought had just occurred to her, she couldn't believe she hadn't thought of it earlier. "Baby," she said, grabbing her shirt. "Baby, *what about Jeff?*"

"Well, what about him?" Baby took a bite of her oatmeal out of the tin cup.

"But don't you love him?"

"Sure I do," Baby said. "But he's not here. Anyway this doesn't count. It doesn't mean anything, believe me. Nothing happened anyway. Just forget about it." She went to sit next to the captain. Already, she was his favorite girl on the raft.

Harriet remembers wanting Baby to be wrong. She had wanted that night to mean something, to mean everything, but as the days passed the meaning slipped away and it began to seem that maybe Baby was right after all, that Noah and the night in the woods had been mostly a dream, like *A Midsummer Night's Dream*, in fact, time out of mind, like Shakespeare.

So why is it more real to Harriet at this moment on the *Belle of Natchez* than her own real life, her exemplary life, all those years of taking care of Alice and teaching and mentoring and serving on committees and volunteering? Why does all *that* seem improbable, ephemeral, when it is, in fact, her life? Right now, Harriet feels more like the girl on the porch in Natchez than herself. She can almost taste that coffee with chicory in it. She takes off her nightgown and goes into the tiny bathroom. She'd better go ahead and wash her hair now, before she does any sightseeing, since she's got — oh Lord! — a lunch date.

Mile 364.2
Natchez, Mississippi
Tuesday 5/11/99
1335 hours

Often Russell Hurt wakes up into his life like it's a strange house in another town, and he walks through the rooms and recognizes nothing, not the things of his life that are there nor the people who seem to know him. This has been happening for some time now. Yesterday, in Vicksburg, the tour guide told an anecdote that sums it up: There was a wounded Confederate officer — Russell has already forgotten his name — who was brought home from the war only to fall into a coma which lasted for weeks. His wife sat at his bedside during all this time, pressing gruel and water to his lips, fanning away flies. Though all in the household believed he could not recover, at length the officer opened his eyes to behold the haggard yet lovely countenance of his faithful wife. "Ah," he said, sighing deeply, "My dear, pray tell me, where and who are we?"

Russell often feels this way, recognizing only the face of Catherine, his beautiful Catherine, whom he does not deserve. And sometimes failing to recognize even *her*, as today, at lunch, when suddenly everything she says gets under his skin, the way she and her friends are going on and on about the goddamn plantations. Russell fails to see the romance of it. To him, Natchez epitomizes the worst of the South, just as Catherine epitomizes the best of it. A monument to slavery, that's what Natchez is.

Russell has read that right before the war, it was home to more millionaires than anyplace else in the country except New York, though it had only six thousand people. Thanks to slavery. With the invention of the cotton gin, the slave population in the South had increased from seven hundred thousand to four million. The biggest cotton crop in history was produced in 1861. Abraham Lincoln had been elected in 1860, amid rumors of war. (*"Stop lecturing,"* Catherine had whispered into his ear at lunch. "Why can't you just let us enjoy ourselves? You're not our teacher.")

Russell threw down his checkered napkin and stood up at the table in the Pig Out Barbecue. "Hell, don't mind me, girls," he said. "I'm just nuts, Catherine will tell you that. To quote Woody Allen, I've got an inadequate denial mechanism, that's all. Go on and enjoy your afternoon. I think I'll head back to the boat. Catch up on some reading." He blew them all a kiss from the screen door before stopping to think that *this* might embarrass Catherine, too. But she dimpled prettily and waved as the door slammed shut behind him. He shouldn't have lectured them. He shouldn't have eaten all that barbecue either. But he just couldn't quit. He can never quit anything, that's his problem.

Russell needs to get off this boat, to get back home and back on his schedule. Everything depends on his schedule. All this random eating and drinking is insane, it's wrecking his digestion, too. Thank God for Tagamet. And yet he *wants* a drink, goddamn it, right now. All these bars are killing him. The more you drink, the more you want to drink, and Russell considers himself a carefully controlled alcoholic at the best of times, always has been, always will be. He never wants to tip the balance, to fall over into alcoholism, because then he'll have to stop drinking, a thing he cannot imagine. It has been his drug of choice ever since he was a boy — thirteen or fourteen, getting beer from the pretty widow woman up the street.

Russell cannot imagine doing without women either but luckily he's never had to. Women like him. This is because *he likes them,* which is immediately obvious to a woman. And sex is not all he likes. He likes to talk to them, too. Draw them out. Women like that. Most men — Russell has learned this from women — don't really like them and don't really want to talk to them. Especially in the South. Women don't think enough of themselves either. They never think they look good, for instance. Even the most attractive women, it doesn't matter. "My face is too fat," they'll say, "look at this," pinching their own sweet cheeks. Or they think their butt sags or they have too much hair on their arms. It's ridiculous. Now if Catherine would just grow the hair out under her arms, she'd be perfect. Russell has been trying to get her to do this for years. He can't say why she won't. Just thinking about it turns Russell on. Damn. He might as well have a drink, just one, to settle his nerves when he gets back to the *Belle.*

Russell walks down the hill as briskly as he can, considering his hard-on and the heat which is like a golden weight now on his head and the arthritis in his feet which is considerable. They wanted to operate on his feet at the Mayo Clinic, maybe he'll let them sometime. But right now all he wants is a drink and a look at the Weather Channel, *goddamn it!* Enough is enough. A man can do without a phone. In fact, Russell has enjoyed being somewhat out of touch with the office. But a man can't do without the Weather Channel.

Russell checks it out at least every couple of hours, more on the weekends when he's home. At the office he's got one of those tiny TVs in his top left desk drawer, which he can close if anybody comes in. At home he just clicks the thing over to the Weather Channel whenever a commercial comes on, which is all the goddamn time, it seems like. They have about three times as many commercials as they used to, and they're louder than the programs. It drives him wild. All he ever watches besides the weather is ESPN and the Discovery Channel anyway. "Fuck!" he screams, clicking it around the dial. They've got a million channels now, too, and the shit they put on TV is just amazing. Here's a big-haired lady evangelist, or maybe it's a man in drag; there's some surgeons performing an appendectomy; some babies starving in Ethiopia; there's two huge wrestlers pretending to fight, now one of them is hitting the other with a table. A table! Shit!

"Why don't you just turn it off?" asks Catherine, sweet reason personified.

But he never does. He can't. Instead he clicks over to the weather, which calms him down immediately. He loves the music on the Weather Channel, for one thing. All that light jazz. Or maybe you call it fusion. It's so upbeat, that bouncy vibraphone. He loves the pleasant weather girls in their nice little suits or sometimes a dress and jacket, he loves Dr. Stan Goodman, the lightning expert from NASA. He loves to know the temperature in Dallas, in Richmond and Seattle and Rome. He loves the Doppler radar system and the lake effect snows. His love for the thirty-six-hour forecast is exceeded only by his love for the extended forecast which covers five to seven days, now *that's* what Russell calls a forecast! It's encouraging to think that anything can be predicted five to seven days ahead, it gives him hope for the future, strength to carry on. The Weather Channel is what Russell has instead of prayer.

"It's going up to eighty today," he might call out to Catherine as she goes down the hall with a load of towels. Or, "Light rain predicted for afternoon."

"It's *already raining*," Catherine called back once over her shoulder. "Why don't you just look out the window instead of at that damn television all the time?"

But Russell merely shook his head, clicking. She doesn't understand. And actually, Russell knows that the weather is random: weather is the basis, in fact, for chaos theory. Edward Lorenz's work at MIT in the early 1960s provided a lot of insights into systems with nonlinear properties, such as the weather. Lorenz showed that as one parameter changes, others alter in a way that is not in direct proportion to this change. This means that the weather will *never* precisely repeat past patterns, and deep down, Russell knows this. The weather cannot be predicted.

Yet the "butterfly effect" seems true as well: the theory that one tiny disturbance in the air can create a major weather occurrence elsewhere at a later time, because of the interconnectedness of the atmosphere. Makes sense to Russell. He's lost a couple of women and several clients this way, through tiny insignificant indiscretions that have come back against all odds to haunt him. And a lot of good things have happened to him, too, possibly as a result of some kind little thing he did for somebody else, years ago, if he did any. He thinks he did. He hopes he did. Like a little deposit in the karma bank, creating a positive butterfly effect. Makes more sense than believing in some big God guy up in the sky zapping people left and right just whenever He feels like it, whether they deserve it or not. If such a God does exist, then He's a shit, and Russell doesn't want to have anything to do with Him. But hell, if you think about this stuff too much, you'll go crazy. Better to kick back, go with the flow, let that sweet jazz wash over you along with the five-day forecast . . .

"Good afternoon." Russell nods to the purser as he crosses the gangplank onto the *Belle*. He takes the steps two at a time — Cabin Deck, Texas Deck, Promenade Deck. Then he heads for the stern, where the only TV he can remember seeing on this whole boat is located at the open-air Calliope Bar. Sure enough, there it is, tuned to baseball. Shit. Some old geezer in seersucker pants and a red bow tie sits slumped over the bar, talking to the bartender, a muscular young man who's snapping towels and moving things around industriously despite the off hour and the heat. "Yes sir!" he says to Russell, startling him.

"Jack Black on the rocks," Russell tells him. He climbs onto a stool. "Hello there," he says to the old guy, clearly a drunk, beside him.

"Afternoon," the old guy says. His nose is red and bulbous, spread out on his face like some kind of growth, or maybe it *is* a growth. Russell can't stand to look at it.

"How about switching over to the Weather Channel?" Russell asks the bartender, who nods and says, "Just a minute," snapping his towel in the air. Actually these are not ideal conditions for watching TV, you have to lean way back in your chair which is really a stool with a back on it, the kind of chair that could tip right over, exactly the kind of stupid accident that could happen if you're not careful. The world is full of these accidents just waiting to happen. And then where would you be? Miles from a hospital, out here in the middle of this muddy river — but then Russell remembers the forty ENT doctors from Indianapolis, and calms down. He sips his drink.

"You watching the game?" he asks the old guy who says, "Hell no," as if the whole idea is ridiculous. He's got some kind of stuff in his hair, it's all matted down on one side. Russell is not even going to imagine what that could be. And yet the old guy looks familiar. A former client? Hell, could be anybody. "Hey, buddy," he says to him, "where you from?"

"What the hell business is it of yours?" The old guy draws himself up with some dignity to stare at Russell. His eyes are filmed, rheumy, yellow. Might be age, might even have hepatitis and not know it. Hepatitis B.

"Aw, don't pay any attention to Mr. Stone." The bartender flashes a healthy white grin at Russell. "He's been drinking ever since we left Memphis. He doesn't mean any harm. The only thing worries me is, I don't think he's eating much of anything either. I went and got him a hot dog for lunch today but he only ate two bites, that's all I've ever seen him eat. His wife comes by and checks on him every now and then."

"He's got a wife? On this boat?"

"Yes sir. She's playing bridge on the Texas Deck, most likely. That's what she does all day, while he's drinking." The bartender finally points the TV gun at the TV and clicks the channels, Russell would give anything to do it himself. "We can't pick up as many channels out here, even with our satellite dish," the bartender says. "Let's see —"

But here it is, and here's the weather girl, Susan Abernathy, one of Russell's favorites, in a bright green suit, predicting rain. She has wound her hair up into a severe knot on top of her head, as befits a meteorologist. Sometimes Russell wonders if any of these girls are really meteorologists. Once when he was in law school in Chapel Hill, he met a weather girl in a bar who confessed that she didn't know a damn thing about the weather, all she did was turn on the Greensboro station and then repeat whatever *that* weather girl had said one hour earlier. Weather moves west to east, she had informed him, something Russell hadn't known back then, in the prime of his youth. He thinks he fucked her, too, but maybe not.

"I said, *how's that,* sir?" the bartender says in his ear.

"Oh. Fine," Russell says. "Thanks. And I'll just have another one of these, while you're at it." The bartender's sparkling white dress shirt is too tight across his chest. Russell used to be young once, too, and strong. Strong as an ox. He could walk all day long which he did on his first honeymoon, with Iphigenia in Scotland, striding across the moors. He married her because she was named Iphigenia as much as anything, though he loved her wild curly golden hair and her thick glasses and shyness and her devotion to literature. Russell in those days was devoted to the idea of literature while being actually more drawn to pussy, a shame and a failing. He used to quote Yeats to Iphigenia: "Only God, my dear/Could love you for yourself alone/And not your yellow hair." Finally he was too much for her, wore her out. Now she is a poet, he saw one of her books the other day in the bookstore: *The Moons of Jupiter.*

Actually Iphigenia reminded him of his mother, another shy retiring woman he loved to shock, he just couldn't help himself. His very birth had been a surprise to his parents, quiet people long told they could never have children. They taught at a communal school in New Hampshire where they raised their own food, organically. As a child, Russell mixed the granola. In adolescence he came to hate this life, the same way he hated his pasty-face father's calm voice saying "Son" which was what he always called him, never "Russell." He hated his mother's blue-veined hands and her long thin braids and all the quivering hope in her face.

At fourteen Russell rebelled and went to public school where he played football and turned into a jock. His parents sat in the bleachers at every game but did not cheer. Russell had it on good authority that his mother covered her eyes when he carried the ball. Russell wrecked two cars and got a girl pregnant while still in high school, things his father took care of without getting too upset either, it must be said. In fact, he seemed almost proud of this huge bad boy they had raised up to be so different from themselves. When Russell went off to college, it was an immense relief to them all. After college Russell taught at a prep school for a couple of years to avoid the draft (here he met Iphigenia), and then entered law school when the marriage ended.

Sometimes we fall into situations we are made for, as was the case with Russell and the law. He could twist it, he could turn it, he could dodge to the side, he could feint left and go right, he could surprise everybody with a power surge straight up the middle, just as he had carried the ball in high school. He graduated sixth in his class, edited the law review, then clerked for a famous judge. He joined a prestigious firm in Washington, right on Connecticut Avenue. But here his cock got in the way, as it so often has since.

Women have been Russell's undoing all along. At the law firm, he fell hopelessly in love with one of the secretaries, Shannon Steele, she of the enormous tits and the big happy grin. Before he knew what hit him, they were doing it in the coatroom, and he was taking her on sandy, passionate weekend trips to the Eastern Shore. When she left her husband (Dusty, an electrician) to marry him, Russell was the happiest of men. He loved Shannon beyond imagining, his parents never could see why. At least Iphigenia had made sense to them. But Shannon had not gone to college. She did not read; she did not care a thing about politics. She did not see the big picture. But she proved to be a genius of the everyday, a connoisseur of the moment, of the right tie and the best coffee and the matching fabric. She loved things, and Russell was well on his way to providing her with a lot of them. Best of all, she was naturally content, glad to be pregnant, glad to stay home with the children. Lauren was an easy baby, followed by Russ, who was not. Looking back on it all from this great distance, Russell remembers these as the happiest days of his life, Shannon and the babies at home, himself shooting up the ladder in his firm.

He was amazed when, twelve years into the marriage, Shannon proclaimed her boredom, then her depression. She took a job as office manager for a group of accountants. Then she fell in love with one of them, exactly as she had fallen in love with Russell, and left Russell for him. Once this happened, it seemed inevitable to Russell, who felt he should have seen it coming a mile away. He guessed it served him right. He entered a hazy and prolonged period of joint custody and serial women, one of whom — Diane — actually married him, over his not-so-strenuous objections. The truth is, he had a moment of weakness. He was exhausted. He wanted to be taken care of, and Diane seemed the girl for the job. She believed she could change him, shut him up and shape him up, and turn him back into a model middle-class husband, which was foolish, of course. He had been through things. He took a dark view. Plus, nobody can ever change anybody else, something Russell's spidery little mother remarked shortly before her death, which was soon followed by Russell's father's death, both of them dying quickly and neatly and causing him virtually no trouble at all, leaving him a pile of Coca-Cola stock he had never known about.

Too late, too late, Russell mourned them. Now he was alone in the world, nobody to stand between him and the abyss. Nobody, nothing. Russell teetered on the edge of a black hole larger than the Grand Canyon, filled with despair. Diane left him. "I have loved you, Russell," she said from the door, "but you bring me down." Russell had heard this before. Diane came and went with such speed that she scarcely affected happy-go-lucky Lauren or Russ, a go-getter all the way. They stayed in Chevy Chase with their mother to finish high school when Russell moved to Tuscaloosa to join his old mentor, Judge Hancock. He had been there through several years and several unsuitable women when he met Catherine, the love of his life.

Sometimes Russell can't believe he met her so late, mourning the years they have already lost. Other times he can't believe he met her at all, wanting only to be with her constantly. He'll do anything she wants to do, such as come on this stupid boat trip, which is turning out to be kind of a kick, actually, though Catherine has turned weird on him and it's not really Russell's cup of tea anyway. Russell likes ruins, which turn him on, as opposed to dolled-up plantation houses, which do not. He likes picnics. Last summer he took Catherine to Tuscany where they found enough ruins and picnics to satisfy even him, though all those cobblestones in the hill towns hurt his feet and he was having trouble with his digestion then, too. Reflux, which can lead to esophageal cancer.

But he remembers one magic afternoon — it was almost exactly a year ago — when they picnicked in the vast sunny ruin of the unfinished cathedral San Galgano, how the light looked falling on the thick wild grass through the high round rose window; and the low, musical thrumming sound of the pigeons, oddly familiar, like a sound you think you've heard before somewhere, only you can't remember where. At that moment Russell would have given anything to be twenty-eight again, to come here at dusk with a girl and a blanket and a bottle of wine, to be here when the light goes and the stars come out and you could look up at them through all these arches . . . San Galgano was real.

This is not real, these idiot white women in the columned mansions or these idiot black women selling pralines and boiled peanuts down by the boat landings, calling out "Please missah, please missah, please missah" exactly as if the Civil War and the civil rights movement had never happened. No wonder the South is so stereotyped. Southerners — black and white — insist on stereotyping themselves. They were selling Rebel flags and "Forget, hell!" bath towels and black mammy salt-and-pepper shakers at the battlefield shop in Vicksburg. Why, a Northern person on this boat, or a Californian — and there are plenty — could travel down the entire Mississippi River and go back home without ever having seen anything of the real South where people live and die and play out their personal dramas just as they do everywhere.

Trips are good, though. Russell likes to get Catherine away from home, her friends, her work. Russell sees each of their days together as pearls on a string, shiny and round and precious, though he has never told her this. Maybe he will. Maybe he'll buy her some pearls in New Orleans and tell her then.

"Fill 'er up?" the bartender asks.

"Sure." Russell glances over at Mr. Stone who has fallen asleep on the bar now, face turned toward him, cheek smashed flat, mouth open with a little drool and a little ratty snore coming out occasionally. Russell shudders. It won't be long. Russell's got a place on his forehead that he forgot to show the dermatologist, and it's almost time for another colonoscopy. You can't be too careful with this stuff.

"Here you go, sir." Actually the bartender reminds Russell of his son, Russ, an uncomplicated hustling kind of a boy now getting his M.B.A. at Duke. Plans to go into Internet sales. Has got lots of plans, in fact, big plans. Russ has rebelled against Russell by becoming a salesman and a Republican, two things Russell hates above all others, except for maybe computers and corporations. Russell prides himself on being a throwback, a Luddite, a Don Quixote. Over the years he has become known for taking on the impossible cases, the cases nobody else wants: the death penalty cases, the civil rights cases, the sexual harassment cases, the little guy against the big company cases. Helping people set up charitable nonprofit corporations is his sideline specialty, pro bono. Russell believes in what he has done, yet he is not proud of himself. He has changed nothing.

The harder you work, the more things go to hell, the farther the culture slips down the tubes. And deep inside himself Russell fears that maybe Russ was right in their last "discussion" — *fight* is more like it — when Russ told him he'd never have done any of this stuff if he had really had to make a living. That pissed Russell off royally, but it may be true.

Russell read in the paper the other day that the most useful phrase in the English language is "You may be right." Which is not a total capitulation, actually, when you think about it. So maybe he'll start saying it all the time, and kick back some, and quit pissing everybody off so much. He needs to act better and quit embarrassing Catherine. Other guys get old and calm down, don't they? Attain a sense of equilibrium? Retire. Grow roses. But *not golf.* Russell will never play golf, which symbolizes most of what is worst about America in his opinion, despite Tiger Woods; just look at how they're fucking up the deserts in Arizona right now so they can grow grass on them, so they can make more golf courses, so people can play more golf. Jesus Fucking H. Christ!

Russell takes some deep slow deliberate breaths. He turns his attention back up to the TV where — *damn!* — he sees Susi Sergi, his favorite weather girl of all time, with her black cascading curls and the little dimples at the corners of her full red mouth and the big breasts which she doesn't try to hide though she doesn't try to display them either, as would not be seemly in a meteorologist, and Susi's the best. She's a professional, specializing in thunderstorms. Russell hated it when Susi took that maternity leave a couple of years ago, it lasted so long, hell, she should have come back to work and let the husband take care of the kid. Damn! Susi Sergi looks hot today. Dynamite red dress with a matching red jacket, an expensive-looking gold necklace. Maybe Catherine would like a gold necklace like Susi Sergi's. Russell is *sure* Susi Sergi grows out her armpits, it's an ethnic thing. He loves the way she holds her pointer, like a majorette with a baton, pointing at the concentric circles of a low pressure system.

"Yes, we're having a wet time today in the Southeast," she announces cheerily, "with severe thunderstorms bringing three-quarter-inch hail in some cases. Central Texas, it's heavy rain for *you,* with an accumulation of three to five inches, ending your drought watch. And Montgomery, you've seen less than a quarter inch of rainfall this summer, so it's good news for you. You're still working on a two-year rainfall deficit — and you're also enjoying some wet weather today. Las Vegas, you'd love that, wouldn't you? You're presently at 103; Phoenix, you're at 101 and rising . . ." Russell admires the bossy, familiar way Susi Sergi addresses the cities and regions of the whole United States directly. He wishes he could fuck her, to feel, even for an instant, that assurance. But right then an underling hands her a piece of paper, breaking news. "Take cover immediately, everybody in *Charles County, Maryland!*" Susi announces dramatically. "Two funnel clouds have been reported in your area. A tornado warning has been issued until 3 p.m. Everybody in Charles County, Maryland, take cover *immediately.*"

One reason Russell feels so close to Susi Sergi is that she's the one who announced the severe weather warning for Alabama when he and Catherine had just moved out into the country, soon after their marriage. Russell had never paid too much attention to houses before, but he loved the huge old trees out there, hickories and pecans and oaks and pines, and Catherine needed

401

more space for her work.

"Now, exactly what are you looking for?" the real estate lady had asked them pertly.

"An old farmhouse," Catherine said. "With a big barn."

"I want a house I can die in," added Russell, helpfully he thought, though the real estate lady had swiveled her pixie head on her skinny neck to stare at him. Later, in the garden of that very house, Catherine was "oohing" and "ahhing" about the big swooping limb of some tree. "We could put a swing here for the grandchildren," she cooed.

"Or I could hang myself," Russell said, offending the upbeat real estate lady so much that she went to sit in her car, while Catherine collapsed on a garden bench in laughter.

They hadn't been in the house two months when Susi Sergi came on with her dire news. "A supercell thunderstorm warning has just been issued for Tuscaloosa, Alabama."

"Catherine!" Russell yelled, "Catherine!" still hanging on Susi's every word. In some crazy way, it even made sense to him, that once he was finally living in a house he owned with a woman he loved, the weather would do this to him. No matter how much you watch it, it doesn't care. Okay, you sorry bastard, it's thinking. You got complacent, didn't you? Well, how do you like this? And this? Thunder rolled as the sunshine dimmed. "Catherine!"

"Honey, what are you yelling about now?" Catherine had stretched luxuriously, looking up from the crossword puzzle on her lap. Because she is a woman, she views the Weather Channel as mere background noise.

"We've got a severe thunderstorm warning in effect right now, that's what! With the possibility of tornadoes —," which punch out from the top of the anvil-shaped thundercloud, Russell knew this cold.

"I repeat, Tuscaloosa, Northport, and the surrounding area, take cover immediately. Make sure all pets are inside. Go to the safest part of the house, often a bathroom floor or a stairwell, and stay there until the thunderstorm has passed. Do not, under any circumstances, go outside. If you are in your car on a highway, pull over to the side of the road. Do not leave your vehicle." Susi Sergi was dead serious. It was her shining moment, her big chance to prove herself more than a pretty face, more than a bimbo. Russell rushed over and threw open the French doors. "High winds and flash flooding will be associated —," Susi continued before dissolving into an electronic crackle on the screen. The TV went dead. The lights went out.

"Oh, honey!" Catherine dropped her puzzle on the floor and came over to Russell.

"Oh my God, this is it, baby, this is the big one," he said as the sky darkened and the wind picked up and rain came slashing down in sheets across their yard. The umbrella and two folding chairs from the patio sailed off in the air.

"Maybe I'd better . . ." Catherine made a move as if to go outside, but Russell held her back. "No," he said. "Stay here. Just stay." He closed the French doors and locked them and stood with his arms around her as the wind increased until the rain stopped falling down and drove into the panes of glass with a rat-a-tat noise like BBs shot from a pellet gun. The whole sky turned black. Then, was it a siren? Or was it the wind which began to wail with an awful screeching noise, followed by all those explosions, cracks as loud as bombs going off, and then more thunder, and a sudden close flash of lightning that had lit up Catherine's face.

"Oh, Russell, what is it? It sounds like a war."

He kissed her. "It's a tornado, honey. I always knew we'd get one sooner or later."

"But Tuscaloosa *just had* a tornado, not even three years ago," Catherine cried. "It isn't fair."

"No, baby, nothing is fair," Russell said. Even the old saying that lightning never strikes the same place twice is not true; it strikes the top of the Empire State Building about five hundred times a year. Even if you've got terminal cancer, you can still die in a wreck. "We don't get any guarantees," he told Catherine just as something heavy hit the roof.

"What was that?" she cried out in the darkness. And, "Russell, what do you think you're *doing?*" though she knew perfectly well. And why not? What better thing to do while rain washes down your road in a river and trees fall all over your dream house? And afterward he must have fallen asleep because it was late afternoon by the time he opened his eyes again to see Catherine sleeping beside him spread-eagled in her bra and panties on the Persian rug.

"Shoot," she said, sitting up suddenly. "I can't believe it. I've got rug burns." She was rubbing her elbow. "Oh my." Miraculously, the French doors were not broken, though all you could see was leaves. Green light filled the room. Russell pointed the clicker at the television, but nothing happened. He picked up the phone. Dead. He stood up and pulled on his pants, then zipped them. Sirens started someplace. Horns sounded. It was over, though it would be five more days before the power came back on. A long time without Susi Sergi. A helluva long time without air-conditioning. Finally Russell and Catherine fled to the new Phoenix Hotel in town for the last two days, what the hell.

Here Catherine was soon fully occupied, calling roofers, calling tree surgeons, calling yard service crews, calling God knows who. Lying on the king-sized bed in the Phoenix Hotel watching her (watching Susi, too), Russell was knocked out by Catherine's secret organizational capacity. If she weren't so domestic, so artistic, she could be running Microsoft. Their house wasn't hurt much, actually, once they got the trees off it. Some damage to the roof, the gutters, the porches. Russell didn't care about the house. But the yard broke his heart. They lost fourteen trees, including the biggest, the most beautiful one of all, the giant hickory right in front, the one Russell had always identified with: old but upright, still here. The hickory had fallen to the right, splitting the largest maple tree where it remained lodged at a forty-five-degree angle, half its root ball exposed.

"What do you think about pulling it back up?" he asked the tree guys when they finally arrived.

"Can't be done, sir." The man took off his hat to scratch his sweaty head. "Won't work. It's a goner. But I'll cut it up and get it out of here. A thousand bucks, that'll run you. Let's say around seven grand for the whole property." For a Southerner, he was dismayingly definite, even terse.

"I'll tell you what. You go ahead and deal with the other trees. I'm going to see if I can't find somebody to jack this fellow back up for me. I believe it'll grow." Suddenly Russell, too, was decisive; and he stuck to his guns though Catherine wept and begged him to let them cut it up and get it out of there, it was such an eyesore. "Catherine," he said, imitating John Wayne, "I'll deal with it."

Eventually he found a fly-by-night crew from South Carolina, young boys, who swore they could do it with a couple of tractors, and cable to fashion a "come-along." Russell had thought the job would require a crane. But the boys said they had stood lots of trees back up before. "Trees this big?" asked Russell. Oh, sure, they said. No problem. "We can handle it if we can rent the tractors," the blond boy, their leader, told Russell. "No sweat." He wore a red bandanna around his head like a pirate. Russell believed them because he wanted to. He didn't realize how unusual it was to stand a tree back up until the boys set to work and soon the road was lined with spectators. Some of them brought their lunch. Catherine was distraught. "I was just down at the post office," she reported to Russell, "and everybody in there was talking about us."

"What do you mean, talking about us?"

"About you trying to save this tree. They didn't know it was me, I mean, they didn't know I was a person who lives here. They think we're fools, honey. *Fools*."

The boys attached cable from the fallen tree to two other trees, then to an iron spike they planted in the yard, forming a rough triangle. "This way," the blond boy explained to Russell, "it'll fall *away* from the house if it falls."

Russell was out in the yard with them, drinking heavily. "What do you mean, if it falls?" His question was drowned out by the arrival of the two big tractors and a dump truck, which they hooked up to the tree as well. The crowd grew. The boys from South Carolina posed for group shots of themselves beside the tree, beside the tractors, and in front of the house. The minute the cameras came out, Russell realized they had lied. They had never done this before. A reporter from the newspaper arrived. The boys ostentatiously retied the laces on their boots and drank a lot of bottled water. Two of them got onto the tractors, backing them into position until the cables went taut. The man who owned the dump truck drove it out onto the lawn and got in position, too.

"They're ruining the grass!" Catherine wept. "Russell, *what* do you think you're doing?"

"Saving the tree," Russell answered grimly. He nodded to the blond boy on the tractor, who took off his bandanna and waved it in the air above his head. Engines roared. The drivers started backing up. The cables quivered. Everybody strained forward to see. The great tree shook and groaned, losing leaves and even branches as they pulled it up. Half the maple shuddered, split, and fell. "Keep it coming, boys, keep it coming," Russell yelled over the noise even though no one could hear him. He had always wanted to yell something like this.

"I can't watch." Catherine ran inside.

Slowly, groaning and creaking, the big tree rose. The crowd cheered. More men ran out to secure the cables. People came across the yard to shake Russell's hand. The man from the newspaper interviewed him. Later, Russell would receive a citation from the Arbor Society. He would become a local hero. For the next four months, he watered the tree every night, all night. His water bill averaged $595 a month. He didn't care.

For the tree still stands: in fact, it is flourishing. Russell drinks his coffee out on the porch every morning so he can look at it, which gives him great pleasure. A big new shoot just popped up from the base this past spring.

"Travelwise, it's a pretty good day across America," Susi Sergi says now, above the noise at the Calliope Bar on the *Belle of Natchez*. Susi Sergi turns from side to side as she sweeps the pointer in a wide arc across the weather map. But wait a minute! Russell leans forward on his bar stool. Either Susi has gained some weight, or —

damn! Susi is pregnant again! That red dress and jacket is actually a maternity outfit. "Susi, you slut!"

"Pardon, sir?" The bartender wheels to face him, with concern.

"I'll take one more . . ."

"Sir, I hope you'll excuse me for saying this, but maybe you've had enough for right now."

What do you know about it, you little —, Russell wants to say. Instead he says, "You may be right." Relieved, the bartender smiles at him. "You may be right," Russell says again, with more conviction. He could get into this. And it's true that he wants to control his anger, he wants to live a long time, to grow old with Catherine, to grow old, old, old, filled with concentric ever-expanding circles like a tree. Russell has already lived a long time. He's seen most kinds of weather, from floods to rainbows to New England blizzards to hurricanes in the Caribbean to the Santa Ana wind in California and sun dogs over the desert. But he has never seen the famous green flash just at sunset, over water. He'd like to see that sometime. Hey! Why doesn't he take Catherine to an island next winter? *Carpe diem.* "Better grab the wife, buckle up the kids, and make that trip to

Grandma's," Susi advises everyone, "before these storm systems collide beginning June 12, next Thursday." *Seize the day.* The cables are holding up pretty good but there's a helluva lot of weather still out there, Russell thinks as he pays up and leaves the Calliope Bar to go in search of Catherine.

"Everything's good here, actually. Frances Barker runs a great kitchen. I try to stop in every chance I get." Pete leans across the pink-linen-covered table in the Magnolia Grille where he and Harriet sit on the screened porch. Downriver, the *Belle* rides at anchor, flags flying, big red paddle wheel glistening in the sun. It looks like a floating party. Harriet looks at everything except the Riverlorian, right across the table from her. Close up, Pete Jones is disturbingly large, disturbingly male, he even has hair growing out of his ears which Harriet has read someplace — she thinks it was Marilyn vos Savant's column in Sunday's paper — is a sign of lots of testosterone or too much testosterone or something. She tries to read the menu.

"May I recommend the crab-cake sandwich?" Pete has a gallant old-fashioned

413

manner of speech.

"Fine, I'll take it. I love crab cakes." Harriet's voice sounds squeaky in her own ears. Who was that hippie killer? Squeaky Fromme.

"Maybe a stuffed artichoke to start off with? That's one of Frances's specialties."

"Fine, I'll take it. I love artichokes."

"And what if I also ordered you a blackened catfish and a chicken pot pie?"

Finally Harriet looks straight at him.

"Would you take those, too?" He's smiling at her, well, he's just some old guy, after all.

"No, I . . ."

Pete puts his menu down and touches her hand. "Hey, I'm just pulling your leg, just funning with you, as my daddy used to say. Actually, I'm pretty harmless." But he keeps smiling at her. Why, he's got a gold eyetooth, of all things! Harriet can't believe she didn't notice it before. She smiles back. "The stuffed artichoke and the crab cakes sound delicious," she says. "You'll have to excuse me, too. I'm a little bit out of my element here." To put it mildly, she does not say.

"What element is that? What do you mean?" Behind the glasses, Pete's eyes are sharply blue.

"Oh, I teach school, I live very quietly, so this is all new to me." Harriet sips her water. "I guess I'm a little bit nervous."

Pete orders their lunch from Frances herself, who calls him "hon," and pushes her hip against his shoulder as she writes it down. She's a big woman with curly black hair, wearing a tight pink pantsuit. "So what do you teach?" Pete hands their menus back to Frances.

"Oh, you wouldn't be . . ."

"Sure I would."

"Well, I guess you'd have to say I teach English, but it's not literature or anything, though it's not just grammar either. I work with these returning students —"

Pete leans forward while she explains; by the end of her recital, Harriet is exhausted, but she actually feels interesting.

"I used to teach school myself," he surprises her by saying. "High school history, like my father before me."

"Where?"

"Cairo, Illinois."

"Why, I've been to Cairo!" Harriet says. "We stopped there the first time I went down the river."

"Oh, you've traveled with us before?"

"No, I was on a raft with a lot of other girls, it was the summer of 1965. This trip we're on right now is kind of a reunion for some of us."

"Well, I was wondering about that, trying to put you all together. You don't look like sisters, or like you might be having a family reunion — we get a lot of those. A raft, you say?"

The stuffed artichoke is good and so is the Chablis he ordered to go with it, but Harriet barely touches her appetizer while she tells him about the raft trip. She's embarrassed when Frances comes over to clear away Pete's appetizer plate and flashes her an accusing look. "And what about *you?*" Harriet asks him. "I mean, I was wondering how you — how a person, I mean — just up and becomes a Riverlorian. It seems like such an unusual occupation to choose." Now she sounds like a fool.

But he smiles — Harriet loves his big square teeth! "Well," he says, "the truth is that I fell into it by accident, the way most people fall into things." Do they? Harriet thinks. *Do they?* "Here's the way it happened." Pete leans back in his chair, nodding at Frances who brings in his grouper and sets it down before him with a thud. "I grew up right there in Cairo, then went down to Ole Miss and played a little football, then hurt my leg and turned to history. I always liked history. Went into the navy, then went back to school and got a master's degree. Married my childhood sweetheart Lois and settled down to live in Cairo for the rest of my life, five streets over from my parents'. Finally had a little son, Clifton, named for my father. Loved Clifton, loved Lois." Inadvertently, Harriet glances down at his hand: wide gold wedding band, *oh no*. "Lived like this for years and got used to it. Used to having her there every evening, when I'd get home from school . . ." Pete was also the football coach, so that took up a lot of time. "My boy played football, too, grade school through eighth grade. He was a real chip off the old block in those days."

Oh no — in her peripheral vision, Harriet sees the girls peeping around the screen door at the restaurant entrance — damn them! Why did she ever tell them she was having lunch with the Riverlorian anyway? Catherine puts her finger to her lips in an exaggerated "ssssh" gesture, Courtney wiggles her fingers in a little wave, while Anna tiptoes over to the rest room, looking outlandish in a huge African print dress.

Pete leans back and laughs. "Yes, I see

them," he says without turning around. "Just checking up on you, I guess. Want to give them a little shock?"

"Well, *sure*," Harriet has scarcely said it when suddenly Pete leans forward across the little table and grabs both her hands and kisses them. Or she *thinks* he's kissing them, there's something wet going on, so he must be, but mostly it just tickles. He's got that Mark Twain moustache. When Anna comes out of the rest room, they all scuttle out of the restaurant like crabs, eyes big as plates.

"That got 'em!" Pete says.

Harriet, flushed and laughing, does not withdraw her hands. "You were saying —"

"I was saying I had a life, a good life, there in Cairo. It was so good I never thought about it, if that makes any sense to you" — Harriet nods, it does — "Me and the missus, we owned our own home, she had a nice little C.P.A. business down-town, doing people's taxes and such. On the weekends we'd ride up and down the river here in my Boston Whaler, maybe we'd fish a little. Lois liked to fish, too. Our boy was doing good in school, oh, he got in a few scrapes, but nothing unusual for a teenager. Got into skateboards, then into dirt bikes, that was okay by me as long as

418

he kept up his grades and stuck with the football. I guess I thought of life in terms of football in those days, this must sound simpleminded to you. I reckon those early years were the hardest, but they were the most exciting, too, when we were building the football program from scratch, building the team. Then in 1975, 1977, 1980, 1982 and '83 we were conference champions. Nobody could touch us. You know, high school football means a lot to people in a town like Cairo, people that work all day long in a mill, say, or a factory, or in a machine shop. They come out to a game on Friday night and they can leave all that behind them. They can *win*. And of course they've all got an opinion as to what the coach did, or what he didn't do, they've all got something to say about it. Well, it means something, is what I'm trying to say. It means more than what it is. But I was so wrapped up in it, I didn't even understand that until it was over."

"What happened?"

"Lois was diagnosed with multiple myeloma in the summer of 1986. I didn't know what hit me. I didn't really have time to take it in. Five months later, she was dead." Pete shakes his head, looks down.

"Oh, I'm so sorry."

"You think, oh, there were so many things we were always going to do, you know, but we just never did get around to them, like go to Nova Scotia, Lois always wanted to go to Nova Scotia, don't ask me why. We were going to remodel the kitchen, too. I know that sounds stupid, but there's these little things that come back to haunt you in a time like that. But that Lois, now — she was sweet, she was something, a fellow ought to pay more attention to a woman like that."

"I'm so sorry," Harriet says again. These crab cakes are delicious, but it would be trivial to mention it now.

Pete wipes his moustache with a napkin, then pours himself another glass of wine. "All hell broke loose after that," he says matter-of-factly. "Some of it was my fault, and some of it wasn't. Bottom line was, my son got on drugs while Lois was dying. See, she was over there in the hospital and so I was over there, too, every minute I could spare from school, I wasn't home much, I reckon. And then I was one holy mess after she did die, and I swear I never even noticed what was going on until the police showed up knocking at my door. They had caught him red-handed, him and some other boys breaking into a 7-Eleven to get money for drugs. Old story. It was crack cocaine, what it was. He was selling the stuff, too."

"Good heavens," Harriet says, though she has heard similar stories from the women in her classes. "What did you do?"

"Well, it was all out of my hands by then anyway. But I was hard, too hard, on him. They jerked him out of school and shipped him off to rehab, and when that didn't work, I sent him off to another rehab, but he turned eighteen while he was there and said he wanted to come back home, and I wouldn't let him. I said he had to stay. To make a long story short, he left anyway, and bummed around for a while, and got back on the stuff, and shot somebody, and ended up in federal prison in Atlanta. Wouldn't see me while he was there. Said if I didn't want to see him, he didn't want to see me. Now this would have broken his mother's heart, thank God she didn't have to know it."

"Where is he now?"

"I don't know, that's the hell of it, though he sends me a postcard from time to time." Pete takes a billfold out of his back pocket and opens it and unfolds a postcard with a Montana postmark on it. The postcard is folded in fourths. "Hey

Dad," it reads, "Hope you are okay, I'm hanging in. Big sky out here. Yours, Cliff." Pete looks at it for a minute. "Lois saw to it that he had good penmanship," he says. Carefully he folds the card back up and puts it back in his wallet. Pete looks at the river while a younger waitress — not Frances, maybe Frances has given up on him — clears their plates. "Dessert?" she asks. "Oh, I couldn't," Harriet says, and Pete says, "None for me." He looks really far away now.

"You still didn't tell me how you got to be a Riverlorian."

He turns back to her. "Things had kind of generally gone to hell, as I told you, what with Lois dying and my boy gone, and I just didn't give a damn, frankly, about football. It all came to seem real silly to me. And I was being casseroled to death by the merry widows of Cairo. I was drinking like a fish, too. So you can imagine what kind of coaching job I was doing. Finally my old friend John, the principal, came over to see me and offered me a paid leave of absence from my coaching duties and my history teaching, just for a year, so I could get myself together. But I never went back. I couldn't. Oh, I fell down into a dark place indeed, let me tell you. Finally, in desperation I started to read. It had been years since I'd had time to read, but now I found that it calmed me. It interested me, and nothing else had interested me in a long time. I read biographies, I read history. I read everything I could get my hands on about the Mississippi River, and that's when I ran into Mark Twain. Now Mark Twain *really* interested me. For he was dark, dark as me by the end of his life, you know, his entire family having died on him, and I reckon I identified with that. With him.

"Then one day I was in a bar down there in Cairo by the docks when some people off a steamboat came in, and one of them asked me, she said, 'Say, aren't you the guy who does the Mark Twain show on our boat?' And I had to tell her no, of course, that I wasn't, but it got me thinking. So I let my moustache and my hair grow out a little more, and the next time they came through, I went down to the levee and walked right onto the boat. I figured I had nothing to lose, one way or the other. And son of a gun, it turned out that the company was actually looking for more Mark Twains right at that time. In fact, they were kind of desperate because one of their Mark Twains was going to have this big back operation, leaving them shorthanded for the next few months. 'Fellers,' I said, 'Sign me up.' 'Do you know anything about Mark Twain?' they asked me, and I said, 'Well, by coincidence, I do.' 'Can you do a Mark Twain show?' they asked me, 'if we can get you a script?' and I said yes. I had nothing to lose, as I said. I had already lost it all. So the next time they came through, I was waiting down at the dock in a three-piece white suit with my satchel, and I just walked on board, and that was it. Been with the company eight years now. It's a fine job. I make, oh, six to eight runs a year. I enjoy it. Rest of the time I read, garden, teach a dance class over at the senior center, do my show around the state, at schools and rest homes and such, I can vary it for any age group. Eat the casseroles, kiss the widows. I'm still waiting for my boy to come back, and I'm still waiting for the right woman to come along." He winks at her. "In the meantime, I have to admit, I'm enjoying myself. I've enjoyed myself here at lunch today." He hands his credit card over to the waitress.

"So you think this date went okay?" Harriet is horrified to hear herself ask.

He starts laughing as the waitress brings

him the bill; he signs his name with a flourish, then looks up at Harriet from underneath his heavy white eyebrows. "It went just fine," he says. "And I hope I may buy you a drink tonight, after Mark Twain's lecture, perhaps?" He stands. She stands too, knees wobbly.

"Well?" he puts his hand on the small of her back to guide her out. People at several tables wave, nod, or smile at them — they're all from the *Belle*, they recognize the Riverlorian. Giddily, Harriet waves back. "Well, *sure*," she tells him.

Pete opens the door and suddenly they're back in the real world, it's unbelievably bright out here, like coming out of a movie, Harriet thinks, a movie about somebody else's life.

Seated at the little desk in her stateroom, wearing the pink peignoir, Anna's already on Chapter 4. In 5, she will "break the back" of this novel. That's how she thinks about it anyway, though she has never revealed her secret tricks of the trade to anyone. After 5, the chapters will become progressively shorter in length so as to enhance the aura of suspense, of the characters rushing ever more rapidly toward their destiny. For the reader, the novel will thus pick up speed until she is literally unable to put it down. Or so one hopes. Anna sneaks a look at the clock, then plunges her pen deep into the inkwell again for what must be her last lines of this writing day:

For no reason at all, Jade Cameron stirred in sleep and then opened her eyes. Only 2 a.m., yet she felt strangely, violently awake. Pulling the creamy satin robe around her nude body, she stood and crossed to the long window giving out upon the brooding mysterious swamp now ethereally lovely in the light from the full moon hanging low upon the horizon. Jade opened the heavy latch. Cicadas whirred. Night birds called. The live oaks groaned while their curtains of Spanish moss waved gently in a sudden breeze. Without pausing to reflect, Jade stepped out into the moonlight. She was walking forward, her bare feet sinking deliciously into the soft carpet of damp moss, when suddenly —

"Oh, I'm sorry, Miss Trethaway! I'll come back later!" It's Huckleberry, carrying the evening tray of Perrier, mints, and a clean glass for her bedside table.

"That's perfectly all right, dear. Just go right ahead and put it down, as long as you're here."

He does so, pausing to turn down her coverlet and plump up her pillows while Anna watches him. His shirt is white and crisp, his hands are tan, his tie is crooked. Freckles fan across his cheek. He really is extravagantly handsome in the most wholesome sort of way. He places a Godiva chocolate on her pillow.

"Will there be anything else, Miss Trethaway?"

"*Well* . . ." Anna puts down her pen and purses her plummy lips and looks at him. He looks back. But the dinner bell sounds; footsteps and voices fill the corridor outside the flimsy stateroom door. The moment has passed. "*Ta-ta!*" Anna wiggles her fingers at him. "Until tomorrow, then —"

Arriving at the Calliope Bar a little late for their ten-thirty meeting, Courtney's surprised to find Harriet already sipping a huge New Orleans hurricane, served in a ridiculous fat-bellied brandy snifter. "Isn't it a little bit early for that?" Courtney climbs onto the bar stool next to her.

"Hello there, young lady!" The old man on Courtney's left has the face of a drunk, but he's wearing a beautiful seersucker suit. Courtney ignores him.

"Harriet? Hello?" Courtney nudges her. "I said, isn't it a bit early for that?"

"Oh, Courtney," Harriet sighs in an otherworldly sort of way. "Pete wants me to stay over in New Orleans, instead of flying straight home. He says he wants to show me the French Quarter and take me dancing."

"Well, do it!" Courtney was planning to

order coffee, but now she decides to have a vodka and orange juice instead. "Why not? You've got no husband, no family, to hold you back and keep you from having a good time." This comes out more bitterly than she expected, but Harriet doesn't seem to notice. "I'd certainly do it if I were you."

"Oh, I just don't know." Harriet swishes the umbrella around and around in her Hurricane, creating a scary little whirlpool. "I mean, I don't think I can. I mean, I can't. I've already got my plane ticket."

"Change it." Courtney takes a big gulp. "It'll only cost you seventy-five to change it. Well worth the money."

"Oh, Courtney —"

"Good morning, girls! Have you met my good friend, Mr. Stone?" Here's Russell in a crisp white shirt and a Red Sox baseball cap with binoculars and a camera slung around his neck. The old man sways on his stool, nodding at them all. He looks like he's about to fall off.

"Oh yes, we certainly have met Mr. Stone, haven't we, Harriet?" Courtney nudges Harriet who stares off into space in the mooniest possible way. Honestly! She doesn't have the sense God gave a house cat.

Russell orders a Bloody Mary in a plastic

cup. "I've got to go," he says. "Time for the USS *Kidd* tour. Catherine will be along in a minute. She wants to go to the swamp with you."

"What is the USS *Kidd* again?" Harriet asks.

"It's a restored naval destroyer. The reason I want to see it is that it's the ship my uncle served on in the Pacific."

"Now I was a ball turret gunner," Mr. Stone says loudly, suddenly. He sits straight up with a light in his eye.

"No kidding, old buddy?" Russell turns to him with interest but he has slumped back down over the bar already, face turned away. Russell shakes his head.

"I couldn't possibly do it," Harriet says hopelessly to herself.

"Enjoy yourselves, girls." Russell is off. "Don't let a gator get you."

"We'd better go, too. Here, this'll cover both of us." Courtney pays up and practically drags Harriet away, the little dunce.

"Oh, look," Harriet says suddenly as they pass the Grand Saloon, where a billboard announces the Marriage Game in progress. "That's Leonard and Bridget, right up on the stage there. They must be contestants. Let's go in for just a minute, Courtney. Don't we have time?"

Courtney consults her watch. "I guess so. But just for a minute, okay?"

They take a seat in back with a good view of the stage where Leonard and Bridget sit comfortably on a love seat, along with two other couples on two other love seats. Melinda Post, one of the Steamboat Syncopators, is dressed as a judge. "Okey-dokey!" She bangs an oversized gavel on the same desk used by Mark Twain last night. "Okey-dokey!" she says with fierce gaiety into her microphone. "Okey-dokey! For the first question, what is the color of your shower curtain at home? Oh, look at the guys, they're all thinking — but you can tell they don't know. They don't have a clue! All right — Bart! Where you from, Bart?"

"Pasadena, California."

"And what is the color of your shower curtain at home, Bart?"

"It's — ah — blue."

"Okay, let's go to Liz, his lovely wife of how many years?"

"It'll be forty on Thursday."

Applause for Liz and Bart.

"Okay, Liz, what color is that shower curtain?"

"We don't even *have* a shower curtain, you idiot! We have a shower stall! You dummy!" Liz hits Bart over the head with her big straw purse while the crowd goes wild.

Judge Melinda bangs her gavel. "And now for our next pair of lovebirds, Eleanor and Bud Patkin. Where are you from, folks?"

Eleanor and Bud from Rochester, New York, get it wrong, too; but Leonard and Bridget get it right, winning one hundred points. Their shower curtain is silver. *Silver?* "How does Bridget know how to do this so well?" Harriet whispers to Courtney. "How do they all know how to act?"

"From TV," Courtney whispers back. "This is based on that old show *The Newlywed Game,* didn't you ever see that? It's been around for years."

"I guess I don't watch much TV, really. I've got one, though," Harriet adds hopefully.

Judge Melinda asks the husbands to "name something of yours that she would really like to throw away. Oh, look at their faces, folks, they're thinking. 'Now *what* could *I* possibly own . . .'"

Bud picks his lawn-bowling hat, Bart picks his handgun, somewhat ominously, Harriet feels, while Leonard picks his old robe.

"No, honey, it's your computer," Bridget says. "I hate the way you spend so much time with it now instead of me."

"Awwww," goes the crowd.

"Come on." Courtney pulls Harriet to her feet. From the door they hear Judge Melinda's next question. "Okay, boys, which of your wife's girlfriends is the best looking?"

"Living or dead?" Old Leonard leans forward to ask. It seems to be an honest question, but the crowd cracks up.

"Oh Jesus." Courtney pushes Harriet out the door. Old Leonard gives her the creeps. Gene has just *got* to change his mind. Courtney can't believe he's being so silly.

"Anna! What a nice surprise!" Harriet says as Anna flaps across the concrete landing in sandals and long skirt and peasant overblouse, necklaces and red hair flying out behind her like a flag. It's only the second time Anna has been seen outside during daylight hours since the trip began. They all board and take seats facing each other in the very back of the tour bus.

"Thank God for air-conditioning." Anna spreads her skirts out around herself, then fans her red face with a notebook. "I felt I should come and take notes, since I'm actually setting my new book in the swamp, after all," she explains. "I've never been in a swamp, but of course I've never let that kind of thing stop me before!" She throws back her head to join in their laughter.

"Can you give us a little preview of the plot?" Catherine asks.

"Oh, sure —"

In no time the bus is pulling into a large leafy glade beneath enormous live oaks that shade several ancient-looking buildings. Why, it looks like some kind of a shanty-town! Although it is, well, *adorable,* as Anna announces upon alighting. The bus is welcomed by a young accordion player and a fiddler, sawing away at that New Orleans–style music, and they're adorable, too. But it's all so foreign back in here, it makes Harriet even more nervous. It's a different world, it might as well be Europe, it might as well be France. That old playground rhyme comes into her mind: I see Europe, I see France, I see Harriet's underpants! *Good Lord.* The live oaks droop over an open-air restaurant with weathered picnic tables under a tin roof. Loose chickens run everywhere, pecking at the ground around their feet. A big orange tabby cat lies sleeping on a giant stump. Old men play checkers at a battered table. And right beyond the bait shop, beyond the canoe rental shack, lies the swamp itself, another world. The musicians turn out to be their tour guides, too, the owners of Alligator Bayou. Bill, the little one with the curly dark hair, runs the canopied launch *Alligator Queen* while Sandy, the larger, blond one, tells them about the swamp, pointing out cypress hardwoods and resurrection ferns, which disappear in dry spells but come back out when it rains.

"Today," Sandy says, "Alligator Swamp Refuge protects 901 acres of land that is home to alligators, snakes, turtles, owls, white-tailed deer, black bear" — "BEAR!" Anna writes in her notebook — "and more than 250 species of birds." The *Alligator Queen* cruises out of the still bayou and glides onto a silver lake. "Here you'll see egrets, herons, ibis, cormorants, and anything else that happens to be migrating along the Mississippi River flyway, depending on the season," Sandy tells them. "And if you'll look closely, you'll see a lot of ratlike animals, about as big as cats, up there on those cypress knees. Look — right there! Yes, ma'am. Those are nutria. They are not native to this habitat, and they have become the scourge —"

436

"Oh, gross. Aren't they awful?" Anna exclaims, writing fast.

"I used to have a nutria coat," Catherine says. "All the girls in Birmingham had nutria coats, it was quite the thing."

Anna thinks of having her heroine tied to a stump, nibbled by nutria.

"Now right ahead of us, just to the left, see that log? This is actually a huge male gator, we call him Fred, he likes to hang out over here." The *Alligator Queen* rocks as everybody moves up to look at Fred. "Oh, he's huge!" "How can you tell it's a male?" Giggles. Anna alone still sits in her seat, writing.

"Don't you want to go up and look at him, ma'am?" Bill asks from the wheel at the back of the launch. "We're right on him. You'll get a good view."

Anna finally looks up, focuses, smiles. "Oh heavens no," she says. "There are many things which I really prefer to imagine, and this is one of them." It's so humid out here she's about to faint, and who really cares about all these slimy animals and birds and things, except insofar as they provide *atmosphere* anyway? Especially who cares about their sex lives, which Sandy seems determined to go on and on about.

"Alligators mate very gently, in fact that's the only time you can ever see the difference between the male and the female, the only time you can tell their sex organs, which only come out for breeding."

"I think that's lovely," Catherine says, as they all return to their seats.

Anna can't possibly use any of this distracting information, though she does like the way Sandy and Bill wear these big lace-up hiking boots with their khaki shorts, sort of a Crocodile Dundee look, very attractive. Now they have left the lake and headed up another dark bayou which really is primordial, though Anna is aware that she has used that word too much in the novel already — well, it's almost *intestinal*, isn't it, or *reproductive*, like the dark bayous of the body —

"Oh my God." She has been so absorbed that she didn't even notice Sandy coming back to stand by her end seat with a real live alligator, a little one, wiggling in his arms. He gets a better grip on it, strokes it, and it closes its heavy-lidded eyes which look ancient, even though it's a baby.

"Wanna hold it?" Sandy asks.

"No, I certainly do not!" Anna says.

He steps closer. "I don't mean the alligator." He gives her a big wink. Even Anna has to laugh. "Hey, no kidding, it's not slimy at all, in fact it's dry and kind of leathery. Come on, just touch it —"

"You don't have to do that, ma'am," Bill yells from the rear of the launch. Honestly, these guys are like the Smothers Brothers, or Cheech and Chong, or those car guys on NPR.

Suddenly, Harriet sticks her hand out and strokes its back.

"See? It's not slimy at all, is it?" Sandy asks.

"Not a bit," says Harriet firmly, flushed with success.

Then Sandy changes the subject to birds, which Anna couldn't care less about. She must have dozed a little, for when she opens her eyes again, he's back up at the front of the launch wearing a — what is that? It looks like a washboard hung around his neck, like they used back in West Virginia to scrub their clothes clean in the creek.

"Zydeco music is like a good jambalaya," Sandy says. "It's got a little bit of everything in it. Basically, it's an accordion, a scrub board, and a fiddle, playing a waltz tune. But it's a waltz tune with a difference. You'll hear some African rhythms in it, some country-and-western swing, and some Delta blues. But mostly this is Cajun music, Cajuns being those French-speaking Acadians who were exiled from Nova Scotia in the mid-1700s."

A lively accordion melody comes from Bill at the back of the launch. Everybody claps. Sandy joins him on the washboard as a huge white bird lands on the dark water ahead and the giant cypresses close like a canopy over the launch. Sandy dips and sways, scraping on the washboard with two forks and singing, "Jambalaya, crayfish pie, filé gumbo." Sandy dances all over the deck in spite of those hiking boots. "Gimme a little more music, copain!" he yells to Bill. "I feel like dancin' today! Let's show them how it's done." Bill starts a new melody on the accordion. "All right! *Laissez les bon temps rouler!*" Sandy yells. He takes off the washboard. He kicks up his clodhopper heels. "I need me a *woman!*" Eyes closed, he sways across the deck with an imaginary partner, holding one hand high and the other around her waist. Harriet's heart starts to race in her chest. In confusion she looks away from the dancing Sandy to the nearest bank of the bayou where a red-flowered vine trails down from a tree and a log slips into the water and glides away, giving Harriet a cold chill which runs up her spine exactly like Emily Dickinson described in that poem, "The Snake (A Narrow Fellow in the Grass)." *Oh my God.* Didn't anybody else see that alligator? But no, they're all watching Sandy dance.

"I said, I need me a woman!" he cries with his head thrown back, eyes closed. The accordion notes jangle in Harriet's head and she's not even surprised when he moves her way, dipping and weaving, eyes still closed, engaged in some mysterious yet inevitable selection process. This is the end of the world, she thinks. *Le bout du monde.* Full circle, Sandy wheels around. He comes to a stop at the end of their row. *"Ma cherie?"* Now he's looking straight at Harriet. He bows low and holds out his hand. Harriet rises. She slips past Catherine and Courtney and Anna. Sandy pulls her to him, putting his other hand firmly around her waist, until they're cheek to cheek. Her right hand stays high in the air, gripping his. "Good girl," he says into her ear. His breath is hot. He smells like sweat, like swamp. "Just follow me. Ready?" Harriet doesn't have time to reply. Bill cranks the accordion into another chorus and they're off, *step* step step, *step*

441

step step, dipping swaying and swinging around in a circle *step* step step, *step* step step, *step*. Harriet is actually sorry when the song winds up with a flourish and it's all over. Sandy bows, still holding her hand, while Harriet curtsies low to the crowd as if she's been doing this all her life.

Mile 229.4
Baton Rogue, Louisiana
Wednesday 5/12/99
2300 hours

The Chocolate, Chocolate, Chocolate late-night buffet features chocolate mousse, German chocolate cake, chocolate hazelnut cake, profiteroles, chocolate-glazed pears, Mississippi mud cake, and chocolate truffles, among other things. Courtney, sitting alone, takes the very last bite of chocolate pecan pie, holding it on her tongue to savor it for as long as she can. She closes her eyes. There's really nothing quite like chocolate, is there? But then Courtney feels someone staring at her, sure as the world. She opens her eyes and turns around to see Anna, two tables back. Anna smiles conspiratorially beneath her smoked glasses. She stands and rustles toward Courtney. "I caught you," Anna says.

Courtney jumps right up. "Actually, I —"

Anna puts a heavy hand on Courtney's thin arm. Close up, Anna smells like, what is it? Patchouli or something, the way it always smells in Pier 1. "It's okay," she says. "Forget it. Come on, let's go out on the deck and have a smoke."

They take two rockers at the stern looking down on the wake which streams out in a giant V behind them. The Mississippi is narrower here. The banks on both sides are dark and mysterious, though a few lights dot the shoreline. The moon, almost full, has turned a dark, peachy yellow. "Pollution," Courtney offers, waving her cigarette to indicate it. "All that pollution from Baton Rouge, not to mention these refineries and chemical plants. I guess it'll be like this from here on into New Orleans."

"I expect so." Anna's match flares. "Where's Harriet?"

"I haven't seen her since the show," Courtney says. "She went somewhere to have a drink with Pete."

"Oh my." Anna sucks deep on her cigar as the moon dips under a cloud. They smoke in silence until Harriet's soft voice cuts into the night. "Hi! I thought I'd check — I can't believe y'all are still up." She slips into the rocker next to Anna.

"So, did you have fun?" Courtney just has to ask.

"Yes," says Harriet. "Yes," she repeats

but not really to Courtney, as the yellow moon pops out to sail forth across the cloudy sky.

"I'm so glad," Courtney says. This is not true. She puts her cigarette out and stands up. "Good night, then," she tells them abruptly.

"In spite of all her good manners, sometimes she seems almost angry, doesn't she?" Anna says after she's gone. "What's going on with her, do you know?"

"Hawk is having some medical tests this week, maybe that's it. Maybe she's just worried about him."

"Probably. Ah well, we've all got our little histories, haven't we?" Anna takes a drag on the cigar.

Harriet turns to look at Anna's face, smooth as a Buddha's in the moon's yellow light. Of them all, Anna has changed the most. They're the only people out on the deck now. "Oh, Anna." On impulse, Harriet reaches over to touch her plump, ringed hand. "Anna — whatever has happened to you?"

"What do you mean?" Something inside Anna that has been expanding, opening up, quivers and stills.

"Obviously your first marriage didn't work out, to Kenneth Trethaway, I mean.

But what did you do after that? Did you ever remarry? You *did* find someone eventually, didn't you? Something you said earlier made me think that."

"Oh yes." Anna's face flares up as she lights another cigar; she looks softer now, smiling in a way they haven't seen. "He was the love of my life," she says simply.

"And —"

"And I can't talk about it," Anna finally says, "not even to you. It's too awful, too sad. I simply can't go there. This is why I write romances. They end at a certain point. Every true story ends terribly, if you follow it far enough, I mean. Don't you know that?" Now her voice is shaking.

"I'm sorry. I didn't mean to pry. It's late anyway. I believe I'll go on to bed now." Suddenly Harriet is almost too exhausted to stand up, walk back to her stateroom. "Good night." She squeezes Anna's shoulder.

"Good night, dear."

Anna feels years older than Harriet, watching her slim back disappear down the deck. She feels a whole generation older. A snatch of music comes over the water. A cluster of lights appear on the riverbank, twinkling like jewels, then disappear. A little town. A whole town full of people asleep in their beds, dreaming, or not dreaming, not asleep, worrying, remembering. Each one filled with love, pain, joy, loss, whatever. Anna is shaking. Real life is entirely too much to bear. Sweet, innocent Harriet: *Anna, Anna, whatever has happened to you?*

Terrible things, my dear.

Which will come to us all eventually, though in Anna's case they came sooner than most . . . ah well. Whatever doesn't kill us makes us stronger, she believes. She has to believe this. But of course she has never believed in talking about it either, preferring to grow strong in silence, in darkness and privacy, as she has done. Her books speak for her now, and they are a comfort, to herself as well as to her readers. She has written so many — so very many — books. She will write many more. She has to. And yet in some ways it still feels like yesterday when she wrote the first one, just after leaving Kenneth Trethaway.

She arrived at Piggott's Island, Georgia, just at sunset, wading ankle-deep into the ocean in spite of the cold, stretching her arms out to the wind. *Stretching her arms out to the wind,* she thought. She could probably get the hang of this. She drove around until she found the Flamingo, a peeling, pink-painted boardinghouse set down in the dunes, with a cheap vacant room and two old sisters who loved to feed people. When they found out she was pregnant, there was no stopping them. Crab cakes, smothered chicken, she-crab soup. Anna swelled up like a tick. She got dimples. She wrote the book in the mornings and walked miles on the beach in the afternoon. Every man who stayed at the Flamingo made a pass at her; she knew she had never looked better.

Her money lasted about as long as her pregnancy.

When the time came, the sisters drove her to the hospital in Savannah. "Spare no expense!" they screeched at her astonished old doctor, who had assumed all along that she was married. She went into labor laughing.

It lasted all night and into the next day, until Anna really thought she could bear it no more, until the town clock struck noon and suddenly her body bent up double like a nutcracker and then there was her baby in the old doctor's arms, long and — blue? — but just for a second, and then the doctor gave Anna a shot, and then she went to sleep. She woke up in a sweat, a panic. "Where's my baby?" she screamed at the soothing nurse.

"Now, now," the nurse said.

"I want my baby!" she was crying.

"Miss Todd," the old doctor said. "I regret to tell you that this infant was dead upon delivery. It happens sometimes. It is nobody's fault. That is all I can say. I'm terribly, terribly sorry." Dark lines cut into his face; his hooded eyes were bloodshot. He had been up all night, too.

"I want to hold her," Anna said.

The old doctor nodded to the nurse.

When they brought her in and put her on the pillow beside Anna, she unwrapped the soft white blanket and touched her baby's lips, her nose, her funny spot of reddish hair — "Little carrot-top," she whispered. She counted her baby's fingers and toes. Mothers are supposed to do that. She gently opened her baby's eyes and as she had expected, they were blue, not a pale misty blue but a bright solid blue, like wooden beads. "Your name is Anna Carolina," Anna said. "Anna Carolina Todd." She closed the little eyelids and bent down to kiss both cheeks. "Can I have that bag over there?" she asked, and somebody jumped to get it for her. Anna opened it and dressed her baby in the long white dress with the blue cross-stitching that she had brought to take her home in. She tied on the little blue hat. "Oh God," somebody said. Somebody else said, "Isn't there *anyone* . . ." But there was not. And she had killed her own baby, strangled her to death with the cord.

Anna doesn't remember the whole next year. For some months she was in the mental hospital in Milledgeville, then she was back at the Flamingo, then she was in the hospital again, then she was back at the Flamingo again. One of the sisters had died and the other one, Miss Bette, was having a hell of a time keeping the bank from foreclosing on the property. When Anna got well enough to understand this, she knew she must pay Bette back. She thought of asking her old friends for money — Baby, who was so rich, or Courtney, who had married well — but somehow she just couldn't do it. She couldn't even imagine doing it. She thought of her days at Mary Scott as days in another world, a sunny blue enclosed world like that model of the Globe Theatre she had built painstakingly with popsicle sticks for extra credit in English while she lived with Miss Todd. She couldn't even imagine how to tell her friends what had happened to her or where she was. Also it seemed to Anna that once you set out on a course, you had to finish it. You had to keep going forward, not back.

In the end she took a job housecleaning the luxury rental estates at the end of the island. This got her back into shape, though she was heavier now, and it paid well, and best of all, it was solitary, as the maids went in when the renters left or before the owners came, so she never had to talk to anybody. These houses had everything: huge TVs, king-sized beds, ice makers, trash compactors. They had signed art on the walls, and hot tubs and gas grills and little green plots of grass in front, with sprinkler systems. Anna liked cleaning these houses. She liked opening the bottom dresser drawers and looking in the closets and finding their scrapbooks and family pictures and financial statements and trying to figure out what the owners were really like, since she never met them. She felt that she could reconstruct them completely just from the contents of their medicine chests and desks and bookcases and storage sheds. It amused her to think that she was a reconstructionist, the exact opposite of

Kenneth the deconstructionist.

One day she reconstructed a family with a wife who looked somehow familiar in their family photographs. Digging further in their master bedroom closet, she came upon a Mary Scott yearbook. The woman had graduated two years behind Anna, who had not really known her. But the yearbook was filled with pictures of people she did know, including . . . herself, as a junior. Anna stared and stared at her own pale face, surrounded by all that long curly hair. She'd been living for art then, and look where it had gotten her. Now she was cleaning houses. Still, she used to be a writer. She really did. Look at her here, holding on to the stupid daisy chain in the *Calliope* photograph. Maybe she'll find that manuscript she started when she came to the island — isn't it still under her bed?

Anna turned back to the faculty section at the front of the yearbook and looked at Mr. Gaines. He must have been younger than she realized — he looked like a boy himself in this photograph, sitting on his desk, leaning forward, laughing. He looked so *nice* — engaged, interested, expansive. He *was* nice, damn it. She should never have written that anonymous letter to the dean. Anna shut the yearbook and pushed it back onto the shelf she had taken it from. She stood up, shaken. She cleaned their bathroom.

It was a while before she reconstructed anybody else.

But finally she *had* to; cleaning houses was too boring otherwise. She started to snoop again. She was especially fascinated by the marble monstrosity situated on the prime lot at the southern point of the island, a house which made no architectural concessions at all to the fact that it was located on an *island,* for God's sake, reportedly full of expensive antiques and Oriental rugs and huge arrangements of silk flowers. From time to time it was rented by corporate clients for high-level strategy weekends. Anna could not imagine who would have built such a pretentious house, or why — it seemed out of sync with everything else on the island. Finally the service assigned it to her.

The guys went in first, to vacuum and haul out the garbage and hose down the decks and carport.

"Thanks!" Anna yelled after them, starting in on the kitchen which was fairly tidy anyway since the last group had apparently brought their own chef along. This kitchen had black marble countertops, white cabinets, and a restaurant-sized stove. Anna scrubbed everything. Out the window, she watched the long line of green surf where the outgoing tide from the marsh behind the island met the ocean. It was the best view on the island; she should know. She'd been in enough houses.

Anna worked her way through the guest rooms, each with its own bath, putting fresh sheets on each bed. The house slept sixteen. It was afternoon by the time she reached the master bedroom suite (described in the brochure as the "solarium suite" in the "aerie") on the top floor. She was tired, but curious — surely there'd be *something* to indicate who these owners were.

Carrying her basket of supplies, she rode up in the elevator, emerging into darkness. All the draperies in the semicircular master bedroom were pulled shut, hiding the view, which must be spectacular. Anna set her bucket down with a clatter, inching her way over toward the windows in the dark. She touched a switch and the draperies slid open to reveal the sky, the beach, the ocean, and the huge king-sized master bed with a man in it, half covered up by a wad of sheets.

"What the hell!" He sat up abruptly.

Anna screamed.

"Shit," he said. He was huge, his massive chest and back covered by black hair, like a bear, like a monster. He shook his big head back and forth to clear it.

Anna screamed again.

"Calm down, honey," he said wearily. "I ain't gonna hurt you."

"What are you doing in this house?"

"I own the goddamn house," he said.

"You do not." Anna was as sure of this as she had ever been sure of anything. She backed up against the wall.

"You wanna bet?" Now he was grinning at her through his black moustache. "I built this lovely house for my lovely cultured princess bride who has now run off with the kids' fucking shrink, pardon my French, who never even liked the goddamn house anyway, preferring the place in Maine which is just as goddamn cold as she is. So the divorce is final this weekend, and she got this house. She got all the houses."

"But the cleaning service —," Anna started. "You can't just —"

"So I didn't tell the cleaning service I was coming, all right? I can't be bothered with every goddamn thing. Besides, I don't even know the name of the damn cleaning service."

"Merry Maids," Anna said automatically.

"Oh yeah? And who are you? Little Miss Merry Maid?"

"Actually I'm a writer," Anna said. She couldn't imagine why she'd said it.

"Sure you are, honey." He threw his big head back and laughed, a laugh so contagious that Anna found herself smiling too before she remembered that she was furious.

"I'm going to call the service," she said.

"No, you're not. You're going to have a drink with me. I came down here to drink, and I'm still drinking. I'm a long way from through." He climbed out of bed stark naked and walked over to the wet bar. He had a huge dark hairy torso with scars running all over it and thick white legs. The scars were raised and puckered like somebody had squirted toothpaste on him.

Anna turned away. "Put your pants on," she said.

"Oh, come on," he said. "You've seen one, you've seen them all. Besides, it doesn't even work." He turned his back and she stared at his hairy ass while he poured two tumblers full of scotch and handed one to her.

"Lou Angelli," he said, clicking his glass

against hers. "Angelli's Delis, maybe you've seen them? All up and down the east coast, mostly Florida and New Jersey. My story is, I went public too soon. You're a pretty thing," he went on. "I don't mind a big girl."

"Please!" But Anna was drinking the scotch.

"Don't I know you from someplace?" He gave her a broad wink.

"I doubt it," she said, and of course it was just a line, but the funny thing was, she felt she *did* know him from someplace. She recognized him. Somehow they were two of a kind. "I'm Anna Todd," she said. "Now put your pants on," and he did, and they sat out on the deck and drank until Mrs. Baggett from the cleaning service, along with the island's one policeman, Harry Renfro, arrived to evict them.

"I sure am sorry, Anna honey," he said. She played bingo at Harry's church on Tuesday nights.

"Oh, that's okay," Anna said cheerfully, sunburned and drunk.

"You're fired," Miss Baggett said.

"Bitch," Anna said. Then she and Lou cracked up, staggering along his wife's deck. Harry gave them a ride back over to the Flamingo in the cop car, turning on the blue light and siren at Anna's request. She woke up after noon the next day with the worst hangover she'd had since college — dry-mouthed, heart pounding, terrified that she was back in the hospital and none of it had happened at all. But then she looked over and there was Lou, lying on his back in her own bed with one huge arm dropping all the way down to the floor. She kept on looking at him.

Her door opened just a crack to reveal Miss Bette's sharp-nosed old face. "Anna, is that a *man?*" Mrs. Bette said in a loud stage whisper, over the sound of the window air conditioner.

"Yes," Anna whispered back.

"Good." Miss Bette shut the door.

Anna showered and brushed her teeth and took four Anacin and put on her yellow sundress, wincing when the spaghetti straps touched her shoulders. She made coffee on her hot plate and got her manuscript out from under the bed while Lou slept on. She read what she'd written so far. Not bad, she thought. Or, *bad.* But bad enough? Anyway, it beat reconstructing families. Hers could *never* be reconstructed, face it, none of her families could ever be reconstructed, so she might as well write books where it all happened again and again just the way it was supposed to: boy meets girl, sparks fly despite the mad underlying attraction, et cetera, et cetera, until it all ended happily ever after, again and again and again.

In this book, her heroine, a missionary schoolteacher, comes to the mountains to do good but encounters a wildly dangerous, darkly handsome moonshiner who won't let his brilliant crippled daughter attend school. Her heroine, Rosalie Peach, puts on a little bonnet and kicks the old mule into a spirited trot heading up Devil Mountain to confront him. A shot rings out —

Lou sat up. "Jesus," he said.

"How do you feel?"

"Like shit. I feel like shit." But he was grinning at her. He had a snaggle tooth, which she had always found attractive in a man.

She put down her pen. "It really doesn't work?" she asked.

"There are other things to do," he said, and they did them all afternoon, coming downstairs finally just as Miss Bette's last story of the day was going off the TV. "Well, hello, look what the cat dragged in," she said.

"I can cook," Lou said.

"Cook, then," Miss Bette said.

From then on, nothing was ever like it was supposed to be, except in Anna's books, where *everything* was. Lou and Anna never married. They stayed on at the Flamingo for her first three books. Lou shopped and cooked and cleaned while Anna wrote, reading each day's section aloud to Lou and Miss Bette (and whoever else happened to be staying at the Flamingo) in the late afternoon while thunderstorms raced across the ocean and they all drank Ramos gin fizzes whipped up by Lou. Some of the guests got so involved in the story that they stayed on for days. Miss Bette was a devastating critic, always right. She said the first one, *Mountain Magic*, was "entirely too arty," and sure enough, it was rejected by Sunset Romances on those very grounds. Anna took all the symbolism and semicolons out, and it was subsequently published by another publisher, Heartline Books, under the title *Devil Mountain Man*. Anna wrote a sequel, *Return to Devil Mountain*, which had a supernatural angle, and then *Come Home My Heart*, which made them rich.

They paid off the Flamingo and went to Europe, which led to *Toujours Toulouse* and *¡Arriba! Baby* which was translated into eleven languages, making Anna famous. Upon their return, they sold the Flamingo property to a German developer for a fabulous sum of money, buying the apartment in New York, the condo in Vail, and a wonderful old house in Key West which needed a lot of work.

This is where they found Robert, a decorator: in the Key West yellow pages. Robert had spiky peroxide-blond hair and beautiful manners; he was a Southern boy, from Charleston. He took care of their houses while becoming a massage therapist on the side. He was very gifted. Lou handled the money while Anna wrote the books and made personal appearances. She hired an assistant (Della Rosen, with tortoiseshell glasses) to make reservations, shop, answer the phone, and deal with the mail. Della saw to it that every fan heard from Anna personally. Depending on the tone and the degree of intimacy claimed in the initial letter, Della sent Response A, B, or C, beginning, respectively, "Of course I remember you"; "The life of any writer is such a lonely one, how heartwarming it is to hear from a reader like yourself, and to know . . ."; or "Alas, we may not meet!" Anna endorsed a line of cosmetics, then scarves.

After a while, Lou hired a financial manager named Martin Dean Marquette who had come to Key West for a Merrill Lynch convention and never left. Martin Dean Marquette took care of all their business for them, wearing a jeans skirt. Lou took up art. He specialized in wacky copies of famous paintings by modern masters, changing their signatures accordingly: Loutrillo, Loucasso, Loutrecht, Loualt . . . Above each signature he put his trademark black moustache, two quick strokes of the brush. Soon these paintings became collectible; then they were all the rage. Lou opened his own gallery on Duval. They bought the house next to theirs on Margaret Street, erecting a tall bougainvillea-covered pink picket fence around the entire compound which eventually housed not only Anna and Lou but also Robert, Della, Martin Dean Marquette, Miss Bette and her private nurse, and one of Lou's daughters with her illegitimate child, Susannah, whom they adored. Guides on the conch train pointed out the "House of Romance," as they called it, on sightseeing tours. If Anna happened to be working when they came by, she'd trail a pink chiffon scarf at them from the window of her tower study.

But Anna got Lou for only twelve years. Since his heart attack, she has never had another man although she has imagined a slew of them, romantic hero after hero, as she must, to support her entourage. She was with Lou on the satin sheets in their big round bed beneath the turning ceiling fan on the day he died — too young, at sixty-four — while making what passed for love.

Courtney slips into a denim sundress with a smocked bodice, then snaps a denim band over the crown of her straw hat. There. She applies clear red lipstick which is always so cheering. She straightens her shoulders, adjusts her hat. She has been looking forward to St. Francisville, where she has signed up to tour the antebellum plantations Oakley and Catalpa. The rest of the town is supposed to be very pretty as well; there'll be a lot to photograph. John James Audubon lived here in the 1820s, tutoring children at Feliciana plantation; here he made more than eighty paintings of birds and wildlife. It still looks wild out there even now, jungly and snaky. And it's hotter today than expected — already eighty-five degrees and it's not even 9 a.m. How did they ever do it, all those plantation ladies in the hoop skirts and the crinolines with their waists pinched in until they looked like wasps, like hourglasses — hourglasses marking time, counting the silver, waiting to die. Oh dear. Whatever is *wrong* with her this morning? Gene Minor has no business talking to her like that.

But she really must call Hawk this very minute before she does one more thing; she really cannot evade her responsibilities any longer. For once, she gets the outside line on the first try. Far away at Magnolia Court, somebody picks up the ringing phone, but says nothing. "Hello?" Courtney asks. She can't tell if anybody is there or not.

"Courtney?" Oh God, it's Hawk after all, the one person she hasn't talked to since this trip started, actually. The center of the action, the still point of the storm. "Courtney?" he says again. His firm voice sounds exactly the same. He sounds *fine*.

"Hi, darling," she says. "I'm so glad I caught you. We're docking at St. Francisville right now, so I'm off for a morning of photography. It's getting hot, though. There's a big difference between North Carolina and Louisiana weather, let me tell you. It's a lot more humid down here."

"So are you having a good time? Enjoying it?" It's unlike Hawk to be so solicitous.

"Oh yes, it's wonderful, but you would have hated it, you're too type A. It would have been too slow for you. Though there is a fitness center and there are a few people jogging around the deck every morning including Russell Hurt, you'd like him anyway."

"Who?"

"Russell Hurt. He's married to Catherine Wilson, don't you remember her? He's the only man in our group, actually. I think he's enjoying it, though — well, *they're* enjoying it —" *A lady never lets a silence fall.* Miss Evangeline's motto rings out in her head like a bell.

"I remember Catherine Wilson," Hawk says when she finally lets him speak. "Pretty girl from Birmingham. Got married the summer after we did, left the church in a horse and buggy." Hawk chuckles. Obviously, there's nothing whatsoever wrong with him, if he can remember all this. Maybe Ellen Henley is just as prone to exaggeration as Vangie.

"That was her first wedding," Courtney says. "Hawk, how are the tests going? Has the doctor said anything?"

"Hell, you know, they never say anything. It's a power trip, basically. They take off all your clothes and strip you of all your dignity and then they ask you a lot of stupid questions and insult you and you pay thousands of dollars for the privilege, thank you very much. That's the way it works."

"What kind of questions?"

"Oh, stuff like what is your mother's maiden name, or who is the governor of this state? What is today's date? What is your birthday? You wouldn't believe these questions, what a waste of a man's time."

"But what kind of tests, Hawk?"

"You name it, I'm taking it," Hawk says. "EKG, MRI, CAT scan, PETT scan, pee in the cup, blood tests up the wazoo. Close your eyes and touch your face. Jesus Christ."

"Well, you certainly sound like your old self, at any rate. But they must have said something . . ."

"So far it's inconclusive, that's what the guy said, Dr. Famous Fucking Levinson. A lot of the tests haven't even come back yet, of course, but so far, based on the best of his famous fucking expertise, it's inconclusive."

"But what does that *mean?*" Out her window, Courtney sees people streaming onto the landing and into the two waiting buses. Oh well. There's no help for it now.

Courtney sits down on her bed. "What did Dr. Levinson actually say, Hawk? Doesn't he have any idea what's going on?"

"Oh, sure. The guy's full of ideas. Maybe head injury, maybe stroke, maybe frontal lobe disorder, maybe thyroid, maybe meningitis, maybe depression . . ."

"Depression! Oh, surely not." Hawk is the least depressed person Courtney has ever known.

"Don't be too sure," Hawk says somewhat mysteriously. "Guys like me, we're falling like trees all over America, but nobody's there to hear us yell when we go down."

Courtney can't quite make the connection.

"Just read the statistics," Hawk goes on. "Who do you think is eating all this Prozac?"

"Dr. Levinson didn't put you on Prozac, did he?" Courtney has never heard of anything so ridiculous.

"Sure, Prozac and a bunch of other pills. One day you're a man, the next day you're a laboratory," Hawk says. "But he really won't know much until next week. I've got an appointment on Thursday afternoon."

Thank God, she'll be home. "I'll go with you," Courtney says, feeling better immediately, though she doubts that he'll actually let her do it.

"Great," Hawk surprises her by saying. "That'd be just great. And when are you coming home?"

God. What is *wrong* with everybody? The schedule has been up on the refrigerator for weeks. "Monday night," Courtney says for what seems about the tenth time.

"And when does your plane get in?"

Look at the *schedule,* she thinks. "Seven-forty," she says.

"I'll tell you what. Why don't I pick you up at the airport and take you out to dinner? What do you say? Just the two of us. No reason to rush right home, am I right? I'll see if Tom can give us a table at the Starfish Grille. You can tell me all about the trip."

Just the two of us? Years before, Courtney used to dream of Hawk saying something like this to her, but then she stopped dreaming of it, and now, it's funny, but this is the last thing she wants to hear, the very last. Her heart starts beating too fast.

"Baby? Have we got a date on Monday night?" Hawk pauses, clears his throat. "This thing has got my attention," he says.

"I'll be looking forward to it," Courtney

sings, "and you take it easy in the mean-time, you hear? I hope Mary Bell is taking good care of you."

"Mary Bell is driving me fucking crazy."

Courtney laughs. She puts the receiver down and gathers her things; her heart is still beating too fast.

Courtney keeps up a lively pace in spite of the heat and the road's steep grade into town. What was it Miss Evangeline used to say? Horses sweat, men perspire, and ladies glow. Well, she's surely glowing today!

Theatrically beautiful lilies bloom in the swamp down the hill to her left; she stops to take her camera out of its case and focus it, using the zoom lens. *Click:* the deep freckled pink lilies have dark mysterious centers, black stamens. When photographing flowers, Courtney likes to fit several into the frame. She's not going after anything sexual, no weird Georgia O'Keeffe stuff. She catches a monarch butterfly on a yellow flower, which pleases her, *click*. A white egret stands like a ghost in the murky water near the shady bank, *click*. And then *click* again as it skims the blue flowers, rising over the swamp. She'll call this one "Bird on the Wing." Really this is the most satisfying aspect of photography, the way you can stop time, freeze action forever within the frame. Courtney hastens up the hill, dripping sweat, feeling faint, as if her period is about to start, only it's not of course, she's got her pills timed so she won't be having it in New Orleans as it is not conducive to romance. She attains the top of the hill.

St. Francisville is chock-full of beautiful homes surrounded by live oaks draped with Spanish moss, just the way they're supposed to be. Inviting porches hold wicker furniture and languid green ferns. Everybody on the street nods and smiles, friendly: people down here know how to act, which is not always true back in redneck North Carolina. Courtney snaps first one house, then another. She's *glad* she missed the bus; this is much more fun. She decides to focus on *fences,* as there are so many different kinds of pickets, some of them very original. She can frame them all alike and hang them in the hall, six or eight of them, say, in a nice little grouping. *Click. Click. Click.* Courtney circles the town, stopping in the Button Shop for more film and some lemonade. She buys a brooch made out of antique buttons for Mary Bell, even though it's much too expensive. *A lady doesn't care what it costs. Click,* old men

471

on the bench; *click*, old lady tourist scratching her butt, Gene will get a kick out of that one. She will not think about Gene. *Click*, the guy from the boat in the red muscle shirt stands before a house that he would never be invited to enter, not in a million years. She'll name this one "Louisiana Irony." *Click*, the dusty road starting back down the hill, *click*, the beautiful little United Methodist Church, she grew up Methodist before she became an Episcopalian to marry Hawk. She won't think about him either.

Courtney has already taken three rolls of film by the time she heads back down the hill toward the landing, but she can't resist ducking into the old cemetery here to the right. Suddenly she remembers how her father used to ask, "Now who do you think is in that cemetery?" whenever they passed one on a car trip. And how she and Jean would ask, "Who, Daddy?" and then crack up every time when the answer came: "Dead people." This was their daddy, that sweet old drunk. Courtney scarcely remembers him. Also Gene is a fool for cemeteries, they used to have cemetery picnics all the time. How he'd love this one, the most beautiful cemetery Courtney has ever seen. The old live oaks stretch out their long furry gray arms to form a canopy over an ancient little brick Episcopal church and all the old graves that disappear into the shadows there at the edge of the frame: *click*. White stones rising into consciousness like ideas, like memories, like ghosts; darker, older stones with names too faint to read, souls long lost to time. *Click*. Time has stopped dead in here, this high dim leafy tent where it's always cool with a little breeze that makes a sound you can almost hear as it sighs through the Spanish moss. The trees are so tall that they creak, leaning toward each other, telling old, old secrets.

Courtney stops to reload. *Click*, a wingless angel ("Louisiana Irony #2"). *Click*, a marble boy with his marble dog. *Click*, a marble tree cut down before its time, stump draped in a marble shroud, Louis Chenier, age seventeen years, C.S.A. *Click*, a marble rose that could be paired with a photograph of a real rose from one of these beautiful gardens, "Life and Death," a study in contrasts. Gene said, *"You can choose."* Courtney is the only live person in this cemetery, why is that? She needs to get back to the boat. Is it possible that they would embark without her — just steam away downriver leaving her forever in this poky backward town? Security is certainly lax on the boat, that's for sure; nobody checks you off or on when they dock. So who would know? Her heart starts to flap in her chest like a bird at a windowpane. But she just has to have a drink of water before braving that sun again. Maybe the church is open. Her feet sink down in the long soft grass as she goes around to the front. Thank God, the red door gives inward; Courtney pushes it and steps inside the stone vestibule which smells like her own church, Saint Matthews, the very same smell as every other old Episcopal church in the world. Damp and holy and utterly familiar. But it's dark as a tomb in here. Surely there's a water fountain someplace. She finally finds it in the dimness, a silver cylinder against the wall by the coatroom. The water is icy and bracing. Well! That's better. Courtney dabs it on her temples, too, and at her throat.

She pushes the frosted pane of the door into the sanctuary, where all is light. Not bright light — there is no bright light anywhere beneath this canopy of oaks — but a soft, muted light which seems to rise from the polished shining pews curving in toward each other in a timeless embrace like the oaks themselves; from the white linens on the altar; the gleaming pipes on the old-fashioned organ; the white lilies and baby's breath in the urns, very nice, she has to admit, being an old hand at the altar guild herself; the gold-and-cream-satin standard; the glowing golden cross. Before she knows it, Courtney has knelt and placed her hands on the cool brass rail. A rose glass window shines softly behind the altar. The side windows are stained glass arches depicting familiar scenes: the woman at the well, Jesus holding a woolly sheep. One of these windows has been opened at the top for ventilation, so that a shaft of light falls on Courtney's folded hands. Her wedding ring flashes in the sun. Oh God. What is this, some kind of a sign? But signs don't come to women like her, they come to tacky fat women in revival tents with scraggly hair and flip-flops. Courtney has run the Altar Guild and served on the vestry all these years because she felt she *should*, not because she was hoping for some kind of actual religious experience. Oh God. She remembers Gertrude Marshall, the totally innocuous old maid who served as Saint Matthews's deacon for years, thin little Gertrude Marshall who nevertheless announced from the pulpit that she had had a vision and then proceeded to speak in tongues for the rest of her sermon. Later she started a woman's prayer group named Sisters on Fire. Well! Gertrude Marshall did not last long at Saint Matthews. Episcopalians simply are not into that sort of thing, which is one reason Courtney is an Episcopalian.

Hawk gave her this ring in August after the raft trip; they married in September, at Saint Matthews, of course, in a much smaller ceremony than they would have had if she had been somebody else, somebody more suitable, or if she had stayed in school to graduate. But Hawk was a boy accustomed to getting what he wanted, and right then he'd wanted *her*. And Hawk loved her, he really did; she didn't force him into anything. Even Miss Evangeline seemed pleased, or at least she had borne her disappointment bravely, promising aloud to "do all in her power to uphold these two persons in their marriage," as exhorted by the *Book of Common Prayer*, which has a service for everything. Your whole life is covered by the *Book of Common Prayer.*

Courtney didn't mind not finishing Mary Scott either; she'd had enough school by then anyway, and she'd certainly never needed that degree. Oh God. How many times has she knelt at an Episcopal altar, how many times has she received communion? And yet, as now, she has always been thinking of something else — who to invite to dinner, what to wear, whether she can get a plumber on Sunday afternoon, the little things of life that are holy, too, or so she has always thought, oh, how she loves to set the table with Miss Evangeline's heavy silver, for instance — she sets the loveliest table in town, and it gives her great satisfaction to do so. Gene Minor said her life is a lie, but it's not a lie, it's just complicated. Him and his crazy New Age ideas, his ridiculous demands! Her ring shines like a headlight into the shadows.

Here in this dim old church, everything becomes very clear. Courtney's husband is ill; she needs to fly straight home on Saturday to take care of him. She folds her hands, then bows her head, then stands. Strangely enough, the words come to her in the voice of Gertrude Marshall, who had this little lisp that used to drive Courtney crazy: "The Peath of the Lord be alwayth with you." Courtney turns and walks back up the aisle and out into the oak grove which strikes her now as yet another church, a big leafy cathedral. She feels dwarfed by the giant scale. She reaches for her camera, but stops. This is a picture she can't take, because she's in it. But suddenly she sees herself in the frame anyway, a tourist in a hat, a silly woman in a silly hat in a large, serious landscape — a little figure whose only function is to show perspective, to demonstrate how big the trees are, how ancient it all is, how insignificant she is, we all are. She'll have to call Gene, too.

AT THE CEMETERY

praying hands
crosses
hearts, vines, roses,
doves, lambs,
even a dog or two
the tree cut down
in the prime of life
draped with a shroud
and angels
angels everywhere
fat cheeked cherubs
angels on urns
archangels
angels with trumpets
(you are my angel, he said)

Beyond Care
Friend To All
He hath come and gathered his jewels.
Precious Memories
Our Darling At Rest
Beloved Brother
To forget is vain endeavor,
Love's remembrance lasteth ever.
Blessed be the pure in heart
for they shall see God.
(But do they want to see God?
He scares the hell out of me)
In Loving Memory
In the Bosom of Abraham
At Rest

I was once
as you are
and as I am now
you also shall be

TIPPLING

Mama keeps that little jelly glass
with her all day long
it's never empty
it's never full
When we work in the flowers
it nests in the grass

When we go in the car
I hold it for her
When she reads in the sunroom
it casts rainbows on the wall
pink yellow purple red
It makes everything
             pretty

FOR JEFF

             He's so good
he makes me want to
do bad things
shout bad words
put a cherry bomb
in the crèche
shoot off guns
the way we used to do
on Christmas

NECESSITY

ashes to ashes
dust to dust
come on baby
we must we must

OLD SOUL

Mama said, There's nothing
wrong with Ricky
He gets it, that's all
Ricky is an old soul
You are too
Now be a dear
and bring that jelly glass
over here

CAMERA OBSCURA

How do you do,
Ricky Ballou?
You never knew
How I grew.
The eyes of the dead
are red.
Photographs
of catastrophy.

WATCHDOG

Jeff brings out
the bitch in me.
I try to keep her locked
behind the chain-link fence

where she paces
back and forth.
She's worn a path
in my yard.
When he comes over,
she goes crazy —
charging the fence
leaping over,
tunneling out.
She goes straight for his throat.

THE TRIP TO FRANCE

She passed away
is what we say.
But in point of fact
she died drunk
in a wreck
on Highway 43
heading for Mobile
with her lover.
She left a note behind.
It said she loved us.
Also she loved flowers,
peignoirs, shoes.
Once she had lived in France.
He always drove too fast.
Hit a tree
just south of Demopolis

doing ninety.
Mama died instantly
her neck snapped
just like that.
Today he's a restauranteur
in Boca Raton, Florida.
She didn't even make it
across the county line.
Mama, you slut
you darling

Somehow Harriet has gotten on the wrong bus. Here she is taking the Rosedown and Myrtles tour without anybody else from their group. They must have taken the other tour or the shuttle into town. Somehow she misunderstood. But it's oddly relaxing to sink down into this blue plush seat all by herself, nobody next to her. She doesn't have to talk. It's an enormous relief. All this talking and talking is too much, this is why she feels so hot in spite of the air-conditioning, in spite of her hysterectomy. It's hard to go from living alone to being part of a group — no wonder she's exhausted. Or maybe she needs to have her estrogen adjusted. Maybe she's taking too much. This might account for her silly reaction to the attentions of the Riverlorian, for instance. She knows it's not a big deal, he's just a widower looking for a little company. She tries to pay attention as they tour Rosedown, which really is lovely, especially the gardens, twenty-eight acres in all. Fanciful topiary boxwoods (a duck, a dog, a bell) line a crushed-shell lane winding down to a lily pond ringed with roses. By this time the sun is killing everybody, but the roses love it, you can tell, thrusting their red faces greedily up for more. This part of the garden makes Harriet think of Alice in Wonderland; she scurries back to the bus. She hated the Red Queen.

The Myrtles, also antebellum, is much better, smaller and less grand, set on a gentle hill. It is furnished with French antiques, including a chair that once belonged to Napoleon. Harriet doesn't quite get its bee motif needlepoint upholstery; what did bees have to do with Napoleon? Yet they seem appropriate here, where real bees buzz in and out of the open windows and butterflies flit about the garden just outside.

Harriet lets the tour go on ahead of her. She wanders into the grand hall, empty now, though voices sound like music, or echoes of music, from other parts of the house. She's drawn to the spiral staircase. Soon she's up on the first landing, looking down through the little leaded panes at their silver bus, then she's up on the next landing where she can see the river. A cool breeze comes from somewhere. It lifts the hair off the back of her neck, it touches her skin in a way which is both intimate and familiar. Someone is here. Harriet does not move. The light through the diamond panes grows brilliantly, blindingly bright until it's like an explosion. Harriet whirls around, but she sees nothing. Though someone is still here, very close to her, and then not. Harriet puts her hand on the wall to steady herself while she waits for her vision to clear. Down below they're calling her name. But again her eye is drawn upward, where she perceives a kind of shimmering brilliance, a white radiance on the top landing. The single door beyond it closes silently. Immediately Harriet can breathe again. She can see. She runs down the steps like a girl. In the wide hall below, she almost collides with one of the Myrtles hostesses, a tiny trim silver-haired woman who stares at her curiously out of shiny black eyes like seeds. "Are you all right?" Her voice is sharp.

"Yes," Harriet says after a minute.

"You're not supposed to go upstairs." The woman comes closer. Her minty breath is overpowering. "Did you see something?"

Harriet pulls back. "Why?" she manages to ask.

"This house is haunted, everybody knows it," the woman says matter-of-factly. "Sometimes, certain guests . . . well. We have the ghost of a young woman from New Orleans forced into an unwelcome marriage to the son of this house, who died here mysteriously on her wedding night, whether murdered or killed by her own hand or the hand of God we shall never know; yet she is seen from time to time about the house and stairs, dressed in her wedding gown. Now, did you see her? Did you? Is this what you saw?"

"No." Harriet pushes the little woman aside as easily as if she were a curtain, and rushes out into the day.

"Miss," the woman calls from the door.

But Harriet swings up into the bus whose doors close behind her in a pneumatic wheeze as they pull out.

"Some people don't even consider the rest of the group," a woman's nasal voice says acidly.

"Hey, are you okay?" somebody else asks.

"I'm fine," Harriet announces, which is not true. She's all wrought up. She crumples into her seat. Of course she would be the one; of course it would know her. It *is* her, the way this trip keeps forcing her back again and again to stand outside that door. Perhaps, in a certain way, she even knew this would happen if she came. Miles pass in the steady rumble of the wheels beneath her feet. Voices rise around her; a man laughs. *Ashes to ashes, dust to dust. Come on, baby, we must we must.* Holding her breath, closing her eyes, Harriet pushes the door open.

She'd gone back to school a few days early in the fall after the raft trip, to set up the *Redbud* office and help with registration, one of her scholarship duties. Courtney was already married. Anna was still in West Virginia, teaching drama to kids at some arts program. She'd be back tomorrow. And Baby? Nobody had heard from Baby since New Orleans, and Harriet still hadn't figured out exactly what she'd say to her when she saw her again. Didn't she sleep with that civil rights guy in Natchez? Didn't she?

And why hadn't she called? Or written — at least a postcard? As least to let them know when to expect her. Honestly, she was the most spoiled, most irritating, the most prima donna person Harriet had ever heard of. Harriet hadn't heard from Jeff either, but at least he had a good excuse. He'd been on maneuvers. She wondered when he'd be back, and what would happen next.

Harriet had waked abruptly that night at about 2 a.m. from a sound sleep to see Baby silhouetted against the yellow rectangle of light from the hall door. She knew something was different, something had changed, just from the way Baby stood there, hip cocked, leg thrust out at an angle.

"Hey. Are you asleep? Harriet? Are you asleep?" Baby whispered fiercely, tiptoeing forward.

"No." Harriet sat straight up. "I mean yes, I was, but I'm not now." Then she did exactly what she had promised herself *not* to do. "Oh, Baby, why didn't you write me back? Or call me? Did I do something, say anything, to make you mad? I didn't know what to think."

"Oh no, oh not at all, oh sweetie, I'm so sorry." Baby dropped her bags on the floor and sat down on the edge of Harriet's bed. "I'm sorry, I *should* have called, but I wanted to see you, to tell you in person."

"Tell me what?"

"Don't hate me," Baby said in her little-girl voice. "You've got to promise you won't hate me."

"Hate you! What are you talking about?"

Baby grabbed Harriet's shoulders, hugging her hard. "I broke up with Jeff."

It was funny how Harriet was not surprised. What was it that her mama used to say? "Waiting for the other shoe to drop . . ." In a way, Harriet realized, that's what she'd been doing for some time. Waiting for the other shoe to drop. "When?"

"Last week. I called him when he got back to Richmond from his little war games. I knew before that, but I couldn't get in touch with him to tell him. I knew since the raft trip, actually." She held Harriet tightly to her. "So don't hate me."

"Oh, Baby," Harriet whispered into her smoky hair. She felt that she would burst, literally explode with feeling, yet she couldn't tell, honestly, what emotion it was. Fury? Pain? Hope? A tiny piercing light started burning a hole in her brain. She struggled to get free from Baby, to stand up.

"Harriet — what's the matter?"

"Let me go."

Baby sat back.

Harriet finally stood. "You bitch," she said.

"I can't believe you would do this to him."

Baby stood up, too, her back still to the light; Harriet couldn't see her face. "I was no good for him, Harriet," she said. "He thought I was — oh, I don't know — he made me feel so — he actually wanted me to *marry* him — can you imagine? I mean, can you imagine living on a military base in some godawful place like East Jesus, Georgia, or something?" Harriet could imagine this. But Baby went on. "Listen, he'll be better off, you know he will. He didn't have any business with somebody like me."

"What does that mean, somebody like you? What do you mean when you say that?"

"Nothing. I don't know. I don't mean anything."

"You think you're so special." Harriet was surprised by her own voice.

"You hate me, don't you? You hate me, too." Baby took a deep, ragged breath. "I don't blame you, any of you."

"Oh, quit being so melodramatic! What is it, you met some other guy, is that it?"

"No, I told you, I just *decided*, that's all. This is the only good thing I've done in ages, and now you're trying to make me feel bad about it."

"So who's the new boy?"

"There's not any new boy, I'm telling you. I mean, I *did* meet somebody, actually, but he's not a boy, he's this businessman from Memphis that knows Daddy. Anyway, I'm not going to marry him or anybody else. Jeff got too damn serious. I just want to have some fun, what's wrong with that?"

"But you're not —," Harriet started.

"Not what?"

"Not having fun."

"I am, too!" Baby stomped her foot. "I am so having fun. I always have fun. What do you know? You don't know anything about it." She was breathing hard in the dark room. "Okay, so this guy is my kind, and Jeff was not my kind. But that doesn't have anything to do with me and Jeff. You know me better than anybody in the world, Harriet. You're my best friend. I don't know why you're being so mean."

Harriet went over and sat at her desk, looking out at the dark campus, at the dark moving trees, at the light from the lamp-post making its shiny path across the duck pond. It seemed — almost — no. For a second, Harriet thought she had seen something moving beneath the water. She turned back. "Look, what does Jeff have to say about all this?"

"He doesn't get it either, not yet. But he will. You know I'm right." Baby put two cigarettes in her mouth and lit them and gave one to Harriet. Her face flared up for a minute in the light from the match.

Harriet inhaled deeply. It made her a little dizzy. It helped.

"Hey," Baby said after a while. "I forgot to tell you, I've got this cute new little car, wait till you see it. It's a red convertible."

Of course it is, Harriet thought.

The next afternoon Baby talked Anna and Harriet into shooting some pool down at the Cabin on Route 86, where she was a favorite with the locals. "Hi, Freddie," she called to the proprietor, big and grinning, who brought them three beers on the house and then stood there moving his mouth.

"H-how are my g-g-g-girrls?" he finally said.

"Great." Baby had a glint in her eye as she broke the balls, pounding her cue stick on the floor when the four ball went into the corner pocket. Harriet was sure Baby knew that those two old truckers were standing behind her, watching her shoot, sure that was why she paused for so long with her ass stuck up in the air. "Two,"

493

Baby said, and made it, and made the five ball and the six ball, too. She ran five balls before she missed. "Not bad for the first day back at Freddie's," she said, lifting her beer to him before she drained it.

"You drink too fast," Anna said, chalking her cue.

"I drink as fast as I drink." Baby sat back down at the table with Harriet and they shot pool all afternoon, and Baby did not mention Jeff then or later, not once during the whole next week, so Harriet didn't either, though she thought about him all the time, wondering how he was taking it, wondering what he was doing, how he felt. She thought about the time he cried for his father and how he looked in his uniform. She thought about the little vertical line that appeared between his eyebrows when he was worried or when he was figuring something out. Harriet found herself making excuses to stay in the room, by the phone, but he didn't call. Of course, he would never show up in the middle of the night yelling for Baby outside the window like that boy had done freshman year, that was not Jeff's style, but Harriet had thought at least he'd call. At least he'd call *her*. But he never did. Two weeks passed. Harriet thought about calling him, just to see how he was doing, but she couldn't, somehow. Another week went by.

"Tell me again where you're going," she said to Baby, who was in a turmoil of packing on a Friday afternoon.

"I told you." Baby slammed her suitcase shut. "It's a hotel named the Homestead, in Virginia. A resort, actually. It's very famous."

"I never heard of it."

"Well, so what? You wouldn't have, necessarily." Baby was brushing her hair. She made a face at herself in the mirror. "He likes makeup," she said. "Look, he bought me some." She showed Harriet the silver bag full of little silver tubes and pots, then poured it out on the top of her dresser. Baby outlined her eyes in black, followed by mascara. "Well, what do you think?" She batted her eyelashes at Harriet in the mirror. "Come on, try some of it. He got it in New York. It's very expensive."

"I'll bet." Harriet went to stand beside her, then chose the green eyeliner and drew it across her eyelids.

"Oh, wow," Baby said, looking at her. "Here."

Harriet put on the mascara.

"Now look at yourself," Baby said. "Don't you look pretty?"

"No."

"Oh, come on. Of course you do! And now for some lipstick. He likes red." Baby's mouth turned into a bright slash. She giggled at herself in the mirror. "Oh God, I look like a whore. Don't I look just like a whore?"

"Yes," Harriet said. Then she said, "Just kidding," when Baby threw a tube of lipstick at her.

"I was just wondering," Baby said in a carefully offhand voice as she pulled the black sweaterdress down over her head, "if you've heard anything from Jeff." Her face was covered up by the dress when she said his name.

"No, why?" Harriet tried to sound as casual as Baby.

"Oh — I — I just wondered. Sometimes I really miss him," she said, smoothing the dress down over her hips.

"You need to wear stockings with that dress," Harriet said. Anna stuck her head in the door.

Baby made a face. "Oh, y'all know I can't stand them," she said. "Not even to go to the Homestead. Okay!" She put on her leather jacket and grabbed her bag. "See you Sunday." She looked really glamorous, like a girl in a magazine.

"Baby, this is stupid," Harriet said.

"Don't you know how dangerous those little planes are?" The man from Memphis was picking her up at the airport in his private plane.

"Yes," Baby said.

"Don't we get to meet him?" Anna asked.

"*No*," Baby said. "Honestly, you wouldn't want to," and then she was gone. Anna went to the library.

Harriet sat on her bed and stared at the phone until it rang, startling her. It was as if she had willed it. "Hello?" she said, picking it up. "Hello?" No answer. Harriet hung up. Wrong number. Or . . . her heart started pounding and everything around her went into sharp relief. It was up to her. She should go over there and tell him what Baby had said. Then they'd get back together. She stood up, trying to breathe. She went over to Baby's dresser and looked at herself in the mirror and put on some lipstick, a dusty pink, and some blush. There now. "Okey-dokey," as Jill used to say. Then she walked straight over to Miss Auerbach's house and asked to borrow her car which turned out to be an ancient humpbacked Vauxhall, a kind of car Harriet had never heard of. Miss Auerbach called the car "Jane Austen."

Jane Austen slowed down to forty miles per hour on the uphill grades of Route 81, which was okay, since Harriet needed to slow down anyway, to fix this day forever in her mind. Luckily it was beautiful. There were times when the Blue Ridge really looked *blue,* and this was one of them, the huge blue mountains spiking the horizon, then closer, grassy hills rolling out like waves, dotted with farms and cows and fields and dark-green patches of standing trees. In a week it would be autumn. But for now it was summer still, the noon sun spread out thick and golden as butter over everything, the sky a vast dome which reminded Harriet of some cathedral from art history, Della Robbia blue.

But it was a football weekend in Lexington, with home games at both SMI and W&L. The hilly little streets were jammed with cars, and guys and dates with their arms entwined, jaywalking haphazardly. " 'Lo Harriet!" yelled Frannie Kernodle from the *Redbud* staff, while one of the W&L Dekes that Harriet knew slapped the Vauxhall's puke-green flank in greeting, as if it were a horse. Harriet had been hoping she would not run into anybody she knew, especially not Trent Ogilvie, a Phi Delt, who had asked her up this weekend. Trent was a nice enough guy, no sense in hurting his feelings. Harriet drove past the infamous Liquid Lunch, where things were already hopping, and turned left down Washington Street to the big old brick house on the corner where Jeff and a couple of other cadets had rented the basement apartment, dirt cheap. The house, owned by the historical society, was due for renovation next year. In the meantime, wasn't it nice to have these upstanding young cadets as part-time caretakers? Harriet could imagine how the initial interview had gone, the wonderful impression Jeff had made. *She* would have rented it to them, that's for sure, and closed her eyes to the girls who showed up on the weekends and the occasional beer cans, always picked up later, in the overgrown formal garden. Harriet loved this garden with its old stone walls and its mossy green fountain, a boy holding a fish which dribbled water down the boy's chubby tummy. She parked on the street and entered the garden through the heavy wooden gate. She didn't really expect anybody to be there — after all, it *was* a big weekend. Shenandoah Military Institute was playing Virginia Polytechnic Institute from Blacksburg, down the road, a traditional rivalry and a very big deal. Harriet didn't really expect to see Jeff. He'd be over on campus. Maybe he even had a date. She could just leave him a note.

But first Harriet sat down on the big warm rock at the top of the garden in the sun, feeling curiously drowsy. Bees buzzed. Sunflowers nodded by the wall. As she sat on the rock, surrounded by bees and mint, Harriet's head felt as heavy as a sunflower. She might have slept for a little while. In any case she woke up filled with energy, heart in her throat, pulse pounding just behind her temple. She could hear a band playing somewhere. Down the hill, the garden lay gold and dreamy in the sun. The blue hydrangea bush by the back door was dusty, droopy; a scarlet leaf came spiraling down through the crystal air to land like an arrow, pointed at Harriet's foot. She stood, looking down at it. I'm going to remember this, she thought, for the rest of my life.

She walked down the hill and pushed the door open. "Hello?" she called. "It's me." Somehow she knew he was there. She made her way through the pizza boxes, beer cans, and Coke cans which littered the kitchen floor. Flies buzzed around an overflowing trash can; the sink was full of dishes. An open copy of *Steppenwolf* lay on the kitchen counter. She kept going.

Jeff half lay, half sat up against the pillows in the old brass bed in the first bedroom, holding a water glass. The bed had been pushed against the open window. He turned his head toward Harriet, but slowly, as if he were blind. With its gray stone walls and its only window blocked by branches, the bedroom was almost dark. Of course they were partly underground. Jeff was looking at her. He had several days' growth of beard.

"Harriet," he said. "You're here." He did not smile. His dark eyes had circles under them.

Harriet sat gingerly on the edge of the bed. "You look awful," she said.

"I haven't slept," he said.

"Since when?"

"Since, oh . . ." His voice trailed off.

Harriet tried again. "Shouldn't you be at the game?" she said. "Don't you have to march or something?"

Jeff smiled at her, a tired smile, as if he were very old. "Oh, honey," he said, "I'm through with all that." He lifted the glass and drank and Harriet saw the pint bottle of Gilbey's gin on the windowsill.

"What do you mean?" she asked.

501

"I quit." His grin was weird, jagged, different. "In fact, I'm going to enlist."

"Soldier boy," Harriet said before she remembered that this was what Baby had always called him.

"Soldier boy," Jeff said.

"Don't do that. Don't enlist."

"I have to," he said. "I have to do something."

"Can I have a drink?" Harriet edged closer, across the dirty sheets.

"You don't need a drink."

"I want one."

"No, you don't." Jeff drained his glass and turned to look at her. The light coming in through the leaves was a pale, strange greeny-gold. "What *do* you want, Harriet? Why did you come over here anyway?"

"I wanted to tell you . . . I wanted . . ." Harriet couldn't talk.

"What?" Jeff's eyes were like holes in his head.

"You," Harriet said simply. "I've always wanted you." It was the truth. She held her breath. Jeff turned to her with a groan, his eyes dark and unreadable. "Look at me," she said. Jeff came close to her then. He touched her face, cupping her chin for a moment to stare in her eyes. He put his hand on her knee then ran a finger up the inside of her leg. He was going away but it didn't matter. *This*. She would have this, touching the little hollow at the base of his neck. "Oh, Harriet," he said into her hair. Then he was unbuttoning her blouse and it was on the floor. She was all wet "down there," as Alice always said, whatever went on down there? Harriet used to wonder but now she knew it was the Fourth of July, the bright explosions and sparks spinning off into darkness. "My God, Harriet," he said and she was lying across his bed, she had never wanted to be anywhere else in the world. She knew it then. He would go away but she didn't care, this would be hers, this open window this droning bee the hot little wind like a zephyr from a poem the smell of the mint and honeysuckle. His face above her, the boyface she had always loved. He moves over her now like a storm, like the pouring rain. She can't see a thing but him. He kicks off his cutoffs, oh, he can do whatever he wants. This is Harriet rising to meet him, it's Gypsy Park and they're swinging in the late gray afternoon higher and higher, higher and higher, up even with the bars then out into the sweet open air and they're flying through it up and up and up into the endless sky. She kissed his face and tasted salt. "Oh Harriet honey," he said into her neck. Later he made a funny little noise that was not quite a snore but more like a bird flying, like the rush of a bird's wings, while he slept through the long afternoon, his arm flung across her chest. Harriet did not sleep. She stayed awake while a beam of sunlight came in through the curtain of leaves and moved slowly across the room to touch the satiny heartpine floor, the dully glowing brass bedrail. Harriet rubbed her fingers back and forth on the rough stone wall, her toes on the gritty sheet, listening to the faraway sound of marches.

She sat by the phone for the next two weeks, willing it to ring, willing it to be for her. But it was always for Baby. "Just a minute," she'd say, handing the receiver over, or "I'll see if she's around," if it was somebody Baby might not want to talk to, or "She's not here right now, can I take a message?" when she was out. She was out a lot — with James Flood, the rich mysterious Memphis businessman who kept flying over to see her in his private plane; with Lap-Dog Brown, a Sigma Nu from W&L; with Red Robertson, a local greaser, a mechanic she'd met at Freddie's.

"Oh, come on," Baby teased her. "You know I like a little rough trade." But Harriet hated the way Red wore his T-shirts too tight, cigarettes rolled up in his sleeve, she hated the way he looked at you, she hated his hooded eyes. Harriet sat by the phone reading long English novels for Miss Auerbach's class, trying not to imagine Jefferson Carr in his bed in his room across the mountains, all that pale green light. She wrote a pretty good paper on Thomas Hardy. She flunked her chemistry midterm. She did not climb Morrow Mountain on Mary Scott Day, watching the other girls instead. First they all converged upon the front quad, wearing crazy clothes, to the traditional ringing of the bell which announced the surprise cancellation of classes. Then they set off up the country road for the mountain in a long straggling line, later to be glimpsed as little figures up on Scott Knob, toy girls, waving their tiny hands across the sparkling air. Harriet could barely see them.

It was finally fall. Harriet had found him again last fall, a million years ago. Now other girls and their dates sat on the grass around the duck pond, as *they* had once sat; Harriet watched them from her window. She imagined their conversations.

Leaves drifted down past the window, turning slowly in the air. Wasn't there some O. Henry story about some sick girl who believed she wouldn't die until all the leaves fell off the tree outside her window? And then some artist went out in the cold and painted one leaf onto the window so she wouldn't die but then he caught pneumonia out there and died himself? Miss Auerbach would *hate* that story if anybody wrote it and turned it in now — Miss Auerbach hated trick endings. She considered them cheating. Also, trick endings were not postmodern.

"Oh Lord." Baby came in, dropped her books, and sank down on the bed. "I keep wondering how he is."

Harriet's heart began to flutter in her chest. "You mean Jeff, I take it?"

Baby nodded, biting her lip, staring out the window.

"Well, I'm sure he's just fine, why wouldn't he be?" Harriet said.

Baby looked over at her. "What's the matter with you? Are you mad about something?"

Harriet shook her head no. "Of course not. Let's go on over to the dining room and eat dinner early," she suggested, but Baby said she was on her way to the Cabin and left, jingling her keys.

The phone rang.

"Is this Baby?" a somehow familiar voice asked.

"No, it's Harriet. Baby's not here right now."

"This is Kyle" — one of Jeff's housemates, Harriet held her breath — "Listen, I know they're supposed to be broken up and all, but I thought Baby might have heard from Jeff or something. Fact is, he's disappeared. Nobody knows where he is."

"What do you mean, disappeared?"

"He's just *gone*. It's the weirdest thing. I guess we didn't realize it at first because he left all his stuff here, or lots of it anyway." Kyle had a flat Midwestern accent.

"What kind of stuff?" Harriet asked cautiously.

"Clothes, books, you know, the works. Albums. Everything. But he's definitely gone. No note, no nothing. We can't figure it out. I thought Baby might have heard from him."

"No, she hasn't." Harriet's own voice rang hollow in her ears, distorted, as if she were calling down into a well or a tunnel.

"Harriet?"

"Sorry, I'm here."

"Yeah, well, please call me if you or Baby hear from him, or if anybody else does. You can get me at school, or on weekends at the house. You know. Or you can call Price." Rick Price was the other housemate. "I think Jeff will call her. It's her fault anyway. Man, is he ever messed up! You haven't ever seen anybody so messed up."

"I know."

"This whole thing is such a bitch because once you're out of the institute, they act like you're dead. They act like they never heard of you. But I guess I'll have to go over to the office anyway and try to get his sisters' phone numbers, and call them," Kyle said. "You know both his parents are dead."

"I know," Harriet said again. Later, she could not remember the rest of their conversation.

After they hung up, she lay down and stayed there all afternoon, skipping supper. Finally Baby came back and went to sit on the edge of Harriet's bed, stroking her hair. "Harriet, are you awake? Harriet?" She smelled like smoke.

Harriet breathed in deeply and kept her eyes closed.

"Harriet?"

"Oh, hi. I'm not feeling very well," Harriet said, which was true. She sat up on her elbows and steeled herself to do it. "Listen, Baby, you got a phone call."

Baby sat back. "Who was it?"

Harriet hesitated. Then she said, "Elise. She said to call her back tomorrow."

"Oh. Okay. You want me to get you a Coke or anything? I can run down to the snack bar."

"A Coke would be great," Harriet said. "And maybe some nabs?"

When Baby had left the room, Harriet sat up and snapped on the light. The clock read eight-thirty, that's all, she'd thought it was later than that. She looked around the room as if she were seeing it for the very first time: Baby's bed piled high with clothes and books, her jumbled desk; Harriet's neat desk, her own closet door neatly closed. Her own framed print of Monet's *Water Lilies* on the wall. Baby's Janis Joplin and Elvis posters, the Slow Children sign she'd ripped off the road by faculty row, the dead roses in a florist vase. Harriet saw all these things as if they held a secret that could be decoded, as if she were an anthropologist. Everything seemed significant. This was our room, mine and Baby's, she said to herself, at Mary Scott College,

1965. That kind of thrumming began behind her ears and then she was gulping air and then Baby came back.

"Here," Baby said, handing over the Coke.

"Thanks." Harriet sipped it, and the hard bright edge went off of things. "Thanks," she said again. She looked at Baby. "So what have you been up to? You and —"

"Red." Baby took off her T-shirt and dropped it on the floor. "Same old thing." She grinned. "Actually we went up to the quarry."

Where you went with Jeff and me.

"You know what Red can do?" Baby asked.

"What?"

"He picked up this green lizard? This little green lizard that was running across the rock out there? And then he said, 'Watch this,' and held it up to his head and the lizard bit his earlobe and hung on like an earring. It stayed till he took it off. It was the most amazing thing."

"I guess so." Harriet could see it all: the dark water, the rocks, the iridescent lizard swinging from Red's ear.

"So, are you getting up or going back to bed or what? I mean, I can read out in the study room —"

"Oh no." Harriet sat up and swung her feet out of bed. "I've got to study for French. So stay here," she said. "With me."

Several days later, Harriet came back to their room from the library, dropped her books on the floor, switched on the light, and jumped to find Baby sitting in a chair at the window looking out at the late gray afternoon. "Oh!" she said. "I didn't know you were here."

"I'm not, really," Baby said. She turned slowly to look at Harriet. She was wearing her old jeans jacket. "Jeff's in the army," she said.

"He is? How do you know?" Harriet sat down on the edge of her bed.

"Rick called a little while ago."

"But where is he, exactly?"

"He's in basic training, I guess, in some horrible place. I mean, *I* don't know. I don't care. I don't even know why Rick called me anyway, it's got nothing to do with me. Nothing, nothing, nothing. That's what I told him, too. I said, just leave me out of it. I don't care. It's none of my business. I don't give a damn." Now Harriet could tell that Baby was quietly, terribly, agitated. She stood up so abruptly that her chair fell over. "I'm going out to the Cabin for a while," she said, jingling her car keys. She slammed the door and was gone.

When Harriet went over to pick up the chair, she saw the crumpled slip of paper half under the bed: Jeff's address at Fort Benning, Georgia. She smoothed it out and put it in her desk drawer.

Harriet had written him several letters, with no response, when the phone rang early on a Tuesday morning just after Thanksgiving break. She sat up in bed and looked over at Baby who was still sound asleep, face lost in the dark tangle of her hair. Outside it was barely light. The phone rang again. Harriet got up and grabbed it. "Hello," she said.

"This is Marianne Carr Kingsley," Jeff's older sister said in her cultured Tidewater drawl. "Could I please speak with Margaret Ballou, er, *Baby?*"

"This is Baby," Harriet said immediately, looking over at Baby who did not stir.

"I'm afraid I have some terrible news." But the sister's voice remained neutral, expressionless. "Jefferson is dead. He was killed in a helicopter accident down at Fort

Benning where he was in basic training. But I guess you already know all that."

"*What* happened?" Harriet can't seem to talk right.

"I'm sorry — I can't hear you."

"What happened?"

"We were notified two days ago by a summary courts officer, a man who also knew him, apparently. Basically Jefferson was on a training mission. It was a troop lift in a Huey helicopter which had just taken off with a full load of fuel when it crashed into a field and burned. They're still investigating, but they think it was hydraulic failure, the man said. We haven't gotten the full report yet, of course. He said everybody on the helicopter died instantly, the pilot and six recruits. Nobody even got out before it went up in flames. It was at night, Friday night." Then Jeff's sister seemed to choke or strangle. "This never would have happened if he'd stayed at school. If he hadn't signed up," she said. "He could have had a commission. He'd still be alive. What did you do?" Now she was screaming. *"What did you do to him?"*

Harriet replaced the receiver carefully and got up and went to stand at the window. In a way, Jeff's sister was right. But it was *her* fault, it was all her fault:

Harriet's fault, not Baby's. She could have told Jeff that Baby missed him — it was all she had to do. He would have driven straight over here, they would have made up, he wouldn't have dropped out of the institute, he wouldn't have joined the army. "Soldier boy, oh my little soldier boy, I'll be true to you." The words from the pop song ran through her head. She had danced to that song at a recent fraternity party at W&L with a boy she had never seen before and would never see again.

Harriet looked out the window at the cold, overcast campus. The still surface of the duck pond shone like pewter. A girl in a black raincoat walked down the path between the boxwoods and was gone. Shivering, Harriet hugged herself, squeezing her arms to make sure she was real. For suddenly she *was* that girl, disappearing entirely into the boxwood hedge. And it was cold in here, too. Harriet stared down into the dark where Jeff blazed up suddenly out of the blackness, outlined in flames, his burning arms outstretched as if to push her away, his mouth a round black screaming O. NO — a round black screaming NO. Harriet wanted to go to him but she was cold, just so cold, and she couldn't get there, her feet wouldn't move. All she could do was cry, or maybe that was Baby crying. Now Baby was crying, too.

Harriet was sick then. First she was sick in bed, then she was sick in the infirmary where Nurse Pam gave her tapioca pudding and said she would be all right (*liar, liar, pants on fire*), then she was sick at home with Alice flitting in and out of her bedroom, the front room she had shared for so long with Jill, Dr. Piccolo standing lugubriously in the doorway. He had a way of clicking his teeth that Harriet had never noticed before, it drove her wild. "Call me Ed," he always said, but Harriet never could. She went back to school and took her exams but then she was home again. It was like she had never left except that Alice had suddenly grown so old. She looked like a crumpled pastel doll version of herself, or like an ancient child, one of those children that have that weird disease that they're born old, whatever it's called.

"Ed!" Alice cried from Harriet's bedside. "Whatever is the matter with her? Can't you do something?"

Dr. Piccolo shook his head and clicked his teeth. Alice smoothed Harriet's top sheet, patted her shoulder, and followed him out of the room. Harriet looked around. There sat her foreign doll collection on top of the bureau, her schoolbooks in the nightstand, Jill's paperweights on their shelves in front of the window. She saw the same view out the window from her bed as always: the red neon Jefferson Hotel sign, the white branches of the birch tree which grew beside the entrance to the sewing shop below, the Lucky Strike sign on the top of the Connor Building across the street, the roofs of the taller buildings beyond it, and someplace in that direction, someplace she couldn't see from here, Gypsy Park. Harriet closed her eyes but could not sleep.

Dr. Piccolo brought her three kinds of medication: a flat yellow pill, a round red pill, and two pale green capsules to take at night. They helped. She stayed in bed and read the books she could find in the apartment: *Babbitt, The Call of the Wild, How to Win Friends and Influence People, Butterfield Eight.* Dr. Piccolo came into her room at night and touched her face and her breasts. Harriet pretended to sleep; this seemed easiest. But then he began doing other things to her, too. Once she decided to tell her mother, but when she got up her nerve and went in the kitchen she found him and Alice playing rummy at the round oak table, bare feet entwined beneath it, in the rosy glow of the hanging Tiffany lamp. "Call-Me-Ed" was in an undershirt; Alice wore the pink silk wrapper of another day.

"So whaddya got?" Dr. Piccolo's hairy back was to Harriet, who stood in the dark. "Huh? Whaddya got?"

"Gin!" Alice slapped the cards down with a flourish, then burst into giggles. She ran around the table to sit in his lap. "So you've got to pay up, big boy. Now what have you got for your little girl?"

Harriet backed silently into the bedroom. The next day she answered an ad in the paper and got a part-time job in medical records at the famous hospital up on the hill where Jeff's mother had stayed for so long. That summer she also took four courses, two each session, at UVA's summer school, sharing a dorm room with a Mennonite nursing student.

Back at Mary Scott for senior year, Harriet moved into the single room she had requested in Ransom Hall. Anna had a single room in Cabell while Baby roomed with Catherine Wilson, in Oglethorpe. Four new freshmen had the Tower Suite in Old South. Harriet got a good look at them as she drove past the familiar old dorm in the Volkswagen that Mr. Carr had bought her from beyond the grave. Three of the new Tower Suite freshmen were carrying an old red leather sofa across the grass, while the fourth shouted encouragement down from the front window of what used to be Courtney's room. The new girl's long blond hair hung down from the window like Rapunzel's, in a golden rope.

A note from Courtney had been waiting in Harriet's mailbox, written on heavy new informal stationery, engraved with her new initials, C. G. R. Harriet tore it open in the post office. "Of course I have not gotten any sleep since Scott was born," Courtney wrote, "but somehow I don't even care. Isn't he cute??? I don't need to sleep, I am so happy. I never knew I could love anything or anybody so much as I love this baby. I will bring him up to see you all later on. XOXOXO, Courtney." The baby's picture was inside: a funny little thing with a pointed head like a little cap, and squinty eyes.

"Oooh! Let me see!" It was Catherine, grabbing the letter, hugging Harriet. "Oh shit, look at his head! Do you think he's all right?"

"I think Courtney would tell us if he

wasn't, don't you? She's always been pretty up front about things," Harriet said.

"I guess so. But my goodness, just look at *you!*" Catherine hugged Harriet again and then held her out at arm's length. "You look different," she announced. "What's different about you? Aren't you doing something different with your hair?"

Harriet shook her head no. "You just forgot," she said. "I haven't seen you all for almost a year, remember. It's just the same old me."

But Catherine continued to peer closely at her as they walked out under the giant oaks of the front quadrangle. "That's not true, is it?" Catherine said. "Something has changed. What is it, Harriet?"

Harriet shook her head. *"Nothing,"* she said. "I told you, I had mono, remember? And then it was too late in the semester to come back to Mary Scott so I got a job and went to summer school at UVA."

"So, how's your mom?" Catherine sat down on the miller's stone and lit a cigarette.

"Fine."

"And the doctor?"

"Hirsute as ever." Harriet sat down beside her on the huge stone, still warm from the day's sun.

Catherine laughed. "That word was actually on my college board test. And now we're graduating. Well, I'm ready to be out of here. You know, Howie has already gotten two raises at his job. And he loves it." After one of the world's longest engagements, Catherine's wedding was still nine months away. "Exactly like a pregnancy," she said, scooting across the rough stone to hug Harriet. "I'm just so glad to see you! But now tell me the truth — what's with you and Baby?"

"What do you mean?"

"She says you never wrote her back or answered her calls or anything after you left last year. It really hurt her feelings, Harriet."

Harriet studied the grass, too green.

"Harriet? Tell me?"

Harriet sighed and took off her sandals, digging her feet into the grass. "It's a long story," she said.

"Well, *she* still wants to be friends. You know she got pretty messed up after Jeff died, everybody did, but she took it the hardest, of course. She got skinnier and skinnier and Nurse Pam made her go see this psychiatrist in Roanoke twice a week, or they said they would send her home. But now, guess what?"

"What?"

"She's engaged, too! To this older guy named Charlie Mahan that she's known all her life practically, I think he may even be her cousin although of course I'm sure it's her third or fourth cousin once removed or something like that. Baby says he's from 'the Delta' like it's a big deal or something."

"Charlie Mahan?" A sudden image of Charlie Mahan came into Harriet's mind as he had appeared when she went down to Alabama for the cousin's debut party, sophomore year — Charlie Mahan showing up at the airport in his big blue pickup truck, throwing Harriet's suitcase into the back, helping her up into the cab in courteous, cowboy fashion. Baby always claimed Charlie wasn't "all that smart" but he was clearly nice, one of the nicest boys Harriet could ever remember meeting. Too nice for Baby, went through her mind. Somehow she remembered that he had dropped out of Ole Miss to go home and run his family's farm when his dad got sick.

"The wedding is set for the end of June, three weeks after mine," Catherine said with evident satisfaction that hers was first. "Just after Howie and I get back from Bermuda."

"I always thought Baby would go to graduate school," Harriet said.

"No, she's not," Catherine said. "You know what I think? I think she's just *tired,* Harriet. I think she's all worn out. It's real hard to be Baby. I think she wants a normal life now, somebody to take care of her, and I must say, I don't blame her. I, for one, am real happy for her. Didn't you know she dropped out of the writing workshop?"

"Really? When?"

"Oh, way back last spring. Well, look, speak of the devil, here she is now! You'll see. She's missed you, Harriet." Catherine touched Harriet's hand lightly for emphasis; Harriet jumped back. Baby! In a way Harriet could not explain, she felt that Baby had died, too. She was as dead as Jeff, though here she came, loping across the grass with her big stride and her big lopsided grin. Harriet shrank back on the miller's stone.

"Hey, *Harriet!*" Baby leaned down and hugged Harriet fiercely. Her hair was much shorter, cut in a trim pageboy. She had gained weight. She didn't look so haunted.

Even her hands looked different, ragged nails now manicured. She wore a short flowered shift and sandals, legs as long and bare and tan as ever. "Oh, Harriet, I've missed you so much — how are you?"

"Fine —" Harriet said, then stopped cold. She swallowed. She remembered what Mama used to say to Jill: Cat got your tongue?

"Well, I've got to go see the registrar, right now. See y'all later." Catherine stood and left.

"Me too." Harriet jumped up.

Baby looked at her quizzically. "So, is that how you feel? You don't want to be friends anymore? You don't want to see me now?"

"Of course I do," Harriet was lying. "Don't be crazy." Though actually she couldn't really see Baby at all from this angle, with the sun in her eyes.

"That's exactly what I'm trying to do — not be crazy," Baby said.

"Well, did it ever occur to you that maybe you ought to try that on your own? That maybe you don't have to have a boy around all the time?" Harriet was amazed to hear herself actually say this, though she knew immediately it was true.

"Charlie isn't a boy, he's a man. He's really nice. Don't you remember him? He picked you up at the airport that time you came at Christmas for Nina's party?"

"I didn't really talk to him," Harriet said.

Baby moved over so the sun was no longer in Harriet's eyes and looked straight at her. "Oh, come on," she said. "Charlie *knows* me. He knows all about me. And he still loves me. Don't you want me to be happy?"

"Sure. Great. Be happy. Now I really do have to go over to the registrar's office, I've got to make sure I get credit for those summer school courses I took" — Harriet stopped — "Oh, Baby," she said. "Why did you do it? Why did you ever break up with him anyway?"

Baby threw her arms around Harriet again. "I'm sorry," she said. "I'm so sorry. Sometimes I just run out on people, I don't *know* why. I just can't help it. Please don't hate me anymore."

"Hate you? I don't hate you," Harriet said into her hair.

"So we're friends again? We're okay?" Baby sounded doubtful, pulling back to look at her. She ran her finger along Harriet's cheekbone.

"We're okay," Harriet said, giving Baby

everything she wanted, everything she had to have, and oddly enough it *was* okay, though it would never be the same, and that was as close as they would ever come to talking about it.

All during their Friday morning tour of
River Road Plantation, Harriet keeps whispering that she doesn't feel well. Courtney
practically has to drag her down the long
alley of arching live oaks, almost like a
tunnel, back up the levee and onto the *Belle*
for lunch.

"I really think I ought to just lie down,"
Harriet says as they enter the dining room.

"Nonsense." Courtney seats herself and
wipes her face with her napkin. She
doesn't care if all her makeup comes off or
not, she's too *hot* to care. Plus there is certainly nobody on this boat she wants to impress, that's for sure. "You need to eat
something, preferably something with
some salt in it."

"I could order the gazpacho," Harriet finally says.

"The gazpacho would be perfect.

Actually I have two really good gazpacho recipes, remind me to send them to you. They're both real easy — basically, just a big can of tomato juice and some vegetables in a blender. I often serve it on the patio in the summer, in a cup, before we go to dinner." Somehow, since Courtney has renounced romance, it comforts her to think about her house: about her beautiful slate patio, for instance, with its big urn of flowers, its ferns, its bougainvillea trellises.

Maurice crosses the dining room toward them with his pigeon-toed, athletic gait.

"I think we should go ahead," Courtney says. "Why should we wait for the others? Who knows when they'll be here?"

"Good afternoon, ladies. Ready to order?" Maurice asks.

"I'll take the club sandwich and french fries and a glass of Chardonnay, please." Courtney orders crisply. She sits back. She's beginning to feel better.

"Ma'am?" Maurice turns to Harriet.

"I'll have the gazpacho and, well, I haven't quite decided . . ."

"Oh, go on! Just pick something. Pick *anything!*" Courtney's fed up with Harriet's constant indecision. It's ridiculous, really. It's hard to see how Harriet ever gets anything done at all, much less hold down an obviously demanding position at a college, even if it is only a community college.

"How about a beverage, then? I can come back later for the rest of your order."

"Sweet tea," Harriet says.

"No wine?" Maurice's pen is poised over his order pad.

"Oh, come on, drink a glass of wine with me." Courtney touches Harriet's arm.

"*No!*" Harriet says, then flushes. "I mean, no thanks, just tea for now, please, and I guess I'll just do the salad bar." That way, she still doesn't have to decide anything. "Honestly, I've never had as much to drink in my whole life as I have on this trip. It's making me feel funny."

"What do you mean, feel funny?"

"Not myself. I'm not quite myself," Harriet says. "Haven't you noticed?"

"Well, I must say, you seem to have relaxed a little since we left Memphis, but that's the whole point of a cruise, isn't it?"

"No, it is *not* the whole point. You know what the point is." Harriet grips the edge of the table.

"I know." Courtney takes a sip of her Chardonnay. "Of course. But there's nothing wrong with enjoying the trip, Harriet, no reason why you shouldn't appreciate Pete's attentions, for instance. He seems to be a perfectly nice man, as far as I can see. What's wrong with him?"

"Nothing. That's the problem." Harriet twists her napkin, looking down. Bright spots of color dot her cheeks making her look, for all the world, like a Raggedy Ann doll.

"Then why don't you just try to have a little fun, for a change? I would, if I were you. Anybody would. Come on. How many unattached men do you think you'll meet, at your age? You'd be a fool to pass up a date in New Orleans, especially with a man who really knows the city."

"But —" Harriet looks absolutely miserable.

"But what?" Courtney leans forward to grab her pointy elbow. "Harriet, look at me. This is not normal. What's wrong with you?"

Tears stand in Harriet's eyes when she finally raises her head. "I don't know," she says.

"Well, then." Courtney has to talk fast; the dining room is filling up with other sightseers, straggling in. Soon, the rest of the chairs at their table will be filled except for Anna's, of course. Anna refuses to have any fun either. She's always shut up in her stateroom, working. "Harriet, just listen to me. I've got a room reserved at the Royal Orleans for the weekend, in my name. Since I'll be flying on home, you can have it."

"Oh, I could never —"

"Free. With my blessings!" Courtney speaks from a great saintly distance.

"Courtney, it's not the money —" Actually Harriet has got plenty of money in the bank, more money than anyone would ever believe. She lives so simply, she's just never thought of anything she wanted to buy with it or any way to spend it on herself, though she has given a great deal of it away to her favorite charities, anonymously of course.

"Well, hello there!" Russell, Catherine, Leonard, and Bridget converge on their table simultaneously which is too much for Harriet, who falls over to one side in her chair.

"Hey now! Look out now!" Maurice cries, arriving with a sweating pitcher to fill their water glasses. He puts it down and rushes to Harriet's side.

"Oh, she'll be all right." Courtney's in control of this situation, dipping her napkin in her water, wiping Harriet's face. "She's okay, it's just the heat," she tells everybody clustered around. "Bring her a glass of wine," she directs Maurice, "and another one for me."

"Harriet, Harriet." Catherine sits in the chair on Harriet's other side and leans over to hug her. "Honey, are you really all right?"

"Oh, yes, sure —" Harriet blinks and sits up. "I'm fine, I'm so sorry, don't mind me."

"This is just so *Southern!*" Russell erupts. "I'm only dying, don't let me interrupt anybody's lunch —"

"She's not dying," Courtney says.

Leonard and Bridget merely turn their blank polite Midwestern stares at Harriet before they order. Leonard wears a natty yachting cap today. Bridget wears an aqua linen sundress with seashell buttons on it, and matching seashell earrings. She's a very good-looking woman. Ready Freddy, indeed! Courtney kicks Harriet under the table.

Harriet jumps in her seat.

"Honey, what is it? What's the matter?" Catherine hugs her.

"Nothing," Harriet whispers, looking at Courtney.

"A toast, then," Russell suggests, raising his Bloody Mary. "To the death of the Confederacy."

Several people chuckle at nearby tables.

"I'll drink to that." Leonard raises his glass. His pretty blond Bridget is the only person in the dining room who doesn't appear to be at all bothered by this heat, not a hair out of place in her French twist, makeup impeccable.

"Russell just hates all this plantation stuff," Catherine tells everybody.

"Well, shit, what about the Whistle Walk?" Russell already had two mint juleps on the verandah at River Road.

"Watch your language, honey," Catherine says.

"Sorry."

"What's the Whistle Walk?" asks Bridget.

"Oh, it's at River Road Plantation," Catherine says smoothly, aiming her easy smile across the table. "You know, it gets so hot down here in the summers that all these big plantations had a kitchen built separately from the big house, so the cooking wouldn't heat up the whole place. At River Road, for instance, the kitchen is right out back, separated from the house by a brick walkway. So the servants —"

"*Slaves*," Russell puts in.

"The slaves who carried the food from the kitchen to the dining room had to whistle all the way," Catherine continues. "That way the owners could be sure that they weren't sneaking bites of food."

Russell shakes his head and signals Maurice for another drink, an irony that is not lost on him.

"We should have called Suzanne ahead of time." Courtney eats her french fries one by one so they'll last longer. "I'm sure she would have come up from New Orleans to see us. I left a little note for her at the River Road office, just saying we'd been there."

"Good." Catherine nods. "But her schedule must be amazing. Russell says she's been written up in *U.S. News and World Report* a couple of times."

"Really?" Harriet finally finishes her gazpacho.

"Well, certainly. She's a legendary businesswoman. She owns a big piece of the French Quarter, too. You're not surprised, are you?"

"No." Courtney remembers that Suzanne St. John was even more organized than she was on the original raft trip, the only girl whose clothes stayed dry, because she brought each item individually bagged in plastic. Courtney hadn't thought of that. "I wonder if she ever married. They've interviewed her in the *Alumnae News*, but they never mention a family. She's certainly done a great job with River Road, though."

"Oh, Courtney, I think River Road is awful!" Harriet bursts out. She's been thinking this all morning long.

"Hear, hear!" Russell says.

"Really?" Courtney turns to look at Harriet, who will never cease to surprise her.

"Well, yes. I mean, all those huge fake Southern houses on half-acre lots, and all those condominiums, and the golf course — I'll bet they had to dredge the whole swamp to build that golf course. And even the main house, it's just dreadful now with all those awful fake *ladies* in every room, and it's all commercial, they're selling everything in the world — River Road cookbooks, River Road china, River Road aprons and T-shirts and hats, River Road jewelry, River Road perfume —"

"Perfume?" Bridget asks.

"It's gardenia, very heavy." Harriet goes on, "River Road cheese sticks and benne wafers and fudge and cookies, River Road doorstops and ashtrays and notepaper —"

"Why, Harriet, the notepaper is actually quite lovely," says Courtney, who bought some.

"But I just can't help remembering the way the house was when we came before, on the raft," Harriet says. "It was so beautiful, don't you remember? It was all completely empty then —"

"We ran through the whole house just at twilight," Catherine adds.

"And made a big fire on the levee and watched the moon come up. It was a full moon," Harriet says softly. "I remember looking back up at the house and it was so lovely, you could see it so well in the moonlight, it was like it was floating on the mist and the shadows. It seemed to glow out in the night."

"It's still beautiful," Catherine says. "Even today, you can see what it was."

"Wait a minute. How long ago was this trip?" Bridget asks.

"Some thirty years ago," Courtney says briskly, "so as you can imagine it was very different. Why, River Road was virtually a ruin at that time. Nobody could afford to keep it up. I think they had some sort of a retainer, or caretaker, or whatever, living there then, and maybe they were leasing out some of the land for farming, but that was all. It was deserted. However, it had been in our classmate's family for many, many generations, so that's why she was able to get permission for us to stop by. The next day we went on into New Orleans."

A silence falls over their table in the midst of the noisy dining room.

"Angel passing," Harriet says.

"What?" Bridget asks. "What was that?"

"Harriet?" Courtney didn't get it either.

"Nothing." Harriet looks down, remembering how Baby pirouetted the length of the verandah in the dusk, her hair swinging out on the turns.

"Now are you really finished, Missy?" Maurice removes Harriet's uneaten salad. "Can't I bring you a little piece of cheesecake? Or some pecan pie? How about some pecan pie with a little ice cream?"

"That sounds good. I'll take some of that," Bridget speaks up.

"Me too," adds Russell.

"Missy?" Maurice stands there looking at Harriet.

"No . . . thank you . . . I'm fine. That gazpacho was delicious," she says. "Isn't he nice?" she asks the others when he leaves.

"Well, of course he's nice!" Courtney snaps. "It's the end of the cruise, he wants to get a good tip. Tonight's dinner is our last real meal on board. Breakfast is just doughnuts and coffee on deck, and then we're all off by 9 a.m. So you better believe he's got that tip in mind."

"But he *is* nice." Harriet is blushing again.

"Don't kid yourself," Courtney says.

Maurice comes back with three pieces of pecan pie and puts one down deftly in front of Harriet. "Just in case you change your mind," he says. He gives another to Russell. "And this one goes to — " He waves it in the air, a question.

"Right here." Bridget picks up her fork.

Catherine orders coffee for herself and Russell, who obviously needs it. "Now what's the plan for tonight?" she asks at the risk of being rude to Leonard, who seems out of it anyway, and Bridget, busy wolfing down her pie.

"I think we'd better do it just as we come into New Orleans," Harriet says. "Actually, I asked Pete and that's his suggestion. He said there'll be too much activity in the morning. We'll wake up docked at the Robin Street wharf with everybody unloading the baggage and restocking the boat and everything."

"Tonight, then." Russell drains his cup. "We'll go up on top after dinner, have a drink."

Catherine looks at him.

"Be right back," he says, heading for the bathroom.

"Okay." Harriet nods. "Pete says we'll be entering the port of New Orleans about ten-thirty. Maybe we should do it at ten, while we're still actually on the river, before we really get into the city." She glances over at Leonard and Bridget, deep in whispered conversation.

"What about Anna?" Courtney asks.

"I'll leave her a note right now," Harriet says.

"No, *I'll* leave her the note," Courtney decides. "You go rest this afternoon. Read a book, take a nap."

"Maybe I will." Actually, Harriet still doesn't feel too good. She rises, fumbling with her purse.

"Here. Let me walk you to your room." Catherine follows her.

Courtney stands to leave, too, just as Russell reenters the dining room and lurches somewhat alarmingly back toward their table. Catherine should have stuck with Howie, in Courtney's opinion. But there's no accounting for taste, as anybody will tell you. Look at old Leonard here, for instance. Look at Gene Minor. *Oh God.* "Baby? Baby?" Russell takes in the nearly abandoned table, then turns on his heel abruptly. Honestly! He's just as rude as he can be. "Baby?" He rushes off. Maurice shakes his head, clearing dishes. Courtney leaves by herself. Under the tablecloth, Leonard puts his hand on Bridget's thigh.

Mile 139.2
Dutch Bayou, Louisiana
Friday 5/14/99
1400 hours

An hour later, feeling pretty frustrated, Russell slides onto a stool at the Calliope Bar for a quick much-needed hit of weather. He needs the weather girls, too — needs their easy warmth, their open, carefree manner. The weather girls are immediately accessible, unlike his Catherine, who has gotten so moody on this trip. And distant — at least to Russell. This is not like her. He can remember plenty of trips when they'd jumped into bed at the first opportunity; trips always seem to turn her on, one reason Russell agreed to come along on this one in the first place. Since when does she "need to rest"? Since when does she have a headache?

Mr. Stone occupies his accustomed place at the corner of the bar. Actually he's all sprawled out across its marbled surface, face turned toward Russell. His cabbage nose is squashed sideways against his cheek; his mouth, partly open, is squashed, too, so it looks like a baby's mouth. Russell used to squish Lauren's little mouth together like that with his fingers until her lips made a bow, a baby-doll mouth. "Chubby baby! Chubby baby!" he'd say. Lauren hated it. And now she has chubby babies of her own. But Mr. Stone doesn't look so good today. His color's not good, though his crisply starched white shirt and striped silk tie could break your heart. His feet in their white bucks dangle down from his knees in a loose way that makes Russell nervous. But it's none of his business.

"Hi, Nick," he says to the bartender. Nick has got the overhead TV tuned to baseball, as usual. Braves versus Cubs, top of the fourth.

"Good afternoon, Mr. Hurt! I hope you enjoyed your morning." Nick sounds like he really means it. The kid's got a great future in business — what's he doing on this boat?

"It was okay," Russell says. "But I'm ready for New Orleans. What about you?"

Nick flashes his white grin. "Yessir!" He wipes off the bar, then mixes a Jack Black on the rocks and sets it down in front of Russell. The *Belle* is in the center of the river now, steaming south. Oil refineries

541

rise up like tinker toys beyond the trees on either bank. Docks, tanks, smokestacks, and other structures clog the shoreline. No more nature, they're in the petrochemical corridor now. Russell has read something about the cancer rate in this part of Louisiana, maybe in his Johns Hopkins Health Letter, something grim. No telling what carcinogens he's breathing in right now. Mr. Stone makes a little sighing noise. Nick watches Smoltz strike out Marvin Benard and then turns back to Russell. "Weather Channel, sir?" he asks respectfully.

"Just for a minute, if you can stand it."

"No problem." Nick clicks the pointer and — yes! Damn if it's not Susi Sergi herself in a clingy black knit outfit that outlines her swelling stomach. She will never get ahead in the world of meteorology if she keeps having all these babies. And as a scientist, doesn't she want to do her part to stop the world's overpopulation? But of course Russell knows she's not really a scientist, she's a little slut. Still, he wants the best for her. It's interesting how the girls of today just let it all show, Russell can't quite get used to it. He remembers those big ugly checkered blouses that pregnant women used to wear, with white collars and bows and shit. They looked like shit. That's how they thought they were *supposed* to look when they were pregnant. Russell knows it's an advance, this modern attitude. Women shouldn't be ashamed of their bodies, but damn if they ought to go around throwing them right up in your face either. Russell guesses it's hard to find a happy medium, as with anything.

Today Susi has pulled her hair back and up from her face on both sides, fastening it with gold barrettes so it cascades down to her shoulders in a swoopy wave. Russell likes the barrettes. Susi wears gold earrings and that gold chain he also likes so much, he's got to remember to get one of those for Catherine. Susi smiles straight at him. "So it's another sunny day across the South, with a light wind from the West and some isolated afternoon thundershowers along the Gulf."

"Sounds pretty good," Russell remarks to Nick.

"Yes, sir. Mind if I switch it back over to the game now?"

"No, go ahead." Actually, Russell had hoped to catch the five-day forecast, but you can't have everything. You don't even *want* everything. The minute you get too much of whatever you think you really want, the Big Guy zaps you. Better to lie low, not try too hard or achieve too much, so as not to attract His attention. You pay for everything. The *Belle of Natchez* goes under a big highway bridge. Smoltz is still on the mound pitching to Sammy Sosa now. Sosa hits a long drive to left center and Jones is going back, back, back — he's got it with an over-the-shoulder catch. Mark Grace trots out of the dugout. Russell sips his Jack Black and considers another one but no, it's a long day still ahead, and a big night. Jesus. Maybe he'll rest a little, too. Catch a nap. *Then* see if she's in the mood. He looks up at the TV just in time to see Mark Grace hit a line drive when suddenly Mr. Stone makes a kind of whooshing noise, like air being let out of a tire, and slides off his stool sideways but slowly, slowly, it's all agonizingly slow — to lie curled on his side on the deck. Now he sounds like he's strangling. He keeps his eyes closed. Nick picks up the telephone.

"Mr. Stone!" Russell falls to his knees at Mr. Stone's side and touches Mr. Stone's face which has a curiously malleable, plastic feel to it, as if Russell could shape it however he chose. The skin is damp and pale. From somewhere, from some booklet he probably saw in some doctor's waiting room, Russell remembers a phrase, "The ABC's of CPR." But he can't remember what they are. "Mr. Stone! Mr. Stone, can you hear me?" Russell says in his ear.

Mr. Stone doesn't say a thing.

With a superman leap, Nick is over the bar, jostling Russell aside, pulling at Mr. Stone's shoulders until he's got him laid out flat, tilting his head back, jerking his jaw forward, feeling around inside his mouth. Mr. Stone looks awful. Nick throws Mr. Stone's tie aside. He gets down and puts his ear to Mr. Stone's open mouth. Then he rips his nice white shirt open. He rubs his knuckles roughly on Mr. Stone's bony little chest.

"Stop it! You're killing him," Russell says.

Nick doesn't even turn around.

"Where is he?" One of the ship's pilots bursts through the ring of hushed on-lookers who have gathered around the Calliope Bar. "Breathing? Pulse?" he asks.

Nick shakes his head no.

Russell remembers that the B of the ABC's is *breathing*. But what was A? Maybe *air*?

"Shit." The pilot struggles out of his white jacket and flings it on the floor. He pushes Russell aside and positions himself on his knees beside Mr. Stone. He nods to Nick. Nick sits up for a second, wipes his mouth with the back of his hand, then leans back down to put his face over Mr. Stone's face, his mouth to his mouth. *Chubby baby*, Russell thinks. The pilot pushes down, hard, with both hands on Mr. Stone's chest. Nick makes a loud breathing noise, then turns his head to spit. He makes the noise again. Russell sits back on his heels, shaking. He doesn't think he can stand up. His own heart is going a mile a minute, these guys will probably have to do him next. He glances up: the sun is still shining, the TV's still on, Tyler Houston's at bat. The river stretches wide beyond the rail. "I don't know why they have to do this right out here on the deck in front of everybody," a woman says in a nasal voice.

But it goes on. It goes on forever, it seems to Russell, Nick and Mr. Stone locked tight in their long and terrible kiss. It goes on until another man, a swarthy man Russell has not seen before, arrives with an emergency pack. This guy's wearing a khaki uniform, maybe he's come up from the engine room. He kneels, sets up some kind of monitor, and positions two things with black cords coming out of them on Mr. Stone's battered chest. "Okay," he says.

Nick sits back. "Shocking paddles," he tells Russell.

The man yells, "Clear!" He pushes a button and Mr. Stone twitches horribly, violently, though he does not open his eyes. "My God," Russell says. The man is looking at the monitor. "Hell," he says. He shocks Mr. Stone three more times and then quits trying. "Good work anyway," the man says to Nick. "Damn good job, all you can do." He packs up his kit. He has short, blunt fingers with black hair on them. He looks like that actor who used to be on TV all the time, playing a detective, what was that guy's name? Some one-eyed guy. Nick gets up and brushes off his pants. But Russell can't stand to see Mr. Stone just left splayed out on the deck like a frog in biology lab, so pathetic and vulnerable. Death has no dignity. He moves forward to button up Mr. Stone's nice white shirt. Peter Falk, Russell remembers suddenly. "Peter Falk," he says. But nobody cares, nobody's paying the slightest bit of attention to him. The swarthy man shakes Nick's hand and says he'll send some guys right up. Nick goes back around the bar and starts mixing drinks, he's got a crowd now, all talking, glancing over at Mr. Stone and then quickly glancing away. Mr. Stone seems to be shrinking. He looks littler and littler there on the deck. Russell looks around. A few of the rockers by the rail are occupied by women in hats, reading. One old man has fallen asleep, his newspaper down at his feet. He's snoring loudly. Two more women, smoking cigarettes and occupied in intense conversation, don't even notice when Mr. Stone, covered now by a tablecloth, is carried unceremoniously right past them, one guy grabbing him under the shoulders and another guy holding his feet. Russell finally stands up. He feels okay as far as he can tell, though now his own heart is beating in a slow, thudding, scary way. Nick grins at him across the heads of his customers. "Hey, Russell," he calls. "One on the house! Come and get it, you deserve it."

People stand aside so Russell can get to the bar. Somebody gives him a stool. Nick hands him a drink. "What's the matter?" a woman asks, that pretty woman from Florida, Russell has noticed her before, and somebody else says, "Had a heart attack," and Russell says, "Damnedest thing, he was sitting right here" and tells them all about it. Telling it makes him feel better. From time to time he looks back down at the deck where Mr. Stone was lying just minutes ago, but he's gone now, of course, and there's not a trace of him left, not even a skim of moisture on the shiny blond wood floor, nothing. Not a thing. Mr. Stone is gone. Absolutely gone, as if he had never existed, and anybody who thinks otherwise is a fool. Nothing else happens after death. An image comes to Russell: we drift through the world like dandelion puffs on the wind, we spread our seed and disappear, and the world doesn't care. The world doesn't even notice. The world is not about us. Finally the crowd thins out, the Braves win, and Russell gets a chance to ask Nick, "Has anything like this ever happened on board before? Since you've been a bartender, I mean."

Nick smiles. "Oh, sure," he says. "Happens all the time. Though not right here, not at my bar, specifically. This is a first. But they drop like flies on this run. That's why we all have to get trained in CPR before they'll hire us."

Russell shudders, though this knowledge makes him feel better. "What will we do now? Stop?"

"Nah." Nick shakes his head. "They'll

just ice him down and hang on to him. We'll be in New Orleans by midnight anyway. They can sneak him off while everybody's asleep."

An open boat filled with pretty girls goes by, all of them waving enthusiastically at the *Belle of Natchez*. One blond jerks up her halter top to show her breasts, round as apples, white against her tan. "Hey, man, am I dreaming? Did you see that?" Nick asks. Lil plays a short chorus of "Dixie" on the calliope as Russell and Nick wave back.

Russell has a little trouble navigating by the time he finally decides to leave the Calliope Bar and go back down to check on Catherine. He could definitely use a nap himself. Or maybe she'll be waking up now, stretching, her breasts lifted, he can just imagine it, she'll be rested and rosy-cheeked and in the mood. But when he finally gets the damn key to work in the damn lock, she's gone, bed as smooth as if she had never lain there, as if *they* had never lain there with the curtains open, brown river and changing sky and leafy shore passing by their window like a film on the Discovery Channel. "Well, damn." Russell sits heavily on the side of the bed but he doesn't feel like sleeping, he feels like he might never wake up if he goes to sleep now. He can't think what to do next. Her name comes into his mind. He fumbles his way back out into the corridor, then up the Grand Staircase. He gets one quick, shocking look at himself in the floor-length mirror on the landing — maybe he ought to go back to the stateroom first, clean up some. But then he thinks, Nah . . . He goes out to stand at the rail, sun pounding on his head. But isn't the sun on the wrong side of the *Belle* now? Or has he gone crazy? He's feeling really disoriented. That bridge overhead, for instance, didn't they just pass under that same bridge a little while ago? What the hell is going on here? Russell is headed for the pilot house when he literally runs into Pete, coming down the narrow metal staircase from the Sun Deck.

"Hey, Russell. Everything all right?"

The very fact that Pete asks him this worries Russell. "Sure, yeah —" He shakes Pete's outstretched hand. But hell, what's the point of pretending? Behind the square lenses, Pete's eyes are shrewd and curious.

Russell hangs on to the metal banister. "I couldn't help noticing —," he begins. "I mean, it seems to me that we just went under a bridge that we already went under, earlier today. Correct me if I'm wrong."

But Pete grins at him, shaking his head. "Damn if you haven't caught us out," he says. "Good for you, buddy. First time in three or four trips."

"What do you mean?"

"You're absolutely right. It's the Luling-Destrehan highway bridge which we passed under earlier, going south." Pete consults his watch. "It's now 3:40 p.m., and we are, indeed, heading upriver, or north/northwest, to be exact. During dinner, we'll make a nice slow swing around a big island at about mile 135, a turn so slow you'll never notice it, and then we'll be headed south again. So we'll pass under the Luling-Destrehan bridge yet another time as we ease on down to New Orleans, still going as slow as possible."

Russell doesn't get it. "So what's the point of all this slowing down and back and forth? Why don't you just go straight to New Orleans?"

Pete throws back his head and laughs. "Hell, it would only take us two days, total, from Memphis to New Orleans if we did that. We are enhancing your experience, man. Don't you feel enhanced?" He pokes

Russell in the shoulder, a kind of man-to-man solidarity touching which Russell remembers from football. Russell laughs, too.

"Say," Pete adds, "how about putting in a good word for me with Harriet? I'm trying to get her to stay over, let me show her the town." Pete winks at him.

"You got it," Russell promises, though he cannot, for the life of him, see the mystifying attraction of Harriet. There's no accounting for taste, as Catherine's mother was so fond of saying. Catherine. Now where is she?

"See you later, buddy," he tells Pete. "I'll work on Harriet for you," he throws back over his shoulder.

Russell strolls around the entire Promenade Deck twice, nodding to various people, waving to Nick at the Calliope Bar, without seeing anybody in his party. Finally, on his third lap, he looks into the Grand Saloon through the window and sees the backs of their heads — Catherine, Courtney, and Harriet seated near the door in back while some other godawful thing starts up on stage. He goes inside and grabs a seat behind them.

"Hey, baby, I've been looking all over the place for you," Russell has just begun when Catherine starts shushing him. Up on stage stands Captain John Dulaney, resplendent in his gold-braided uniform and million-dollar smile, along with the Syncopators, all decked out in black tuxedos, and a round table holding an enormous wedding cake flanked by candelabra blazing away despite the bright sunshine outside the windows. Captain Dulaney nods to Alabama Huey. Alabama Huey raises his baton, and the Syncopators launch into the Wedding March as ten or twelve old men come hesitantly onstage left, joined by their wives who enter right. Everybody is all dolled up: coats and ties for the men, dresses for the women. The men look embarrassed. The women carry bouquets. Now Russell remembers what this is. "My God," he says.

"*Sssh.*" Catherine, Harriet, and Courtney hiss as one.

Captain Dulaney treats the crowd to his dazzling smile. He raises his arms. "I, John Dulaney, by the power vested in me as the captain of the *Belle of Natchez*, now pronounce you man and wife. Gentlemen, you may kiss your brides!" A giant kissing session ensues which is really pretty damn sweet, all those old geezers and their ladies. Russell reaches for Catherine.

"No!" she pulls away. "Russell, come on. Cut it out. These people are serious. Quit being such a jerk."

"Hey, you must have the wrong guy. This is me, Russell, I'm not a jerk. I am serious, damn it! Come on, honey. We were signed up to do this, too, as I recall — weren't we, girls?" Russell glances darkly at Harriet who giggles, blushing. "So let's *do* it. Dance with me?" Out on the parquet dance floor, couples glide and whirl. A few of them mostly stumble and sway, but some of them are splendid dancers, better than Russell ever was or ever will be. Some of them are probably better husbands than he is, too.

"Baby?" He puts his arms around Catherine from behind, chair and all, awkwardly. "Can I have this dance for the rest of my life?" he sings off key.

"Russell, stop it. You are really embarrassing me now." Catherine sounds like she means it. "You're drunk. And these people are *sincere*."

"I'm sincere, too. Why won't anybody ever believe me when I'm sincere?" But Russell already knows the answer — it's because he's been ironic all his life. He's like the little boy who cried wolf so much that no one believed it when the real wolf came.

Catherine keeps trying to pry his arms loose. "Hush," she says.

"Okay, then fuck it. Just fuck it, baby." Suddenly he's fed up with the whole thing. "Pardon my French," he says to Courtney, that bitch, she looks like she's got a poker up her ass right now. She looks away. Russell stands up. "You'd better stay over in New Orleans, honey," he tells Harriet, who opens and closes her mouth rapidly, like a baby bird. Like a little baby wren, that's it. These women look like See No Evil, Hear No Evil, Speak No Evil. Russell pauses to grab four plastic flutes of champagne, two in each hand, from Maurice as he goes past with a huge silver tray.

"Hey, buddy, they've got your friend all wrapped up in a tarp and laid out on the Main Deck now, dead as a mackerel. Gonna unload his ass in the Easy, first thing." Maurice disappears into the crowd.

"What friend? What's he talking about? Did somebody die?" Catherine finally stands up and turns to Russell.

"Yeah. It was Mr. Stone, you know, the old guy who's always out at the bar. I introduced you, right?"

Catherine nods. She comes around the chair and takes Russell's arm. He looks terrible. "What happened?"

"Heart attack," Russell says. "I was right there, sitting at the bar with him. Shit, baby, it was awful. Everything you ever thought about a heart attack, it's true. It's all true. In spades. Except it's even worse than you can possibly imagine." Russell follows her out of the Grand Saloon. "It's so gross. So undignified. They strip you, they stick stuff on you, they stick other stuff in you, they hit you . . . *Jesus*. It's the end, the absolute end, of privacy." Russell is fanatic about his privacy, he hates to have strangers in his house. Hell, he even hates to have *friends* in his house. He holds on to Catherine's elbow going down the Grand Staircase, then along the corridor. She stops in front of their stateroom door and fumbles in her purse for the key. Russell encircles her waist from behind and buries his face in her lemony hair. He closes his eyes. "Mr. Stone was fucking *dead*, honey," he tells her. He breathes in deeply, raggedly. "Russell —," Catherine starts to say when suddenly Russell's dick rises up out of this long weird confusing scary day, rises of its own accord to push insistently against Catherine's soft butt in the denim skirt. "Ready Freddy," he says, making a joke. He had a girlfriend one time who called it Mr. Happy. His hands move up to her breasts.

"Russell!" Catherine pushes his hands down and breaks away from him. She goes to stand at the window, looking out. Right now they're fairly close to a densely wooded island with an old boat wrecked on its muddy half-moon beach. Bleached wooden ribs curve out from the boat's rounded spine, like bones. The mud looks pretty good there, actually, around the wreck. Dense, dark, clay-ey. Suddenly Catherine knows exactly how it would feel to scoop up a handful and squeeze it through her fingers. This was where she started making things, on the riverbank at the river house, long ago. Figures — little people and animals, some real and some not real, bowls, plates, a tiny perfect pitcher. She wonders whatever happened to that tiny pitcher. It was just her and Wesley then, wasn't it, just her and Wesley in the river house before it all got started, periods cramps boys dates birth babies, *the works*. Oh God, before Wesley left her and then suddenly somehow Catherine got surrounded by all these other people. Husbands, children, grandchildren, friends — where did all these *people* come from is what she'd like to know.

"Honey," Russell says. He's looking at

her. He holds out his arms. He looks drunk, disheveled, pathetic. But he gets it now. Something's wrong. "Baby, come here. Just come over here to your old man, I won't do anything you don't want me to, you know that."Crossing the room, Catherine feels like she's underwater or like she's a girl in a dream. "Yeah. Just let me hold you like this." He strokes her wild hair. "Baby, what's the matter? What the fuck is wrong with you anyway?"

Catherine takes a deep breath and lets it go. "Oh Russell, I've got this lump in my breast, see, feel it, it's right here. I just found it yesterday, and I've been feeling so weird ever since —" The dam crumbles, the water rushes through.

"Where? This? Oh Jesus, oh my God, you're right. Oh honey, oh baby, oh my love. But why didn't you tell me?" He pulls back to look at her face. "Catherine? Why didn't you tell me immediately?"

"Oh, I don't know. I guess, I didn't — I didn't want to spoil your trip" though that's not the real reason, Catherine knows.

"Oh, fuck! I give up. Mary Bernice would be proud of you for once, you're finally turning into her. *My* trip? *My* trip? Oh Jesus." He folds Catherine up in his arms where for the first time in days she feels like herself again, and this is Russell after all, her old buddy, her old flame, her old man. Whatever was she thinking? But it's all about holding back and letting go, isn't it? Pulling apart and getting back together, keeping and giving, on and on, that's the way it works, that's the real story, and there's no beginning and no end to it either.

"We'll get the best doctors," Russell says. "We can go to the Mayo Clinic, Houston, anyplace you want. We'll go straight to the top." The irony of this is not lost on Russell, of course: the hypochondriac's wife gets cancer, the fire chief's house burns down. He imagines the Big Guy up there getting a real chuckle out of this one. *Shit head.*

"Hush, I'm sure Birmingham will be just fine, and we can't do anything about it until Monday morning anyway." Catherine seems like her old practical self again. "Also, it might be a cyst, or it might be benign, or — who knows? Let's wait and see. Anyway, whatever it is, they'll get it, I'm sure. They can almost always take care of breast cancer these days." It's the first time she has named it.

"Well, they'd better. Because I can't

fucking live without you, you know that, don't you? Baby?"

"Yes," Catherine says, "yes," again, as he pulls her T-shirt over her head and throws it down on the bed. The stateroom fills up with sunset. Now she wants him. She wants him terribly, and for a drunk guy, he does fine. Then he wraps one leg around her legs and hugs her tight all over. This is his sweet Catherine, the one he loves. "Buddies?" he asks. "Buddies," she says, the last thing Russell hears before he falls instantly, deeply asleep, mouth still open, snoring slightly.

Catherine sits up on one elbow. She pushes his heavy leg off her. She looks up from the sleeping man beside her to watch the sun make its fiery trail across the water straight to their window, a shining path so wide and straight that she imagines stepping out onto it and walking across the water and into the trees on the other side. She imagines the mud and the vines and flowers, and the smell of honeysuckle and rotting fish. She knows exactly how it would be there. She looks down to stroke his cheek.

What a nuisance — everything except hand luggage has to be packed and set out in the hall before bedtime, so Courtney might as well do it now, before dinner. And speaking of dinner, she'll have to get a picture of the whole group tonight. Maybe she can get Bridget to snap it, so she can be in the picture, too. Actually, it's just as well that this trip is finally almost over, in Courtney's opinion — for her, the whole point of it was to have a stolen weekend in New Orleans with Gene. She takes the new baby-doll pajamas out of the drawer, hesitates, then buries her face in the emerald green silk. Never worn, never will be. She thinks she ought to feel good about her decision, but she does not. On impulse, she reaches for the phone and sits down on the bed to call Gene one last time.

"Ay-up," he says in some sort of cowboy

voice, you never know what he's up to.

"Gene, it's me. Courtney."

"Why, yes it is!" He sounds much cheerier than she would have thought. He's supposed to be brokenhearted.

"What are you doing?" she asks, with a sudden stabbing desire to picture him there in his crazy house.

"Oh, nothing much, you know me. Just been out in the yard racing these two wisteria vines. I started one on each side of the trellis by the pond. So far the left one is ahead, but I've got my money on the right."

It's just like Gene Minor to be totally involved in something nobody else would give a damn about.

"Actually," he goes on in that oddly cheery, manly tone, "I'm so glad it's you. I was just going to try to call that WATERCOM number and leave you a message to call me."

"Yes?" Courtney's heart leaps up to her throat. So he's changed his mind, after all! Everything else falls away. But what if she can't change her airline reservation back again? *A lady doesn't care what it costs.* At least she's still got the room, she'll tell Harriet she can't use it after all. She won't even try to offer an explanation, she'll just let Harriet think that the reservation got inadvertently screwed up somehow. *Never apologize, never explain. Just talk real sweet and you can have whatever you want.* She says, "Gene, honey, I'm so glad you've changed your mind."

"Whoa, baby," he says immediately. "Who says I changed my mind? I was just thinking, though, that since I've already got my nonrefundable ticket and you've got a room you're not using, I might just fly down to New Orleans anyway and meet Rosalie."

"What?"

"Rosalie." He sounds pleased as punch with himself. "You know, I told you, Rosalie Hungerheart. Incidentally you were right, it's not really Hungerheart, it's Patterson. Anyway, she lives in Atlanta and she's got all these frequent flyer miles saved up and she's never been to New Orleans either."

"No! You can't do this to me, I'll cancel the room —"

"Then meet me, babe. Last chance — my way or the highway. I don't care where we stay. Just meet me and go back home with me and be my love and we will all the pleasures prove. You know I've always loved you, ever since I was a lad."

Courtney is trying to breathe. "No," she finally says.

"What a shame then, what a fucking shame." Gene sounds old and tired. "You're just not up to it, are you?"

"Gene, you know that's not it, you know I have to . . ." But Courtney feels both furious and foolish, with none of the resolve she had felt in the church at St. Francisville.

Click.

"Gene!" she cries into the phone, then click, then buzz, then nothing.

Anna steals a glance at her little jeweled travel clock. Oh no — what has happened to the afternoon? After a week of furious work, she has almost finished *The Louisiana Purchase*.

Though she should start getting ready for dinner now, especially if she really intends to shampoo her hair, she just can't bring herself to stop writing. She takes the last miniature Nestlé Crunch from its blue wrapper and pops it into her mouth. She crumples the cellophane bag and tosses it into the wastebasket. She can't quit now.

Propelled by a sudden sense of urgency too strong to ignore, Jade throws the gold pen down onto Jean St. Pierre's huge mahogany desk. She jumps to her feet, scattering the contracts.

"Darling! What's the matter?" Alarm gathers in Jean's penetrating blue eyes.

"Ooh! I just don't know — I have this feeling —" Jade presses her hands to her heaving breast. "I can't really explain it. It's just the most powerful sense of — of—"

"Here, my love." Swiftly he has rounded the desk and pressed her back down into the leather chair, while four lawyers and his secretary look on in surprise. "Some water for the lady, please," he barks, and the secretary races out to obtain it.

He strokes her hair. "Now, Jade, you do realize that these contracts must be signed today, right now in fact, if we are to have the financial backing of the powerful Japanese firm Unagi in developing our island —"

"Jean, stop it! Just — quit — *patting* me!"

Obviously embarrassed, Jean stands back up and straightens his power tie. "Women are often emotional at times like these," he remarks to all.

"I am *not emotional!* It's just — I just —" Jade closes her eyes and sways slightly in her chair. Deep in her ears she can hear the faint melody of an old fiddle tune, her grandmother's favorite, *"Jole Blon."* In her mind's eye she sees an old-fashioned couple waltzing across the wide bare floor

567

of an ancient wooden house . . . Jade rubs her fists in her eyes and stands again, clutching her purse to her chest. "I'm sorry," she blurts. "I can't sign these contracts right now, there's something else I have to do first. I'll sign them later. Please excuse me." Then before anyone can stop her, she has bolted for the door and run across the parking lot and down the grassy bank to the dock where Jean St. Pierre's sleek motor launch sits glistening in the sun. Jade leaps aboard despite her stiletto heels. She turns the key and the engine roars to life. The Playboy key chain dangles from the lock as the *Mermaid* heads into the bay. Back on shore, Jean St. Pierre jumps up and down in fury like a puppet in a Punch and Judy show.

Jade points the bow into the waves and races toward the island. She cannot help but notice the gray clouds that have suddenly appeared from nowhere it seems, rolling across the horizon toward her at alarming speed. Now the sun is obscured and the wind picks up. Waves slap against the boat. Jade kicks off her shoes and holds on to the wheel with both hands. Soon she is drenched with spray, her white silk blouse all but transparent in the gathering gloom. Lightning flashes. Thunder rolls.

The boat rides up and down the troughs of enormous waves. And yet — despite the fearsome noise of the storm — she can still hear the fiddle tune in her mind, ever more clearly.

At last! Through the curtain of rain, she spies the island. Fighting the wheel, she maneuvers the launch into Frenchman's Bayou and cruises up to the rotting pier of her grandmother's house. Now the song is ringing in her ears! Quickly she secures the boat as best she can and climbs out, heading for the house, tripping and falling as pesky vines grab at her feet. At last she reaches the wide balcony, crosses it, and pushes at the old cypress door.

"Ma cherie!" Adrian Batiste drops his fiddle and leaps forward to cover her wet face and her throat with his burning kisses — the kisses she has secretly wanted ever since the first day she laid eyes on him. Even the furor of the raging storm outside is muted by the rising music — music, music everywhere, as Adrian takes Jade in his arms and waltzes her across that old pine floor.

There! Anna throws down her pen. She stands and stretches, as stiff and sore as if she had just run a marathon, which — in a way — she has. The world comes back; she hears voices in the corridor outside her door. It must be dinnertime already. She'll have to forgo that shampoo but it doesn't really matter anyway, does it? She can always put her hair up. Tonight she'll wear the jungle dress, with ivory combs in her hair, very *Heart of Darkness*. She unbuttons her pink dressing gown and throws it across the bed, then crosses to the mirror in her rose satin panties and bustier to pin up her hair for a quick bath.

"Oh, Miss Trethaway! I thought you would have already gone to dinner! Pardon me —" Huckleberry drops his tray to the floor with a resounding crash. "Oh my gosh! I'm so sorry —" He falls to his knees and starts scrambling after the china and silver, which has spilled everywhere.

Anna grabs her robe and slips it around her shoulders, but not before — she hopes — he has seen her enormous breasts. Boys like breasts. She clutches the robe at her neck in a show of primness. "Here, now, get up — you can just come back later to get those things and straighten the room up." Finishing a book always makes her feel sexy.

"*Later?*" But Huckleberry stands up immediately, an obedient boy, a puppet. The red blush under those tan freckles is adorable. He gulps for air. "Actually, I've been trying to get up the nerve to talk to you for the whole trip," he says. "I mean, I've been wanting to *really* talk to you, ma'am."

"My name is Anna." She takes his sweaty hand. "And I've been wanting to really talk to *you,* too." She loosens her robe just the slightest bit. "Tell me all about yourself."

His Adam's apple quivers. "Of course I know who you are. We *all* know who you are. And I know I'm not supposed to bother you. But I wanted to tell you — I'm a writer, too. I just got my M.F.A. from Florida State, and my thesis was a novel which I'm revising right now so I can submit it for publication. I don't want to impose or anything, but I was wondering if you might have a minute to look at my query letter and my synopsis and maybe the first chapter, that's all, just to see what you think before I send them off, a professional opinion, you know, I'd really appreciate it." Huckleberry pats the pocket of his uniform, why, he's actually got the envelope with him, the little polecat! He smooths it out on his knee.

Anna stands up. "No, I'm sorry, I can't do that," she says crisply. "My agent doesn't allow me to look at any manuscripts — or synopses or any *letters* —," she adds. "In fact, he strictly forbids it, on pain of *death*. That way, no one can ever accuse me of stealing an idea, and this is something that comes up frequently in my field, you'd better believe it. So if you'll excuse me, I am — as you see — late for dinner."

"Oh, sure, oh yes ma'am. I'm sorry!" Huckleberry stands up, too, folding the pages furiously, jamming them back down into his jacket pocket. "I'm sorry I bothered you."

"You haven't bothered me a bit, you silly boy," Anna says from the bathroom door with a brilliant smile. How could she ever have been so foolish? So — so *deluded*. Why he's young enough to be her own son, her own little baby . . . "And you can just clean up all that mess later, when I'm not here. Good luck with your work, and now — *adieu*." She flutters her fingers at him, then closes the mirrored bathroom door and sinks back against it until she has slid all the way down to the floor where she sits propped up like a rag doll with her fist pressed against her mouth.

Harriet goes into her stateroom and kicks off her heels, feeling under the edge of the bed with her toes for her sandals. There. That's better. She crosses over to the mirror and stands in front of it and looks at herself still wearing the Mardi Gras beads — three shiny strands, one purple, one green, one gold — over her white sundress. Actually, they become her. But the last dinner was strange, definitely strange, in spite of the excellent New Orleans food and the determined Mardi Gras gaiety that the staff was trying so hard to create. Anna didn't even show up; nor did Russell. Catherine just smiled when they asked her about him. "Oh, he's all right. He's still napping. He'll join us later, I'm sure." Catherine had a certain Mona Lisa gravity about her at dinner, striking long gray hair pulled back into a knot at the nape of her neck. She was less talkative than usual, though, and Courtney, too, seemed out of sorts, edgy and abstracted.

But Leonard and Bridget were in fine form; they'd even imported some friends from another table to take Anna and Russell's empty chairs. Harriet wondered if *they* knew about Leonard's pump. The new guy, Phil, said he was a member of the Toastmasters Club of McMinnville, Tennessee, and told four awful jokes in a row to prove it. Luckily, conversation was kept to a minimum by the entire Syncopators band which had joined Little Bobby Blue tonight for the grand finale, playing loud zydeco music as costumed kitchen help and waiters danced between the tables. Maurice was particularly stunning, all decked out in whiteface as Pierrot. Now there's somebody who can really dance! But it's racist to think so, isn't it? Oh dear. And Harriet still hasn't told Pete definitely whether she'll stay over in New Orleans or not, even though Courtney has given her that room in the Royal Orleans, and even though she wants to, she really *wants* to. She hasn't told Pete about the room either. Then he'd really put the pressure on her. As it is, his kidding has been bad enough. *"Laissez les bons temps roulez,"* he'd said into her ear that afternoon, coming up behind her while she stood at the rail.

"Oh my gosh!" She'd jumped a mile. His bristly moustache tickled her neck.

"Hey, now, steady there, didn't mean to scare you!" He put a hand on each shoulder to steady her, which had the opposite effect.

"Listen, I'll talk to you about it right after the — ceremony," she'd said finally, for lack of a better word. "I just can't get my mind around anything else until that's over with."

"I understand." His blue eyes behind his glasses looked like still water. His gaze held hers calmly. "Of course I understand." He touched her hand. "And speaking of that, I wanted to tell you that I'll be there too, tonight, if it's all right with you. I thought I'd just stand guard by the top of the steps to keep any other passengers from wandering up there and interrupting you."

"Oh, that's so nice." Harriet had barely breathed then.

"I *am* nice." He grinned down at her. His gold eyetooth gleamed. "I'll show you the time of your life in New Orleans. You ought to take me up on it. It's hard to find an old bird like me, that's why you see all these women going on tours with each other all the time — there's no men left. I may not be much, but at least I'm *alive,*" Pete said.

Then Harriet started laughing and she laughed so hard, he had to pat her on the back. She smiles now, in her stateroom, just thinking about it. And it's true, he is so nice . . . So what's wrong with her? Harriet sighs. She slips the Mardi Gras beads over her head and drops them in a shiny little heap on her bed. There's a part of her that already knows what her answer will be.

In any case, she has things to do now. It's time. The open FedEx box is the only thing left in its dresser drawer; all her clothes have been packed in the bags which already stand outside in the corridor. She puts the FedEx box on the bed and takes everything out of it: the unopened white envelope, the black lacquered wooden box with its gold fittings and its gold key. It looks like an Oriental jewelry box. Chinoiserie. "To Harriet and the Girls, from Charlie, To Be Opened at Maggie's Memorial" is written in black ink on the white envelope in a firm, flowing hand. She looks at her watch, then gets a glass of water from the carafe and takes it over to the chair by the window, along with the rest of the poems. There's time yet. She settles down to read.

BOURBON STREET

The bride wears her ivory linen
going-away dress
in the Ladies.
She says she's never
been in one of these places before.
She thinks it's awful
that Bobby has actually dragged her
into one of these places
on her honeymoon.
I don't know.
I could stay here —
ride that pole, the velvet swing —

or I could go to graduate school

FOLK ART

you're so pretty
they always said
you're so pretty
aren't you lucky
you're so pretty
you're so rich
but I'm such a bitch
deep inside
where I hide
it's a godawful mess

look like I done been hit
with the ugly stick

VESPERS

The statue behind the cathedral
is Christ or somebody
I don't know I'm drunk
with some boy who goes to Tulane
his father is a jeweler
in Indianola, Mississippi
his mother has cancer
Oh Lord
It's always something with these boys
He lays me down
but not to sleep
in the statue's shadow
enormous on the cathedral wall
a giant Christ, a huge whoever
I lie in his arms
on the soft damp holy grass

SALE AT THE HOUSE OF VOODOO

un noir cadeau
pour Marie Laveau
The gift came from her mother.
Born with a veil

across her face,
seventh child of a seventh child
what chance did she have?
always, second sight
always knew too much
little snake wrapped around her leg
for company.

I can cure
high blood, low blood
chills and fever
High John the Conqueror
is my familiar
Gimme all you got:
black candles
beef brains
red hot peppers
(his fingernails, his underwear)
cat bones, ashes
chicken foot, feces
I'll make you a mojo hand
Honey he ain't got a chance
We gonna make him
Dance, dance, dance

But once I said
Mama, I don't want to do it
She said, *Hush your mouth, child*
Get to it.
Only thing to it
is do it

The snake grew as she grew.
It killed her, finally.

THE UNDEAD

If they buried you underground
in New Orleans,
you'd float up,
sail down the flooded street
to the Quarter.
So they put you in a concrete bunkbed
in this vast dormitory
of the dead
instead.

(After every funeral
I fuck somebody)

Harriet stirs in her chair and then jumps up, disoriented but calm somehow, and rested. Impossible as it seems, she must have fallen asleep, at least for a few minutes. Sometimes she sort of blanks out when she's really stressed. She looks at her watch. Nine-forty-five. Thank goodness — at least she's not late. She brushes her teeth and freshens her lipstick in the bathroom mirror, then fluffs up her hair which looks exactly the same when she's done as it did before she started. That's the story of Harriet, isn't it? Stasis. Slice of life. The deep, world-weary voice of Lucian Delgado sounds in her ear: "Every story must contain the possibility of change, my lovelies. If there is no possibility of change, there's no conflict, and if there's no conflict, there's no story." The story of Harriet is no story at all.

But it's time, isn't it? Isn't it time? In the view from Harriet's stateroom window the river looks busy now, almost congested, with boats and lights and the reflection of lights in the water. She puts Charlie Mahan's letter into her purse. She slips the purse strap over her shoulder. She takes a deep breath and runs her damp hands down her body, over her thighs; she picks up the Chinese box and straightens her shoulders and opens the door and goes into the corridor, sidestepping bags, as she makes her way forward to the Grand Staircase leading up to the Promenade Deck. She nods to several people, shipboard acquaintances on their way down. She nods to Captain John Dulaney who stands on the landing ensconced in a bank of potted ferns: photo opportunity. Everyone is taking advantage of it, queuing up to pose with the captain. Flashbulbs go off like fireworks. "Good evening, sir . . . Good evening, ma'am . . . If you enjoyed your voyage, tell everybody; and if you didn't, just keep your damn mouth shut!" What a character! He winks at Harriet. His eleven-year-old son is dying from cystic fibrosis. Harriet knows this from Pete. The captain never stops smiling.

Finally Harriet slips through the knot of photographers and makes it to the final flight of stairs. She hates all the gaudy flowered carpeting everywhere, it's making her dizzy. She rushes past the Steamboatique with its huge LAST CHANCE SALE banner and greets the Syncopators, all decked out now in flashy Oriental silk saris, headed back toward the Upper Paddlewheel Lounge where they will perform as Chop Suey Huey and the Won Tons. Melinda and Suzette have pulled their long hair back and wound it into tight knots on top of their heads, anchored by chopsticks poking out in every direction. They look lethal, with bright red lipstick, rouged cheeks, and eyes ringed severely in black.

Harriet pushes the door to the deck. The air itself seems denser now, filled with the smell of oil and the heavy promise of rain later on. It's so humid on deck that by the time Harriet makes it all the way forward and starts climbing the iron stairs, she feels damp all over, as if she's been sprayed by one of those fern misters. She stops for a minute on the Observation Deck to get her breath before heading up the final, smaller flight of stairs to the Sun Deck where they will all be waiting. She hopes. She looks up the stairwell to see stars in the sky and a white blur at the top of the stairs. Her heart stops still. Then she remembers: it's Pete, just Pete, dressed up in his Mark Twain suit for the last night's photo opportunities. He extends his hard square hand which Harriet takes, allowing him to pull her up the few last steps onto the Sun Deck.

"You made it," he says from behind his moustache. "I was beginning to wonder."

"Well." Harriet smiles up at him. "I'm here now."

He gives her a practiced bow, an old-fashioned, courtly gesture, and steps back. Harriet moves forward to where Courtney and Anna and Catherine and Russell have pulled four deck chairs into a semi-circle. She pauses to get another one for herself, but Pete's already there; he picks it up and puts it against the rail for her, facing the others. "Thanks," she tells him. "Hi," she says to them.

"Hi yourself," Courtney says tartly. "Where have you been? We were about to give up on you."

"Oh, they were taking pictures up on the landing, and I couldn't get past. It always takes longer than you think it will to get anywhere on this boat."

"That's the damn truth." Russell nods, sipping a tall mixed drink with a lot of fruit in it, for the vitamins. He wears a wrinkled Hawaiian shirt with huge red tropical flowers on it. The shirt is buttoned up wrong. His hair sticks up in some places and lies flat in others. He needs a shave. But Russell and Catherine are holding hands now, publicly, solidly, their hands clasped on the little glass table between them.

"Is *that* it?" Courtney points to the small black lacquered box which Harriet balances carefully on her knees. Harriet nods. Anna takes a deep breath, shudders, and looks away. Catherine squeezes Russell's hand.

"Let's do it, then," Courtney says through her teeth.

But a boat's horn sounds over the water from someplace ahead of them and is answered by the *Belle*, several short blasts of the steam whistle right above their heads, it's deafening. Harriet's ears are ringing when it's over.

"For God's sake!" Anna cries. "Can't we do this someplace else? Can't we do it *later?*"

Harriet looks up across their heads to Pete, who shakes his head no. He points to his wrist. "There isn't time," she says. "We'll be coming into New Orleans soon, and then there'll be too many people around. This is okay, Anna, really. It won't take long, I promise. But I have to read you this letter first."

"*What* letter?" Courtney asks.

"Charlie Mahan enclosed a letter, addressed to all of us, along with *this*." Harriet touches the box on her lap, then puts it down on the deck beside her chair and gets Charlie's letter and her reading glasses out of her purse. She's settling back in her chair when the P.A. system crackles alarmingly above their heads and "Bobby's Girl" blares out into the humid air.

"Oh hell!" Anna jumps up in fright, then rearranges herself and settles back down. "This is just impossible."

"I want to be Bobby's girl" comes across the deck at top volume.

585

"Hang on there, folks, don't move. Just a minute," Pete yells, disappearing up the iron ladder to the top level, the Pilot House.

"Who's this, the Chipmunks?" Russell downs his drink.

"What?" Courtney cups her ear with her hand.

"I said, is this the fucking *Chipmunks?*"

"I think it's the Everly Brothers," Anna calls out, surprising everybody.

First Catherine starts laughing and then Harriet starts laughing too, what else can you do? Harriet thinks she'll never stop laughing. Anna's rocking, she's gone someplace back in her head, but Courtney sits straight and prim in her deck chair, staring ahead. (At least, *she* knows how to act!) Harriet laughs and laughs while "Bobby's Girl" fills the air and a hot little wind lifts her hair off the back of her neck. On shore, across the dark water, oil refineries lace the skies with strings of white lights; it looks like Christmas. Some of them move up and down like carnival rides. It's really very beautiful up here. But it seems shockingly quiet when "Bobby's Girl" cuts off suddenly with a scratchy noise that makes you grit your teeth, like nails on a blackboard.

"Sorry, folks." Pete drops back down on

their deck. "That wasn't supposed to happen, obviously. Just a little cut from the 'Times of Your Life' — it's this oldies program they keep going up here on the Sun Deck all day long. People seem to like it. Okay, now. You may proceed." He nods to Harriet across the others' heads.

Harriet rips open the envelope, unfolds the letter, and sits back. "Well, I won't say anything first. I'll just read you this letter, as it is really intended for all of us. Okay. Here goes." They lean forward in their chairs to catch Harriet's soft voice.

May 5, 1999

My dear Harriet,

First I must offer you and the others my deepest gratitude for undertaking this journey and carrying out our beloved Maggie's final wish. I hope it has been a pleasant trip for you as well as a duty. And now I must confess that Maggie's request was not stated in our joint will, that document having been drawn up many years ago. No, it is my own idea, and I shall tell you exactly how it came to me. For several months preceding Maggie's death, she had been thinking of her college years, especially the trip down the Mississippi River. She spoke of the trip, and of you, many times, regretting that she had never been one to attend reunions or "keep in touch," at least not in close touch, taken up as she has always been with the demands produced by our family and the farm. At this point I made a suggestion. Why not call up "the girls," I said, and suggest a return voyage down the river on one of those steamboats? She seized upon my idea with alacrity, planning to contact you all after Christmas. She was, I might say, thrilled by this prospect. The intervening tragedy put a stop to the plan, of course, and yet I could not get her excitement over it out of my mind. I resolved to help her make the trip, if at all possible. Hence my request to you, a request that I hope you do not now consider dishonest in light of these disclosures.

Maggie's college years were precious to her despite some times of unhappiness and those lifelong difficulties that you are aware of. In fact, as the intervening years passed, her time at Mary Scott seemed to become ever more dear to her. In a reflective moment last fall, she told me that she "just felt so *alive* then." I was struck by this remark at the time, for I believed her life here at El Destino to be filled almost to bursting with passionate life: our five children (and now two grandchildren); our farm, where she has always been my "right-hand man"; and her active role in our little community, where she was known and revered by all. I realized even at the time that she meant, then, something else; and after thinking about this matter a great deal, as you must imagine I have done, I believe this memory of "aliveness" derived not only from the natural exuberance of youth — and oh, yes, she *was* exuberant, wasn't she? So filled with "passionate intensity," to borrow a line from W. B. Yeats whose volume of *Collected Poems* lies even now in its accustomed place on her bedside table — but also from the warm and true friendships she formed at Mary Scott with the other girls, and especially with *you*, Harriet.

I have heard it said that the friends of our youth are the closest friends we will ever have, and I believe this to be true. Certainly it has been so for me. The boys of my childhood are the men I rely on now. For at no later time are we ever so open, so ready to offer up all that we have and all that we are, to allow others real access into our very souls. The friendships we make in later life are friendships of a different order, it seems to me. The Mississippi River trip came to symbolize Maggie's whole college experience for her. I do realize, as well, that Maggie could have gone on to graduate school and who knows what further academic honors had she so chosen, and yet she chose to marry me rather than pursue that course, *despite my pleas.* It was not an either-or choice. Loving her as I did, I always wanted to give Maggie whatever *she* wanted. Indeed, it is true to say I have devoted my life to this purpose, and been richly rewarded for it. I had loved her since she was a child. I loved her simply, from the bottom of my heart, and she knew it, and knew that she could depend on me when times of trouble came, as they did periodically. We weathered them together. Perhaps our union was even strengthened by them. We were closer than ever at the time of her death.

Her tragic accident last December was the shock and sorrow of my life, totally unexpected, of course; in fact, we had planned a trip together in January. The airline tickets had just arrived.

What can I tell you of those final days? They were as full as all her days have been, perhaps *more* full. Maggie was in the midst of "doing Christmas" as she always called it. This process involved preparing the house for the arrival of our four children who had left it, with only Merry remaining at home in her final year of high school. All five children and their various mates would be with us for the holidays. Furthermore, Maggie planned to give our traditional "at home" on the 26th, Boxing Day. The invitations had been sent out the week before. I had more than once suggested to Maggie that all this might be too much for her, and had earlier offered the idea that we take them all someplace else for Christmas, such as Sanibel Island, for a change, a suggestion she had thoroughly pooh-poohed. She was feeling wonderful, she said, the best she had felt in years. The new medicine was terrific. Nothing would do but the traditional Christmas, and as she pointed out, she had "plenty of help," something I, of course, made sure of.

Under her supervision, then, the house had been garlanded outside and inside. Our customary trees were decorated — one in the parlor, one in the library, and a magnificent cedar in the hall, easily twenty feet in height, all of them cut on our land. Maggie always did the stairs and mantelpieces herself, with greenery from our woods. She was known for her artistic touch. She and Princess had been baking for days; the rum cakes were lined up on the marble slab in the cold corner ready for distribution to all the people she gave them to each year: the yard men, her hairdresser, our minister, the girls at the bank, my foremen, an ever-expanding list of all those — not even family — who touched our lives. I mention these details in the hope of giving you a true sense of the fabric of her life.

The day of her death was as busy and productive as all our other days have been. I had awakened early to find that a promised ice storm had, indeed, arrived overnight. The farm was encased in ice — every fence rail, every twig, every blade of grass. I got up and made the coffee, as usual, and ate my cereal with Merry, who then left for school in the car we had just given her for her seventeenth birthday. Maggie never ate breakfast, as you may recall. In that respect, she had not changed. By the time I put her coffee on her tray and took it in to her, the sun was fully up, transforming the entire farm into a glistening fairy-tale landscape.

I put the tray down on the hassock and

opened the draperies. "Maggie," I said, "wake up." Which she did, first rubbing her eyes and then springing up with delight. "Oh, Bunny," she exclaimed — her old name for me — "oh, Bunny! Just *look!* Isn't it beautiful?" As indeed it was. We stood together at the bay window with our arms wrapped around each other for the longest time. From that window, we looked past the sundial and the old *garçonnière* and Mr. Ruel Green's house and the old store, past the white hedges down the long lane of icy pecan trees and across the shining fields. The sky was a deep clear blue. Having work to do, I moved to go, yet she held me to her a bit longer.

"Oh, Bunny," she said, "help me memorize this moment. It'll be all gone by ten o'clock." As it was, and I have always been glad that I stayed with her there by the window until she glanced at the clock and gave a little cry, for she had planned to drive to Jackson for some last-minute shopping later that morning. I was out in the office at the time she left, but she gave me her customary toot of the horn as she rounded the circle, and I can assure you that the roads were perfectly clear of ice by that time. I did not think twice about her driving. Except when she was in her very worst periods — and that had not been for some years now — she drove herself everywhere, and enjoyed doing so. She always drove too fast, but I had gotten used to this over the years, and she was a very good driver.

I remember looking up from my desk to watch her car — a white Saab, last year's model — as she flashed down the lane and out of sight. Something also flashed at the corner of my vision, something silver, peripheral. I stopped to rub my eyes and it was gone. But I have thought about it since. A lot of things will come back to haunt you in times like these. Mr. Green and I worked steadily until noon, when the state trooper car pulled up to the office and parked, with two men in the front seat. The minute I saw their faces, I knew.

Maggie had stopped at our little Sweet Springs post office in town to pick up the mail, then stayed to have a cup of coffee with Rhoda Frye, the storekeeper and postmistress, a great old pal of hers. Maggie was in very good spirits, Rhoda said, joking about President Clinton and other things and describing the new curtains for Melissa's room which she planned to pick up in Jackson, along with the completed portrait that Roland Hart had painted of her — this was to be my Christmas present, and I am looking at it now as I write. Painted in the somewhat impressionistic style for which Hart has become justly celebrated, it depicts Maggie leaning out one of the windows of our antebellum carriage barn, wearing the tan suede jacket we bought in Spain. Her face is turned to the side, almost in profile — you can't see what she's looking at — and she is laughing. He has captured her perfectly: her animation, that sense of constant movement framed by the splintery silvering wood of the ancient structure. I hope you will come to visit El Destino again one day, Harriet, so you can see this lovely likeness for yourself. I believe you will see she was still your good old friend after all these years.

After visiting with Rhoda for twenty minutes or so, Maggie got back in her car and drove out the old Houma road instead of just taking 115 up to the interstate, which would have been a faster route but far less scenic, I suppose, and she had mentioned several times to Rhoda what a pretty day it was for a drive. The Houma road winds through a wood, then becomes a causeway through the swamp where anyone would agree, it is picturesque all right, the stark white trees, the black water, all the birds. Then it climbs up through what we call the "red hills" before it crosses the Houma River and joins up with the interstate maybe twelve miles later.

Maggie never made it across the river. She drove off the shoulder of the bridge going approximately sixty miles an hour, rolled off the rocky embankment into the river, a seventy-foot drop, taking the guard rail with her, crashing upside down into that giant rock which marks the old swimming hole that every kid in this county knew about, including myself. Many's the time I jumped off that rock, which is as big as a small house, hence its name, House Rock. The car's tremendous momentum caused it to flip off the rock into the Black Hole, as they call it, the broken windshield allowing the car to fill with water and sink instantly. She might not have been found for days were it not for two teenaged boys who were skipping school to smoke a little morning marijuana on the river bank and reported the accident.

Harriet, what more can I tell you? What

more beyond this? She died instantly, as best anybody can figure. Was the accident due to a patch of ice, shady and unmelted on the steep approach to the bridge? Or due to a crucial second of inattention on Maggie's part, as she turned her head for a moment to see the river, or look at a flying bird? We will never know. I will never know. I will tell you this, however: no man ever loved a woman more than I loved Maggie Mahan, nor has any woman ever been so mourned. The hole she has left in my life, and in the life of this community, is incalculable — even now, as I write to you five months later. So many people came to her funeral on that gray, drizzly day that some of them had to stand outside in the cold. I wanted you to know that. Her ashes were not buried in the church cemetery as is customary here, but were sprinkled over El Destino by Mr. Green and myself as per the instructions in her will, which upset her brothers, yet I enforced her wishes to the letter, as I believe that I do now in sending a small portion of them to you.

I want you to know also that the children are doing as well as can be expected. I thank God that Merry (Meredith Troy Mahan, our youngest, of course) is still here with me, though she has been accepted to Mary Scott, as you may already know, for the coming fall. I will give you an account of the others, as follows: "Mac", or Charles MacFarland Mahan IV, our oldest, is in the sugar business in New Orleans, doing well, with a wife and two little boys who were the apples of Maggie's eye. She thought the sun rose and set on those little boys, as do I. "Richie," Richard Ballou Mahan, is a stockbroker in Atlanta, married, too, last year, no children yet; Melissa (Melissa Mills Mahan) is up at the University in Oxford, working toward a postgraduate degree in psychology. Our youngest son, Ross (John Ross Mahan), will graduate from Auburn University next year. He plans to come back here and join me in working this farm, for which I am most thankful, as I consider this place a trust as well as a living. I also want you all to know that the children and myself are establishing a full scholarship at Mary Scott in memory of Maggie. And you know you will always be most welcome, Harriet, should you care to visit me here at any time. This goes for the other "girls," too. Please give them my very best, and my deepest thanks, for helping me to fulfill her wishes. It makes me happy to think of you all on the river, together again.

I remain your faithful,
Charlie Mahan

For a minute, nobody says a word. The *Belle* slides under the Huey P. Long bridge, an arch of lights above them. Then, "My God," Anna says, "he's smart, isn't he? Charlie Mahan, I mean. I had no idea. I mean, he's a farmer, for God's sake. But I have to admit, that is a brilliant letter. Very moving."

"He called her Maggie." Harriet speaks up involuntarily. "As if she were a different person from the one we knew."

"Maybe she was," Catherine says. "But he really loved her, obviously."

"I sort of thought she'd killed herself, didn't you?" Courtney asks.

Anna nods. "But now I don't think so. He's convinced me. And it actually sounds like a wonderful marriage."

But it's always the storyteller's story. Harriet knows this from her COME-BACK! students.

"Well, you never know," Catherine says softly, sensibly. "I mean, who ever knows what anybody's marriage is really like? Or what's going on in anybody's head? But it certainly doesn't *sound* like she killed herself. I guess it really was an accident, don't you think so?"

"Yes," says Courtney firmly.

"Absolutely," says Anna.

"Sure." Russell stands up. "Okay. Great. Let's get it over with, then."

But Harriet can't open the box — she just can't. She holds it out toward Russell who takes it from her and opens it with the key and then hands it back to Harriet where she stands now against the rail.

"We have to say something." Courtney sounds very definite. "We can't just throw her in the river without a word."

"Why not?" Russell asks. "Sounds to me like Charlie said everything there was to say in his letter. And this is what she wanted, presumably, according to her husband. And he doesn't give us any instructions for a ceremony."

"Only thing to it, is do it," Harriet whispers. *Of course* Baby killed herself.

"What? What did you say?" Russell asks.

"Nothing." Harriet clutches the box.

"At the very least, we have to say the Lord's Prayer. I just can't stand it if we don't," Courtney declares.

"Well, I certainly don't care," Anna says. "*Whatever.* Whatever you all want to do."

"Let us pray, then." Courtney clasps her hands together and bows her head. "Our Father, who art in Heaven," she begins.

"Wait!" Harriet practically screams. "Wait. I mean, how am I supposed to do this? Just throw the whole box overboard? Or empty it over the side? Or scoop it out bit by bit? Or what?" Close up, Baby's ashes are not like she expected, not all like powder, but some of them grainy, like kitty litter.

"Poor Harriet. Here, we'll help you. We should all do it anyway, shouldn't we? I mean, we're all in this together." Catherine comes over to scoop out a bit, then Courtney, and finally Anna, holding her breath, averting her eyes. They line the rail with Russell standing just behind them. The lights of New Orleans rise in the distance ahead.

"Well, look who's up here!" exclaims Bridget, as she and Leonard appear in the stairwell. Pete stops them at the top.

"Our Father, who art in heaven," Courtney begins again, "hallowed be thy name. Thy kingdom come, thy will be done, on earth as it is in heaven." They're praying straight into the wind. "For thine is the power and the glory, for ever and ever, Amen." They fling their open hands to the river and let her go. Harriet throws the box in after her, for good measure. What would she ever do with it, later? It vanishes into darkness; the water is too far down to see it sink.

"Oh my God! She's coming back. Oh no!" Whirling, Anna swats at her skirts as a little puff of ashes floats back like smoke on the wind.

"Well, shit!" Russell bursts out laughing.

Courtney dusts her hands briskly together. "That's that, then," she says. But she really should have brought along the *Book of Common Prayer* herself so that things could have been done properly; she should have known Harriet wouldn't be properly prepared. There's the deep froggy tone of a tugboat off to their right now, and then another, why for heaven's sakes, they're coming into New Orleans already. And Courtney won't even have a chance to see the city. First thing in the morning, she'll go straight out to the airport, having given up her expensive hotel room to that little twit Harriet. She hears Gene's voice singing "Heartbreak Hotel" in her ear. She sees his face, his house, his room, his bed. She knows she will never meet anybody else on this earth who is racing wisteria. She sees his crazy cat clock, his kitchen, his wild garden in contrast to her own garden at Magnolia Court which has been so carefully maintained, it has been preserved, right next to the antebellum cemetery where even now the magnificent Berry monument rises from its square marble base straight up to the sky. On one side of it are listed the accomplishments of John Berry, architect and statesman, holder of many offices and winner of many honors. On two sides are carved the names and dates of the Berry children of whom there were eleven in all, though four of them died before childhood's end. On the back side is engraved the name of John Berry's wife, Cornelia Branch Berry, the dates of her birth and death, and this legend, SHE HATH DONE WHAT SHE COULD, in capital letters, which strikes Courtney suddenly as awful, as too sad to bear, though it's not, of course, it's admirable. So why does Courtney feel this terrible sense of desolation sweeping over her suddenly, there on the deck of the *Belle*, when all she has ever done is the *right thing?* She closes her eyes and sways in the wind and sees the Berry monument standing white and pure and straight as any arrow against the evening sky, above the surrounding tombstones and the dark encircling trees.

Courtney turns away from the rail as the loudspeaker crackles again. That's that, then. She takes out her camera.

"Speaking of the songs of my life!" Russell says into Catherine's ear as the theme from *A Summer Place* fills the air. "Let's dance, shall we?"

Catherine wipes her hands on her skirt and comes toward him, putting her left hand on his shoulder where it goes. She touches Russell's ear, his hair, his beard, that little place on his neck right below his ear where the hair doesn't grow and his skin is smooth as a baby's. She looks out past Russell's bristly neck and watches New Orleans come closer and closer, all those colored lights.

"*Excuse me!*" Anna's trying to push her way across the crowded little deck but they're all dancing now, Russell and Catherine, Leonard and Bridget, and that awful Toastmaster couple from Tennessee — dancing at a funeral! Anna is horrified. In her novels she always makes it rain at funerals or the sky is somber and leaden or the day is drear. Everyone wears black. Though it is true that when Lou died, she and Robert chartered the schooner *Wolf* and sailed out into the ocean and cast his ashes over the side (still in their silver urn, of course, not blowing all around, for God's sake). Anna said, "Good-bye, my love," while Robert held her. Then the sun did that wonderful thing it does just before it sinks into the ocean off Key West, it sort of spread out at the bottom and swelled up bigger and bigger until its rosy light filled the entire sky and kept the undersides of all the puffy clouds lit up while the schooner tacked and sailed back to Key West, into its dock at the bight. Now that might not have been traditional but it was certainly very moving and appropriate for Lou, what a guy. To her distress Anna finds herself sobbing right out loud on the deck in the middle of all these dancers. It's true that when anyone dies, the other dead rise up and die all over again. She sees Lou's dark liquid eyes, his sideways smile. "Hey, baby," he says. "C'mere."

But it's only Harriet hugging her, only Courtney patting her arm. *They* think she's crying for Baby. What a joke. Everyone always made so much of Baby while *she*, Anna, was the talented one. She has published thirty-four books; she has been translated into fourteen languages. Baby never published a word. *And he loved me, not her.* For just one awful moment, Anna entertains this thought: what if she had not listened outside Mr. Gaines's door on that Saturday morning so long ago? What if she had taken that fellowship and gone on to Columbia in her ignorance and had consequently never married Kenneth Trethaway? What then? Doubt and confusion envelop her like a dark cloak. She should never have come on this trip.

"Anna, my goodness," Courtney says, embarrassed by such large grief.

But Anna can't stand to think these things. Finally her mantra comes into her mind: *que sera, sera.* What's done is done; whatever *should* be, *is.* Touch, see, smell, hear, taste, feel. *Be here now.* This is her mantra, and how could she ever have forgotten it, even for a moment? Anna wonders as the *Belle* makes her way into the crowded harbor past the giant Port of New Orleans sign. The whistle gives two piercing shrieks. Bells clang. People throng onto the decks below them, lining the rails. Through her tears Anna sees the lights of the city ringing the harbor on every side.

Huckleberry turns to Francesca as the changing light makes shadowy patterns on the snowy sheets. "We're coming into port," he says.

"Oh, my darling, we've not much time left then, have we?" Francesca's husky voice seems to swell up from the very night.

"No ma'am, but thanks for everything!" Huckleberry tries to be brave, though his freckles are slick with tears. "Only, only — I know it's not cool, but the problem is that I really love you, ma'am. I really do. I don't think I can live without you."

"Oh, my little darling." Francesca strokes his wet cheek and smooths his wrinkled brow. "Of course it seems this way to you now. But you are young, and life goes on. You'll see. You will love many women, and one day there will come that special woman, who will walk with you hand in hand through the rest of your life."

"But I want her to be *you!*" Huckleberry wails. "I can't live without *you!*"

"Now, now. It cannot be," Francesca utters throatily. "But get up now, and come to the window with me, and look as we enter the city. It is *your* city, my young friend, it is *your* world, yours for the taking." They stand together and watch as the ship maneuvers her way toward the dock.

"And you?" Huckleberry cries out suddenly. "Where will *you* be?" But when he turns to find Francesca, she is gone. She has slipped away into the night, into the past, leaving him even in his heartbreak a wiser young man. And though he will search for her through all the streets of all the cities in the world for the rest of his life, and though he will remember her forever, he will never, *ever*, see her again.

Anna leans back against the rail as the music changes to Creedence Clearwater Revival's "Bad Moon Rising": "Don't go around tonight, Well it's bound to take your life, There's a bad moon on the rise." Without missing a beat, Russell and Catherine swing apart and start to jitterbug. They are very, very good at this. *Click*. Courtney snaps their picture, then takes one of Anna at the rail, which ought to be interesting if it turns out right, somber Anna silhouetted against the brilliant good-time skyline. *Click*. Leonard and Bridget are doing the electric slide which they have learned in dance class. The couple from Tennessee are dancing, too, but soon stop, as he suffers terribly from gout.

"Gets you in the toe!" the Toastmaster shouts to Pete over the music.

"What?" Pete shouts back.

"Gout!" the Toastmaster yells.

"You may be right!" cries Russell, spinning his wife around.

"Harriet?" Pete calls over them all. "Harriet?"

But Harriet seems not to hear him or anyone else, leaning over the railing just at the point of the bow like a figurehead, facing into the breeze. Courtney snaps a picture of her like that, in profile, with her hair streaming back from her face, and one of Pete, a step or two above the rest of the group, hanging on to the Pilot House ladder. "Harriet," he calls.

But Harriet hovers just above the deck, hating herself. For now she has changed her mind, and she wonders how she could ever have been so egotistical as to presume, even for one minute, that her own actions were of such importance in lives where her presence had been only incidental. Baby grew up, that's all — while she, Harriet, did not. And now she must rethink her whole opinion of Charlie, seeing him as passionate and articulate, seeing Baby's marriage as a good choice instead of a cop-out. Though on the other hand, Harriet can still imagine Baby's death as a choice, too . . . but who knows? Who can ever know which story is true? Maybe they're *both* true. Harriet feels an utter fool for torturing herself all these years, for blaming herself, punishing herself for Jeff's

609

death and the wreckage of Baby's life when maybe it wasn't even wrecked. According to Charlie Mahan, it was happy and filled with love. Baby is dead now, but at least she *lived* . . .

Maybe Harriet's own life could have been full and happy, too, if she hadn't felt so guilty. But this is such a scary thought that it sends Harriet shooting up even higher, many feet above the Sun Deck of the *Belle of Natchez* and even above the smokestacks, so that she can look down and see her friends and Pete as tiny toy figures, windup toys, moving round and round in their little dance. She sees the busy port and the lighted city and the wide dark river beyond, going all the way down the Mississippi Delta and into the sea. From this distance it is also possible for Harriet to see that she was sort of in love with Baby herself, as well as with Jeff, and that Jeff's death was, in a sense, her own.

> I was once as you are
> and as I am now
> You also shall be.

Harriet looks down on the city's twinkling lights until she can almost see patterns like all those constellations so long ago — Courtney's heart-shaped corsage, Catherine's Civil War dog, Anna's little finger bones — and there, yes, it's his constellation, it's Jeff blazing out in the night. He's burning to death. Every inch of him is blazing, his mouth that huge black O that Harriet is pulled toward inexorably, it's where she's been headed of course all along, it's what she wants. "Harriet!" Pete yells again and with a sudden cry she turns on her heel and runs back down the starry sky almost colliding with the ghost of Baby who sits on a little star swinging her long bare legs, dangling her loafers, wearing her old cutoff jeans.

"Don't be a fool, Harriet." Baby's laughing, smoking a Salem, as in life. "How many English majors ever got a chance to fuck Mark Twain? You better go for it, girl —"

"Oh, I'd never do *that*," Harriet says immediately, but then all the stars are moving, they're dancing like the snowflakes in Jill's paperweights so long ago, and Baby's star explodes before her eyes. *Click.* "Got it!" says Courtney. Pete puts his arm around Harriet's waist. *"Okay,"* she says. "Okay." *I hear hurricanes ablowing, I know the end is coming soon.* The Robin Street Wharf lies right ahead, the black river slides under the *Belle*. They're almost there. Funny how it seems like practically no time at all has passed since they first left, since they went running up that hill, since they set out upon the water like a dream.

In all ways remarkable, the rest of the girls —

"I've carried more tonnage, but never a more valuable cargo."

Capt. Gordon S. Cartwright
June 10, 1965

Jane Gillespie Reed has just moved into her mother's house on Three Chopt Road in Richmond's West End, only two blocks away from the private girls' school they all attended: her mother, herself, her three daughters. Jane married her childhood sweetheart, Royster Reed. Their daughters are perfectly healthy, though none has turned out exactly as expected, best not to dwell on this too much. Best to go about her day exactly as she always has, as her mother went about *hers* in this very same house until her sudden death. Mama had been sitting by the fire, with Jane across from her in the matching wingback chair, when suddenly she twitched violently, upsetting the glass of water on the little table. "Oh!" she cried, her hand flying up to her mouth, and she died with her eyes wide open. Whatever Mama saw on the other side seemed to surprise her. This worries Jane. Mama's death was a year ago, but Jane has felt unsettled ever since. Royster is no help; he thinks she's just going through the Change. The girls are no help either, involved with their own busy lives.

Today Jane thinks of driving downtown for lunch so she can catch at least a glimpse of Fontaine, their youngest, her favorite. Fontaine and her Japanese husband, Tommy Chiba, own a popular sushi bar down at the Shockoe Slip. Three months pregnant, Fontaine runs the cash register, wearing a kimono. Tommy Chiba cuts the fish. Fontaine has told Jane that each chef has his own sushi knife, which no one else is ever allowed to touch. Jane imagines Tommy Chiba's sharp knife slicing into tuna. She shivers. Best to stay home, make herself a tuna salad sandwich, unpack another box of china as the afternoon light moves across her mother's lovely Oriental rugs.

Busy *Suzanne St. John* alternates between her condominium at River Road Plantation and the lovely apartment on Chartres Street in New Orleans where she has lived alone ever since David Maynard, her husband of sixteen years, left her for his personal trainer. An estate attorney, David is a dry and predictable man who never showed a single sign of leaving her before he just up and did it.

He never showed a sign of getting a personal trainer either; he imported wine by the case, and loved his étoufée. Now Suzanne can see him any morning she chooses to look through the plate glass window of Gold's Gym across from her parking building. He's running on a treadmill, watching a television suspended from the wall above him, eyes raised as if in prayer. This suggestion — that he has found some meaning in it all — infuriates Suzanne. She feels very much alone. Suzanne and David never had children, as he already had three, from his first marriage, when she met him. These children visited in the summers and at holidays, but Suzanne is not in touch with them now. Nor does she have close friends. And as the head of River Road Corporation, she cannot confide in any of her employees. She doesn't have time to go on trips, join clubs, or take a course in order to meet new people. But she doesn't see any reason why she should feel so alone at this stage of her life. So something else has come into her mind. In secret, in her office during the day, or late at night, at home, she has found herself clicking onto those personals sites. Why not? What's wrong with that? Soon she will answer an ad, and then something will happen to her.

Whoever thought a nomadic, urban creature like **Ruth d'Agostino** could ever settle down so happily on this ramshackle Florida farm out here in the middle of nowhere? Up before dawn, walking down the sandy road to feed the Charolais cattle, three dogs romping around her feet, Ruth whistles a little tune through her teeth as the sky grows light. She has been astonished to find this rolling, grassy plain in central Florida, with occasional trees that rise up like billowing smoke. It's like another country here.

A former bond trader, Ruth has never married. She buried her longtime lover (colon cancer) four years ago in New York. Then she almost ran Lane down while rollerblading in Central Park, occasioning coffee. Lane was only in the city overnight, for an art opening. Ruth took a little, much-needed vacation. Three months later she returned to pack and move to Miami, where Lane held a faculty position. When Lane's father died, they took over the family farm, against all advice. But Lane is painting better than ever, and Ruth can manage all their business on the Internet. She could live anywhere, really. Now she leans against the split-rail fence and watches the sun come up red as a blood orange. Rain later, this afternoon. She calls the dogs, heads for the barn, gathers the eggs.

When Ruth gets back to the low, tin-roofed house, the smell of coffee fills the kitchen. Ruth leaves her clogs at the door and walks barefoot across the smooth terra-cotta tiles to the sink where Lane is running water.

"Tim called," Lane says. "Lucy's gone into labor."

"When?"

"Last night. They're on their way to the hospital right now. He'll call later, of course."

Ruth squeezes her shoulder. Tim, Lane's youngest, lives in Louisville. Ruth puts the enamel pan of eggs on the counter and pours herself a cup of coffee. She has just sat down at the kitchen table and opened the paper when Lane says, "Oh, Ruthie!" with a certain tone in her voice. Lane turns from the window and holds the blue bowl out so that Ruthie can see it, too: a double-yolk egg, its yolks shot through with red like the sun, each of them perfectly round, tightly and perfectly joined. "Just look," says Lane. The sun is in her hair.

Dr. Mimi West Worthington, 49, of

11 Hobbyhorse Circle, Winston-Salem, N.C., died Wednesday, March 12, 1985, at Baptist Memorial Hospital following a brief illness. She was born April 5, 1945, in Silver Spring, Md., to the late Frank and Elizabeth West. She graduated from Mary Scott College in 1966, and from dental school at the University of North Carolina, Chapel Hill, in 1971. Following a postdoctoral fellowship, also at UNC, she moved to Winston-Salem where she entered private practice at Forsythe Dental Care, remaining active there until her sudden death. She was a member of Grace Street Methodist Church, serving in many capacities including Sunday School teacher and Methodist Youth Fellowship leader. She was elected to membership in the Xi Psi Phi Dental Fraternity and the Academy of General Dentistry. She served as head of the Winston-Salem Dental League. One of her joys was providing dental care to needy children at the Forsythe Saturday Clinic, which she started. A devoted mother, she is survived by two sons, Patrick West Worthington, a student at the University of Colorado in Boulder; and James Justin Worthington

of Boone, N.C.; a sister, Mrs. Laura Miller of Baltimore, Md.; a good friend, Michael Ridge; and a multitude of devoted friends and patients. Funeral services will be conducted at Grace Street Methodist Church on Saturday, March 15, at 2 p.m., followed by burial in Evergreen Cemetery. Memorial contributions may be made to the Forsythe Saturday Clinic, the American Cancer Society, or the Grace Street Methodist Church.

(But what of her ex, not mentioned in this yellowed clipping? or her older son's diabetes? What of the men she loved, the books she read, or her famous beef carbonnade? What about how she swam at the Y on Tuesday and Thursday mornings, and played tennis with the same three women for fifteen years? What of that time when she and Michael were hiking in Arizona and the sun came up and all the earth turned red?)

Her years at Mary Scott were the exception in **Lauren DuPree**'s quiet life; now, she marvels at them, as if they had happened to somebody else. A shy child who stayed mostly at home with her frail, bookish parents, she returned to Mobile after college and has lived here ever since, taking care of them and of her blind uncle Bernard who lived in the garden house now completely covered in wisteria, as well as her alcoholic sister from time to time and her sister's children (beloved nephews!) at various points in their lives. It may not seem that such a sheltered life could be interesting. But au contraire it has been filled with joy and, yes, love; Lauren feels we are here for a purpose, to seek God's plan for our lives. In the poorer quarters of the city where she has long worked as a public health nurse, Lauren is considered a saint.

Oh, but she's *not* a saint, for she once loved a man with all her incandescent heart; however, he went away to England for graduate school, returning only to break the engagement. That man's daughter, now a young matron, came up to Lauren on the street long after his death and said, "He always loved you, you know," which filled her with wild sorrow rather than the pleasure she's sure the daughter intended. Well, never mind. She has her work, she has her little dog. And God's purpose has been further revealed since her parents' deaths.

They were very rich; she's giving it all

away. To charities and to individual persons she knows who are in need, and to strangers who show up on her doorstep looking for money. She gives it to them in spite of her nephews' injunction. There are so many good causes and needy people in the world, and not enough money to go around. The more she gives away, the lighter and smaller she feels. She is finalizing plans to give this house to Pansy's church; Pansy was her parents' housekeeper. It will be used as a shelter for women and children. Lauren loves the idea of children running through this courtyard, up and down the stairs, along the iron balconies. She will hear them. She will live here, too, in the garden house with Smoky, her little dog, taking up less and less room.

My name is **Bowen Montague** and I am an alcoholic. I grew up in the Belle Meade section of Nashville, Tennessee. My father was a Fugitive poet and my mother was a dissatisfied aristocrat with impossible expectations who drove everybody crazy, so that we children all left home as soon as possible, for prep school and then for college. But yet I repeated her life, returning to marry well, open a gift shop, and finally have a daughter, a life that might have sufficed well enough if our daughter had not been murdered at age twenty, the summer after her sophomore year in college. Murdered! Missing for weeks, then found raped, strangled, in the woods near Percy Priest Lake. Never solved, though in the investigation it became clear that drugs were involved and that she had led another life with people of whom we had had no knowledge. Or had we? How much did we know and *not know?* This tormented me. I felt I must know more than I thought, that at some point I would remember something, and things would click into place. I drove the streets looking into the faces I encountered, wondering, *him?* Is he the one? I kept her room exactly as she had left it, though the things said about her during the investigation bore no relation to this room, our life. They said terrible things. My husband wanted to move away, but I could not, and so he moved without me; and I started drinking sherry and then switched to vodka, and sold the shop. Soon I rarely left the house. I rarely ate. Finally my parents and my brother did an intervention, putting me into rehab. By then I was almost dead, skin and bones. I hated everybody. It took me a long time to come around.

But here I met Jerry Rusher, a musician, twelve years younger than I am. Jerry has a big smile and a long ponytail and a way of grinning at you with his eyes. The first time this happened I thought, Well I *know* him! which turned out to be true, even though our backgrounds could not be more different. Jerry grew up dirt poor. He was a heroin addict for seven years, in prison for five. Now we live in a mobile home on his sister's land, out near Columbia. He and his sister are getting a band together with some young boys. They all want to play with Jerry because he's a legend. Sometimes I sing high harmony with them. But mostly I cook and take care of his sister's kids, twin boys with dimples, age ten. They're a handful. My parents and my brother will have nothing to do with me. They drove all the way out here to say this, and would not even get out of the car or speak to Jerry. They're waiting for me to "come to my senses" and "come back home." Don't hold your breath! I say. I say, I am the fugitive now.

I have a garden out here by the road where it gets lots of sun. I'm growing lettuce, beans, tomatoes, yellow squash, and zucchini. These zucchini are taking over! I'm going to make zucchini bread later today, I cut the recipe out of the *Tennessean*.

Not much is known of **Susan Alexis Hill**, though her photographs can be found in major exhibits throughout the United States. Born in Atlanta, she'd never been out of the South until she went to Maine with her young husband, visiting Castine where she fell in love with the light and with an older man, a photographer, who took her under his wing. She stayed. Theirs was an austere life which she got a taste for, staying on after his death, teaching sometimes, traveling often, traveling light. She never thinks about the past. But only last month when she was in Texas, photographing along the Brazos near Waco, there was something about the afternoon light, about the way it fell through the vines, and a bend in the river that reminded her of the Mississippi, and of their trip down the river years ago.

Acknowledgments

First I want to thank the women with whom I shared the real Mississippi River raft trip in 1966 — my Hollins College classmates Allison Ames, Nancy Beckham, Anne Boyce, Virginia Clark, Vicki Derby, Margaret Hanes, Kathy Hershey, Lee Harrison, Anne Jones, Anne MacKinney, Alice Meriwether, Mary Poe, Ann Megaro, Mimzie Speiden, and Tricia Neild — as well as Captain Gordon Cooper, and our "cabin boys" Robert "Rosebob" Whitton and Jimmy Middleton. What a time we had! Although a few traces of our actual experience may be found here and there in the pages of this novel, it's truly fiction — the events described are imaginary, and the characters are fictitious and not intended to represent specific living persons. But the idea of river journey as metaphor for the course of women's lives has intrigued me for years.

627

I'd also like to thank noted writer and lecturer Dennis Brown for his informative, lively, and thought-provoking talks on board the *Mississippi Queen*, as well as all the staff and employees of the Delta Queen Steamboat Company.

For great lines, insights, or inspiration: Stella Connell, Bland Simpson, Annie Dillard, Doris Betts, Roy Blount, Steven Burke, Jackie Seay Sergi, Nancy Demorest, Lucinda MacKethan, Joshua Seay, Buffy Morgan, Hal Crowther, Karren Pell, and Dorothy Hill. For their support during the writing of this book: Paul Ferguson and my fellow "Good Ol' Girls," Jill McCorkle, Matraca Berg, and Marshall Chapman; and Debbie Raines and all the Grundy High School students who worked with me on our oral history book project.

Thanks to Dan and Carol Mayfield for putting me up in Memphis; to Clyde Edgerton for his helicopter expertise; to Dr. Michael Ferguson, my medical consultant; to Callie Warner, whose iron furniture, artwork, and sculpture have found their way into these pages; to Virginia Bullman and Lanelle Davis, whose giant concrete women are likewise here described; and to Anne Weaver, who made a handsome contribution to the Heart Fund so she could be a character.

Special thanks to my wonderful agent, Liz Darhansoff, a saint, who believed in me and in this book; to Nancy Demorest and Hal Crowther for their invaluable feedback; to my editor, Shannon Ravenel, for her good humor, extraordinary insight, common sense, and literary sensibility; and to Mona Sinquefield for her patience, skill, and help with research and manuscript preparation.

The employees of Thorndike Press hope you have enjoyed this Large Print book. All our Thorndike and Wheeler Large Print titles are designed for easy reading, and all our books are made to last. Other Thorndike Press Large Print books are available at your library, through selected bookstores, or directly from us.

For information about titles, please call:

(800) 223-1244

or visit our Web site at:

www.gale.com/thorndike
www.gale.com/wheeler

To share your comments, please write:

Publisher
Thorndike Press
295 Kennedy Memorial Drive
Waterville, ME 04901